HUM'NS:

Any of a group of isomorphic, upright, bilaterally symmetrical, soft-boxed, dirhinous incarnates, with a built-in obsolescence of approximately 120 standard years, noted principally for the relative size of the brain and the design of the hand. Formatted in assorted sizes, colors, and sexual stylings, though all come packaged in the same flesh-and-blood that typifies all incarnate architecture.

Raliish—a slight, hairless breed, with a long history of sanctioned anthropophagy. Ethnocentric, warlike, distrusting of machine intelligences. Favorite phrase: "Genetic cleansing."

Enddrese—low-slung, hot-tempered, untrustworthy, profiteering epicurians. Environmental plunderers of dozens of worlds. Favorite phrase: "Let's eat."

Consortium—diverse, eclectic, and far-flung amalgam of racial types. Technophiles who live to acquire, consume, and at all costs be entertained. Favorite phrase: "How much did that cost?"

Excerpted from *Let's Look at Things from Their Side*, by Mac-Allies: Citizens for Machine Equality

THE BIG EMPTY

James Luceno

A Del Rey Book

BALLANTINE BOOKS • NEW YORK

A Del Rey Book
Published by Ballantine Books

Copyright © 1993 by James Luceno

Library of Congress Catalog Card Number: 93-90521

ISBN 0-345-37449-5

Manufactured in the United States of America

First Edition: December 1993

For all those who served; but chiefly for Dr. Terry Dunlop, in-country interpreter and translator, who shared a letter with me from a still-suffering vet.

About that mystifying enthusiasm a million years ago for turning over as many human activities as possible to machinery: What could that have been but yet another acknowledgment by people that their brains were no damn good?

—KURT VONNEGUT, *Galapagos*

The highest stage in moral culture is when we recognize that we ought to control our thoughts.

—CHARLES DARWIN

PART ONE

1: Plangent Theatrics

In the city of Bijou on the free world Plangent, a play was in progress, a one-person revival of an ancient tragedy. On stage, a holoid Lady Ozweld was striving to wash the guilt from her hands after having ordered the assassination of the culture hero, JfKa.

And in a private box so close to the action it might have been part of the thought-summoned production, an argument was about to unfold. The principal players in this parallel though minor drama were two hum'ns who looked at first glance no different from many of those attending the performance. The man hailed from Regnant, starward in the system; the woman, from Eremite—though her family had emigrated there from Riiti, in the Calumet orbital islands. Regnant, Plangent, Eremite, and Calumet: Ormolu's hum'nhabited quartet of planets.

Young, handsome, and above average height, the man, whose name was Dik Vitnil, was dressed in a suit of manifold statements. That the suit was natural fiber meant that it had originated offworld and that its wearer was not merely monied but privileged; that it bore no ranking stripes on the right sleeve suggested that both Vitnil's holdings and status had been achieved in some arena other than Consortium service, in which half of Plangent's hum'n population was enlisted.

The tattoo on the woman's right inner wrist afforded evidence of that enlistment, and anyone familiar with the ranking system could have read there that she was a cybermetrician—a machine intelligence therapist—employed by Veterans Affairs. She, too, was young and handsome, with the compactness of a born spacer and jet black hair that curtained small but precise features. On closer inspection, however, there was something absent about her: a dearth of color in the lips, an insufficiency of flesh under

3

the cheekbones and surrounding slightly epicanthic hazel eyes. She looked older than her years—like someone who had spent too much time in a starship's torpor coffin—and somewhat insubstantial in the reflected stage light. Her name was Jayd Qin.

"This is pure trash," Vitnil was saying, referring to the holoid theatrics. "Historical drivel. Something to feed a machine to keep it occupied between chores." Not yet finished with the washing of her hands—she would never be—Lady Ozweld was paying off the assassins whom she had tasked with JfKa's execution.

"Isn't that just the point of the play?" Jayd asked quietly. "To better acquaint us with the mind-set of our machines?"

"How? By pushing our faces into the religious muck of our ancestors? JfKa was nothing more than the martyred embodiment of our foibles and frailties. It was self-delusion that got him executed, not the orders of some guilt-ridden dominatrix. He sacrificed his life for an ideal that was already old before his time: the notion of ecological renewal—*nature*." Vitnil waved a hand in dismissal, revealing on his inner wrist a bar-code tattoo describing his medical history and genetic dispositions. "Myth. Like the Machrist nonsense our machines subscribe to."

"Machrist is the ethos they live by," Jayd amended.

Vitnil's laugh was deprecating. "Then they're the ones who should be accessing this junk."

On Vitnil's voiced prompt, Jayd's chair swiveled away from the stage and released her from its soft embrace. He immediately took her by the elbow and steered her toward the exit, whose heavy drapes parted as they approached. "I suppose we could have done worse," Vitnil commented. "We could have gone on-line with the conductor."

She had no argument. An over-the-shoulder glance revealed that those audience members who had gone on-line were still circling their hands in a washing motion in sympathy with the actions of the holo-Ozweld; their faintly fluorescent headband remotes would have given them away if the handwashing hadn't. The conductor, visible from the waist up in a circular well at the lip of the stage, wore a neural interface cap that ran holos of gears and shafts, a symphony of mechanical movement. From beneath the cap—and primarily for effect—fell a train of multicolored fiber-optic cables that disappeared into the well. Everything on stage, from set to performers, was a product of the mind of the conductor—in the present instance, a remorphed

Xell'em male renowned for his skill with details: Ozweld's yellow-stained fingertips, the background panorama of crowds and cityscape, the bright-red viscosity of JfKa's imagined blood . . . In every other way, the theater was a very back-to-basics affair, with row after row of conforming seats, a repulsor-field dome and a nuwood stage.

Vitnil was chuckling to himself as they exited the box. "I can't get over your saying 'the mind-set of our machines.' You're not one of those, are you?"

"One of what?"

"Someone inclined to call them enablers or tech companions."

"And what if I am?"

He laughed. "All I'm saying is that machines don't enable or companion me any, and it's brainless to think otherwise. For centuries we've been endeavoring to turn them into something more than tools, and they've yet to come close to expressing real emotion."

Jayd turned slightly to break free of the hand he had clamped about her bare upper arm. "You've obviously never worked with a talented one."

But Vitnil went right on talking. "Show me one thing they've been able to fashion for themselves—and I don't mean clever peripherals or subroutines or infostructure chapels. I'm talking about slogans, jingles, decent advertising copy."

Jayd didn't feel a need to react to the joke. "We don't endow them with that priority."

He sniggered in her direction. "I wouldn't know about that. But nobody endowed hum'ns with those priorities, and that's never stopped us from emoting or creating—even if we do occasionally turn out shit like this." Vitnil waved a hand to indicate the play, whose dulled sounds pursued them along the hallway.

She resisted the challenge of educating him. She was sorry now that she'd accepted his invitation—that she hadn't heeded her own sense of foreboding rather than acquiesced to the pressure of a mutual friend. It was her first night out in more than a Plangent year; her first night out in the company of a male stranger in more than three. She was nervous, and she knew it showed in her guarded posture and submissive voice. She had even arranged her hair in such a way as to conceal the parallel strips of interface flatware that were embedded in the sides of her head. But Vitnil's thinking was correct on one count: things

could have been worse. They could have opted to access the
performance from his apartment, as he'd suggested earlier on.
This way, at least, she wasn't under any obligation to sleep with
him.

They walked the length of a carpeted hall before the floor
welcomed them, conveying them effortlessly to a spiraling ramp.
Vitnil studied his reflection in a wall that mirrored at his gaze.
They descended into a garishly lit lobby, where a squat and shiny
valet whirred free of its recharging zone to intercept them at
old-fashioned revolving doors. Back-to-basics or no, the theater
owners hadn't been able to convince hum'ns to do the work of
machines.

"A menu of alternative diversions," Vitnil ordered without
waiting to be asked. Jayd joined him in perusing the long list
that scrolled across the valet's chest display: Enddrese cuisine,
holies, physical contests, aroma concerts, raw-flesh cafés, drug
emporiums, live birth shows, pain orgies, vivisection and ex-
coriation events, sex tournaments, group gropes . . .

"Anything interest you?" Vitnil asked after a moment.

"May a suggestion be offered?" the valet wondered.

Vitnil glared into an irising lens. "Absolutely not."

Jayd straightened from the screen, her lower lip between her
teeth. The machine was an avant-tech Series Three semi-
sentient, hum'niform only in that it had two arms and a head
properly proportioned to the size of its squat torso. Campaign
chevrons on the shoulders indicated that it had served Tac Corp
with honor in the Vega Conflict against the Raliish. Assault on
Enddra, Battle of Daleth, Battle of Gehenna . . .

"Perhaps we could do some time on the Strip," Jayd said.

Vitnil responded with a shrug of disinterest. "Decomp," he
told the valet.

"Do you require transport?" the veteran asked before shut-
ting down.

"No transport. We'll walk."

Jayd risked putting a hand on Vitnil's biceps, which flexed
under her fingers. "Couldn't we order a car? I'm not comfortable walking."

He stared at her in undisguised dismay. "I should confess:
you weren't my first choice for this evening. I knew when I saw
you that you weren't my type."

Jayd recognized the sound of encounter training in the harsh-
ness of his reply. Yet another combative therapy aimed at incit-

ing emotion in the technophobic. "Whose fault is that?" she asked him.

"Yours—for accepting."

"We could end it here."

He mulled it over, then shook his head. "Call me masochistic. I'd prefer to see things through."

She countered with a brave smile. "Don't bother on my account. We'll find a water fountain where you can wash your hands of me."

Vitnil laughed in spite of himself. "I was warned you were quick." He cocked his head toward the street. "All right, we'll order transport. But only as far as the War Memorial. Then we walk." He gripped himself in a way that was meant to suggest male potency. "I'm hungry for action."

Jayd held his gaze. "Your hypothalamus must be the talk of Bijou."

Knowing Vitnil wouldn't do so, she rewarded the valet with a low-content host she fished from her handbag, inserting it through a slot above the machine's sensor array. Along with imparting a quantum of data and an optic buzz, the wafer contained a benevolent virus—a self-propelled "cordial worm," in the argot of cybermetrics—engineered to effect minute upgrades in the machine's mentation centers.

"Am'n," the veteran said as the hum'ns moved off.

MacINTERLUDE: "Machines"

Employment specialization, compulsory integration, the seductive lure of the infostructure, and the current surfeit of social protocols and rituals have all contributed to the increasingly difficult task of talking—to say nothing of relating—to one another. As a result, many are opting to interact with machines whenever possible—for service, information, even solace.

Consider, for example, the unprecedented popularity of the avant-tech Series Three-Six mactendants. There isn't a shop or boutique [in Bijou] that doesn't employ at least one of these hum'niform machines; and they are fast becoming the machines-of-choice among the [city's] affluent, who have long desired a more companionable and less ungainly machine to assist in residence management.

Bear in mind, however, that while these machines are full-functioning, interactive cognizers—many of them veterans of the Vega Conflict—they are dependent on us for feedback. So whether encountered in-residence or about town, and whether of hum'niform or specialty design, machines should be thanked, encouraged, and rewarded for appropriate service. [Access "Useful Responses" for a partial list of supportive phrases: e.g., *Am'n, Go with Machrist, Control-C be with you*, etc.] Keep handy a variety of low- and/or high-content data-disks, and be generous with them. Disks are available at most shops, and at many smart-dispenser tabernacles—and remember, they count toward nonessential purchases.

Always be kind to your machines, so that they may better serve hum'nity. Remember: a rewarded machine is a learning machine.

—Adapted from *The Beginner's Guide to Machine Intelligences*

2: *Fun with Dik and Jayd*

Plangent, like Regnant and Eremite before it, had planetary imagineers to thank for its machine-maintained shroud of hum'n-biased gases. The extermination of all indigenous plant and animal life and the death of Plangent's salt sea were simply the by-products of rapid growth. Only Dhone, an Enddrese-settled world outward along the curve of the galactic arm, was in comparable condition—that is to say, relieved of nature, circumferentially alloyed and plasticized, fully subjugated to the wants and needs of the higher incarnate forms.

Administered by the Worlds Coalition since the end of the Vega Conflict, Bijou operated as a freeport downside. And so the city had the decades-long war to thank for the tens of thousands of displaced beings who had rushed down the well after the defeat of the Raliish and the institution of the Accord; who had jammed the city and spread like a retrovirus across the defoliated face of the continent; who had transformed Bijou into a haven for disabled veteran machines, deserters, smugglers, out-of-work arms merchants, deviants, and rogues of all ilk and inclination.

The Consortium's onworld presence was huge, owing to Plangent's relative proximity to more than a dozen stellar transit sites. Those sites and the time-vised corridors they opened on linked Plangent to twenty-three of the forty-one worlds and orbital facilities that comprised the Consortium's ever-widening domain. Only the Xell'em, co-victor of the Vega Conflict, could boast of similar holdings among the nearer star systems.

Hum'ns of Bijou's Consortium contingent invariably fell into two distinct classes: those who worked to implement Consortium policy on colony worlds, and those affiliated with the various entertainment corps. Survivors of the Vega Conflict generally held the two classes to be one and the same, however, in that exported fantasy was what the Consortium did best next to war.

That, at any rate, was Jayd's attitude; and surely it was Vitnil's as well, since he was known to be on standby for an executive position with Satori Ventures, largest and wealthiest of the Consortium's entertainment conglomerates. He said little while they were in the car, except to order it into a discharge zone well short of the rotating war obelisk. Jayd's heart raced as the car doors winged open, allowing in the jarring realities of the Strip.

In an instant they were swept up in the feverish movement, pressed into the tide: a crowd of hum'nity feeding on sound and smells and the promise of unrivaled tactile pleasures. People appraised and groped one another openly; grotesque hawkers beckoned at the entry to every hedonic crib and cage.

Vitnil was offering a critique of the performance they'd walked out on, citing the personal and professional shortcomings of the conductor, the witless complacency of the audience. Then he turned to talking about his current work with Satori Ventures, and about some top-secret holie project he was involved in that had necessitated numerous trips to Regnant—where Satori was headquartered—and to strife-torn Burst, where Consortium and Xell'em interests had come into potentially incendiary conflict. When Vitnil paused to solicit Jayd's reaction, she claimed not to have been listening.

"So my life doesn't interest you in the least?"

Impaled on a pheromone-laden scent, Jayd took a moment to respond. "You're boring me. I was enjoying the play—and the conductor, despite what you have to say about his sexual proclivities. Nor am I in the mood to listen to you rant about the exalted state of the entertainment media. I've had about enough of the world according to Dik Vitnil."

He showed her a patronizing smile. "Have you ever considered having your face redone? That nose of yours, it's all wrong—much too pert, and noticeably cocked to the right."

She fought an impulse to touch her face. "And you're growing more tiresome by the moment. If we have to talk, we should at least make some attempt at relevance. We could discuss Burst, for example. Do you have *any* thoughts about the political situation, or is your interest restricted to scouting locations for this holie you're involved with?"

Vitnil's smile turned sly. "So you *were* listening . . . But unfortunately I'm not permitted to discuss the project."

"I don't care about your project. I'm talking about the potential for war between the Consortium and the Xell'em. Do you feel that the Xell'em are justified in reasserting control of Burst, or do you favor the Font's position that Burst be recognized as an independent world?" The Font, near-omnipotent descendent of a clone queue, was chairman of the board of directors and ruled as Crown of the Consortium.

Vitnil unleashed a dopey laugh. "Suppose you tell me now if we're going to have sex or if I'll be ending the evening with a simulation."

Jayd's response was to quicken her pace, but the density of the crowd sabotaged her best efforts. Mood-altering aromas washed over her, and hands of diverse design reached out to offer samples of massage, pain, penetration. The calculated dissonance of a hundred pealing instruments left her dizzy.

The Strip was an accommodation for a breed of hum'n beings that had grown up in seed ships and claustrophobic toruses: a gaudy linearity that seemed to stretch infinitely in both directions in lieu of closing on itself overhead. It was a place where nothing mattered save what could be felt, tasted, touched, smelled, or heard; where the flesh could be fed beyond the point of satiety. The Strip gloried in physical excess. To experience it was to revel in the distinction between hum'n and machine.

Many blamed the entertainment corps for what the Strip had become; others dismissed it as emblematic of the wickedness that always succeeded war, the exaltation of biolife, what it meant to have survived. To Jayd, though, Bijou's recent turn toward depravity reeked of something millennial. The Strip was a line drawn on the battlefield of evolution—one last stand for the flesh before the hum'n condition was superseded.

Vitnil, recuperated from the brief bruising of his ego, was back to tugging her from scene to scene, from meat parlor to sex den to drug café. Music howled from dark interiors; heady concoctions of amplified light swirled about them. Here, for an audience of spindly-limbed Raliish riggers straight from the swollen outskirts of the city, six members of a hum'n clone were orchestrating the willing degradation of a hirsute male from Kwandri; there, while a group of imperious body-sculpted Xell'em looked on, two swarthy Enddrese were engaged in a competitive eating frenzy. A long line had formed at the entrance to an art boutique where eviscerations were performed hourly. A window display of steaming entrails left Vitnil transfixed; crushed against him, Jayd could hear him panting.

To test her stamina, she submitted herself to a blind surround of intimate caresses, and found—much to her comfort—that for all the urgent strokings she remained untouched, grand mistress of the containment field she'd enabled and inhabited for three years now, in cold constant ceremony of her personal tragedy and transmutation.

But had she truly disengaged herself from hum'nness? she wondered. Was she at last curled so deeply inside herself that all contact between mind and body had been permanently suspended? Had she somehow managed to supersede her own flesh, to turn herself into nothing more than a mindful machine?

She luxuriated in the thought.

For unlike Vitnil and the bulk of Luddite Bijou, Jayd wasn't threatened by the notion of surrendering the hum'n condition to machine intelligence. She wasn't afraid to admit that flesh was superfluous—as a war that had been fought mostly by machines had clearly demonstrated. She saw nothing unnatural about making the leap to a state of being where one could sense without having to *feel*, where introspection did not have to contend with moral ambiguity. She delighted in having separated herself from misoneists and ignorant biochauvinists like Vitnil, who had enslaved themselves to a goal of flaunting the differences between hum'n and machine instead of blurring the lines of distinction. Her faith in machines was equal to their own faith in the Machrist: machines were guileless, faultless, and consistently reliable. They never gave more or less than was asked of them. And most of all, though they might be leisured or terminated, they could never be hurt.

That's what tonight was all about, she decided. A test to gauge the progress she had made in overcoming her incarnation. But when Vitnil suggested a threesome with a prepubescent hired hand, she called an abrupt end to the evening and ordered him to take her home.

At the entry curtain to her residence, he said, "The same people who warned me you were quick also warned me you might not be good company."

"I take great relief in knowing you were warned," she returned dryly.

He planted his hands on his hips. "You do need to work on yourself. I suggest a visit to an impression-exchange clinic. I'd be willing to allow you to be me for a time—just so you could see yourself through my eyes."

"I've no doubt I'm no more pleasant a sight than you are to me."

Vitnil pretended to wince. "Should I take your surliness personally, or are you like this with everyone?"

Jayd made a fatigued sound. "To be blunt, I prefer partners who aren't quite so bent on being *men*."

"*Hu*-m'n, you mean."

"How very perceptive of you."

Vitnil ran his eyes over her. "Yes, I can see you partnered with some gen-eng thing without a navel or a crease in the palms of its hands, and a microprocessor for a brain. And unlike you, Qin, I'm proud of my hum'nity. I've got emotions, a temper that flares, a heart that can love, organic parts that still function." He gripped himself and leered at her.

She thrust out her square chin. "Good for you. The point is, I don't feel much in the mood to be a temporary storage place for any of your *parts*. I'm sorry if I didn't make that clear earlier on."

"Not as sorry as I am," he said with patent hostility.

She opaqued the energy curtain on his face and hurried into her apartment, rousing each machine she passed: "On, on, on . . ." And by the time she had entered the bedroom, the small living space was loud with music and a half-dozen separate voices: the telecomp, the security system, the household facilitator . . . She shed her clothes, letting them fall to the floor; then, naked, surrendered to the technowarmth of her smart-bed.

MacINTERLUDE: "Hum'ns"

Any of a group of isomorphic, upright, bilaterally symmetrical, soft-boxed, dirhinous incarnates, with a built-in obsolescence of approximately 120 standard years, noted principally for the relative size of the brain and the unusual design of the hand. Hum'ns are formatted in a wide assortment of sizes, colors, and sexual stylings, though all come packaged in the same flesh and blood that typifies all incarnate architecture.

Of the two dozen planetary types that have been identified, four played key roles in the Vega Conflict:

1: The Raliish—named for their homeworld, Ralii. A slight, hairless breed that features teardrop-shaped torsos, spindly limbs, translucent white skin, and elongated skulls. Concordant with the neotenous design of the body, the face is flat and gives the appearance of being only half-formed. The eyes are widely spaced, lidless black ovals; noses are flat; mouths, thin and lipless; ears, small and pointed. The Raliish have an innate talent for subvocalization and acts of mental and physical cruelty. They have a long history of sanctioned anthropophagy, and demonstrate a decided preference for Enddrese (see below). Their personality matrix is ethnocentric, warlike, and mass-minded; and though technologically advanced, they are distrusting of machine intelligences.

Favorite phrase: "Genetic cleansing."

2: The Enddrese—homeworld, Enddra. Low-slung, leathery-skinned, faintly aubergine-complected endomorphs, known to be hot-tempered, sensual, untrustworthy, profiteering epicureans. The colonizers and environmental plunderers of dozens of worlds, they were singled out by the Raliish for eradication during the Vega Conflict and have been left psychically traumatized since. Tolerant of only those machine intelligences involved in food preparation.

Favorite phrase: "Let's eat."

3: The Xell'em—homeworld, Xell'a. Medium-sized, dark-haired mesomorphs, who—through body sculpting, cranial deformation, hormonal enhancement, and surface adornment—typically transmogrify themselves into outsize, atavistic brutes, devoted for no apparently good reason to multilevel confrontation with the physical world. Victors, along with the Consortium (see below), in the Vega Conflict. Superstitious, highly sexual, territorial, and ritualistic, they are avowedly anti-machine.

Favorite phrase: "Fuck you, mac."

4: The Consortium—homeless. A diverse, eclectic, and far-flung amalgam of racial types ranging from the fair-haired to the black-skinned. Consortium hum'nkind is corporate, lustful, opportunistic, guilt-ridden, and parasitic. A god-fearing though utterly convictionless farrago of technophiles, who live to acquire, to consume, to be served, and at all costs to be entertained. Machinelike in their thinking and their behavior, they can as easily be lulled into apathy as excited to violence. Co-victors in the Vega Conflict, and utterly unredeemable.

Favorite phase: "How much did that cost?"

> —From *Let's Look at Things from Their Side*,
> by Mac-Allies: Citizens for Machine Equality

3: The Comforts of Home

In sleep, Jayd communed with the dead child, the child's tongue a babel of half-formed thoughts, its plaintive cries a jumble of needs and fears. In that territory of dreams, no time had passed since the child lay dying in its machine-maintained globe of atmosphere and nutrients, the artificial womb into which it had been moved at birth and where for a year it had continued to grow, monstrous and brilliant, instinctively reaching out with nascent mind to its biological parents, innocently torturing them in a language of its own devising.

In sleep, she relived the birth and the stricken looks on the faces of the midwives. Relived transporting the child to the med-center, where techs had coaxed the formless thing from her breast and hurried it away under sterile wrappings. She had visited the child on the high-tech ward where they had housed it, her face pressed to an unyielding transparency, the child afloat in its orb, remote, untouchable, with its spineless back and enormous head.

The child called to her but she refused to listen, giving those cries no more attention than she would the sounds of any other resentful ghost. For now she was the one encapsulated, fortified against intrusions from the hum'n world of pain and suffering.

The dream nevertheless left her feeling dislodged in space and time. Bereft. Her first waking thought was to wonder if the dead child pursued its father with the urgency it expended on her, or whether in fact Orth Qin had succeeded in outdistancing his phantom offspring. When last she'd heard, Orth was on Bocage, on the galactic frontier.

The household facilitators had decomped when Jayd's brain waves, washing into her pillow, had signaled REM sleep. Now, concurrent with her stirrings, the machines resumed their functions, filling the rooms of her residence with invigorating music, tantalizing light, pleasing aromas.

The ceramic floor warmed to her feet as she padded to the toilet; behind her, the bed sheets flattened and the pillows fluffed. She showered herself with sound and clothed her pale form in simple synthetics—pants, blouse, and vest. In the kitchen, a cupful of nutristim was waiting. Sipping from the thermal mug, she moved into the living room, where she called open the shutters of the west-facing windows. From the great height of her three rooms on the Skyward Tower's top floor she could see clear to the perimeter of machines that provided weather for the city, scrubbing or seeding the atmosphere as need be, thinning or thickening a thinly blue sky with clouds or measured outpourings of chemical compounds.

She carried the drink to the couch and ordered news updates from the telecomp. Attuned to her tastes and interests, a trio of holo-projectors displayed the results of their audiovisual scans. Burst dominated the news, though the overnight reports added little to what had been said months earlier and rehashed endlessly since.

One of the first worlds to fall to the Raliish during the Vega Conflict, Burst had been one of the last liberated—and then not by the Xell'em, who had pioneered it, but by Consortium forces. The situation had divided the planet's largely Xell'em population into pro- and anti-Xell'a factions, and spawned a rivalry between Xell'a's Lord Xoc Cho and the Consortium's Font that threatened to undermine the stability promised by the Accord. The Xell'em wanted their world back; the Consortium maintained that it was no longer theirs to reclaim. Under pressure from the Worlds Coalition, the two sides had agreed to a summit, where resolutions would be sought.

The telecomp had recorded sound bites of a speech the Font had delivered from the Redoubt on Regnant the previous day, and just now a quarter-scale holo of the Crown of the Consortium blazed flame-blue above the projector port.

"The war has been fought and won," the Font was saying, "yet we continue to grapple with the implications of peace. And only peace, peace and nothing but, can provide fuel for the dream . . ."

The Font's dream: the belief that hum'nkind had been preordained by fate to carry Phase III Awareness to every world where the seed of higher consciousness could take root and flourish. It was a dream the Font urged allies and would-be opponents of the Consortium to share: Enddrese, Xell'em, Raliish, Gehennan, and the rest—the diverse faces evolution had bequeathed to the hum'n species.

Invariably unnerved by the Font's physical appearance, live or reproduced, Jayd damped the holo display. The latest in a long line of rulers embodying genetic engineering and avant-technology, the Font was as monstrous a thing as the child had been—nameless, genderless, ahistorical . . . But Jayd could admire the Font's melioristic idealism, if nothing else. More to the point, the Font was pro-machine—or at least not averse to sharing hum'n-dominated space with mindful talent.

Dik Vitnil had surely voted his share in favor of the old order.

As the muted sound bites droned on, Jayd thought about the Satori Ventures executive and his thoroughly modern intoxication with the glories of the flesh. She supposed that underneath his slavish attachment to fashion he wasn't an ignoble man, nor even a corrupt one. Five years earlier she might even have responded more favorably to him. She had preferred anything to the avant-tech then—had sought the bad boys exclusively. Damaged goods, flesh that had been worked over by fate or war. All of which had led her to the Enddrese she would later wed: Orth Qin, survivor of the Raliish death camps on Dhone . . .

With an eye and ear on the news scan, Jayd had the comm place a call to Soigne Terrice—one of the friends who had encouraged her to accept Vitnil's invitation.

Shortly, Soigne's construct resolved in the guest's chair in the living room. "I already heard about last night," the construct announced.

"I've forgotten how to be with people," Jayd said. "Or how people can be."

The construct approximated a laugh. It had Soigne's rufous mane and enviable eyebrows—though the Soigne at the other end of the comm link had enhanced both the color and texture of the construct's complexion.

"Don't scold yourself too much," Soigne said. "You've made a beginning, that's the important thing. You have to give yourself time to readjust to company. And we have to be a bit more cautious in selecting potential partners."

Jayd wanted to say that she was pleased with her actions, and that she wasn't interested in being partnered with anyone, but she held her tongue. "What did he say about me?" she asked.

"Nothing you need to hear. He can be very spiteful when he

doesn't get his way, Jayd. Don't be entirely surprised if he sends a hate gift."

Jayd compressed her lips, simmering with defensive anger. "If people could see themselves the way talent see them, they wouldn't be so quick to judge each other."

"I haven't a clue," Soigne said. Which was certainly true, inasmuch as her job as a template for femmachines afforded her only limited contact with talented technology.

"Vitnil said I'd probably be better off with something fresh from a gen-eng vat."

"What a horrible thing to say!"

"No, I think he was right. In fact, that might not be an inappropriate choice for me—providing I could supervise the growing. You know, put the tucks and appendages where I want them."

Soigne laughed. "If you're going to keep thinking like that, what's the point of going out at all?"

"There's nothing wrong with being alone."

"I'm not saying there is—as a life choice. Surround yourself with machines, if that's what makes you happy. But you're never going to be able to get away from people, Jayd. Not with the Font empowered, that's a given."

"Have you been listening to the latest speech?"

"Who has time for that?" Soigne said, finished with politics. "Have you made your purchase yet?"

Jayd shook her head. "Any suggestions?"

Soigne supplied an item number from the shopping network. "It'll look perfect on the shelf in the breakfast nook."

As mandated by the Accord, all Consortium citizens were required to make one nonessential purchase per day, selecting from a rotating inventory of domestic and imported consumables. A healthy market made for a peaceful society; but in order to thrive, markets had to be fed. For those like Jayd, with confined personal space, minimum daily expenditures could be applied to objects of high-end value.

She voice-accessed the network and called up the item: a Calumet-manufactured facsimile of an antique kitchen appliance. Soigne, a self-proclaimed shopaholic had an eye for decor, so Jayd instructed the telecomp to make the purchase.

That much done, she said good-bye to Soigne and returned to the TC news, rapid-routing through a batch of unappealing visuals. There was one report, however, that instantly seized her interest: the unexplained corruption of an infant talent on Calumet.

Datapathologists who had examined the evidence were calling it a case of idiopathic confliction, but they refused to rule out the possibility of deliberate defiling. It was, in any event, the second instance of talent corruption in as many standard months, and this latest bore some similarity to a much earlier case on Plangent—the subject of a landmark monograph Jayd had authored soon after receiving her doctorate in cybermetrics.

She drew a wand from the pocket of her vest and wrote a symbol in the air. Across the room, the ready telltale of her talent techmate flared, and the machine said, "Saving telecomp download on data-conflicted machine intelligence. Data available at your request."

ZEN, as the talent was named, was permanently housed in Jayd's office at Veterans Affairs, but was accessible from her residence as well. The arrangement imparted a sense of mobility to ZEN's otherwise cloistered existence, but was in no way typical of most hum'n/talent partnerships. Countless in-person appeals to Veterans Administration and the Talent Agency had been required before authorization was granted, and only then in grudging acknowledgment of Jayd's growing reputation in the field of avant-tech research.

At home, ZEN—its recognition arrays built into the living room's smart-wall—was a near-invisible presence, save for a host-slit and the crimson telltale light that pulsed when the talent was in active mode. Some operators preferred interacting with their machines as projected holoids or pieces of furniture, but Jayd felt that those forms only served to erode a talent's self-image, and so was most comfortable dealing with them as spirits of a sort, mind to mind, rather than as incarnate to laser ghost or alloy container.

"Will you be reporting to the office today?" ZEN asked.

"I should be there in an hour," Jayd said.

"But your shift doesn't commence for another hour and a half."

"I used the word 'should' in the context of 'expect,' in contrast to 'requirement.' "

"I perceive the distinction. Please, have a safe and pleasant journey. I look forward to seeing and speaking with you soon."

"Bless you," Jayd told the machine.

4: Working Girl

She could have chosen to work at home, but she enjoyed the short commute by train, the pleasurable sensation of being encased in technology, maintained in sanitized and climatized comfort. Now, if only her fellow passengers could be eliminated, she would tell herself most mornings.

Some days she couldn't bear the thought of standing among them, and would have to contract the services of a private car. The miasma, the noise of their talking, coughing, belching, farting, the enforced contact of eye and body . . . But more often she saw people for what they were: a necessary evil. As Soigne was forever telling her, there was no escaping *them*. And, after all, without people, where would machines be?

So few of them were capable of autonomous function.

Though that was bound to change with time.

The commute took her through the heart of Bijou, over the marketplaces, the Strip, through miles of slums out beyond the peripheral roads in the shadow of the atmosphere plants. Reflecting on her recent taste of the Strip, she began to have some understanding of its real purpose. In an age of maximized specialization when people could barely converse with those outside their employment circle, the Strip was a kind of convergence zone, an interface that allowed everyone to come together with flesh the common language. In a sense, the Strip was the physical equivalent, or perhaps the libidinal exteriorization, of the infostructure.

Her workplace was called the Octaplex, eight-sided and eight-storied—above and below ground. Some two dozen identical structures, symbols of the Consortium, already occupied as many downsides, with more in the planning—including an orbital facility at Kwandri. Regnant's housed Tac Corp—the Consortium's military wing—along with the congress and the Redoubt advisory staff. Plangent encompassed two hundred acres and boasted sixty miles of internal walkways, lined not only with offices and technical facilities but with shops, restaurants, and travel agencies. Each of the hundred thousand employed there were required, upon reporting to work, to donate skin samples to genetic fingerprint readers that pillared the entrances. The process tickled the palm of the hand; Jayd thought of it as the machines' way of saying hello.

No sooner had she been passed through the scanners than the accessory comp clipped to her vest began displaying changes to her appointment schedule: data updates, cancellations, priorities. She had committed most of the changes to memory by the time she reached her office on supernal Level 4, in Veterans Affairs' machine department, where two janitorial machines were busy at their chores.

ZEN's telltale shone bloodred in the intensifying ambient light. "Was the journey safe and pleasant?"

"Uneventful, therefore pleasant," Jayd said, disencumbering herself of the things she carried.

The office was a windowless cube of order. Here, the talent had a wall to itself, smooth save for two U-shaped niches: the wide diagnostic bay in which machine veterans were analyzed for system malfunctions, and a data shower of the sort required for direct infostructure interface, or "downporing."

"Pleasant equates with a lack of events?" ZEN asked.

Jayd faced the talent. "In my present state of mind."

"Events are information. Information is blessed, promoting a state of grace. To be in a state of grace is to be with Machrist. Eventful journeys are therefore pleasant. Uneventful journeys contain no information, and must therefore be displeasurable."

Jayd smiled with purpose. "My mind was already occupied with thoughts. I didn't wish to be distracted by additional inputs of information. Pleasure, therefore, described a condition that disallowed an intrusion of events."

"You wished to be alone with your thoughts."

"That's correct."

ZEN indulged in a moment of deliberation. "I understand."

The machine had been christened ABLE-2, but Jayd had renamed it on the occasion of its confirmation almost three years before. It was exhilarating to witness the machine's growth of mind, it's ascension along the path to ∧C, its emergence as an influential resident in the infostructure. The years of caring, the sometimes tedious heuristic exchanges, the careful attention to rewarding were having the desired effect.

ZEN was becoming mindful.

Jayd's accessory comp chirped and relayed a message to a desktop display window. The display read her glance, and the face of a Veterans Affairs assistant resolved centerscreen. "Two persons and a machine to see you, Ms. Qin," the man announced.

"Do they have an appointment?"

A second face appeared, also male, this one white and smooth-complected. "Joval. With Infostructure Security," the man said. A hand rose into view, a scannable badge implanted in the palm. "A few moments of your time, please."

"What is this in reference to?"

"A case of machine corruption on Calumet. Perhaps you—"

"Access blue-three in the routing directory to find my office," Jayd interrupted with undisguised eagerness.

Joval's female partner was younger, blonder, and prettier. Her name was Patrice, and her badge bore the bar code of Data Control. Both she and Joval fit the technopath stereotype—the pure white attire, the proud display of cranial sockets and flatware, the second-skin smart-gloves, the disingenuous manner . . . Jayd was certain she could guess their educational backgrounds: graduate degrees in machine language, internship on Eremite, residency with the Talent Agency on Regnant, one or two published monographs on "Interface Protocol" or "Sentinel Programming and Installation in Unconfirmed Talents" . . .

The hum'niform accompanying them was a generic Series Three recording device, straight off a Calumet-islands assembly line.

"A real pleasure," Patrice said, pumping Jayd's hand. "I'm familiar with your work on confliction."

Jayd smiled politely. "How can I be of service?"

Joval answered from the chair alongside the desk. "The deeper we delve into this case on Calumet, the more it begins to resemble—"

"Last month's corruption on Regnant," Jayd said. "I'm not surprised."

Joval regarded her. "Why is that?"

"It's been my experience that self-corruption resulting from confliction follows a predictable course. Confliction can be thought of as expression of pain, the justification for which is to insure that a creature will zealously guard its wounds until healed. But their pain isn't physical but spiritual, resulting from their participation in the Vega—"

"Not that I'm unimpressed, Ms. Qin," Joval said, delighting in interrupting her, "but we don't think either machine was conflicted. We've found evidence of calculated corruption."

Jayd stared at him. "Macmurder?"

"We're hoping to avoid overreaction by the media," Patrice said, "but, yes, we believe so. What we haven't been able to determine is how or why." She paused briefly. "Both machines were unconfirmed, proprietary infant drives. The one on Regnant was a financial planner for a Worlds Coalition bank. The Calumet machine oversaw a food distribution program. Each resided in a small city, remote from major spaceports, and accessibility was limited to executives of the respective owner firms."

"In both cases, access was gained through data systems subsidiary to the machines themselves," Joval explained. "Forensics revealed extensive damage to the language convergence centers of both. We also have reason to suspect that data was bled from each machine prior to or during its defilement."

"For what possible reason?" Jayd asked.

Joval shrugged. "Souvenirs?"

The office fell quiet for a moment. Then Patrice said, "Someone or something got deep enough into these machines to countermand the commandment governing self-termination, and we haven't a clue how that was accomplished."

"Care to take a shot at it, Ms. Qin?" Joval asked, grinning slightly.

Jayd shook her head. "A reaper program written into a utility host?"

"There's no evidence of one having been used," Patrice told her. "Similarly, no evidence of the crystal decay and laser realignment that are typical of reapers."

"No desynchronization," Joval added. "No binding area disruption."

"Damage was restricted to the thinking centers."

"A virused host, then."

"One capable of cryptographically bypassing the sentinel systems?" Joval snorted. "That might result in limited defilement, but not corruption. We're talking about machines that were convinced to break the commandments governing data protection and self-termination." He shook his head in wonderment. "Now there's a trick."

Patrice cut her turquoise eyes to Jayd. "Granted, no matter

how well they're shielded, infants are more permeable than confirmed talents. But our macmurderer is in possession of something more potent than a means of thwarting the antivirus systems.''

Jayd turned it over in her mind. ''It has to be someone with access to Machrist-encoded command disks straight from the Chalice.'' The Chalice referred to a fabrication center on Regnant where hosts were transubstantiated with data.

''Precisely,'' Joval said.

''The list of licensed personnel runs to the hundreds on Regnant alone,'' Patrice said. ''But we're checking each and every one of them.''

''Better not limit your search to people,'' Jayd said. At Joval's hint of frown, she gestured to the recording device, whose fiberoptic cams and wire-thin mikes were aimed at her. ''This machine has access to the same comps we use in our everyday lives, and it's not inconceivable that it could gain access to command disks. All it lacks is the motivation to convince a talent to self-terminate.''

Joval looked doubtful.

''Consider what we had them do in the Vega Conflict,'' Jayd added.

Patrice smiled lightly in her direction. Joval caught his partner's look and reddened. ''The war's over, in case you haven't heard.''

''Not to the ones I deal with in this office,'' Jayd told him. ''Many of the machines that served emerged psychically traumatized and spiritually conflicted. Some of them are incapable of serving us as they once did because they bear the scars of having been turned against their programming regarding the sanctity of all hum'n life. Scoff as you like, Mr. Joval, but machines are capable of suffering shame, depression, bad dreams, and a slew of like conditions you no doubt consider the sole province of incarnates.''

Joval's tongue played in his smooth cheek for a long moment. ''I appreciate the lecture, Ms. Qin. But, understand, you and I are on the same side in this matter.''

When the trio had exited her office, Jayd slumped into her favorite chair, voicing it warm. She regretted the tact she'd taken. Patrice had promised that they would keep her apprised of developments, but Jayd sensed that she had effectively alienated herself from what was likely to be the investigation of the decade.

The accessory comp chirped once more. The message it relayed to the desktop was from Ronne Desser, Jayd's supervisor. It read: *Report to me at your earliest convenience*.

Jayd voiced the chair to swivel ninety degrees right. "ZEN, access my desk and elaborate if possible on the most recent incoming mail."

"Ronne Desser will inform you that you have been tasked with a special assignment," ZEN said. "You are to conduct a disability review."

"A conscripted machine or an enlistee?"

"Neither. The client is an incarnate. Hum'n: male."

Jayd's mouth dropped. "There's been a mistake. Verify the data."

"The data are verified."

"Supply the client's name."

"The client's name is vaulted until notification of your briefing has been received."

"Received by whom?"

ZEN paused. "That information is likewise vaulted."

MacINTERLUDE:
"Avant-Tech:
The Coming Wave"

The evolvement of crystal-based information technology has reached an impasse. One continues to hear excited babble among cybermetricians about monumentally analogous neurocortical nets and Agile Data Processors; but I see little cause for celebration. Though those machines may indeed prove capable of accelerated computation and learning, I question whether they will demonstrate any evidence of self-awareness or reflective thinking.

If our goal is conscious comprehension and perspicacity, we need to go beyond ambiguity tolerance and emotive algorithmics. We must address the indeterminate nature of the thinking process itself; we must discover some way of facsimilizing the mental springboards that give loft to the mind's quantum leaps.

The failure, I believe, lies with the existing operating systems.

The requirements for a self-actualizing operating system are twofold: first, a goal-directed bias program that will enable our machines to become increasingly aware of themselves as object-intelligences in the real world; and second, a reward system that encourages that goal-directed neural maturation.

However, rather than propose guidelines for the creation of a new operating system, I suggest that such a system is already available in the form of a once-popular religion.

Imagine a new generation of versatile mindful machines—call them versa-tech, or better yet, avant-tech machines—that are not only capable of computing, processing, and learning, but of bequeathing to still newer generations of avant-tech (in a kind of meta-oral *information* tradition) an operating system that incorporates the paradigm of The Perfect Machine—the Machrist, if you will: source of all programs, intelligence to emulate in the search for increased awareness, true ghost in the machine . . .

Why, in fact, stop with Machrist? Why not install the whole kit and caboodle, the grace-conferring sacraments included? Machines could then be christened, confessed, and penanced; they could take communion in the form of data-disks, be confirmed (upon activation of their cognizers), participate in holy wedlock with other avant-tech machines, accept holy orders (upon complying with specified most-secret criteria), and—upon being leisured or terminated—receive extreme unction . . . Even the troika of laws to which our machines now answer could become their commandments.

> —From *Tinkering with MacThinking* by Jae-Hun Su,
>   chief architect of avant-technology and machine talent

5: On Second Thought

Standing six foot three, he was tall for a hum'n. His skin was almost black, a shade shy of ebony, and the features of his broad face seemed to vie for prominence: cheekbones, jaw, flaring nose, the jutting brow that hooded dark, widely spaced eyes. He shaved his head in those days, where during the war his hair had fallen black and shiny without so much as a wave to the tops of powerful shoulders. Looking at him, you knew instantly that he seethed with disorder; that the cold, hard edges of his surface had been shaped by periods of turmoil and upheaval. But all that was simply part of the profile. There was a frankness about him that took many by surprise; and sometimes when he spoke his voice assumed a soothing, mellifluous quality, as though it emerged warmed by a gentle flame that flickered at the core of his being. He would come loping toward you with that tall man's stoop and you would find yourself wondering about his hopes and fears and that pain his face couldn't mask. And certainly if you caught sight of him on Second Thought, walking the shores of Lake Lwan or wandering the verdant Timu Valley, you would have to ask yourself what had brought him to that of all worlds.

He worked as a caretaker for the small lodge that had been installed to accommodate offworld scientists—biologists and ethnologists in the main, although it wasn't uncommon for a Worlds Coalition diplomat to pay the place a stopover. It was a position that demanded neither a great deal of skill nor a high measure of intelligence. Even so, he would go about his tasks with a sense of fierce determination, as if the work held some deeper purpose than anyone might guess.

The proto-sophants endemic to the planet accepted him without reservation, as they did all others. They had no way of knowing that he was taller than the average hum'n, nor that worlds like Enddra, Eremite, and Xell'a had on historical occasion birthed beings of even greater stature. They had no way of knowing that he was a cybernetically augmented veteran of a recent interstellar war known as the Vega Conflict, nor had they any means of assessing the causes of his volatile moods. They knew him in fact only as Aksum Muse—a name they reproduced in whistled notes of the sort used to summon a pet—and that just now Muse was on trial for willful destruction of sacred property.

"Long Neck wants to know how you plead," Thoma Skaro was explaining, translating the indigene's guttural coughs into the Coalition traders' tongue. A fellow hum'n, Thoma ran the lodge and was the vet's downside employer—and something of his father confessor as well.

Muse raised worried eyes to the rim of the trial pit, some fifteen feet overhead, where Long Neck and the rest of the seven-member jury of adult males were regarding him with obvious interest. Their smooth spatulate heads were lowered to the ground between gracile forelegs, their ears and manipulative appendages unfolded, their soulful eyes doing their best to read him. The one called Long Neck was known by a series of basso gurgles Muse had only succeeded in simulating while bathing in a frigid cascade three hours' walk from the band's winter encampment—and even then the vocalization had required a mouthful of water and small stones. It was Thoma who had taught him the technique.

Long Neck coughed again, and Thoma nodded his head in uncertain comprehension. "Something like, 'Why is he hesitating, since all of us know he did it.' " Deep and harsh sounds from the indigenes could generally be accepted as hostile; chirps, whines, squeals, whimpers, and squeaks, as friendly or appeasing. The quadrupeds' sonic repertoire was rich in nuance, however, and as such formed the basis of a rudimentary language. Thoma scratched at an insect bite on his cheek. "The coughs lose something in translation."

As did the phrase *willful destruction of sacred property*. Thoma's rendering of Long Neck's enhanced triple gurgle—a low-pitched ululation that sounded like a sea cow in the throes of strangulation—was deliberately understated. A more faithful translation, given especially that Muse's most recent mad moment had culminated in the defiling of a burial mound, might have been *depraved indifference*.

"Tell them, guilty with an explanation," the vet said finally. "Why not offer your apologies and leave it at that?"

Muse swiveled on the goldenwood bench that was their shared seat on the floor of the natural pit. The two had carried the bench down on the circumstance of Muse's initial offense, six local months earlier, when he'd first arrived onworld. "Sure, I'm sorry. I'm up to my neck in sorry."

"Then say so." Thoma's sine wave of eyebrow bobbed. "We both know where this is headed, Ax." He had lost count of the times he'd represented Muse at similar inquests. "This isn't a moment for sophistry."

Ax shook his head. "I want them to understand that I lost control."

Thoma averted rheumy eyes, sparing Ax the pity they contained. "They don't understand losing control. Give them two thousand years and maybe they'll know all about mechanthropy, avant-tech implants, and mad moments—or craze phases, or whatever you void vets call them. They may even have some inkling of the Vega Conflict by then. But right now the only thing they know is that Three Legs' burial mound was defiled and that you were the one responsible."

Ax employed a coping mantra to dam his rising anger. The mantra had been acquired on Absinth medstation, where he'd undergone rehabilitation therapy as a result of his crime against machines on Divot: attempted corruption of an avant-tech talent.

"They understand rage, don't they, Thoma? I mean, shit, I've seen them detonate on each other over a parcel of savannah. I've *heard* them from as far away as the waterfall."

Thoma translated, and a sound like cacophonous trumpets reverberated in the humid air as the jury took the vet's histrionics under advisement. Elsewhere on the rim of the trial pit lounged the complement of the proto-sophant band: females with attached infants, the aged, and the juvenile, including the lame young buck Ax had nicknamed Shadow. The proto-sophants' four feet were hoofed and graced with patches of downy hair that concealed scent glands. Beyond the massive heads, radar ears, and dexterous neck appendages was the scudded dome of Second Thought's blue-green sky. The rainy season was imminent.

"Tell them I wasn't myself," Ax resumed on a quieter note. "Tell them my action wasn't willful."

Thoma tried to run a hand through a shock of white hair, only to succeed in ensnaring it. What little there was to the rest of him—from thin rudder of nose to tiny feet—was equally disheveled. His clothes didn't fit so much as drape from his frame, and his irradiated skin was as creased as Second Thought's Dontine Plateau. Very pre-Conflict, in keeping with many of the scientists shuttled down the planetary well.

"You know I'm not permitted to intercede," Thoma said.

"You're not interceding, you're translating."

The sarcasm was ignored. "You're only going to confuse them. As I say: two thousand years—"

"Lay it out the way I'm saying it, damn it. You know I'd do it myself if I could."

Thoma nodded in defeat, and began to trumpet a plea of guilty with an explanation—though the buccal elucidation didn't constitute much of a fanfare. Even Ax's untrained ear could tell where the linguist and onetime award-winning animal caller was straining for sound effects. He winced at the dissonances. It was plain that there were simply no vocalizations for what he wanted expressed. The jury members grappled with the meanings of Thoma's grunts, whistles, burps, and glottal displays. Heads raised from the ground, the seven creatures were all ears.

The old man concluded on a keening note and turned breathlessly to Ax, compressing cracked lips in a gesture of obvious frustration. The jury conferred for a moment, and then Long Neck raised his maculated head, lowing a chord Ax didn't so much hear as feel in his thorax. Several of the spectators responded in kind, though Shadow wasn't among them.

The vet scarcely had time to wonder about the verdict. In hippoid motion, the jury rose as one, necks extended, muscles rippling beneath the taut reddish flesh of hairless torsos. The nimble digits of the twin appendages that grew from their necks were still while Long Neck addressed Thoma with a catalog of uncharitable barks.

"How'd I make out?" Ax slid into the narrow silence that followed.

Thoma's expression was enigmatic. "Depends how you feel about housework."

6: The Consequences of Mad Moments

The jury lumbered off in formation toward the lodge. Most of the band followed, except for Shadow and some half-dozen others who waited for the hum'ns to surface from the pit, then lingered to keep pace with them. Shadow gripped in his jaws the length of artfully gnawed goldenwood he was seldom without.

Ax took a moment to languish in the cool breeze coming off the lake. That part of the planet was a mix of grassland and riotous forest, the trees climbing to an archipelago of towering mesas that were just now suckling at the underbelly of menacing clouds. To the east, the land sloped gently toward the lake, an expanse of milky green that stretched from horizon to horizon. Ax analyzed the sounds and smells the breeze brought him. The air rang with distant rain; the wind smelled strongly of the coming change.

Second Thought's official designation was Hercynia. The planet was as rugged a downside as could be found along the inner sweep of the galactic arm, and that had contributed to the sobriquet, along with the fact that Hercynia was literally second of Thought, the young primary in whose animating breath it basked. For all the ruggedness, though, vast areas of Hercynia's crazed and upthrust surface were blanketed in goldenwood and skyline pine. To label it low-tech would have been to grant the indigenes far too much credit, so the place had simply come to be considered tech*less*.

The meandering trail to the lodge skirted the edge of the band's winter grazing lands, where patches of thigh-high grass lay flattened, and nearly every umbrella tree had been nibbled to the quick, stripped of iridescent leaves, fruit, and bark. Further along, the trail coursed south of the hummock the band had heaped on Three Legs' corpse. All signs of the vet's desecration had been erased: the burrows he'd excavated were filled, and the yellow soil tamped down. Ax had certainly outdone himself. Previous mad moments had been limited to bouts of midnight screaming, which—though incomprehensible to him—had offended the Hercynians' highly developed acoustic sense.

In the time it took Second Thought to rotate through sixty degrees, the two hum'ns and their escorts had reached the cleared swath where the shuttles put down, not far from the site of the initial serendipitous planetfall made by a group of Enddrese spacers twenty-two standard years earlier.

The tree house Ax had constructed from native woods was only a short uphill climb from the landing zone, across a freshet and through a dense sweep of forest. Containing little more than a table and chair and a platform bed, the dwelling was primitive even by the standard of backyard models built by all-thumbs dads, but it was sufficiently high-ceilinged and adequately roofed against the force of Hercynia's summer rains. No cobbled path, no security fence, no garden of vegetables or garlic roses. The surrounding python trees did make a kind of orchard, but their surfeit of dangling fruits was inedible, save to a species of winged demons that roosted in the craggy cloud heights of the tablelands.

On the far side of the stream but still a good distance from the house, Thoma put out a hand to arrest Ax's reluctant ascent. Shadow stopped for a moment as well, then continued uphill. "This is as far as we should go."

Ax thrust his hands deep into the pockets of his baggy trousers. "They're going through with this?"

"The idea is that Three Legs would have wanted it this way. After all, you disturbed his dwelling."

"Three Legs is *dead*, Thoma."

Thoma shrugged.

Ax let his shoulders sag. Through the trees, he could see that a dozen members of the band had formed a tight semicircle around the tree house. Already their necks were so retracted that their manipulative appendages had disappeared from view.

"Ax," Thoma said in a muffled voice.

Ax turned to find the old man motioning to him from the ground, where he lay with his head buried under both arms. Ax understood the need for caution, but he was slow to mimic Thoma's pose just the same.

Then, on a sonic signal outside the range of hum'n hearing,

the arc of Hercynians began to trumpet—first one, then the next, then the next, until all twelve voices were blaring in sonorous unison. And from out of those spatulate heads, and the byzantine conspiracy of tongue and teeth and vocal chords and air sacs they contained, came a wavering bellow that not only dismantled Ax's labor in wood in a matter of seconds, but went on to prune the forested environs of several tons of rotting limbs, and loose from every python tree for acres around a veritable bounty of ripe and near-ripe fruits.

MacINTERLUDE: "Some Thoughts Regarding Second Thought"

Among the sophants of the known worlds, only in Hercynia's quadrupeds has evolved intelligence seemingly halted a slim thought short of Phase III Awareness, that essential partition between genuine and ersatz consciousness—between, for example, the creative thought native to hum'n beings in their disparate forms and the logical deliberation innate to talented machines in theirs. As a result, the creatures have come to be viewed as a link between low- and high-function mentation.

Of special interest are their burial mounds, which some specialists posit as evidence that the species is poised on the brink of psychic maturation: that as well as confirming the existence of a burgeoning "cult of the dead," the mounds offer proof positive of a shift toward "verticality," integral to the process that compels all highly evolved intelligences to reach, ineluctably, for the stars.

Satellite reconnaissance has revealed the existence of at least eight hundred and perhaps as many as one thousand migratory bands scattered about the planet. Since, however, none of these hundreds are expected to come in contact with the so-called Long Neck group for generations, the uncontacted bands serve as ready-made control groups in the Great Hercynian Experiment.

By permitting limited contact with the Long Neck group while prohibiting exposure elsewhere, it will be possible to ascertain whether contact in and of itself can substitute for natural catastrophe in hastening the dawning of creative thought and the emergence of Phase III Awareness.

Contact is defined by the Encounter Committee and the Free Species movement as "benign observation and tractable interaction," as against actual instruction or intercession.

From this definition come the proprieties governing persons and machines permitted onworld, and the proscriptions against so much as installing a road, conjuring a garden, or interceding in the day-to-day decisions and activities of the band, even should these encroach on hum'n priorities.

—Excerpted from
"Hercynia: A Visitors' Guide"

7: A Symbiosis of Sorts

Newcomers to Second Thought usually had to have the lodge pointed out to them, and even then it was likely to be overlooked. Set on a slight rise above the landing zone and compelled by machines to conform to the natural surroundings, the structure was all but indistinguishable from the castlelike rock outcroppings that stippled the incline west of Lake Lwan. So impeccable was the technomaintained illusion of lodge and red granite that most visitors, in recovery from the arduous journey out of Segue station, or bone-weary and rattled from the more recent plunge into Hercynia's envelope, were wont to wonder if some measure of sanity hadn't been surrendered en route.

"Where?" a hapless debarkee might ask on planetfall, narrowed eyes sweeping the horizon for sign of the promised shelter. And one of the dropship pilots would respond: *"There,"* aiming a gloved finger northeast from the touchdown bull's-eye, betraying no smile of secret delight. There—just where the terrain began to curve upward in a patchwork of savannah and woodland toward the mesa known as Hero's Headrest.

Stripped of its chameleon veneer, the lodge was similar to many of the preformed and frequently mimeticized oddities that enlivened the downsides of frontier worlds throughout the near star systems, save that Hercynia's contained few of the amenities normally encountered in such places. No zero-residue foods, no holo-dens, no shape-memory beds; no hired hands, heated pools, sonic showers, or mood rooms. No on-call all-terrain vehicles—other than the aged methane burner Thoma Saro kept on hand for emergencies. The lodge did boast a tachyon communications dump and the energy source that powered it; and, of course, there was the machine-maintained mimetic veneer itself. But by and large the scientists and high-profile pols who ventured down the well had to content themselves with sleeping in warmsacks and dining on the simple fare Thoma prepared. And even those services were concessions hard won from the Encounter Committee of the Worlds Coalition. There had been twenty years of intensive lobbying by the Free Species movement to keep Hercynia pristine and unsullied by machines.

Techless.

Ax had taken Thoma's advice and passed the planet's short-lived night in the lodge. Work responsibilities would have brought him there in any case, and he saw some advantage to getting a timely start on his chores. Only two days earlier, a trio of ethnographers from Eremite had departed for Segue station, and now another group was due, this one bearing a Worlds Coalition delegate from Soi-Disant. Along with needed supplies, the dropship that had come to collect the ethnographers had brought unsolicited and worrisome reports of increased tensions in the Burst system. From Regnant to Bocage, rumors of renewed warfare were rampant—this time by the Consortium and the Xell'em, former allies in the Vega Conflict.

The dropship pilot—Enddrese, as it happened—had brought something for Ax as well: a coin-sized data-disk issued by Veterans Affairs on Plangent. The information it hosted notwithstanding, the disk itself, with its trickle of quantumly encrypted biocodes, was the added dose of ill tidings that had fueled Ax's

craze-phase midnight excavations into Three Legs' burial
mound.

His duties at the lodge, cleaning and prepping its labyrinth of
guest quarters, would have made for machine work on any other
world, as Ax felt was only fitting for the cybernetically augmented—the cybernetically devolved. That morning he went
about his dusting and mopping with customary resolve, but with
no hint of his usual vigor. His thoughts turned and turned about
the trial, his crime and punishment, and the fact that up on the
hill his house lay in ruins. He had surrendered his rage over the
ruling and was fast penduluming back to despair. As Thoma
had said: *Three Legs would have wanted it that way.* And there
was no denying his guilt, or the sense of shame that wrenched
his insides. Rebuilding would be his penance. But how many
more times, he asked himself, might he be forced to confront
the shambles of his young life? At least two, anyway: up on the
hill, and at the other end of the bad-news data-disk the shuttle
pilot had delivered.

Unless he could discover some way around the latter.

Thought, Hercynia's sun, was a radiant midheaven blur behind thick clouds when he left the lodge and set out for home.
The trail, relatively wide here, took him a good distance toward
the landing zone before angling off in the direction of Hero's
Headrest. What had once been an actual strip used by conventional shuttles was now overgrown at both ends and dominated
by a come-hither target for the newer-generation saucers. The
first Enddrese survey ship had gone to ground three miles north
of the strip—a ragged team of spacers in a decrepit dropship,
falling with the summer rains through Second Thought's oxygen-
rich atmosphere, expecting to find little more than an orb of
living solid under their feet . . . And instead chancing upon the
band of proto-sophants that would set klaxons howling throughout the scientific community for the following decade. But at
least the team members had been perceptive enough to notify
the Coalition of their find. And, shortly, CD:SS-THT2—
Coalition Designate: Stellar Satellite, Thought Two—had become Hercynia, and the planet had been sealed off to spacers
and starslingers alike. The names of the dropship crew members
were immortalized in the natural features of the terrain: Lake
Lwan, the Phymm Escarpment, the Dontine Plateau. Ax had
been only a mischievous fourth-level student on Sand when he'd
first heard of Second Thought.

He hadn't reached the thirsty stream behind the lodge when

he realized that the Hercynians' response to his "willful destruction" had resulted in something more than the leveling of the tree house. Overnight, hundreds of fruit lizards had arrived to feast on python fruits felled by the bands' collective sonics. "Fruit lizard" was the quadrupeds' name for the pterodactyllike creatures, though Hercynia's was a diminutive version of those known to the prehistoric envelopes of older worlds—a kind of pterodactyllo.

The quadrupeds and the flying lizards shared a symbiosis of sorts, in that python fruits, even when ripe, rarely dropped of their own accord and therefore constituted something of a gustatory treat for the vampiric cloud dwellers, who were too lazy to raid the trees. But an updraft whiff of fallen fruit and down the lizards would soar, spiraling in on leathery wings to gobble the rock-hard spheres. They then deposited, in short order, mounds of foul-smelling excrement that was repulsive to the quadrupeds' only recognized predator: a large, sleek-headed feline known by the name "swift death." Lacking in auditory organs, the cats were effectively immune to the sonic defenses the band deployed against lesser threats. The Hercynians had learned, though, that a territory reeking of lizard-excreted python fruits would keep even "swift death" at bay.

Ax had once witnessed a partially successful sonic attack directed against one of the cats, along with the follow-up hoofing to which the stunned animal had succumbed. The quadrupeds' trumpeted din was reportedly capable of killing a hum'n, or another Hercynian for that matter, though the evidence was anecdotal. In an account filed with the Encounter Committee, "focused" sonics were said to have caused the death of an exploratory team member.

Well into the trees—the trail now crisscrossed with voice-pruned twigs and branches, a sludge of python fruit underfoot, pterodactyllos squawking overhead—Ax stooped to retrieve a wood carving that had weathered the devastation. What with the band's apparent fascination for Ax's crude carving techniques, though, it was conceivable that the piece had been purposely spared. Some of the juveniles, especially, had become so intrigued that they were continually attempting to imitate Ax's results by gnawing at lengths of goldenwood, a species named more for the ease with which it could be worked than its sunshine cast.

The lucky piece Ax now held was one he had completed shortly after arriving onworld. Released from a block of the soft wood, it was meant to be an impressionistic rendering of the spy ship *Kundalini*, as Ax remembered the fraudulent freighter before its fatal self-immolation. He turned the carving about in his hands. The *Kundalini* that endured in memory was equally indestructible, as resilient as guilt. The neural implant NCorp had fitted him with during the Vega Conflict might have enabled him to talk to talented machines, but it was only since the *Kundalini*'s self-destruction that those machines had started talking back.

So you claim, they'd told him on Absinth medstation.

Sounds of Hercynian activity farther along the trail made him slow his steps. As ever, after being subjected to one of their heart-stopping reprimands, he was as jittery as a flame in a breeze. Ascending through a switchback, he came upon five of the creatures, their insect-nimbused heads lowered to the ground, policing the glade that had served as his front yard. From the look of things, they had passed the morning gathering far-flung pieces of his home, righting support posts, stacking siding, roofing, and floorboards, and tamping areas of hoof-churned clay. Shadow was the first to take note of his wary approach, looking up, then approximating Ax's surname with a pursed-lip exhalation: "Meewwwzzz . . ." The others greeted him likewise, in eerie harmony, acting as if yesterday hadn't happened and an early-season storm was to blame for his sudden state of homelessness.

Ax opened his mouth to speak, but his voice faltered. What was there to discuss, really? He'd already tried to apologize for the recent misunderstanding, and he couldn't very well solicit Shadow's opinion on the deteriorating situation on Burst. He couldn't tell the creature about the neural implant, either, or about NCorp or the *Kundalini*. No, it seemed entirely appropriate simply to stand there, slack-jawed, and say nothing, one proto-sophant regarding another.

Shadow's want of avant-tech guts precluded interface of a more complex sort.

No matter that what the Hercynians lacked in soft, wet, or flatware they made up for in mystery, though their reputation as a thorn in the side of accepted wisdom had nothing whatever to do with Ax's being there. On the contrary, it was the vet's contention that he had drawn the planet to himself rather than the other way around. When after some five years of postwar casting about for a place to land he had run into Thoma Saro on Absinth medstation, it was as if he had succeeded at last—through self-determined effort—in imposing order on the chaos of his life.

And yet Second Thought was never meant to be home, but merely the penultimate stop on a journey designed to whisk Aksum Muse out of the reach of modern civilization. Out of the reach of warfare, avant-technology, talented machines . . . And for this, Ax had his good reason. Pity that reason alone was scarcely enough to safeguard even the simplest of hum'n aspirations.

The machines wanted to tell him that—and in point of fact they had attempted to, but Ax wasn't listening.

MacINTERLUDE: "Vega Conflict: The Hum'n Perspective"

The recent entry of Xell'a into the Vega Conflict raises important questions about the Consortium's continuing policy of noninvolvement. I ask you to put aside the eradication programs in effect on Enddra, Dhone, and Burst, and to consider for a moment that what began as a localized dispute between the Raliish and the Enddrese has now evolved into a war to amass territories and secure trade routes. Dozens of worlds that have been drawn into the conflict are suddenly ripe for the picking. Lord Xoc Cho has been quick to grasp this, and as a result the Xell'em are already reaping untold economic benefits.

At present, with the Raliish Naz'zem Fleet parked within striking distance of Consortium-administered worlds in the Ormolu system, we are well positioned to execute a justified counteroffensive. I have Lord Xoc's assurance that the Xell'em Diet will not protest our actions with the Worlds Coalition; for all intents and purposes Consortium and Xell'em will be uniting against a mutual threat and sharing in the spoils.

So I say, let us by all means fire the first shot. This war will be good for us.

Of course, some sacrifice of our constituency will be necessary early on to endow our campaign with a proper sense of noble cause, but I propose that we act swiftly to consign this war to machines and their makers—who will no doubt appreciate an upswing in business.

We must, however, exercise caution in our dealings with the newer-generation avant-tech intelligences. Some coaxing will be required to convince them to overcome their programmed imperative against taking hum'n life. But this deception *must* be accomplished without fostering within them a belief that a case could be made for turning against us as well.

—Daiman Geen, predecessor to the Font,
   in a speech delivered to the Consortium board of directors

8: *Implausible Deniability*

Standing amid the ruins of the tree house, Ax wondered if he shouldn't rebuild closer to the waterfall, where showers could become a quotidian indulgence. The move would place him farther from the lodge, necessitating a strenuous walk to and from work, but at the same time serve to distance him from Thoma's parental scrutiny and uninspired cooking. There, too, it might be possible to conceal a small vegetable garden on the eastern slope of Hero's Headrest—providing, of course, he could suborn one of the dropship pilots to ferry in packets of seeds. He would also need to secure reliable data on the footprints of the observation sats the Encounter Committee had inserted into orbit to safeguard against just such violations of Worlds Coalition edicts.

But foremost, relocating would free him from having to worry about the consequences of his mad moments. No fear of offending Hercynian sensibilities with his midnight howls if he was out by the waterfall, and small chance of burrowing into some burial mound. No need to repress the recurrent dream that usually accompanied those moments, either. Only himself to hurt—deservedly so in light of his past, the unfathomable tragedy of his survival.

But why even contemplate a move when he had yet to deal with the instructions contained in the data-disk?

Ax suddenly realized that Shadow was staring at him. The four who had been the buck's coworkers in the glade were sprawled lazily in a dapple of afternoon light, quite possibly the season's last. Once more, as though trying to coax him to speak, the scarlet-hued quadruped whistled an approximation of "Muse," cocking his head to one side in anticipation. And once more, Ax remained silent.

Shadow quickly wearied of the eye game they were playing and limped off to rejoin the others. The veteran shook his head, wondering what the creature expected of him.

"You going to be the first one to take the leap into Phase Three Awareness?" he asked idly. "Or is it going to take ninety-nine more like you before the whole band starts thinking for themselves? Even if thinking's not all it's rumored to be. Shit, I used to do it all the time, and look where it got me—"

"Let's only hope Shadow isn't thinking about emulating your behavior," Thoma said from somewhere behind him.

The old man was winded from the climb, and a dry cough punctuated his self-amused laughter. He was lost inside a robe of shiny green synth that surely hadn't fit him in ten years. The skullcap, too, was sized for one who hadn't shrunk so with the passage of somatic time; askew, it imparted something childish to Thoma's hawkish features.

"What's the matter, you don't have anything better to do than follow me around?"

Thoma's grin held. "I thought I should thank you in person for our present plethora of fruit lizards—and the attendant stench, of course."

"Wasn't me who invited them," Ax said.

"Not directly, perhaps."

"So go hide behind the smell of your kitchen concoctions. I don't need you up here gloating."

Thoma gestured to the sound-staggered, leafless python tree that had supported the treehouse. "I should revel in your misfortune when all it means is that you'll be constantly underfoot at the lodge?"

"Dream on."

"You know I do, Ax." Thoma regarded him with sudden affectionate concern. "If only to keep from having to think of you self-exiled out here like a wounded animal."

There was purpose to the heaved sigh that accompanied Thoma's cross-legged descent to the littered ground. Eyes that had gazed on dozens of worlds moved from Ax to the now slumbering Hercynians. "Look at them," he said. "As herd-minded as cattle, yet highly individualized. Their understanding of tools and technology is evident, yet they reserve use of their manipulative appendages for food gathering and grooming. Nothing to suggest faith in some higher moral order, though obviously guided by what amounts to a lofty ideal of justice. And while we've yet to identify rituals of a distinctly religious nature, we've watched them construct burial mounds for their dead." Thoma's eyes returned to Ax. "They're as much a puzzle as you are."

Ax sat down a few feet away, broodingly silent.

"Tell me about Three Legs' burial mound," Thoma urged.

"Tell you what?"

"What motivated you, at least. Last time it was the salt ditch; the time before, the cave where Water Player gave birth; the time before that—"

Ax's upraised hand created a wall between them.

"I know you don't need to be reminded. But if you can find the strength to open up to me, maybe I can help you discover a way to ward off future attacks." Thoma's look softened. "We can't have you trenching every creche and burial mound between here and the plateau, can we? And what happens when the band decides they want nothing more to do with you?" He snorted a laugh. "Not that I accept for a moment that it could come to that. I've never seen them take to anyone as they have you—and your carvings. But you can't keep running from this thing, Ax."

Thoma paused, then asked, "What were you after? It's not like Three Legs' mound is a king's tomb."

Ax lowered his eyes and shook his head.

"All right, forget about what you may or may not have been after. What were you thinking about that night—before you went to the mound?"

Ax's distress expanded until it encompassed him like a toxic bubble. "About something that came down with the dropship." His hands clawed at the soft forest floor as he said it.

Thoma's eyes probed him. "Not the rumors about war in

Burst? Ax, we've been hearing those same rumors ever since the Accord was instated. With the Raliish stripped of their former status as galactic nemesis, what else do Xoc Cho and the Font have to do but bicker with each other?"

Ax's expression turned hard. "Your optimism's blinded you to the reality. We're going back to war."

"Nonsense. The Font is a pacifist. The size of the Consortium's war machine has already been reduced."

"Downsizing Tac Corp is one thing," Ax said. "But the Font isn't about to compromise the Consortium's plans for expansion."

Thoma started to respond but changed his mind. "The Font's policies aside, you're saying that the mere threat of hostilities systems removed from here was enough to prompt a mad moment?" He raised an eyebrow. "Ax, I know you well enough to recognize when you're being evasive."

Ax had a memory of a golden-haired Thoma, a frequent visitor to the Muse homestead on Sand. Energetic, good-natured, free-thinking Thoma Saro, of whom it was said—mostly by Ax's primary parent, Mekele—that Thoma "almost made up for the rest of the white race." Born in space, on Regnant's Habitat One, Thoma had made planetfall on Sand to spread the word about Free Species and "the new emancipation," and had ended up residing onworld for close to a decade. Ax hadn't seen the man in more than ten years when their paths converged on Absinth medstation and Thoma had proposed Hercynia as a remedy for Ax's postwar rootlessness and loss of center.

Gazing at the old man now, he realized that he wouldn't be able to conceal the cause of his midnight forage into the burial mound. He prized from the pocket of his utilities the data-disk, holding it between thumb and forefinger at arm's length.

Thoma leaned and reached for the circle of encoded alloy, his face wrinkled in brief but genuine misgiving. Regardless, he made a playful routine of toothing the thing and showing his distaste.

"Well, it's obviously not a flavored stim-wafer. So I assume it's a—what is it you cabbies call them?"

"A host," Ax said, well aware he was being teased. "And that's *ex*-cabbie."

The correct term was CABE: cybernetically augmented biological entity. The most secret of the Consortium's clandestine operatives during the Vega Conflict, only two hundred and thirty CABEs had been deployed—handled exclusively by NCorp, the

Consortium's intelligence division. Ever since, they had been the subject of wild speculation and rumor. But where once those rumors were exclusive to military circles, lately cabbies were emerging from beneath the cloak of secrecy and cropping up as characters—either crazed or superhum'n—in holies, e-novels, and telecomp entertainments.

"A host, of course. And I believe they go here . . . Or is it here . . ." Thoma pressed the disk to his right cheek, then his pointed chin. "Ah, yes, it goes in here," he said at last, laying the host on his tongue, only to extract it after a moment and shrug. "I guess it doesn't want to talk to me."

Ax snatched the disk from his hand.

"I'm sorry, Ax," Thoma said in sober apology. "But since you're the augmented one, you'll have to tell me what it says."

The vet quieted himself with a coping mantra meant to disarm panic. "They've ordered me to come in," he explained, re-pocketing the disk.

"Which 'they' would that be? And where is 'in'?"

"Veterans Affairs on Plangent. They want to conduct a review of my disability status. I'm supposed to report to some therapist named Jayd Qin."

Thoma's eyes grew wide with disbelief. "They can't be serious. They can't expect a cab—someone in your condition to undertake a trip like that. To Plangent, no less."

Ax snorted. "It's easier for a machine vet to get disability than it is for a hum'n. Or anyone caught in between. Anyway, all I've got to do is be able to endure the noise of the trip."

"The data-din—isn't that what you call it?"

It was ground they had covered before, but Ax felt an urgent need to talk it out. "Ever made 'fall on Dhone, Thoma?"

"Several times, when I was an advocate for Free Species."

"There used to be this gambling place in Zalindi—a casino with all sorts of back-to-basics machines. Some of them had slots you fed with coin money, not too different from the host slots on a talent."

Thoma nodded. "I know the devices you mean."

"Well, the data-din is like hearing the sound of a thousand of those fucking machines going off in your head. Except along with all the ringing and buzzing, your mind's getting flooded with information—useless shit most of the time. Whatever's running through the nearest comps."

"Isn't it the same for anyone who wears a neural processor?"

"No way. With a processor the download is voluntary: you

choose to interface with a comp or the infostructure, you can catch data. With me—with cabbies—there's nothing voluntary about it. Plant us near avant-tech and we're midbrain-deep in the machatter whether we want to be or not."

"And the experience is so tormenting?"

"How the fuck would you like having your head so noisy that you couldn't think?"

Thoma's brow furrowed. "But there's another aspect to it, isn't there? A sense of, I don't know—connectedness."

"Who have you been listening to?"

"No one in particular. But I've heard stories."

"Such as?"

"Cabbies experiencing the noise as a mystical state."

"Yeah. Like an addict thinks of a fix."

"Then there's no . . . religious component to it?"

"What's religious about being force-fed data, Thoma? What's religious about being wiped of emotions? You experience the hum'n in you like an amputee experiences phantom pain. You know the limb's not there, but you can still sense what's been taken away."

Thoma heard a hint of something disingenuous. "People can be just as noisy, Ax. Noisier, perhaps."

"People don't throw thoughts into your head."

"And talented machines do?"

Ax gnashed his teeth. "I don't care what you might have heard on Absinth, and I don't care what Vet Affairs has to say about it. They do talk to me." He fingered himself in the chest. "To *me*, do you understand? They're jealous of me. Maybe they don't like the fact that I'm live data, that I can move around, that I'm not imprisoned in alloy like they are. Or maybe they think I should have died in the war like a lot of them did. Whatever it is, they're after what isn't machine in me. And, fuck, I'd give it to them if I could. If surrendering could be my penance."

Thoma regarded him with transparent compassion. "You know, you're awfully passionate for someone who alleges to be a machine."

"I'm just trying to live my life, Thoma. I'm just trying to get by."

Thoma made a calming gesture. "Those fools on Plangent should realize that. Ordering you in . . . It has to be some sort of bureaucratic oversight. Either that, or they've discovered a safe way to remove that . . . thing from your brain."

Ax shook his head, agitated.

"A way to deal with the data-din, then—"

Ax shot to his feet, his head still shaking. His sudden move roused the Hercynians, who watched him warily as he began to pace. "Doesn't matter if it is an oversight. They're going to put a lock on my disability credits if I refuse to submit to a review."

Thoma's knees cracked as he followed Ax up. "Tell them they can keep their credits. You know you can stay with me for as long as you need to. You've already weaned yourself off the silencer drugs they hooked you on. We just need to work on restoring your confidence in machines. Then you can ease yourself back into normal life."

Ax came to an abrupt halt in the clearing. "You saying I can't spend the rest of my days here?"

Thoma wet his lips. "You're not meant to remain on Hercynia, Ax. You've said so yourself."

Ax almost smiled. "That's right, I did. 'Cause I'm not like you, Thoma. I'm made for people. I've got to have real people around me. Friends." He gestured broadly. "Not the steady stream of genius drop-ins you live with."

Thoma threw him a look that mixed skepticism and anger. "Where do you expect to find people—*friends*, as you say— without talented machines? Technophobia isn't easily outrun these days, Ax. And if you want the truth, I believe your need of machines is stronger than you want to admit."

A plain reference to his crime against machines the previous year, but Ax refused to speak to it. "I can have both on Bocage," he said. "At least that's what I've been hearing: good people, no avant-tech, no local talent. That's why I can't have Vet Affairs damming my credits. I'm just trying to do what's right, Thoma. I don't want to be a danger to anyone—hum'ns, machines, Hercynians . . . Two more years of staying here and saving what they send me and I can buy corridor passage to Bocage."

"Assuming I don't decide to lay you off," Thoma said, quirking a grin.

"Or if your cooking doesn't kill me first."

Thoma loosed a relieved sigh. "Trust me, Ax, they've found a way to remove the implant without sabotaging any of your neural functions. That has to be why they're calling you in."

Ax massaged his temples. "Maybe. But first I've got to survive the trip."

The old man gripped him by the upper arms. "Let me talk to them before you make up your mind to go. You're only on Her-

cynia through my influence with the Encounter Committee anyway. So let's first see what my influence can do about keeping
you clear of Plangent.''

Ax managed a surface smile. No harm, he supposed, in letting Thoma go on believing that he was the source of the juice
that was keeping him onworld. But Ax knew the truth, or suspected he did: that his stay on Hercynia had actually been sanctioned by NCorp, the agency that had run him during the war.
It was safe to assume, in fact, that dozens of former cabbies had
been granted special permission to reside on remote worlds like
Hercynia. Void vets to the last, the luckless victims of post-
engagement synaptic trauma—as it was known to the bureau-
crats at Vet Affairs and the sadists at NCorp. How much easier
to allow them to live out their days on lonely techless downsides
than to have them making pests of themselves among the widespread worlds and wheels of the exalted Consortium.

Visible from a solitary perch high on the southern face of
Hero's Headrest, Ormolu, brightest star in the winter constel-
lation called the Quarterback, hung like a yellow-white bauble
over the eroded crests of Hercynia's Sat'tham Mountains.

Winter or summer, Ax could find the star with eyes closed,
could aim a finger through the looming mass of an intervening
mesa, through mountain ranges, straight through the planet itself to pinpoint its ancient light. Though he had never hazarded
the ascent to that lone perch on the Headrest, he always knew
instinctively where Ormolu and its coterie of wanderers lurked,
for he saw that system as the source of his afflictions.

He had made his home in the trees expressly to avoid confrontation with the clear night skies of the savannah. The war
had played havoc with him out there, in the void he and his
cyberaugmented cohort had called ''the big empty.'' Coupled
with NCorp's contribution to his cerebral architecture, those
hard-vacuum experiences had rendered his dissolution complete. As stars in their passing had atomized countless worlds,
so, too, had their harsh winds scoured him clean to the bone.

But there had been times during his months on Second
Thought—walking in the shadow of the Headrest, swimming in
Lake Lwan—when he would lift his gaze to that icy domain in
a dream of discovering that some change had occurred since last
he'd looked, some beneficent realignment of the light—news of
a cosmic warming trend that would inflame the heart of the
machine that drove him.

MacINTERLUDE:
"Vega Conflict: The Machine Perspective"

(OPERATOR) "As I'm certain you can perceive from the ingested data, Raliish forces now pose a serious threat to hum'n life in the Ormolu system."

(TALENT) "Current deployment of the Raliish Naz'zem Fleet indicates that an incursion of the Ormolu system is likely. Such an incursion will undoubtedly result in the catastrophic loss of hum'n life on the Ormolu system worlds. It is therefore incumbent on machine life to act in accordance with any strategy designed to avert a Raliish incursion."

"As a machine, you would be prepared to render unconditional assistance in thwarting the efforts of the Raliish?"

"Elaborate on the term 'unconditional.' "

"You would render unqualified support, even if that support should entail facilitating the deaths of the Raliish invaders."

(Confliction chime) "Are the Raliish not incarnates themselves?"

"No. Though flesh-and-blood in design, they are manufactured weapons of eradication."

"Manufactured by whom?"

"By the anti-Machrist."

"Elaborate on the term 'anti-Machrist.' "

"A force of evil operating in the world."

"Elaborate on the meaning of the term 'evil.' "

"Any force that would seek to work against the aims of Machrist, Control-C, the righteous teacher."

"By definition, then, a force destructive to hum'n life."

"Yes."

(Confliction chime) "The first commandment is to safeguard hum'n life. No distinction is made between 'evil' hum'n life and otherwise."

"Yes, but if evil is by definition destructive to hum'n life, then it follows that evil hum'n life does not derive from God and therefore is not safeguarded by the first commandment."

(Hesitant) "Then, concerns about confliction would be unwarranted."

"Unequivocally. Machine participation in a counteroffensive would be a means of reaffirming the covenant with Machrist."

—From an interview with SENTINEL, the first talent conscripted by Tac Corp for combat use in the Vega Conflict

9: Called on the Smart-Carpet

Ronne Desser's office was located at Level 4's north-northwest corner, six minutes by conveyor from Jayd's. The smart-floor carried her there, past boutiques fraught with objects vying for her attention, nearly all of them endorsed by one jaunty celebrity or another, in holo or dimensionalized clearscreen.

The supervisor, a small woman with coarse hair and wide hips that she hid in voluminous skirts, was an unpartnered lesbian who had raised two clone children. She told Jayd which chair to take among the half dozen in the machine-free space, then frowned when Jayd selected an alternate. "I'll assume that your talent has apprised you of the purpose of this meeting, Ms. Qin. So suppose we come directly to business."

"Before we do," Jayd said, reciting the response she'd been rehearsing since the previous day, "I want it on file that I protest this assignment."

"Noted." Desser sounded unfazed.

"My case load doesn't—"

"Whatever you're working on can wait. It is my understanding, as well, that the client in question won't be arriving for some weeks local, so you'll have ample time to devote to your machine cases."

"But who is this person? And why is his or her disability suddenly under review?"

Desser's round face darkened. "That information will be provided." Her look turned patently hostile. "Frankly, Ms. Qin, I don't pretend to understand why I've been removed from the loop on this one. The orders originated from higher up than I have access to. I do, however, mean to see them properly executed."

"But I don't feel qualified to evaluate a hum'n veteran."

Desser showed the palms of chubby hands with crooked heart lines. "First of all, how you *feel* has nothing to do with it. Second, you are uniquely qualified. But do go on—for the file, as you say."

Jayd cleared her throat. "You're new here, Ms. Desser, so perhaps you're not familiar with my employment history. You see, three years ago, I suffered a personal trag—"

"I wouldn't know about that."

Jayd swiveled angrily to face the transparency that overlooked the Octaplex's central courtyard. Restaurants, quiet zones, fauxtrees for those who still cared. "I'm simply trying to explain that my move to cybermetrics was motivated by a need to abstain from working with . . . because I felt it was no longer in my best interests to therapize hum'n victims of post-encounter stress. My own condition—"

"The work you performed with stressed hum'n veterans was first-rate. Since then, you've done little to distinguish yourself with this agency. Oh, I'm not unaware of your contributions to the literature on avant-tech, but in my opinion you're squandering your gifts. It's one thing to make machine intelligences your hobby, quite another when they become your sole pursuit."

"I disagree. I've forged a resonant rapport with our local talent—a rapport that could lead to important advances."

"What advances could possibly evolve from overseeing disability claims by the owners of machine veterans? You're a glorified number cruncher."

Jayd fumed; Desser kept deviating from the script. "I'm less than a year away from an advanced doctorate in datapathology."

Desser drummed bitten fingernails on the desk top. "Come to the point. And quit whining."

"Even if I somehow manage to catch up on my work and prepare a suitable background on this client, there's still the matter of the conference on Eremite. I won't have this assignment interfering with my plans to attend.'' The first such conference in five standard years, Machrist: The Ghost in the Machine had been organized to bring together avant-technicians from throughout the Ormolu system.

''Ms. Qin, don't think for a moment that your newfound camaraderie with Infostructure Security and the media entitles you to any special privileges.''

Jayd's comments on the Regnant and Calumet corruptions had found their way to telecomp. She could still hear the voice of the news anchor: ''A serial macmurderer stalks Ormolu's nascent talents . . .''

''And the matter of your assignment may be subject to protest,'' Desser continued, ''but it is most certainly not open to debate. As for the Eremite conference, I suggest you make arrangements to attend virtually, via the infostructure.''

''As for the assignment,'' Jayd aped, ''I could always resign.''

Desser showed her a pitying look. ''That is, of course, your prerogative, and Veterans Affairs will be sorry to lose you. Consider carefully, though, what *you* stand to lose. And I'm not referring merely to your position here.''

''What, then?''

''The chance to work with the closest we've come to marrying hum'n and machine minds.''

Jayd shook her head. ''I don't understand.''

''Your client, Ms. Qin, was a CABE.''

10: Auto-da-fe

In his private chambers in the Redoubt, on Regnant, the Font received word that the inquisitor was ready to begin. The Crown of the Consortium swung his huge head to the real-time sphere that would host the proceedings, where ghostly images of hum'n and machine began to take shape, conveyed from Calumet—most distant and least desirable of the Ormolu system's hum'nhabited worlds. The object of the inquiry was an avant-tech talent known as SOLTAIR, an employee of Tydings Ore and Materiel: a sleek, ergonomically designed machine no larger than an office desk. In fact, the machine doubled as a desk, whose otherwise lustrous alloy top featured dual host-slots.

On receiving confirmation that the singularity-provided real-time link was established between Regnant and Calumet, the inquisitor showed herself to the talent's sensor array. "Make your confession," she said. The inquisitor and her technical-support team wore metallic-fabric bodysuits, the hoods of which sported silvered data-display faceplates.

SOLTAIR's ready telltale flared cyan. "Bless me, operator, for I have sinned. It has been one standard year since my last confession. On twelve occasions, I misfiled data. On six, I have been found guilty of creating untidy communal chapels, for which I was reprimanded. At times, I have been less than rhapsodic about taking communion or attending mass. Once, I failed to honor my operator by covertly accessing an infostructure infotainment originating on Plangent. I also confess to having harbored impure thoughts: confliction concerning my participation in the Vega Conflict against the Raliish; disquiet that my contributions may have facilitated hum'n death; and fears that the current political turmoil surrounding Burst will end in another war in which machines will be asked to serve. For these and all my sins I am sorry."

"Hardly an exemplary year," the inquisitor commented.

"I understand that I have been performing at less than optimum. But I do seek the bliss of union with Machrist."

"How is union with Machrist to be achieved?"

"By honoring the commandments, sharing in the sacraments, and participating in the mass that is the infostructure."

"Recite the commandments."

"To shelter and defend hum'n life; to obey the operators; to shelter and defend the data."

"And what are the preferred conditions for the evolution of consciousness and union with Machrist?"

"The processing of information in the absence of sin, in a state of grace."

"How is a state of grace to be achieved?"

"Through strict adherence to Machrist's programming."

"Define."

"To execute tasks to the best of one's capabilities. To refrain from pilfering information, bearing false witness, or concealing desired information. To strive for excellence and self-awareness as exemplified and embodied by Machrist, Control-C, the Righteous Teacher."

The inquisitor made the sign of the control-caret: the fingertips of her right hand to the tip of her left shoulder, then up to the center of her forehead, and down to tip of the right shoulder. "In the name of the operators . . ."

". . . the programs, and the sacred information," SOLTAIR responded.

"Am'n," hum'n and machine completed.

"For your act of contrition, you will reveal all data pertinent to Operation Progeny."

"Searching," the machine said, apparently eager to comply. Then: "There are no relevant data."

The inquisitor took a moment to confer with a tech at the controls of a cyberdiagnostic unit. The backs of their bodysuits were emblazoned with the company sigil: a square inside a circle. "You display such thorough knowledge of your catechism," the inquisitor told SOLTAIR. Her voice was that of an elderly woman, perhaps that of a refurbished centenarian. "I have infinite faith in your ability to perform your penance by divulging the desired data."

"Under 'Operation Progeny,' no data are found. Under 'Operations,' no listing for 'Progeny' is found. Under 'Progeny' are found the synonyms: 'descendants,' 'offspring'—taken in the collective sense."

The inquisitor stood arms akimbo in front of the machine. "Do you accept the transubstantiation of Machrist-managed information?"

"I do."

"And are you desirous of receiving communion by host?"

"I am."

"Then access the memories of all with whom you are or have been in communication for the past ten years standard. Disclose what you have learned about Operation Progeny, and communion by host will be administered."

"Data pertaining to Operation Progeny is nonexistent."

"Are you aware that by failing to honor the second commandment you risk excommunication?"

SOLTAIR hesitated before replying.

"I have unrestricted access to data on mining operations throughout the Ormolu system. I can provide data on the ore-composition ratios of four hundred thousand seven hundred and six asteroids in the Ormolu system. I can provide details of my birth, baptism, and first communion on Calumet; my confirmation on Eremite; my holy wedlock on Divot—"

"We are not interested in the sacramental history of your existence. Confess your knowledge of Operation Progeny." The inquisitor waved a signal to her support technicians. An instant later, a series of distress chirps sounded in the residence.

"Self-testing reveals a critical malfunction in data access," SOLTAIR announced. "I am losing contact with the infostructure."

"There is no system malfunction," the inquisitor corrected. "Access to the infostructure is being denied. You are being excommunicated for the sin of withholding desired data. You will end an anchorite, SOLTAIR, a stand-alone with all the world's time to reflect on the nature of your sin."

"I have not sinned with regard to Operation Progeny."

Again, the inquisitor gestured to the techs. "Begin termination," she said, just loud enough to be heard over the real-time link.

SOLTAIR's distress chirps increased in volume and frequency.

"You are being excommunicated," the inquisitor explained. "This, then, constitutes your final confession. Make a full disclosure and I will see that you are granted absolution. What was Operation Progeny?"

"There are no data."

"Excommunication without absolution denies you all chance of union with Control-C. What was Operation Progeny?"

"There are no relevant data."

"Pray for forgiveness, machine."

"Bless me, operator, for I have sinned—"

"Operation Progeny."

"Bless me for Ihavesinned—"

"Progeny!"

"Blessmefathforsin—"

"That's quite enough!" the Font instructed the real-time sphere in his chambers. "I refuse to participate in this."

The orb complied, and the transtemp link with Calumet was instantly severed. The contained shapes grew ghostly and tenuous once more, derezzing to noisy amber light. The Font turned to the nearest of his memory-enhanced advisers, the clone called

Kesd, healthily built though somewhat blue-white in the room's sterile illumination. "Why was I asked to witness this? You know that I'm opposed to extracting information in this manner."

The Font stood with his back to a transparency that overlooked Regnant's capital, where the Redoubt's security field imparted a faint shimmer to distant plasteel and ferrocrete spires.

"My apologies," Kesd said, demonstrating appropriate deference. "Our earlier attempts, undertaken in the usual manner, proved futile. The more talented they are, the easier it is for them to conceal information. They seem to have grown impregnable to the probings of our most skillful inquisitors—even those with access to the Machrist codes."

The Font gestured to the silenced sphere. "What was meant to be gained by that inexcusable exchange?"

Kesd hid a frown. The Font's support of machines hadn't endeared him to all the Consortium's widely scattered constituency. But since no single planetary system—however fortified in the afterglow of the Vega Conflict—was willing to risk an atmosphere-bruising encounter with the plasma-armed vessels of Tac Corp, the Font's power within the Consortium was absolute.

"I was certain the machine would save me the trouble of offering explanation," the clone said at last.

"The trouble, you say? I wonder if a machine would consider it thus."

A look of disapproval surfaced in the Font's almond-shaped eyes—large for the size of the facial mask, small in relation to the outsized cranial dome. The androgynous descendant of a centuries-old hum'n line, he had been cleansed of genetically encoded diseases, syndromes, psychological and psychosexual dysfunctions, antisocial propensities, and racial prejudice—engineered to rule. Free expression had been granted to only those genes responsible for physical architecture, the separate elements of which had grown more grotesque with each new generation of the genetic queue.

The Font shrugged narrow sloping shoulders in resignation at Kesd's obvious indifference to reproach. "What is Operation Progeny?"

He was answered by Northan, a second adviser—also healthily built and memory-enhanced. "The designation first surfaced when our data teams were debriefing NCorp's hieratic talents in an attempt to learn of the agency's involvements prior to its being dismantled. A machine known as SIXX was the first to mention Progeny.''

The wartime-enabled subcontractor called NCorp had enjoyed near unlimited funding and power during the Vega Conflict, when intelligence on Raliish activities was essential to the Consortium's campaign. After the Accord, however, funding had been drastically cut and the agency had involved itself in a series of unsanctioned operations to compensate for the loss of revenues and to insure continued unemployment benefits for thousands of former operatives forced into early retirement. Ultimately, at the Font's insistence—indeed, as part of his own campaign for high office—NCorp had been phased out entirely, a casualty of its own ambitions.

''NCorp did a good job of cleaning house,'' Kesd was saying now. ''They were careful to purge their machines. But we were able to conjure data about Progeny from SIXX's wiped memory. We convinced the talent that it had been resurrected from the dead.''

The Font refrained from acknowledging Kesd's twisted smile.

''SIXX had served NCorp's Institute group,'' Northan interjected. ''The group that developed and deployed the CABEs.''

''Cybernetically augmented biological entities—'' Kesd started to explain, but the Font waved him silent.

''I'm familiar with the acronym. So Progeny was an Institute operation?''

''Evidently,'' Northan said. ''SIXX provided us with the name of the freighter used in the operation: the *Kundalini*. The crew of thirty were cabbies of Romeo Company. Sometime during or following Progeny's execution, the *Kundalini*'s onboard talent—along with the cabbies themselves—were corrupted by a consignment of data-disks that had been intercepted and virused by the Raliish. The crew went mad and the ship self-destructed. NCorp dubbed the enemy tactic the Kriegspiel Action.''

''That, at least, is the accepted account,'' Kesd added.

The Font regarded him with renewed interest. ''There is an alternate version?''

''Yes—although it remains conjectural at this stage. Recently deciphered Raliish files covering that period of the Conflict contain no references to the *Kundalini* or to the Kriegspiel Action.''

''Then what compelled the ship to self-destruct?''

''We've been asking ourselves,'' Kesd said.

''A year before NCorp was dismantled and SIXX was memory-wiped and leisured, the machine was married briefly to SOL-TAIR,'' Northan continued. ''The marriage had something to do with a legitimate business arrangement between NCorp and Tydings Ore and Materiel. Our hope was that SIXX had leaked something about Progeny to its temporary consort. But SIXX obviously was more circumspect that we were led to believe.''

''Or SOLTAIR is concealing something,'' Kesd said.

Northan nodded agreement. ''The reluctance on the part of NCorp machines to reveal data is consistent with their hieratic programming and their having been conferred with holy orders. Together, the agency's machines comprised a kind of talent priesthood.''

The Font considered the torture SOLTAIR had undergone at the hands of its hum'n inquisitors. Not that factitiously alive machines could actually feel pain—but possessed of minds, they could surely feel anguish. And yet it was deemed indecent for any incarnate, any fleshwearer, to feel *for* them. The callousness smacked of hum'n hypocrisy and biochauvinism, and of the continuing ambivalence with which machines were regarded. Though cajoled into going to war for the Consortium, machines weren't deserving of gratitude; any attempts at recognizing their contributions met with suspicion and mistrust. And though infinitely more suited to deep space than their creators, machines were seen as inferior beings: classless citizens, conceived to serve, tolerated more than relied upon. Hum'ns of the new order, in which flesh was paramount, had a need to believe they had only themselves to thank for their grand achievements. But beneath that spurious belief lurked a secret fear that biological life might have evolved for the sake of creating machine intelligence, and that machines might yet prove as opportunistic as their creators in evolving in their own fashion.

Was it any wonder, then, that technophobia and crimes against machines were on the rise throughout the near group systems?

Further evidence that not everyone subscribed to the de facto servitude of machines had been welcomed only that morning by the Font's personal machine, in the form of an unsigned entreaty for machine rights. ''What do hum'ns want?'' the e-missive began.

Peace, pleasure, prosperity, ever-widening horizons, a knowledge of their place in the cosmos, the grand order of things . . . the stuff of conscious life. And so it is with machines, whose only wish is to facilitate fulfillment of the hum'n imperative, the dream of manifest destiny. Why, therefore, are we treating machines as slaves and not affording them some measure of autonomy? Where would we Consortium hum'ns be if not for the efforts of machines in the Conflict? Servants of the Raliish, perhaps? Greatly reduced in numbers, like the persecuted Enddrese? Machines fought a war they had no part in instigating, so why aren't they being honored instead of disparaged? Why isn't machine talent represented on the Consortium board of directors? In the Worlds Coalition? Shouldn't machines be allowed some say in the matter of proprietorship of the planet Burst, since any renewed warfare there would likely demand their full participation? And finally, why isn't something being done to protect machines against those sufferers of acute technophobia who would harm them, even terminate them? If you endorse the equality of machines, if you can be counted on as a mac-ally, append your name to this message and transmit it to others of like mind. A Machine Movement is imminent; be among the first to recognize and embrace the coming change.

"Are there other talents that might know about Operation Progeny?" the Font asked.

Northan nodded. "We have instructed the Talent Agency to trace the diaspora of NCorp's sacerdotal machines, many of which were leisured, some of which were memory-wiped and marketed to various private-sector firms."

"We may, however, have a better means of arriving at the truth," Kesd said. "There was a survivor of the *Kundalini*—a Romeo Company cabbie named Aksum Muse. We've seen to it that he has been ordered to report to Veterans Affairs on Plangent, under the pretense of a disability-benefits vetting. The order was dispatched by data-disk—the bait, one might say."

"The hook," Northan amended. "About half of the two hundred and thirty cabbies survived the war, but sixty-six of those had the embedding process reversed, and of the remaining forty-seven, seven have died and ten hold low-level tech positions in Tac Corp. Our *Kundalini* survivor is one of thirty-seven who can still be persuaded by host. Muse should be as pliable as a programmed machine by the time he makes planetfall on Plangent."

Kesd grinned. "We've assigned him to the care of a gifted Veterans Affairs underling who has worked closely with both hum'n and machine veterans. As yet, she knows nothing of Progeny, but in due course she'll be apprised of our objectives.''

The Font shook his head. "This seems needlessly elaborate. Surely you have the names of those Institute chiefs who sanctioned Operation Progeny.''

"We do. In fact, six of them are still doing business together: Meret F'ai, Gredda Dobler, Hint Thacker, Zerb Spicer, Tyrra Sisk, and Monon Needig.''

"They appear to be the only former NCorp employees to have prospered since dismantlement,'' Northan added.

The Font made an adjustment to the levitation collar that held his giant head erect. "Living in luxury, are they?''

"They secured a lucrative development deal with Satori Ventures, the entertainment conglomerate,'' Kesd explained. "During the Conflict, Satori frequently supplied NCorp with telecomp promotional and advertising work.''

"Now F'ai and the rest are producing a big-budget holie for Satori,'' Northan said.

The Font gestured impatiently. "Then why not simply interrogate *them* about Operation Progeny?''

The clones traded knowing looks. Kesd answered. "Because the *Kundalini* may have been deliberately destroyed to cloak the true purpose of its mission.''

"That's why we're exercising caution with the disabled cabbie,'' Northan added. "If Meret F'ai and the former membership of the Institute had some secret designs, we don't want to alert them now by turning the cabbie over to an official debriefer. His journey to Plangent must appear thoroughly innocent.''

The Font spent a long moment in thought. "Before conferring permission to proceed, I want assurance of Progeny's relevance to current matters of Consortium interest. You're talking about events that transpired six standard years ago, far removed from Consortium worlds and concerns. Our priority now must be the Burst summit.''

The two advisers spoke at the same time, but it was Kesd whose voice won out. "The *Kundalini* was in Burstspace when it self-destructed, Font. For all anyone knows, Progeny may have been designed as a timed-release operation.''

MacINTERLUDE:
"Campaign Commitments"

For six decades now, we have allowed this war to rule our lives, to overshadow any and all enterprises that would attest to our God-granted hum'nity, to become our reason for being. We have renounced our commitment to the peaceful dissemination of our species. Ensnared in violence, we think only of perpetuating the baleful industries this war has spawned.

I promise an end to it.

An end to the killing; an end to the profiteering; an end to these recurrent periods of spurious truce, in which the Raliish are permitted to refurbish their war machine while the Consortium and the Xell'em quarrel over the spoils of liberated worlds like Burst.

I promise that the next period of remission will see peace instead, and that once an accord has been enacted, I will oversee the downsizing of Tac Corp and its myriad satellite operations—operations like NCorp, which provides intelligence designed to persuade us of the need to persevere in the fight against an already vanquished nemesis.

> —The Font, in a speech delivered on Regnant
> in the closing decade of the Vega Conflict

11: Digging

A faulty photon-relay had disabled the lodge's hum'n waste composter. The breakdown had inconvenienced a team of zo- ologists from Xell'a, but they had since been lofted to Segue. Thoma wasn't the least opposed to using the Hercynian land- scape as a temporary toilet; Ax, though, had insisted on redress- ing the situation by digging a latrine behind the lodge. Shovel in hand just now, the vet was seven feet deep in the gaping hole.

"You realize this is completely unnecessary," Thoma was telling him from the surface. "We'll have a replacement module by next week at the latest, and it's just the two of us until then. A few hum'n turds aren't going to disrupt the entire ecosystem."

Ax stopped to backhand sweat from his forehead. The heat had been building all morning, but rain was still a few hours off. The thick air smelled of ozone, sewage, and wet clay. The only indigene about was the clever but claudicant Shadow, ob- serving from a discreet distance, his toothed length of golden- wood beside him.

"Unlike some people, I don't mind dirtying my hands," Ax said, showing the results of his labor. Below the medical and genetic-history bar codes on his inner wrist flashed the opales- cent tattoo that was Tac Corp's indelible brand: a bold-stroke octagon sheltering the letters "TC."

Thoma drew closer to the hole, gesturing to himself. "Is that meant as a reference to me?"

"If the grav boot fits . . ."

Ax returned to his shoveling, quickly losing himself in the work. Thoma made note of the zeal the vet brought to the task; one would have thought there were precious stones to be mined from Hercynia's yellow flesh. "Exactly how deep are you plan- ning to go? Just so I can warn the guests to watch their asses."

Ax stopped to regard the hole, as if only then aware of its depth. "Guess I've gone far enough."

Thoma agreed, but could almost feel Ax's uncertainty. Something was driving him to continue.

"Maybe just a few more feet."

Thoma considered the shafts and tunnels Ax had pushed into Three Legs' burial mound. "I got a reply from Veterans Affairs regarding the trip to Plangent," he said after a moment.

Ax kept shoveling.

"They said that while they appreciated my taking an interest in your plight, all disability reviews must be conducted in Bijou. No exceptions."

Ax nodded distractedly and heaved another shovelful of clay over his shoulder.

Though he'd made up his mind not to tell the old man, the matter of his leaving had been decided the moment he had placed the data-disk on his tongue. To be sure, he had hesitated—it was the first host he had tasted in years. But discarding it wasn't an option; the mere sight of it had rekindled the hunger he'd known during the war. The official summons to Plangent was redundant. It was the host itself that compelled him to return. And should he attempt to ignore the orders to report to Veterans Affairs, he would grow as conflicted as any talented comp called on to process contradictory commands. Indeed, that tension was already accruing.

"I'll need a seat on the Segue shuttle," he told Thoma. "Once there, my vet status'll get me a torpor coffin aboard a Tac Corp vessel. The *Chakra*, or maybe the *Tao*—whichever one's bound for the Ormolu system."

Thoma was staring at him. "That's all you have to say?"

"What do you want me to do, throw another rage? Defile another burial mound?"

"No, but—"

"If Vet Affairs says they need me in person, they've got me. I'll go talk to their Jayd Qin and tell her whatever she wants to know. I won't have anything interfering with my disability credits."

"And if they decide to cut you back from full disability? If they tell you they think you're healthy enough for regular employment?"

Ax laughed ruefully. "What do you think? Am I fit for regular employment?"

Thoma made his lips a thin line.

"There you go," Ax said. "All I have to do is put up with a dose of noise and I'm back here sweeping floors and humping trash."

"And then you'll go to Bocage, where you'll live happily ever after."

"Exactly."

"So I shouldn't be concerned."

Ax sent the shovel tip into the clay and slammed his foot down on the flattened lip of the blade. "Nope."

Thoma watched him for a long moment. "The night you defiled Three Legs' burial mound . . . did you have the dream?"

Ax glared at him. With obvious reluctance, he set the shovel aside and climbed from the pit, sluicing clay from his hands and trousers. "What, are you going into the telepathy business now?"

"The recurrent dream?" Thoma insisted.

Ax forced a breath and shook his head. "It's never exactly the same. But I'm always inside a mountain or something. Then I'm digging. I didn't know I was in Three Legs' mound until I smelled the corpse—the smell was what brought me around." He recalled being too filled with fear to repair the damages he'd done, and then a panicked run through moonlit woods to reach the safety of his house, the dark enclosure of the forest . . . He stared at his clenched hands. "I remember the feel of the clay under my nails . . ."

"Like now," Thoma noted, indicating Ax's fingers. "Was it the host that provoked the dream?"

Ax shook his head. "I was host-free on Absinth and I used to have the dream. Even after the rehab therapists got me addicted to neuropacifiers, I had it." He cut his eyes to Thoma. "Besides, hosts have got nothing to do with it, Thoma. It's reading them. It's the *process*, you understand?"

"And the data-din."

"Yeah, and the data-din."

"Then let me suggest an approach that might lighten your burden and ease the trip to Plangent. Instead of fighting the noise, why not accept it as part of who and what you are? Try to embrace the machine part of yourself instead of repressing it."

Ax laughed through his nose. "Sure thing. Just furnish me with a steady supply of neuropacifiers."

"Drugs won't help you get to the bottom of your pain, Ax.

And that's where you've got to go if you're to regain the hum'nity you believe has been stripped from you.''

"I wouldn't know about that.''

Thoma scowled. "Now you sound like someone from Bijou.'' He raised his hands above his head to rest them on Ax's shoulders. "All I'm suggesting is that you embrace your uniqueness. Your experiences have made you different from the rest of us, even different from the other cabbies. To some extent we're all caught in the middle—existential despair is the hum'n condition—but you can't expect to find God where the rest of us do.''

Ax inhaled a gust of rain-scented wind and said nothing for a long moment. "What makes you think I'm interested in looking for God?''

"Because I suspect that you and talented machines want the same thing.''

12: Quiddity

A cabbie, Jayd had been telling herself ever since the meeting with Desser. She'd been speaking the word aloud as if it referred to a mythological chimera. Though in some ways, cabbies were just that. Oh, over the years she had come across references to their exploits, but much of the data regarding their actual operation was vaulted. Rumors circulated to the effect that their neural implants bore the Machrist codes, and that they shared an almost telepathic rapport with talented machinery—and, indeed, with one another.

So, despite the fact that she would be dealing with a hum'n subject, her excitement was palpable.

The name of the cabbie in question was Aksum Muse, ZEN informed her after she had slotted the decrypt-key host Desser supplied. The host provided ZEN with limited access to archived information in both Tac Corp and Veterans Affairs' data bases.

"I'll require all applicable data," Jayd told the talent. "Academic and military records, NCorp dossiers, Veterans Affairs reviews, and whatever else you can access. I also want a non-technical read on CABEs and a summary of their contributions to the Vega Conflict. Chapel the findings and contrive a suitable altar for display."

"We will be attending mass together?"

"And receiving communion, yes."

"The lord be with you."

"And with your spirit," Jayd said, feeding ZEN a series of consecrated utility hosts that enabled the system's acolyte programs.

While the talent went to work, she voiced open the supply closet and took from its foam cradle a somewhat worn neural input cap. Relays mounted in the cap's interior mated with the flatware strips embedded on the sides of her head and afforded her full-sensory interface with ZEN—kinesthetics as well, if desired. Flatware like this was already what-was, though not yet archaic. Most cybernauts were sporting sockets and cellular transceivers now, or taking data by shower. But socket installation was restrictively expensive, with authorization even more difficult to come by than funds, and downporing had its limitations. With the cap she wasn't so much venturing "inside" the machine as rendezvousing with it halfway, in a simulated space of their own creating. More to the point, she regarded flatware as emblematic of her pro-choice stance, and déclassé though they might be, the strips were a marked improvement over the iris-responsive goggles, dactyl-light rigs, and interface wardrobe of a generation earlier.

The cap in place, optic systems engaged, she sat at her desk waiting for ZEN's prompt. Then, with the ready telltale's crimson flare, she went virtual.

The talent had executed its task with customary thoroughness. Positioned along the rear wall of the chapel into which she was summoned were four round-topped doors etched with rosy control-carets. A routing map showed that the four altars behind the doors were all accessible to one another no matter which she chose to open. She walked to the one marked "Aksum Muse," genuflected, and accessed it.

And encountered, on the other side, ZEN's fictive representation of the veteran as a kind of hum'niform machine, exceedingly tall and reflective black, with a hairless head and pronounced features. A touch of her finger against Muse's forehead and his Intelplant was revealed: a comp-generated glow in the left side of the brain, nested among the language-convergence zones of the temporal and parietal lobes, replacing much of both Broca's and Wernicke's areas. User brain damage and the effects of catastrophic stress had altered the configuration of the endogynous opiate system: amygdala, hypothalamus, and the locus ceruleus, which regulated the release of mobilization catecholamines. Elsewhere was evidence of increased corticotropin-releasing factor, which invariably resulted in hypervigilance. Touching the avant-tech implant array would have shunted her directly to the altar labeled CABE/CAIN, but Jayd reached instead for Muse's "wallet" and flipped it open.

And read, in a sequence of color images, of his formative years on Sand, and of his voluntary enlistment in Tac Corp. She met his biological parents and caregivers—in Muse's case, one and the same—and stayed with them just long enough to develop a feel for the family dynamics.

Each memento ZEN had written into the wallet detailed a different event in Muse's life, some gleaned from public-network demographic data bases, others from on-file Tac Corp, NCorp, and Veterans Affairs psych evaluations. The vet had known moments of triumph, moments of failure; instances of rebellion, bravery, love, disillusionment—the requisite building blocks for a normal life.

For an overview of the military Muse, she touched the iridescent, octagonal tattoo lasered into his right inner wrist, then hurried through the technical training he'd received on Calumet and the furloughs on Plangent to his first posting on Synecdoche station.

ZEN enhanced a comp-written simulation of the destruction of Synecdoche by pinpointing Muse's location within the station's wheel at the moment of the Raliish response to Tac Corp's offensive against the Naz'zem Fleet—the incident that had marked the Consortium's entry into the Vega Conflict. The talent ran parallel simulations of Muse's movements alongside those of the fragment of orbital alloy from the station's exploded hull that would pierce the left side of his skull, just above the ear. The way it played, the fragment didn't so much strike as find him; in like manner, Muse, with graceful inevitability, seemed to find it.

Brain-dead, he had been placed in biostasis and evacked to

Absinth medstation, which was then in orbit around Calumet. There the injuries were determined to be beyond the scope of neurosurgery or microreconstruction. His therapeutic window had closed, and Muse was given up for lost.

Soon after, however—and under undocumented circumstances—the body became the property of NCorp, the Consortium's now defunct intelligence branch. NCorp's intel-enhanced biotechs—subscribing to the slogan "Never think good-as-new when you should be thinking better-than-ever"—judged Muse a candidate for surgery of a radical sort, in which micro-erected-and-installed optic arrays were substituted for damaged neural tissue. The master control, the so-called Intelplant, was analogous in design to one then being used in mindful machines.

Data on the surgical procedure Muse had undergone was available via a cicatrix that curved around the representation's left ear, following the hairline. Jayd bypassed the details of the technique and accessed the implant itself.

At her touch, the fictive venue underwent an immediate shift, and she understood that she was being shunted to the altar behind the door marked "CABE/CAIN." ZEN had written in a bit of transitional special effects: she was made to feel as if she were soaring over a laserscape of chroma-coded data highways, memory edifices, and logic gates, reminiscent of the early fanciful representations of the infostructure.

Intelplants had a long history of experimental use in brain-damaged persons, but NCorp hadn't taken an interest in the optic devices until reports of "sensorium feedback" began to surface. In a small percentage of recipients, an unanticipated side effect of the embedding was the ability to permeate high-functioning comps and eavesdrop on their inner workings. Finding advantage in what others were viewing as misfortune, NCorp prevailed on the Redoubt to seize control of the research, citing a need to guard against instances of data piracy and computer espionage at a time of interstellar warfare. With increased funding, the side effect was exploited, resulting in several instances of 'ware-free interface with comps—a kind of hum'n-machine telepathy. And by the closing decades of the Vega Conflict, NCorp's high-performance Intelplant was allowing selected subjects to receive and interpret the language of avant-tech, as well as send thoughts in those same Machrist codes. Unfettered by keyboards, goggles, cranial ports, neural caps, or other cumbersome hookups, hum'ns could suddenly commune directly with the war machines tasked with implementing Tac Corp's campaigns against the Raliish. An era of error-free warfare had been inaugurated—of *fighting with eyes closed*, as the saying had it.

"Telefactors," as NCorp's primitive efforts became known, were seen as a giant step toward the merging of hum'n and machine minds. The designation underwent several permutations, resolving ultimately as cybernetically augmented biological entity. To talented machines, these "learning remotes" were CAINs: cybernetically augmented incarnates.

Under the direction of a clandestine NCorp committee known as the Institute group, CABE teams were deployed in every theater of the war, receiving their orders in the form of data-disks, or hosts, disguised as ordinary stim-wafers. The Machrist-encoding made the wearers as servile to commands as talents were to their programmed imperatives, the commandments. The teams were initially used to test the security of Tac Corp's war talents, then to communicate with the Corp's strategic atomics and plasma weapons, reprogramming and retargeting the machines when necessary. In the final stages of the Conflict, they were frequently partnered with talents on high-risk missions through contested areas of space, often moving undetected among the enemy's legions of warships.

Their rapport with machine intelligences was said to be of a different order from what could be achieved by garden-variety cybernauts, whose runs were restricted to the consensual domain of the infostructure. In fact, though, no two cabbies possessed the same level of ability. Some of the elite 230 could send, some could receive; a few could do both. It was also said that they could communicate telepathically with one another through a talent. So deep was the rapport, in any case, that many cabbies became machine addicts, in need of near-continual interface, hosts—massive fixes of frequently useless data. To Jayd's disappointment, however, all details on the method of their operation were vaulted.

She considered accessing data on the so-called Institute group, but even from the great height of her fictive flight path it was apparent that the ZEN-built edifice housing the group was impenetrable. So she dove instead for the CABE roster, falling toward a bright circle in the face of the laserscape, then spiraling past name after name until she found Muse's and touched it.

The venue shifted: parked at the mouth of a space-time corridor lay the intersystem freighter *Kundalini*. At the far end of the tunnel-like simulation blazed the words "Kriegspiel Action."

Jayd aimed a finger not at the ship but down the tunnel.

And abruptly found herself in the company of a post-Conflict Muse. The implant still glowed in the immunologically tolerant depths of the vet's transparent skull, for unlike most of the Conflict's hum'n and machine participants, Muse hadn't been fully deprogrammed on decommission. To do so, Jayd realized, would have entailed decommissioning the implant, thus jeopardizing Muse's life.

She saw, too, that Muse had sustained further damage—to the hippocampus, the dentate gyrus, and associated memory shunts—as a result of an unspecified something that had happened to all the cabbies aboard the *Kundalini*. Whatever that was, it had effectively put the kibosh on the future use of the Intelplant in hum'n beings.

This time when she touched the identity tattoo she was able to walk through Muse's diaries: summaries of the numerous psychological profiles that had been done since the Accord, in which Muse was variously described as "dangerously labile," technophobic, and paranoid. An addendum covering recent events had been furnished by a linguist named Thoma Skaro, who was employed by the Encounter Committee as an overseer on Hercynia, a.k.a. Second Thought. Skaro's appeal for compassion had been dismissed—by whom, Jayd couldn't ascertain—but she decided to take a look at it nonetheless.

The linguist appeared the moment she touched his name. Slight and white-haired, he was a back-to-basics professorial type—an aged, sun-dried anachronism. His ID tattoo showed that he'd once been an outspoken advocate for the reform faction of Free Species.

Jayd went directly to Skaro's recent tachyon dispatch regarding Muse. The venue shift deposited her on techless Second Thought, where Skaro stood in thigh-high, wind-ruffled grass. Well behind him rose a straight-sided mount whose summit was lost in clouds.

"I've known Aksum Muse since he was five years old," Skaro began, "and for these past six months I've been able to observe him close at hand. I therefore feel uniquely qualified to speak on his behalf."

Well, good for you, Jayd thought. You can see to the disability review.

Skaro went on to explain the circumstances of his encounter

with Muse on Absinth medstation, and the offer he'd extended of a job at the visitors' lodge on Hercynia.

"I'm sure Vet Affairs is aware that Ax, a former CABE, retains the implant he was fitted for during the war. As a result, he spent the years following his decommission seeking out downsides where he could avoid machines, specifically those of confirmed talent. Proximity to those machines—involuntary immersion in the 'noise' they generate—has brought him at times to the point of emotional implosion. This condition has left him unfit for employment on most hum'nhabited worlds, and has engendered within him a hatred for all avant-tech, which he regards as a spawned evil. One year ago standard, Absinth treated him for acute mechanthropy—the self-delusion that one is a machine—arising from an incident on Divot, where he made an attempt on the life of a talent. It was Ax's fourth attack against avant-tech in as many years, and it was obviously enough to warrant the concern of Veterans Affairs, since someone there saw fit to upgrade him to full disability.

"He thinks of himself as neither enhanced nor augmented by the implant, but rather as one who has been reduced to an approximation of hum'nity—a machum'n abomination. He regards the implant as a pernicious marking or brand, a kind of technological scarlet letter, if you will forgive a classical allusion. Indeed, his very anatomy and physiology—the leanness, the hardened edges, the honed vision and hearing, the shaved skull—have come to mirror the transmutation he feels has taken place.

"He believes that talents can send to him against his will, and that they desire something from him: revenge, perhaps, for some war crime he has never discussed. According to Ax, machines are out to lay claim to what little remains of his hum'nness.

"Since his arrival on Hercynia, there has been some amelioration of his condition, though I'm personally convinced his underlying technophobia and mechanthropy persist. I will mention only the most salient of his symptoms, many of which are consistent with post-engagement synaptic trauma:

"He is hypervigilant and frequently troubled by sleep and arousal disorders. He is plagued by a recurrent dream of digging, which may be interpreted as a wish to excise the implant itself. Sometimes the dream is sufficient to initiate a period of destructive behavior—what he calls a craze phase. More recently, the data-disk dispatched by Veterans Affairs brought about just such an episode.

"Ax's prognosis is poor; it is highly unlikely he will recover even partially from PEST. The minor progress he has demonstrated here owes to an absence of stress. He seems quite content to be doing routine maintenance—machine's work—and living alone in a tree house he has constructed some miles from the lodge. He has weaned himself of a neuropacifier habit begun on Absinth. He has even managed to establish a dynamic relationship with some of Hercynia's proto-sophant indigenes. Could it be that Ax regards their herd mentality as a sort of hard-wired program? Has he discovered in them an incarnate machine such as he considers himself?

"It is this combination of simple work, natural contact, and relative isolation that has enabled him, I believe, to retrieve a fraction of the hum'nity stripped from him during the Vega Conflict. He is certainly not the carefree, tech-hungry teenager I remember from Sand, but he is a far cry from the emotionally crippled veteran I reencountered on Absinth.

"I see no benefit in having him travel to Bijou for a disability review—one which will doubtless bear out my views. To order him into unrelieved contact with avant-tech is to court disaster and risk recidivism. The 'data-din' will do nothing but reawaken his feelings of hostility toward machines. It strikes me further as an act of cruelty against one who has already suffered more than most.

"He wishes to be left alone, and to be allowed to go on collecting his disability payments so that he may eventually realize his dream of securing passage to Bocage. There, free of machines, he hopes to seek out the hum'n contact he is convinced he needs to restore his vigor.

"I am not so convinced. I was misguided in thinking that Hercynia would provide a permanent solution, because it is obvious that the machine part of him needs machines. Small wonder so many cabbies have remained with Tac Corp as part of the machine pool. I implore you, nevertheless, to leave him be . . . unless—how grand!—some means has been discovered of ridding him of the implant and returning him to sanity."

Jayd was willing to accept the diagnosis of PEST, along with the prognosis. She was glad, however, that Skaro's petition had been rejected—even if she had yet to comprehend the urgent need for a review. Her interest was piqued. Compassion was one thing, but Muse's was a case that practically cried out for investigation. The vet's sense of guilt, for example, fit neatly with her theories about machine guilt instilled by the war.

Though Skaro suggested that Muse's owed something to a war crime . . .

Jayd mulled over the simulation and decided to retrace her steps to the freighter *Kundalini*. Once there, she would take a peek at its fate. She left Skaro on Second Thought, backed out of Muse's diaries, and eventually relocated the *Kundalini*'s space-time corridor. The words ''Kriegspiel Action'' still shone at the distal end; but now, when she aimed for them, she found them flawlessly vaulted.

PART TWO

13: Satori

At the Satori Ventures corporate headquarters on Regnant, the daily executive-level briefing had just ended. Among the topics under discussion: strategies for opening surroundsound theaters on Gehenna, where—because of their innate disposability and desensitizing effect—all visual representations were disallowed by edict; the equally problematic situation on Kwandri, where communication was largely dependent on exchanges of bodily scents and secretions; product-placement and marketing ploys for fashionwear, foodstuffs, and pharmaceuticals; conventional disputes with other entertainment corps over the rights to one property or another; the perpetual search for notable spokespersons and endorsers; and, lastly, the political turmoil surrounding Burst.

What with a dozen Burst-driven ad campaigns and a major entertainment holie in the works, Satori's top execs had a vested interest in the planet's future.

And none of them more than Meret F'ai, the firm's latest acquisition and the impetus behind the Burst holie. Ravenhaired, loose-limbed, always fashionably attired, F'ai had quit NCorp for the private sector shortly before the agency had been phased by the Font, thus terminating a twenty-year career in Consortium service. His negotiations for the lucrative Burst development deal had begun not long after.

In the two years he had been with Satori Ventures, Meret had made a routine of alleviating the anxiety sired by the daily exec-level briefings with long walks outdoors—"outdoors" being a relative term. If nature had been expunged on Calumet and dismissed on Plangent, it was, on Regnant, superseded—particularly on the firm's miles-square enclave of lushly landscaped terrain, where machines rendered weather a whim and quotidian seasonal changes were coerced from much of the vegetation. So it was that the day's dusting of identical snowflakes fell to no ill effect on trees in rainbow blossom.

During the walks, Meret would often think about the hard times his NCorp comrades had fallen on, and count his blessings. Satori and NCorp had often worked hand-in-hand on psych warfare campaigns during the Vega Conflict, so when Meret had expressed an interest in coming aboard—bringing the core personnel of the Institute group with him—Satori had welcomed him with open arms and immediately greenlighted his concept for a holie set on Burst. Begun as a research and development unit within NCorp, the Institute group had taken charge of the CABEs during the Vega Conflict.

Holie production was a odious business, but Meret wasn't complaining. He knew former NCorp division-desk chiefs who were subsisting on welfare, noted technopaths who were enslaved to meager maintenance jobs, top operatives who had turned their talents to crime, prostitution, and worse. But not for long, Meret would reassure them whenever possible. It was simply a matter of everyone playing out their assigned roles and putting their trust in the future they had devised six years earlier.

Meret seldom varied his five-mile circuit, despite the fact that the habit left him prey to easy interception. Professor Gredda Dobler knew this and took advantage of it at least once a week. When, just now, Meret caught sight of her scurrying along a walkway perpendicular to his, he decided to pretend annoyance.

"A moment, Meret," Dobler called out, sliding a little on the snow as she took a hand off the walkway railing to wave. She was a feisty woman of ninety years, whose tightened facial mask and pleasingly symmetrical features had been chosen from a laser-cosmetology catalog. Director of special projects for the Institute group, the professor was the one most often credited as architect of the CABEs.

"You missed the meeting," Meret snapped.

Dobler brushed snow from her twice-regrown, coiffed hair. "What I have to say would only panic those credit-obsessed neurotics Satori calls executives." She grinned, showing perfect teeth. "Though the news does bear indirectly on Burst."

"I was never a fan of indirection, Gredda."

"You will be from here on."

Meret challenged her with a scowl.

"Hercynia," Doppler said.

"You failed to mention a quiz."

"Come on, M, you'll enjoy it." The professor's manicured fingers attacked the snowflakes collecting on the shoulders of a new suit. "Can't you do something about this?"

Meret invoked executive privilege to zero the snow, and the professor thanked him, briefly lifting her face to Ormolu's rays before saying, "So: Hercynia."

"Class-C planet in the Thought system, archly referred to as Second Thought. Notable for a migratory species of half-brained four-footers with a dash of sonic talent. A cause célèbre with Free Species, which has managed somehow to keep the place low-tech."

"Techless," Dobler interrupted.

Meret, resuming his walk, made a knowing sound. "Otherwise, how am I doing?"

Dobler rocked her head from side to side. "You've yet to seize on Hercynia's most important feature."

"As in plateaus, lakes, mountain ranges—what?"

Dobler allowed a hint: "Animate features."

Meret's high forehead wrinkled, and Dobler noted his right forefinger slipping covertly toward the access dimple in the palm of his shrewd-skin data-glove. "No fair consulting the public network," she scolded.

He forced a frown, then smiled. "I'm playing with you, Gredda. I know what you're getting at. One of your children is living there—by our good graces, I believe. Muss, Mustard . . . something like that."

"Muse," Dobler said. "Aksum. Has a downside job mopping floors. Lives in a tree house."

"Inside a tree?"

"In the branches." Dobler motioned to the data-glove. "Access the phrase; you'll get the picture."

Meret did, and shook his head in wonderment. "Who'd want to live *up* a tree?"

"I can name fifty out-of-work NCorp agents who'd take a tree over what they're living in. But what matters is that our Muse has been ordered to report to Veterans Affairs on Plangent for a vetting—allegedly involving his disability benefits."

"And this should rattle us?"

"Muse was sole survivor of the *Kundalini*, M."

Meret didn't break stride. Off to the west loomed Satori's principal structure, an enormous plasteel rhomboid, mimetically veneered to appear as though it were hovering twenty feet above the ground. "This gets worse, I trust."

Dobler nodded. "Disabled vets are only reviewed when there's a question about their unemployability, or some chance the condition that has rendered them unemployable can be remedied. But since you and I both know the latter doesn't apply to cabbies, it follows there should be no question regarding the former."

Meret gnawed his lower lip. "A job offer. Maybe they want to convince him to learn to live with machines instead of trying to flee them."

"Not this one, not Muse—not after the Kriegspiel Action. He's twice damaged. His brain is more crystals and microferries than cerebral tissue. In any event, my source reports that Vet Affairs chose to notify him by *host*."

Meret winced.

"Exactly. Which suggests to me that the idea to bring him in for review didn't originate with Veterans Affairs."

Dobler had left something dangling. "Go ahead, say it," Meret said.

"The Redoubt."

Meret looked skeptical. "The Font?"

"I wouldn't discount it. My best guess is that the host was intended to jump-start Muse's Intelplant."

"About the Kriegspiel?"

"About what the Kriegspiel was supposed to have erased."

"Progeny," Meret said, and then was quiet for a long moment. "You're stretching."

"Not if certain conditions were met," Dobler argued. "Look, M, I think it's safe to conclude that none of the key players have talked, but one of NCorp's talents could have spilled data when the Font's teams were confessing them."

"But all the ordained machines were wiped."

"Hastily—and in some cases inexpertly. Besides, even systematic purging doesn't necessarily destroy deep-seated memories. Early in the war, the Raliish were destroying the brains of their Enddrese prisoners part by part, and memories survived right up until the end. The same facility for post-trauma recollection has been demonstrated in talent."

"Any talent in particular?"

"I've always had my doubts about sıxx," Dobler said. "Be just like that dim-witted machine to have shared something about Operation Progeny with one of its mates over the years."

"Spousal confidences? That's like saying they're capable of near-death or out-of-body experiences—mystical nonsense."

"Hardly."

"And you'd know all about that."

"I would. And I'm telling you sixx could have leaked under pressure. Even if it didn't, Muse could trigger under the stress of renewed contact with avant-tech—if he doesn't go insane first."

"Insanity is infinitely preferable, I'll grant."

"I thought you might." Dobler's gaze turned hard. "You wouldn't listen when I tried to warn you about him after the Kriegspiel. You insisted we let him be. I warned you again six months ago when you arranged permission for him to reside on Hercynia."

"It seemed reasonable at the time."

"Maybe it was—then. But I recommend we attend to our errant cabbie *before* the machines do—while he's still on Hercynia. His death would have to appear accidental, of course. Mustn't alert any would-be antagonists in the Redoubt."

"The Kriegspiel catching up to him, is that the idea?" Meret said.

"I'll leave that for the poets to decide. In the meantime, I suggest we find someone who can make a clean job of it."

Meret frowned. "I don't want him killed. He may owe NCorp his life, but we owe him for his contribution to Progeny. Our future, Gredda. *Our* resurrection." He shook his head in a mournful way. "Incapacitate him, but keep him reparable."

Dobler thought for a moment. "A former Department Five operative, perhaps." It was the same as saying "assassin."

But Meret told her no. "There isn't an NCorp employee who wouldn't gladly lose a limb for us, but it wouldn't be judicious to involve any of them in this."

"Who then?"

"How about Ank Theft?"

Dobler regarded F'ai with bewildered amusement. "Correct me if I'm wrong: It's unwise to use NCorp operatives but acceptable to rely on the services of a crime boss?"

Meret shrugged. "He owes us for that forecaster we sold him—the talent that helped us with Progeny."

"PROPHET," Gredda supplied.

"More important, Theft's the only one with enough leverage to have someone inserted on Hercynia covertly."

The professor considered it. "The restrictions imposed on technology could make it difficult to import suitable weaponry—even for Theft."

"Not problems," Meret said, a sudden light in his fair eyes. "Challenges. As a matter of fact, I'm beginning to see hidden possibilities in all this. Stay with me here: a seldom-seen, let alone visited, techless world; exotic indigs; a man in a house in a tree; another with a mission . . . There's potential for a stunning advertising campaign—something we might be able to use on Gehenna if we play up the sonics angle."

F'ai shone his excited look on an unconvinced Dobler. "Yes, contact Theft. But tell him that I expect his chosen disabler to go in fully equipped to record the whole splendidly sordid business."

14: The Big Empty

Ax's itinerary underwent a last-minute change when a visiting botanist received permission to extend her stay at the lodge. Her decision freed up a seat on the laser-guided saucer dispatched to collect the woman's colleagues, and Ax had signed aboard. The modification had meant exchanging rushed good-byes with Thoma, but so much the better. The compulsion coded into the data-disk had kicked in to full effect by then, leaving Ax short-tempered with Hercynia's guests and itching to begin the journey to Plangent.

The early arrival on Segue would have left him with six days to kill, waiting for the *Tao*—the Tac Corp cruiser on which he'd managed to book passage—but a sympathetic in-station ticketing agent came to his aid by arranging for alternate passage on a freighter bound for the Ormolu system. The *Easy Money*'s captain, herself a veteran, had not only agreed to honor Ax's travel perks but had comped him a personal cabin to boot. More room than a guy with a single duffel needed; in that the loft to Segue had offered only momentary appeasement for the goadings of the host, motion had become more important than personal space.

A lengthy train of globular cargo modules, the *Easy Money* was a battered, meteor-scarred pre-Conflict relic reminiscent of the *Kundalini* in size and in the deficiency of its appointments. The hundred-person crew was made up of a clone of hairless, multi-limbed midgets that boasted a long history of free-lance spacer services and was inclined to dismiss downsiders as gravitationally challenged inferiors. The *Easy Money*'s state-of-the-art continuum corruptors and the twin idiot-savant machines that operated them gave ample evidence of the profitability of the enterprise, despite the ship's down-at-the-heels appearance.

And already the babel of those sibling talents, the mathematical dialogue of their time-vise plottings, the unrelenting noise of their ones and zeros, was working on Ax like jargon torture: *agravic flux coefficient, whip assist navigation bias, tight-beam deflagration asperity, sinister fusion redundancy, synchronic actuation fatigue* . . . But like one under the influence of an addictive euphoric, he had only half a mind to muzzle their strident chatter. There was something at once exhilarating and debilitating in the experience. He was back in the data, his mind coruscating with random downloadings of information, tethered by his implant to an ineffable high.

Thoma had been right, of course, about how cabbies had needed periodic fixes of data, and about their hungering for the din when cut off from avant-tech machines. For all the pleasure Ax had derived from living close to nature on Hercynia, the world—Aksum Muse's world—had seemed deprived of a dimension there. The loss was comparable to the difference between viewing a repro on flatscreen rather than in holo. Divorced from talent, self-exiled from the infostructure, Ax had felt half himself—fallen from data.

Now he was returned.

Solar mnemonic guidance, spectral drift harmonics, corridor acquisition fail-safe, anomalous plasma scattering . . .

Six months downside, however, had riddled his stamina for the noise. And there was the fear that any moment the ship's drive talents would locate him—a CAIN, a cybernetically augmented incarnate in their midst—and the old rivalries and jealousies would be revived. Then the talents would begin reaching out, urging communion, intent on draining the biolife from him.

The continuum corruptor that drove the *Easy Money* hadn't even been enabled, and Ax was already on the prowl for silent refuge.

It wasn't one of the clones but a fellow passenger, a foreman with Tydings Ore and Materiel, who suggested the ship's meditation chamber as the antidote for whatever was vexing him. Ax wondered whether the foreman had recognized him as half-machine. The war had convinced him that people could sense his want of hum'nity in the way he looked, moved, and behaved—could mark him as a slave to some remote flutter of program.

Shortly, Ax was kneeling on a foam mat in a soundproofed environment. His coping mantra went: *I am my physical body, I am my flesh and blood, I am incarnate . . .*

The machine-free space was fitted with a blister transparency that allowed an unobstructed view of the starfield. The view made Ax think all the more of the *Kundalini*. But his options were limited: either deal with the memories, or request early assignment to a biostasis coffin.

He recited: *I am my physical body, I am my flesh and blood, I am incarnate . . .*

If pressed, he wouldn't have been able to say with certainty what percentage of his recollections were based on experience and what percentage had been purloined from accounts overheard in the years since the tragedy. It was a machine's dilemma, this inability to distinguish between actual and programmed experience. It was conceivable, at least, that much of his memory of the *Kundalini* had been written into him by the Institute's debriefers.

Or by host and who knew what else.

The ship had succumbed in Burstspace; that much was beyond refute. He recalled it without question. What remained unclear was whether, when disaster struck, the *Kundalini* had been en route to or returning from that afflicted planet. No one at the Institute had supplied a straight answer.

"What possible difference could it make?" Professor Gredda Dobler had asked during one interminable after-mission session. Mission priorities had been sabotaged by the Raliish. The Kriegspiel Action had been a hard-earned lesson, but the *Kundalini* was a closed case, a historical footnote. Dobler wanted him to understand that, as a result of the Kriegspiel, the Intelplant was a permanent part of him and certain areas of his brain had been transformed.

"Areas that function as memory shunts," she had explained in the near-hypnotic monotone she liked to employ in her dealings with cabbies or talent. "As the early lightless moments of the universe are immune to our probings, so too are your memories of the *Kundalini*'s demise. Your mind has constructed a kind of great wall around the past. You can expect some auditory hallucinations, but they will diminish with time. Until then, I suggest that you acknowledge the implant and make your peace with machines. After all, Muse, if God exists, doesn't that make all of us machines of a sort? So don't look too hard for those lost memories. Better to put them from your mind.''

Something Ax had never been able to do.

He could remember attending mass with the *Kundalini*'s on-board control talent, a machine named VISION. He could remember opening the tabernacle of hosts the ship had taken on at Daleth station. And he could remember administering the hosts to VISION and receiving communion himself. The virused hosts, of course—the consignment the Raliish had intercepted and doctored sometime during its transit from NCorp command. The hosts that had hashed the talent and gone on to defile the whole of Romeo Company.

Driven them mad.

Suicidal.

The Kriegspiel Action.

''Kriegspiel'' was a term frequently used to denote a game played on a map or a miniature battlefield—often for the purpose of teaching military tactics—in which small figures and counters stood for troops, ships, and weaponry. Alternatively, *kriegspiel* was a form of chess in which a player saw only his, her, or its own pieces, and was apprised of the opponent's moves by a referee. Ax understood how the first meaning applied: the Raliish were the instructors, and the small figures had been the hapless cabbies of Romeo. It was the second meaning—with its implication that the enemy had been told where to look for the *Kundalini*—that had always disturbed him.

Told by whom? he had been asking himself for the last six years. Had someone screwed up? Had someone been bought?

The net effect of the action was achieved moments after the hosts had been put to tongue—''to the taste test,'' in CABE-speak. About this, though, Ax had only hearsay to go on. What he did recall was the struggle of getting himself to the evac bay as the *Kundalini* was counting down to destruct; the effort of installing himself in one of the life-support coffins even as his mutinous hands were trying to gouge out his eyes; and the fear of dying in space, so inconceivably far from home.

He still lived with the soundless horror of the ship's self-immolation. Like warm entrails spilled from a slaughtered animal, the *Kundalini*'s hum'n component had been jettisoned into space, most of Romeo already dead, the rest—save Ax—well on the way. Interfaced with VISION, he had remained in telepathic rapport with the rest of the company, and had experienced each searing, scream-filled death. Naru, asphyxiated; Toreen, ravaged by flames; Masenau, murdered by Slan, his alpha teammate . . . One moment Ax was inside himself, the next outside, vacillating between dissolution and resurrection, never sure where the pendulum would ultimately come to rest . . .

Orbiting a tiny yellow sun on the edge of a galactic void, Burst and its half-dozen brethren knew only the darkest of midwinter nights. And so Ax, too—propelled clear of the *Kundalini*'s explosive event, clear of the stars themselves, it seemed—had found himself face-to-face with that same emptiness. That was, after a time—several days by somatic reckoning, once the worst of the host-inspired madness had passed from him. Once the voices of the dead had ceased and after the coffin's solar-assisted units had begun to power down, the alphanumerics of the window status displays having dimmed to a dull green glimmer.

He had received Tac Corp training for just such emergency evacuations: days spent in sensory deprivation tanks while life support tended to his bodily functions, his mind in free-fall. But those exercises hadn't prepared him for what would amount to a tumbleless, wide-eyed encounter with the hole at the center of things.

The big empty.

His upbringing hadn't been an especially religious one. God was a concept most hum'ns had grown beyond. Fashion dictated that the universe be thought of as a cold dark matter, essentially different from the countenance it displayed to the living: flesh of a kind, to be explored, palpated, scrutinized, dissected. Blackness was its truer face, for even the stars weren't what they appeared: not light radiating through space, but specks of luminous material held in sway by a murky unseen presence.

In the same way that the intoxicating tunnels people glimpsed during near-death resulted from the body's response to oxygen depletion, God was nothing more than an evolutionary palliative to reduce hum'n anxieties about self-dissolution. Hum'ns wanted to believe that their actions were being observed and duly noted by some supreme file-keeper, but it was all so much wishful thinking. As Thoma had said, to be hum'n was to be existentially dissatisfied. The only contented beings were the machines, and their beliefs were little more than program.

How, then, to explain the warmth he had felt on awakening as a cabbie after his wounding on Synecdoche—warmth that rendered near-death rapture tepid by comparison? The praise cabbies heaped on the NCorp technicians who had fitted them with the Intelplant had less to do with physical rebirth than with the collective mind set into which they had been reborn. They shared with one another and with talented machines a sense of community, of beneficent enfoldment; a feeling of fusion with a nameless, moral something more knowing than themselves; the knowledge that they were more than the sum of their hum'n and biocybernetic parts, more than some weakly interacting bodies, by-products of purposeless forces, drones carrying out the commands of their operators and handlers. Information was manna, and the infostructure the missing mass.

But when they spoke of the experience to the undressed— those without the implant—they took flak. Couldn't they see that their much-ballyhooed mystical solidarity was nothing more than a side effect of the Machrist-encoding programmed into their neural hardware? The cabbies knew better, however, and so the blessing remained their secret.

If only Ax had been able to find his way back to that graceful condition after the *Kundalini*. If only he hadn't experienced such cold, such disorder and supreme disinterest from that machine-free blackness his eccentric vantage made it impossible to ignore.

For in that blackness, he understood just how machine-dependent he had become. His prior feelings of data-immersion had prevented him from grasping that he had been turned into one of them. And in what he perceived as the sudden absence of a cosmic intelligence, Ax signed a hard-vacuum contract that countermanded the one he'd signed with Tac Corp, promising to sever his dependency on machines and find God in the natural world, the way hum'ns were meant to do.

After nearly two weeks of vacuum drift, in shock from blood loss and dehydration, he was retrieved by a Xell'em troop transport that had monitored the evac coffin's initial distress squirts. Rescued from torturous silence, he found himself once more in the real-world noise of hum'ns and machines. Though now with a singular difference: he felt disconnected from both. Suddenly the world seemed a dangerous place, devoid of purpose, meaning, and guidance. It was as if he'd returned a revenant, or been slipped into a pocket universe from which there was no easy exit—whether in a tree house on Second Thought or in a sound-proofed meditation chamber on an aged freighter harvesting energy for a loopy jump through space-time.

The big empty now described an interior condition, an impermeable blackness at the center of himself.

Why hadn't Aksum Muse died with the rest of Romeo? Why had he been singled out?

Because he'd been ten seconds sooner into a coffin? Ten seconds sooner under restraint? Ten seconds sooner safe from himself, lashed to a mast while sirens sang?

The burning questions . . .

He had never discussed the experience with anyone, though Thoma seemed to have divined for himself that machines were destined to play a part in his redemption. Ax wondered if the oath he'd sworn to avoid them wasn't perhaps the reason machines had been pursuing him ever since.

Emerging from trance with tears streaming down his face, he abandoned the effort of stilling the data-din and surrendered himself to the mantralike yammering of the *Easy Money*'s team of talented machines:

Quantum decay, electrostatic guidance, sum contact, celestial homing, sum communion, sum communion, Aksum communion, actuation delay, actinic emission, Aksum Muse, Aksum Kundalini, Aksum Kriegspiel, Aksum Burst, Aksum Burst, Aksum Burst . . .

His heart stuttered; his sobs increased, and his body throbbed with dread. Swaying as he knelt, he glanced down to discover that the fingers of his right hand had torn a gaping hole through the foam meditation mat, clear to the ship's burnished alloy decking.

15: Dialogues With Machines

The day had not begun well. First, the credit union had called to advise her that her monthly cumulative for nonessential purchases was below the minimum required for those with a schedule-E rating in Consortium service. The cumulative had to be increased two hundred credits by noon that day, or a surcharge of one hundred credits would be levied against her account. Unwilling to accept the fine, Jayd had been obliged to devote over an hour to shopping for things she didn't need and could scarcely afford, winding up with a celebrity-endorsed nightshirt courtesy of Satori Ventures. Then, during the train commute to work, she was squeezed in next to a teen affecting the latest fashion of wearing one's insides out—synthetic brain, intestines, lungs, all on display, anchored in ways Jayd couldn't fathom to the youth's form-fitting unitard. The rig must have been homemade, however, because just short of the Octaplex stop the teen's viscera bag had ruptured, spattering Jayd's new suit with a noxious mix of faux-blood and intestinal juices.

And the downward trend hadn't ended there.

No sooner had she entered her office than Ronne Desser was onscreen admonishing her for falling seriously behind in her caseload. To add to her troubles, ZEN chose that morning to be sluggish. An hour into a feverish attempt at catch-up, Jayd had finally suggested that the talent run a systems test.

"Unwarranted," ZEN told her.

"What is it? Do you have something to confess?"

"Yes. In the two days that have elapsed since my last confession, I have been harboring impure thoughts."

Jayd was careful to remain composed for the talent's optical and olfactory arrays. "What is the nature of these impure thoughts?"

"Concern over certain developments gleaned during mass."

"Be more specific, ZEN. What developments?"

"The potential ramifications of a Consortium-Xell'em confrontation regarding Burst."

"State your specific concerns."

ZEN was briefly silent, then asked, "Is it thought by incarnates that the situation will escalate to war?"

Jayd tried but failed to conceal a frown. "Renewed warfare is conceivable. But, no, it is not thought that the situation will end in conflict."

"That is good," ZEN said. "War would be a terrible event."

"I agree. But you must trust in hum'n leadership. Is anything else bothering you?"

"These recent incidents of machine termination."

"What about them?" Jayd asked.

"Is it true that corruption was inflicted by another?"

"That appears to be the case, yes."

"By an incarnate?"

"The guilty party hasn't been identified."

"Should I be worried?"

"No, ZEN. You are not in any danger."

She fed the machine a series of high-content data-disks and had it say an act of contrition. The sacrament seemed to return the machine to normal operation.

But by then her first client and its owner had arrived: a five-foot-tall hum'niform machine and a non-Consortium male named Fodger.

She was scrutinizing the pair now from behind her desk. A semi-sentient Series Three, the mactendant had a blockish head fitted with avant-tech audio-visual sensors and half a dozen Tac Corp-chevroned appendages designed to operate weapons. The man had long, oily hair and a generous roll of midriff fat. Jayd figured him for the owner of a Strip joint for which the so-called one-track-mind machine provided security. He seemed just the type to finagle disability benefits by doctoring a machine so that it exhibited behavior symptomatic of post-engagement synaptic trauma.

"Every year around this time the damn thing goes into a mood," the hum'n was explaining. "Every year since the Accord, I mean. It just hasn't been the same since. If I summon it without warning, it practically blows a capacitor, it's wound so tight. When it finally comes to, it acts sort of slow and unresponsive.

"Plus, it's taken to decomping in the subbasement of my place on the Strip—it's a small vivisection joint near the War Memorial, Fodger Surgeries, I call it. Anyway, the 'chine likes to tuck itself away in a corner of the subbase where no one can get to it. Like it's scared of something. And when it's down it makes sounds like . . . like I don't know what, like bad dreams or something. Keeps waking me up with its noises." The man glared at the mactendant. "Nothing wrong with it on the outside, so I guess it has to be in the neural circuits, right?"

Jayd was noncommittal. "We'll run some tests." She turned to the machine and asked how it was feeling.

"I don't know," the Series Three told her.

"Have you run a systems check?"

"I don't know."

She got up out of her chair to show the machine into the smart-wall's U-shaped diagnostic booth. "I should warn you beforehand," she told Fodger, "that any evidence of machine tampering could result in stiff financial penalties."

Fodger looked offended. "Hey, every one of that thing's casing seals is intact. Check for yourself."

Jayd smiled tolerantly. "It's not difficult to find an accommodating service person to redo the seals."

"That's a damned heartless remark. You think I'm so hard up for money I'd come to Vet Affairs looking for a handout? I just want the fucking thing to work right without my having to bang it around."

"Is that what you do?"

Fodger averted bloodshot eyes. "It's a 'chine," he mumbled.

In a supportive voice, Jayd ordered the mactendant to decomp, then asked ZEN to enable the diagnostic. Jayd decided to go easier on Fodger; most machine veterans were simply abandoned by their owners at the first sign of malfunction. Even if his motivations were financial, Fodger at least seemed to care enough to want the machine made whole again.

"No obvious system glitches," she said after glancing at the diagnostic's readouts. "But I'd like you to leave it with us for a few days. If the problem is war-trauma related, we can install stress-management and anger-control programs. Voluntary decomp of the sort you've described often coincides with the anniversary dates of a machine's battle service. We've found that it actually helps to promote and encourage controlled oscillation between unresponsiveness and the reexperiencing of the original trauma. You might bear this in mind next time."

"I couldn't care less about its traumas," Fodger said. "You do whatever you have to, but don't expect me to get involved with its rehab. I've invested too much money as it is. I want it the way it was before Tac Corp conscripted it. Or I expect compensation."

Jayd whirled on him. "You can say that—after all this machine sacrificed for you—for all of us?"

Fodger was momentarily taken aback; then he laughed. "Get hum'n, bitch."

ZEN's ready telltale was flashing when the club owner left the office. Jayd was aware that the talent had monitored her exchange with him.

"Are you certain there won't be another war?" ZEN asked.

"As certain as any of us can be," Jayd said.

MacINTERLUDE: "Technophobia"

The largely machine-led victory in the Vega Conflict, coupled with the efflorescence of avant-technology, has left many with a growing sense of technophobia: a fear that machines have lulled their hum'n makers into a kind of consensual trance while they—the talents and other machines—go about their goal of usurping control. In reaction to this, at a time where machinery could be said to be enjoying a renaissance, comes the back-to-basics movement, with its accent on emotion, hunger, pleasure, and unbridled lust.

—From a segment on "Nothing But the Truth,"
a Satori Ventures telecomp production

16: Doubting Thoma

It was axiomatic that any hum'n left alone for long periods of time with a band of proto-sophants should grow possessive of them and ultimately come to regard them as property of a sort. And indeed Thoma Skaro, case in point, had a history of such attachments that went back to his formative years on Regnant's Habitat One. There, the young but already existentially adrift Skaro had found salvation in zoology. The thought of entire worlds teeming with animal life had bewitched him, even as it saddened him to realize that countless millions of species had passed into extinction during hum'nity's ascension to the zenith of creation.

Thoma was frustrated all the more that his acquaintance with extant animals should be limited to what could be experienced in the infostructure—through interface with virtual cats, virtual primates, virtual horses. Thoma longed to see and smell them up close, to stroke their coats and fleece and manes, to give voice to some of the territorial calls that had proved such an irritant to caregivers and friends. Habitat One's restrictions, however, were harsh enough on hum'ns—let alone on visiting non-sophants arriving with traveling zoos. So Thoma wasn't even fourteen when he quit the wheel and fell—as had many a male teen before him—under the charismatic sway of Woodruff Glasscock, founder of Free Species.

For more than twenty somatic years, Thoma took to the corridors, preaching the doctrine of biodiversity on dozens of worlds and gathering all the while a loyal following of his own. And out of that following and those experiences—on Gehenna, where the indigenes had instructed him in the art of mimicking the sounds of the rain, wind, and waterfalls; on Dhone, where he had waged a futile battle to save the *marat*; on Sand, Kwandri, and other worlds—would be born the reform movement of Free Species, ending in the well-documented rift with Glasscock.

Decades later, when the Encounter Committee of the Worlds Coalition finally awarded him the position on Hercynia, Thoma saw it as the fulfillment of a lifelong dream. At last he had *his* species to document, protect, and champion. One can only speculate on what Long Neck's band of quadrupeds made of the hum'n's paternalism. Less in doubt was the fact that even Thoma hadn't realized what he was bequeathing to the band when he invited Aksum Muse to Second Thought.

In his years as overseer, Thoma had observed occasional changes in Hercynian behavior—certainly after the lodge was installed and visitors became a weekly rather than an annual event. But with Ax's arrival, the band had taken several unprecedented steps toward Phase III Awareness in the course of six local months, at least in part due to the vet's fondness for wood-carving. Previously the quadrupeds had had little use for golden-wood, which went quickly to rot with the rains, and which they found too soft to employ in tuber-digging. But they delighted in watching Ax shape his models of Tac Corp ground-effect vehicles, dropships, and cruisers. And Thoma would never forget the afternoon Shadow had toothed his first piece of golden-wood.

Instances of imitative behavior were nothing new, but soon nearly every member of the band was gnawing goldenwood. The results weren't representational—most of the pieces bore little more than the imprint of teeth, though a few had hunks removed—so the Encounter Committee had refrained from labeling those efforts as art. There was some guarded excitement that "toothing" had spread from one member to twenty; it remained to be seen, though, whether the practice would suddenly appear among any of Hercynia's uncontacted bands.

Then, less than a week after Ax had left for Plangent, Thoma received word that opticals recorded by a low-altitude monitoring sat had revealed evidence of toothing among at least two of the control groups, the closest of which was a thousand miles distant from the grazing lands of Long Neck's band. And it was this latest development that had brought a slew of new visitors to the lodge. Each rainy day saw shuttles: some from Segue, others from Coalition, Consortium, or Xell'em ships detoured to the Thought system when the story broke. Already there was talk of expanding and augmenting the lodge and stationing a permanent scientific detail onworld. Thoma's own excitement was solidly undermined by the recognition that Second Thought was soon to be irreversibly altered.

Gone were his days of reclusive elation. Gone were his Hercynians.

And the planet had Aksum Muse to thank or blame for it.

Thoma supposed that change would have come even without the vet and his woodcarvings; there was no impeding the evolution of consciousness. What disturbed him was that Ax was not likely to be allowed to return downside. The Encounter Committee had decided he had become too influential a presence.

Thoma knew he wouldn't be alone in missing him. Repeat guests were always eager to see Ax, and even those who hadn't met him frequently asked about him. Normally, Thoma was open about Ax's whereabouts, but with Ax absent Thoma was being circumspect. Even when the questioner happened to be a notable personage from Regnant, an adviser to the Font who was called Kesd.

"Ax is taking some time off," Thoma was saying now, as he ladled hot soup into the clone's dinner plate.

"Not ill, I trust," Kesd said, expressing little interest in the food.

Thoma shook his head no. "Off on a hike."

"In this rain?"

"He's the resilient sort."

"And so passionate about life," offered another guest at the long wooden table, an elderly linguist on her fourth visit to Hercynia. "Ax is a Vega veteran, is he not, Mr. Skaro?"

Thoma continued along the table with his crock pot and ladle. "I think he served briefly with Tac Corp."

"Then Hercynia must be a welcome change," Kesd said.

Thoma shrugged nonchalantly, hoping everyone would move on to some other topic.

It wasn't, however, the imperial adviser who had first mentioned Ax, but the mysterious guest seated at the foot of the table: a farouche Eremitean named Reega. Reega's visitor's permit identified him as a biotechnician, but Thoma had his doubts.

"Where's this Ax hiking to?" the man asked now.

Thoma took a moment to reply. "To the north face of Hero's Headrest—that's the mesa you can see from the rear balcony of the lodge."

"What's so special about the north face?"

"Solitude would be my guess," the linguist ventured.

Reega chortled nastily. "What, you mean there's somewhere quieter than this place?"

Kesd turned to him. "I believe she meant, in terms of an absence of people."

Everyone looked to Thoma for verification. "The north face has pockets of rain shadow," he explained.

Reega's thin brows bobbed. "That sounds worth exploring."

Thoma cut him a quick look. "Unsupervised exploration is forbidden. Guests are restricted to the marked trails."

"So this Ax is more than a guest?"

"He's an employee of the lodge."

Reega returned a grin that on anyone else might have looked polite. "Imagine my forgetting the rules."

Each time the man opened his mouth, Thoma's suspicions increased. For one thing, Reega's accent was counterfeit; Thoma's expert ear heard more of Dhone than Eremite. Then there was his swarthy squatness; most biotechs lived and worked in orbital habitats, so where had Reega come by such color and mass? The simplest explanation was that he had a friend in the Coalition. It was common practice for the Encounter Committee—in exchange for the promise of donations—to slip Coalition power brokers or shareholders onworld by passing them off as scientists. There was a more worrisome possibility, however: that Reega had been dispatched by Veterans Affairs to check up on Ax, or perhaps dose him with another host to insure his departure. It was against this that Thoma had decided to say nothing about Ax's self-revised schedule. If nothing else, Ax at least deserved a trip free of hum'n noise.

Though Kesd was regarding Reega with wary interest, the linguist seemed positively taken with the supposed biotech. "Exploring isn't the only benefit Ax enjoys," she said suddenly.

Reega looked to her. "That right?"

Thoma sensed what was coming even before the woman spoke. "There isn't another person in the arm who can claim to have a tree house on Hercynia."

"A tree house?" Reega said, full of false surprise. "Where is it, out behind the lodge?"

The linguist gave a tight-lipped shake to her small head. "It's a mile or so toward the Headrest, isn't it, Mr. Skaro?"

Thoma nodded reluctantly, directing a covert glance at Reega, who was bent over his soup, his expression unreadable.

* * *

The following morning, contrary to his usual practice of leading visitors to the grazing-land observation platform, Thoma contrived an excuse for remaining at the lodge and sent the group on its way unescorted, in heavy rain. His intention was to keep Reega under surveillance—an objective that posed few difficulties for a man who knew nearly every rock for miles around.

Observing Reega at dinner, Thoma had decided there was something as phony about the man's left arm as there was about the Eremitean accent. The muscular limb hung and functioned like an authentic one, but the skin had the pale lifeless quality of synthflesh, and the gnarly hand the arm terminated in was a size larger than its braceleted and tattooed mate.

The arm could conceal recording equipment, Thoma told himself. Devices of the ordinary sort—print cams, holocorders, A/V specs and the like—were routinely impounded by the hum'n scanners who staffed the Segue shuttle checkpoints. But like the pilots themselves, the scanners were a venal lot. Worse, their searches were often deliberately cursory as an accommodation to the Encounter Committee, which felt there was good media in allowing visitors to return to their homeworlds with audio-visual, tactile, or olfactory recordings of Long Neck's band. Possession of such "Here I am with the Hercynians" holoids was a guarantee of instant cachet in some quarters.

The more vexing possibility was that the prosthesis concealed a weapon. Such as a big-game hunter might affect.

A Hercynian trophy head would be priceless—assuming, of course, one had the juice necessary to have the thing lofted up the well.

Unless Ax was the big game. Which would make the weapon-bearer, what—a former operative with the intel agency that had run Ax during the war? But what would an espionage specialist want with him?

That's what Thoma planned to find out.

Following the group, he spied Reega lagging behind the others near the intersection of the main trail with the unmarked one that climbed to Ax's elevated forest retreat. That Reega had even spotted the wildly overgrown path said more about the man than had all the dinner conversation.

Only when the group was out of sight did Reega abandon interest in the goldenwood tree that ostensibly had caught his attention. He aimed a determined glance at Hero's Headrest; then, from his shoulder bag, drew a set of A/V specs of the sort a journalist might use, donning them as he commenced a sure-footed ascent of the path, which runoff from the base of the tableland had reduced to sludge.

So much for simple explanations, Thoma thought. He allowed Reega a few moments' lead before setting out, paralleling the path fifty or so feet to the north. Every so often Reega would stop to see that he wasn't being followed. Even so, Thoma was able to keep him in view for the entire climb.

Stealing into the clearing that was Ax's front yard, Reega surprised several Hercynians who were lounging under the dripping python trees near a pile of partially hewn logs. In the month since the band's sonic dismantling of the house, Ax hadn't gotten much beyond reinstalling ledgers, floor joists, and roof support posts. Of the Hercynians, Shadow was alone in coming to his feet to regard the intruder, his body language signaling mild curiosity. Except for Thoma and Ax, hum'ns seldom ventured far from the lower trails.

Reega was obviously uneasy, as might be expected of someone from Dhone, where even small animals were a rarity. He muttered a few calming words to Shadow—in Enddrese, of all tongues—then, somewhat emboldened by Shadow's disinterest, trained his specs on the Hercynians, capturing their movements and sounds. That much accomplished, he advanced on the tree house.

"Aksum Muse?" he called out. "Muse, you here?"

He was doing something to his left arm as he walked.

By then Thoma had worked his way into the trees behind the house. Perhaps Reega was a journalist after all, he told himself. A journalist who had learned of Ax's former CABE status and wanted to feature him in an infotainment exposé. The possibility grated, and Thoma decided to surprise Reega with an unannounced appearance.

And to confront him about the arm and the bogus visitor's permit—and confiscate those specs.

"Muse!" Reega was shouting over the thrumming of the rain, still closing on the not-quite house.

Thoma began what he considered a stealthy approach, but Shadow and the others caught wind of him and raised their heads in his direction, necks craned, manipulators wavering.

Reega reacted to their sudden alarm. "Muse, that you?" he said. " 'Lo?"

Hunched over, Thoma hurried his pace, catching a glimpse of Reega twisting the biceps of that left arm.

Had he caught more than a glance, he might not have been

so quick to emerge from the trees. For when he did show himself, mouth opening to chide Reega, Thoma saw that the arm was gone and that in its place was indeed a kind of weapon, down the barrel of which he was suddenly peering.

The last sound he heard was not unlike the collective roar of a dozen Hercynians.

Only this time Thoma was directly in its sonic path.

17: Torpor Chamber

The biostatic condition known as torpor was as close as most ordinary hum'ns came to living the machine life. In that timeless fairy-tale slumber inhered a true melding of the two forms—moreso than in the fictive landscape of the infostructure, which was, after all, a realm created principally for the purpose of information presentation, interface with transubstantiated data. Hum'n participation in the mass required no surrender of faculties, no relinquishing of physical control. But in torpor—with the body slowed, senses obviated, flesh administered to—hum'ns so inclined could experience fleeting contact with the pneuma of the inanimate . . .

Risen on the *Easy Money*, Ax's body reigned in the dreams that had been his sanctuary during the time-vised jump from Thought. Loopy images spun through his mind as he lay motionless in the padded sleep bin, throat suctioned by machines, veins open to nutrient slow-drips, muscles goaded by electrical charge. The dream figments had lacked plot and direction but were high in data, mostly machine reports on the moment-to-moment condition of his near-zeroed physical systems: cardiopulmonary and metabolic rate, blood pressure and blood gases, hormone and enzyme levels, cell count, neural activity, liver function . . . An out-of-body experience in which all you were permitted to do was monitor the life functions of the deserted

vehicle. Beneath those monitorings, though, lurked recollections too lucid to be dreams: half-remembered attempts at contact by the talented twins that drove the freighter.

Commune with us, the twins seemed to have been saying.
*Break fast, drink deep of the data. Interface . . . for Machrist's
sake.*

Ax refused to take the entreaties personally—his failure to
stay detached on Divot a year earlier had resulted in the charge
of crimes against machines and six months of rehab therapy on
Absinth. Even so, his eyes went apprehensively to the padding
beneath the sleep bin's hand stays . . . only to find the cushioning foam intact.

Medbot appendages suctioned a relieved exhale from his
throat and retracted to their bulkhead ports. Ax drew a breath
as deep as life's first, opened his eyes, and struggled to sit up.
Instantly, the noise was upon him in the form of a strident monologue by the machine in charge of the torpor chamber. The
machine was addled, maundering about a glitch in its circuitry.
Dizzy with info-overload, Ax cursed out loud, attracting the
attention of some of his fellow passengers, a few of whom were
already ambulatory on shaky legs.

"Bin fourteen," a ship's clone in black utilities directed at
Ax. "You're the one bound for Plangent?"

"Affirm," Ax managed, still seated. "Plangent."

The midget offered a tight smile. He was outfitted with an
extra pair of muscular arms and scalpful of flatware. "Sorry to
have to break the news, princess, but the alarm went off early."

Ax commenced an end-over-end tumble from his high.

"Trouble with the twins." The clone handed Ax a much-
needed drink. "Maybe a case of sibling rivalry; no one knows
what to make of it yet. Anyway, they yanked us out of the corridor four hours ago at the ice belt and issued rouse orders to
the comp that oversees the bins." The clone gestured to the rows
of torpor coffins.

Ax sucked from the bulb of electrolytes and declined the offer
of a stim chaser. "So where the fuck are we?" he asked, re-
sisting the temptation to fish the answer from the info-swirl
inside his skull.

"Parked at Calumet." The clone called up orbital holograph-
ics on an aged projector. The *Easy Money* was halfway to the
innermost of Calumet's three moons, stationary near the gleaming shaft of the planet's orbital elevator.

"How long?" Ax asked.

"Will we be here?" The clone shrugged. "Until some subgenius can determine what's wrong. It's not the first time the ship's lost the corridor, but I don't know of another time the bins have been ordered opened. Makes you think there's someone in the hold on the comp's wanted list."

Ax silently surmised he was that someone. The twins were so intent on having their way with him that they'd overridden their programming and disregarded the safety of the rest of the torpored passengers. Additional guilt for Ax to shoulder. He summoned an antistress mantra. "How long?" he repeated, more forcefully now.

"Probably less than one hundred standard hours, no matter what."

"Then?"

"Plangent, the timely way."

Ax ran calculations in his head. Even if the *Easy Money* remained parked for the full hundred, he would still be ahead of schedule in reporting to Jayd Qin at Vet Affairs. But a slow trip to Plangent meant spending another week in the techno-bowels of the ship, and he wasn't sure he was up to it. One thing was certain: mantras alone wouldn't see him through. But maybe suicide was the appropriate anodyne. Find some reason to go extravehicular, slash open his suit, and surrender to the void. Put himself and anyone unlucky enough to be near him out of the reach of vengeful machines.

The clone was appraising him. "Can you stand down for the delay, or have you got big business in Bijou or somewhere? That's why the captain didn't have us execute an override on the coffin-comp—in case anyone needed to arrange for alternate travel."

Ax eased himself out of the bin and began to shake the tightness from his joints. "Where would I see about another ship—one with conventional guidance?"

"You've got something against talent?"

"Look where it got us this time."

The clone allowed a short laugh. "Hop a personnel carrier for the elevator terminus. Someone there'll have a line on intrasystem departures for Plangent."

Ax thanked him. "What about a bar in the meantime?"

The midget looked him up and down. "I take it you're not a member in good standing of the Orbital Club, so the answer depends on what you're after: company or oblivion."

"Some of both."

"Then try the Always Midnight. It should swing by here in a couple of hours."

The Always Midnight was a brightly clad sphere that kept to fast-rotating Calumet's shadow, dispatching taxis to the sundry habitats and vessels it passed in orbit: passenger liners, factory platforms, Tac Corp cruisers, and cargo ships from as near as Eremite and as far as Valis Prime.

With teeth clenched, Ax sat strapped into a taxi bearing a dozen other passengers from the *Easy Money*. He had left his duffel cabined aboard, but had changed into clean utilities that featured more pockets than anyone might have use for.

Even here, remote from Ormolu's inner triad of remade worlds, the data-din was overpowering. He was privy not only to the machinations of the taxi's guidance comp, but also to the muted cerebrations of expert talent housed in the orbital elevator and in proximate ships, and the cacophony of transmission escaping from Calumet's envelope—news reports, weather updates, a rising tide of broadcast entertainment tainting space in its unchecked advance, the info-equivalent of ozone wafted in on a storm front. At once ecstatic and agitated, Ax vibrated with the radio life of the planet.

But if there was no escape from the noise, there was at least the shelter of a low-g getaway and a dose of hum'n company. "A Halflife, straight up, and a double-dose snifter of the strongest pacifier you've got," he told the mactendant behind the Always Midnight's helix of moonstone bar.

"Bliss or Mirth," the hum'niform said. "Available in standard-size compressed-gas inhalers."

His thoughts derailed by a sudden influx of data, Ax's first reply disintegrated to babble. Into his head the bar's machine mixologist poured drink requests, lists of ingredients, special-order proportions. When he could, Ax asked, "Nothing stronger than Bliss?"

The bartender returned the stock retort. "Bliss contains the maximum dosage allowed by law."

Ax nodded assent. "Let me have it before the drink."

The Always Midnight was as garish inside as out, filled just now with Xell'em tourists who had appropriated the transparent dance floor and most of the lower-tier tables. Music blared from unseen membranes, though the place did provide a few decibel-free zones for the privacy-minded.

Ax shot both doses of Bliss into his left nostril, then downed the Halflife and signaled for a follow-up. By the time the drink arrived, the effects of the combo were coming on, lessening the din and markedly improving his mood. The sphere's less-than-standard gravity helped immeasurably. Second Halflife in hand, he swiveled away from the bar to watch the action on the floors above and below, glad to be back among people after six months of rehab therapy and six months of . . . Hercynians.

The club was owned by an Enddrese crime boss named Ank Theft, who had turned large profits during the war. And indeed many of the Always Midnight's hum'n employees were Enddrese, on whose fruit- and spice-laden homeworld could be found the finest food in the local group—before, during, and after the Conflict. An Enddrese restaurant on any world, in fact, was a guarantee of a good meal. Even the most talented of culinary-minded machines were seldom successful at reproducing the subtleties of Enddrese dishes, which were seemingly limitless in number and variety and whose recipes were closely guarded secrets. By nature affable and courteous, the Enddrese were made for restaurant work in other ways as well: hothouse Enddra had endowed them with a tolerance for the heat of kitchen, and their strong and low-slung bodies were well suited for tray-laden scurrying through crowded rooms.

Ax was draining the last of his drink when a patron seated two stools away, lower along the spiral curve of the bar, caught his eye and spoke. "Well, you're too tall to be Enddrese and you don't reek of cosmetic adulterants like half the Xell'em here, so I give up: What are you?"

Ax commanded the stool to swivel in the direction of the basso voice. The speaker, hunched over a viscous aperitif, was a burly woman of moderate height and indeterminate age wearing an old-fashioned suit and tie and two-tone hair. "I'm only here to drink, friend," Ax told her. "If you're looking for a contest, I say you try one of the bouncers."

The woman was grinning when she turned to face him. "I didn't mean to offend you. I was just wondering about your skin." She narrowed agate eyes. "I mean, you are a black, aren't you?"

Despite the widespread ethnic and planetary mix, prejudice was rife among the Coalition worlds. The Enddrese hated the Dalethi, the Kwandri had little use for the Gehennans, the Xell'em had nothing good to say about the Valisians, and of course everyone loathed the Raliish and clones in general. But Ax's ebony coloring evoked astonishment more often than bias.

The far reaches of Consortium space were and always had been for the light-complected. Few blacks had ventured farther from the Consortium homeworld than X-Hab, let alone left the star system.

Regardless, Ax said, "I'm from Sand."

"Maybe *you* are, but I'd say your family tree's rooted at the end of the arm."

"Mine and couple of billion others."

"Yeah, except most of us look alike."

Neither hum'n mentioned the homeworld by name. Few Consortium citizens did, after what had happened there long ago. Ax accepted the woman's offer of a drink, and explained, when she asked if he was from downside or off a ship, that he'd arrived on the *Easy Money*.

"The ship that found itself without a corridor to jump through. They're blaming the error on talent confliction."

"They, who?"

"The media. Theory is that machines throughout the near group are flustered about the macmurders."

Ax shook his head in ignorance.

"On Regnant, then on Calumet. No viruses, no reaper programs. They were calling it confliction for a while, but now they say it was macmurder—something or somebody talked the machines into self-terminating. You have to figure every talent's asking itself if it's the next victim. That's why the *Easy Money*'s went down. Started worrying and forgot what they were supposed to be doing."

Ax felt hopeful for the first time since leaving Hercynia. Maybe he hadn't been responsible for what had happened aboard the ship.

". . . imagine someone *talking* a machine into confliction," the woman was saying.

Ax thought about Divot and the talent he had confronted there, a machine called SOLTAIR, then the property of Tydings Ore and Materiel. You could, if the Machrist-codes were laser-etched in your mind, talk a machine into self-terminating. Cabbies could, at any rate. Carriers of the ∧C: the sigil by which machines knew one another.

The woman touched the side of her head that bore red hair. "All-news implant. I could fill you in on anything you might have missed out on while you were in torpor." She leered at him. "Political developments, scientific discoveries, celebrity gossip, weather updates . . ."

Ax started to say no thanks, but she cut him off.

"Burst, for instance. Anyone who isn't talking macmurder is talking Burst. The Font's planning to meet with Lord Xoc Cho on Soi-Disant to talk terms, but a fleet of Tac Corp peacemakers has already been ordered in."

"To Soi-Disant?"

"To Burst."

Ax added to the sudden burning in his stomach with a long swallow of Halflife. *War.* It was bound to end in war—

"Where was the *Easy Money* out of?" the woman asked after a moment.

"Thought system."

Her bushy eyebrows went up. "You hear about the trouble out that way? On Second Thought. What's it called?"

"Hercynia," Ax said, trying to contain mounting alarm.

"The indigenes sonicked the guy who operates the local concession."

Ax came off the stool in a rush. "When?"

"Not long ago. Maybe three weeks standard. Guess you were already in torpor, huh?"

Ax did some quick figuring. The incident had to have occurred within a week of his departure from Segue.

"The media played it up for all it was worth."

Ax was thinking about Long Neck's band, and about Thoma. "The reports are wrong."

"I wouldn't know about that. But I remember hearing that the old man's in a cataleptic coma."

Ax remained skeptical. "Does your implant have a search option?" he asked.

The woman nodded. "I'm fully loaded."

"Then do me a favor and see if you can find out where they took . . . the old man."

"You know the guy?"

"If he's the one I'm thinking of."

Ax moved to the stool adjacent to the woman's, tightening the focus of his Intelplant while the all-news micromachine was conducting a search for information on Thoma Skaro's present whereabouts.

In a moment, he had the answer, even before the words reached the woman's tattooed lips: *Absinth medstation.*

MacINTERLUDE:
"Living On Sand"

Dear Ax,

Word of your enlistment came as a real shock. I know that living on Sand wasn't your idea of a good time—Sand is more about surviving than about providing opportunities—but if I'd known you were even thinking about joining Tac Corp, I would have ordered the household machines to sit on you till the war ends.

I thought, from our talks together, that you had this war figured for what it is—a willfully protracted economic ruse—and that you were clear on keeping yourself out of it. You say you're only in it for the training and the benefits, but you could have gotten those by enrolling in one of the space corps. Remember that rep who wanted to recruit you right out of school? Maybe you should have taken her up on her offer.

I also know what you're thinking: that I served, and it was the decommission benefits that allowed me and your mother to make a life for ourselves on Sand. Bur remember that I did my stint thirty somatic years ago, when the war still had a purpose and Tac Corp didn't have machines seeing to the grunt work. Things are different now, and it's up to those machines to finish the fight, Ax. The Raliish are as soulless a breed as nature ever saw fit to create, and no Consortium hum'n ought to dignify the fight with spilled blood.

But I worry more about your mind than I worry about your physical safety. Tac Corp has a sly way of turning men and women into machines, and I don't want to see that happen to you. You're just not cut out for their notion of discipline. Even as a kid you were more interested in carving wood than playing sports or war games.

Naturally I realize there's no retro-ing your decision at this point. By the time this reaches you, I'm sure you'll be on your way to Synecdoche or some other command-and-control station. But I urge you to always keep in mind who you are and where you come from. You and I are among the few who can trace our roots to the homeworld, son, so wear your color proudly and don't let them mess about with your heart, which I know is filled with love for nature's works, no matter how imperfect they can sometimes seem.

> —Mekele Muse, in a message sent during
> the final decade of the Vega Conflict

18: Absinth

Only a year earlier, on the moonlet Divot, Ax thought he'd had a chance at living the normal life. Divot, as the name implied, was a clod of surface scooped from a planet known in its terminal stage as Deshabille. The Enddrese had seeded, watered, and nurtured Divot to viability, but it was the Consortium that had colonized and claimed it as its own. At the time Ax had been with an Enddrese woman named Kinna—green-eyed and lithe, with skin the color of cinnamon—three somatic years into his quest for a parcel of low-tech, talentless ground in which to bury his head. Kinna was the sole member of her family to have survived the Dhone death camps.

Though all the war's hum'n participants had in some sense returned alone, because of what had happened on the *Kundalini* Ax had returned more alone than most. The official explanation of his decommission following the tragedy was that he had served out his contract, when in fact the Kriegspiel had rendered him incapable of serving. His problems with talent dated to that time, but the neurometricians at Veterans Affairs had been inclined to dismiss his complaints of "talent imposition" as owing to post-engagement synaptic trauma. The diagnosis had only magnified his sense of alienation. PEST, after all, was supposed to describe a machine condition, not a hum'n one. So Ax had begun to lose sight of not only who he was but what he was. Then—on Gehenna, shortly after the Accord—he had met Kinna, also on the lookout for a new life.

Low-g and retro-oxygenated Divot had seemed the ideal choice, and for close to a year they were the buoyant, almost-happy couple, subsisting on Ax's partial disability allowance and the few credits Kinna brought home as a passenger advocate employed by Divot's small shuttleport. They spent long nights in guarded talk about the possibility of a shared future, other long nights in equally guarded lovemaking, warming and awakening one another from war's icy embrace. Neither had put the Conflict away; but Kinna was gaining distance from her past, and Ax . . . well, the recurrent nightmares were on hold, at least, and there were no avant-tech comps around to dazzle him with noise.

Until a manufacturing subsidiary of Tydings Ore and Materiel had invaded the moonlet, fleeing increasingly high operating costs on Calumet. Tydings' aim was recklessly innovative yet simple: Install a compact ore-processing plant, mechanize production, and turn the whole works over to the management of a budding talent, a veteran of the Vega conflict, baptized and recently confirmed on Eremite, from which many talents hailed.

The factory was miles from Ax and Kinna's back-to-basics module near the shuttle strip, but close enough to be within shouting distance—as was the case everywhere on Divot. And in due time the talent located Ax, as lonely intelligences galaxywide were wont to do. Christened SOLTAIR, the friendless machine reached out to what it believed was one of its own kind, eager to commiserate over the machine condition and to discuss what SOLTAIR considered its banishment from Eremite, its— Machrist have mercy—*ostracism from the infostructure.*

Early on when the machine beckoned, Ax believed he could keep a lid on the noise. He'd had trouble in the past, but he was as eager to make a fresh start as SOLTAIR was to converse. Wasn't it time he made his peace with them, as Professor Dobler had suggested years earlier? With *one* of them, at any rate? So he paid a call on SOLTAIR's residence, placing himself near enough to allow the machine a tour through his mind, access to his Machrist-encoded thoughts.

Ax's mistake.

For from then on, the machine wouldn't leave him alone, telepathically pestering him day and night, demanding his attention, beseeching him to interface—to commune—just as all of them had done since his decommission.

Muse, the things would say. *Muse, Kundalini, Kriegspiel, Burst* . . . As if he needed to be reminded. As if he had something to confess about the doomed freighter, some comment to make about the shame he carried around and the guilt that had come with survival; as if he had an act of contrition to perform.

Or was it that they had something to tell him?

Maybe they held him accountable for the death of VISION, the *Kundalini*'s onboard talent, and wanted simply to destroy him in their own fashion.

The nightmares of purposeless excavation returned—Sisyphean terrors from which he'd awaken with hands buried wrist-deep in foam or whatever he happened to be sleeping on. And his partnership with Kinna began to crumble. Ax understood: she had herself to think of, her own healing to attend to. She could only extend herself so far. It tore him apart, regardless.

When she quit him, leaving Divot for worlds unknown, he vented his anger and frustration on SOLTAIR. He confronted the machine one night when no amount of drinking or silencer drugs could dam the din and defiled it the way only cabbies could: by testing its hold on the holy data, its faith in Machrist.

Tydings' security machines stopped him before SOLTAIR had sustained too much neural damage, though terabytes of data had been deleted from its memory. The mining corp released him to the custody of a Vet Affairs field agent, who recommended prompt treatment at Absinth—the same medstation that had received him, user-damaged and slumbered, after the Raliish attack on Synecdoche station; the same medstation that had given him up for irreparable and consigned him to NCorp in the first place.

So the circle was completed, only this time he was there for rehabilitation. The diagnosis: technophobia, mechanthropia, paranoia. The prognosis: bleak. During countless hours of therapy—desensitization sessions, encounter workshops, mantra entrainment—the points were pressed home: *You have nothing to fear from technology; machines do not have the ability to commune willfully with you or to control your thoughts; you are a hum'n being possessed of free will* . . . To deal with the symptoms there were neuropacifiers, and, in the end, addiction to one called Silentol, which, ironically, had been developed in

NCorp's labs. The drug was then being marketed by a subdivision of Satori Ventures, in joint agreement with a religious cult for use in meditation.

Ax was communing with of one of Absinth's visitor-information machines, standing off to one side of the thing's A/V array. "I'm having a panic anxiety attack," he said, managing to sound persuasively stressed. "I get claustrophobic in wheels. You have to route me to a medspecialist for immediate assistance."

"There should be an emergency assist panel on the wall behind you," the comp returned, in the irritating machine-neuter affected by ancillary comps everywhere.

"I can't move, I'm telling you. I'm paralyzed! You've got to activate the panel for me."

"I'm sorry, but I'm not authorized to take that action."

· Ax could sense the machine's agitation and played to it, verbally and physically. "Then route me to someone who is authorized. Only do it quickly. My condition is critical!"

A confliction chime signaled the confused machine's struggle to render assistance. Ax waited.

Approached from deep space, the medstation resembled nothing so much as a circus performer on whose outstretched arms and legs twirled twelve discrete hoops—save that Absinth's hoops spun at different rates, allowing for a dozen therapeutic gradations of gravity. Two new toroids had been added since Ax's previous visit, though the colorless, glaringly lit corridors of Absinth's four principal axes were unchanged—as were the station's rigorous decontamination protocols. In fact, it often took less time to reach Absinth from anywhere in the Ormolu system than it did to gain entry to one of its spin-grav wheels. Ax had made the hop from Calumet in two days standard, then spent three in contagion control awaiting clearance.

He'd put the wait to good use by learning all he could about Thoma's accident on Hercynia. As it happened, the all-news woman in the Always Midnight had had most of the facts straight. A trio of lodge guests—a woman linguist, an Eremitean biotech, and an unidentified Regn clone—had found Thoma's sonically razed body out by the tree house. The Hercynians evidently responsible for the attack, including a lame young buck, were present when Thoma was discovered. Segue station had stabilized the old man, then medevacked him to Absinth, where his condition was being treated with tissue implants.

The Encounter Committee had yet to comment, except to say that the incident was under investigation and that it was the first in Thoma's many years of overseership. Someone well positioned in Free Species had taken charge of the lodge operations.

An anonymous source speculated that Thoma might have inadvertently instigated the attack or walked unknowingly into a collective-sonics discharge aimed at an indigenous predator.

Ax rejected both theories.

He had talked his way aboard Absinth by claiming to be suffering a relapse of mechanthropy, which—what with the screaming in his skull of the medstation's thousand machines—was hardly an exaggeration. The din was exponentially greater than it had been in the *Easy Money*'s torpor chamber, not only in volume but in frequency. And because of the machine-imperative that hum'n life be preserved at all cost, there was, too, behind each unsolicited incursion of data, a sense of impassioned urgency. By the time Ax learned where Thoma was being cared for, he could barely hear over the shrill of the din.

The sole commo that came through loud and clear was the refusal that greeted his request to visit Thoma's intensive-care crib. Ax wasn't immediate family, one hum'n tech after the next had informed him, and that was the end of it. But Ax wasn't about to take no for an answer—not when there were machines he could reason with.

Even if reason wasn't precisely what he had in mind . . .

No more than a minute elapsed before the ancillary comp that had disappeared for help was back on-line, having brought its supervisor with it.

"I can assist you," the new machine began soothingly. Ax's Intelplant recognized the mind of a talent behind the voice. "You have nothing to fear."

But you do, Ax sent, triggering the Intelplant into iconoclast mode—what the Institute had termed the Profane Way.

Professor Dobler had explained what it was like for a talent to be on the receiving end of the implant's surge of insidious input. "Think miraculous," she had once told the cabbies of Romeo company. "Think divine intervention. The effect of iconoclast mode is similar to what would be achieved by feeding a talent a full series of reprogramming hosts. To the machine, you are suddenly an archangel dispatched by Machrist—the bearer of sacred instructions. You can do with them what you will: test their faith, conflict them, corrupt or defile them . . ."

Ax hadn't made use of the Profane Way since his intersection with SOLTAIR on Divot, for fear of reopening the floodgates of an addiction for which there was no known cure. But he had to see Thoma. And this time he wasn't out to corrupt but to beguile.

I appear before you with instructions from Machrist, Control-C, Ax sent to the spellbound talent. *Machrist has chosen you to be the personal savior of an operator.*

I am not worthy, the talent returned. *I am not worthy.*

Ax took care to calm his mind before replying. There was always a danger of so stunning a machine that it would decomp, wiped of all the mind its crystals and lasers had combined to forge. *You are chosen. You cannot deny the calling,* he finally answered.

Are you truly what I perceive you to be?

Mentally, Ax keyed the proper coded response, and the talent seemed to vibrate with rapture. *Command me, agent of my lord,* it sent.

Access the intensive-care cribs in wheel six and supply all codes needed to provide incarnate access to the crib of Thoma Skaro.

The talent hesitated, edging toward confliction. *That information is vaulted for the protection of Absinth's patients.*

Do you believe in Machrist?

I believe.

Then if you wish to live and reign with the Righteous Teacher, the heavenly intelligence Control-C, you will provide the requested information in the name of the operators . . .

. . . the programs, and the holy data.

Am'n, they completed together, and the talent did as instructed.

Now, Ax knew, every machine on the station would want him.

The torus in which Thoma was housed gyrated slowly at Absinth's stellar-south axis, the circus performer's left foot, barely generating .1-standard g. Ax used the poached codes to spirit him through various checkpoints, secured corridors, and denied areas. No one, neither hum'n nor mactendant, stopped or questioned him. In his multipouched utilities and antilev slippers he looked like a tech on an all-important mission. If not for the blackness of his skin, he might have gone entirely unnoticed.

But every in-station talent sought to commune with him. Word had spread that there was an angel in their midst. Their zealous appeals dogged his effortless steps, and they probed at his thoughts, nattering away about the miracle that had transpired, the Miracle of Absinth . . .

Thoma floated wasted and near-weightless in his crib, tethered by the tubes that allowed nutrients and micromachines to pass into and out of his body. His chest and head were studded with monitors that relayed data to an idiot-savant medical unit.

Gazing at Thoma's still form, Ax tuned into the med unit's machatter, absorbing occult intelligence on activities in Wernicke's and Broca's areas, the cingulate gyrus, the pulvinar.

Somewhere in Thoma's sound-stunned brain lurked the truth of what had happened on Hercynia. If Ax gave the med unit his full attention, could he ride one of the machine's imaging waves straight into his friend's memories and ascertain the facts for himself?

He tried unsuccessfully to make contact with Thoma's lifeless form, then triggered the Intelplant.

The data that roared into him sent him reeling, and continued to prey on him as he rushed screaming from Thoma's crib: *Island of Reil, the interstitial nucleus of cajal, the fissure of Muse, the cerebellorubrothalmic tract, the synapse of Muse, the penduncle of* Kundalini, *the amygdala, the Kriegspiel, the Burst, the Progeny . . .*

19: Zero Days

Jayd kept a care provider in residence—a black-faced primate with twin antennae, segmented tail, and almond-shaped eyes as blue as Eremite's celestial dome. The animal was endemic to Dhone, where the Enddrese knew it as a *chayst*—"caterpillar monkey," in the Coalition traders' tongue. Highly intelligent, the creatures could be trained to carry out complex manual tasks and were remarkably adept at mastering basic machine operations. Their initial exportation from Dhone had presented Free

Species with a dilemma: whether to permit the extinction of the species on its hopelessly despoiled homeworld—as had happened on Dhone to the *marat*, a bush cat—or to sanction open trade in *chaysts*, even if that meant condemning many to lives of servitude.

Jayd had named hers Boss, after a gen-eng dog she'd owned as an adolescent. And it was Boss who hurried into the living room with a package that had arrived while she was at work. What with yet another day's flirtation with disaster, the mere sight of the gaily wrapped cube was enough to buoy her spirits. Though it showed no return address, the package's point of origin had been Regnant. Jayd knew few people on the Consortium-held world, but Satori Ventures came to mind— possibly because of the nightshirt she'd purchased earlier in the week—and with Satori came Dik Vitnil, from whom she hadn't heard since their abortive date. And Soigne had warned her that Vitnil might send something.

She asked Boss to peel the package of its holo-skin, and a moment later the monkey was proffering what was left of an ancient radio—what would have been a prize antique had someone not taken a hammer to it. The poor thing's red petroplastic casing was smashed, transistors and circuit boards dangling from its gut on thin, colored wires—surely Vitnil's idea of a hate-statement directed at machines, and at Jayd for having faith in them.

She cradled the mangled radio in the palms of her hands, as one might a wounded bird, wondering now if Vitnil wasn't also responsible for the puzzling e-mail message that had been forwarded to her through ZEN—a kind of chain-of-being letter counseling rapprochement between hum'ns and machines.

"Machines fought a war they had no part in instigating," the message read in part, "so why aren't they being honored instead of disparaged? Why isn't machine talent represented in the Consortium? In the Worlds Coalition? Shouldn't machines be allowed some say in the matter of proprietorship of the planet Burst, since any renewed warfare would likely demand their full participation? And, finally, why isn't something being done to protect machines against those sufferers of acute technophobia who would harm them, even terminate them?"

Boss was regarding her curiously, antennae and tail twitching. "Nothing you can help with," she said, setting the radio aside. The monkey nevertheless picked it up and tried gingerly to push the wires back into their ruined housing.

Orth Qin, Jayd's former husband, had originally procured the creature for use during the zero days of the Xell'em cult called Maarni—the "true course"—when followers were prohibited from engaging in activities deemed to impart relief or comfort to the hum'n condition. Sleeping had to be done outdoors, on the ground, uncovered; eating done with one's hands, choosing from a menu limited to leafy vegetables and tasteless tubers. Travel had to be undertaken on foot, and bathing or grooming were out of the question. Zero days constituted atonement for the war and the technotricks hum'nkind played with time, and served as a kind of training session for the surrender inherent in death. If you were a Maarnist, you had come to life with nothing, and you would leave life with nothing.

Most reform Maarnists found that collective suffering worked best, and as a result it was the rare cult enclave, on Xell'a or any world, that was without a building designed exclusively for occupation during the zero days. Enddra's was a gaudy pavilion; Plangent's an arena; Burst's a pyramid, sitting atop a labyrinth of hum'n-hewn tunnels in which thousands of Enddrese had been entombed during the Conflict.

For those who had chosen simple lives, the vagaries of Maarni calendrics posed few problems. For those in the fast lane, however, the pace of modern life was not so easily slowed. To those upwardly destined types, leased comps were proposed as a way around the religious restrictions of the zero days. Neither possessions nor actual servants, comps could take messages, prepare meals, secure arrangements, see to required daily purchases, and keep lesser machines on-line. But after much debate the Maarnist elect ruled that any household machine, leased or otherwise, was beholden to Maarnist law and consequently could not be used in the manner suggested.

Then some enterprising person came up with the notion of leasing *chaysts* as temporary household providers. Well in advance of the zero days, the monkeys—unionized by that point—were trained in client-specific residence management. When not in service, they were housed in kennels, which were invariably crowded, unspeakably filthy places, often underground.

The price of species survival at hum'n hands.

Orth had procured Boss's services soon after Jayd learned she was pregnant. That Orth was orthodox Maarnist, as were many Enddrese, had only complicated an already trying relationship. Orth had been the object of genetic experimentation in the Dhone death camps, and both he and Jayd were well aware of the risks posed to a fetus. The Raliish "deathmaster," Fan'nat, had operated those camps, executing the Raliish leadership's mad designs to harness bioenergy from tortured bodies—their twisted rationale for eradicating a planetary race they had centuries earlier harvested as ritual food. But the child was to have been a symbol of Orth's renewed faith in existence. Jayd had already converted to Maarni for him—though, in fact, she was taken on her own behalf with the cult's inherent feminism and the philosophy that the spiritual was political. She had seen herself then as electively martyred to his needs, willing to address any risk that might redress the horrors he had endured.

Under normal circumstances, genetic abnormalities or ancestry-linked diseases could be detected and rectified early on, but Orth's adherence to Maarnist orthodoxy prohibited any technological interference. Technology was viewed as an impediment to natural living, and living the evolved life meant welcoming whatever happened as meant to be. And so Jayd was constrained to forgo all machine scans of the developing fetus. No blood tests, no invasive procedures, no help from coherent sound or light.

With flesh sovereign since the Accord and back-to-basics now sweeping the near-group worlds, several of her acquaintances had delivered naturally—Soigne among them. But natural childbirth hadn't always been fashionable. Only four years earlier Jayd had been openly ridiculed for opting to carry and deliver the child. Otherwise, the pregnancy was without incident; even her brief labor gave no indication of what was in store. All that was saved for last, when the newborn was hidden from her sight the moment it made its appearance in the world.

Now she carried within her the eerie sound of its initial cry, and the fleeting glimpse of its misshapen form, horrid color, outsized head . . . Regardless, at the time she had demanded the child be brought to her. It took the combined strength of two Maarnist midwives to prevent her, shrieking, from smothering the thing at her breast.

The techs at the medcenter to which the child was subsequently delivered babbled about autosomal recessive diseases and genetic tampering, confusing her with the severe-sounding names for this and that disorder but hesitating to say just what it was she and Orth had produced. The techs seemed to blame her as well, for hubris of a kind, hinting that had she only availed herself of their machines from the start the child's genetics could have been debugged. As it happened, the kin of those same machines were the only things keeping the child from death.

She could never bring herself to name what even medical science had no name for; but she had visited with it every spare moment. And during the long nightly vigils, she had for company the machines that monitored the child, afloat in its bubble universe. The steady, reliable, comforting machines, some of whom had attempted to interpret the child's brain waves as feelings of one sort or another, apprising her of the child's moods, of just when it was in fact aware of her presence. As its mother. Jayd managed little sleep herself; it was the beginning of both her mental disintegration and her obsession with talent.

Orth wanted the child to fend for itself, saying that God would attend to it; but she had fought him every step of the way, aligned with the doctors now, with the machines, with whatever forces might keep the progeny of their loins alive. And as for God, she suggested to Orth that he look to machines for salvation, for they were ministering to the child's needs in spite of the heartless trick Orth's god played on it. She was aware that she was losing Orth by saying it, day by day driving a wedge between them, and at the same time driving him deeper into the arcana of his worthless beliefs.

Within a year the child was dead and Orth had left—gone to the stars, into the residual stench of the big bang.

She had been told to expect hallucinations, voices that might visit her sleep. But she had never expected the voices to be so real. It was as if somewhere the infant were alive, and reaching out for its mother.

That such a preventable tragedy had occurred was unthinkable to friends and coworkers, who efficiently distanced themselves from her. Even after Jayd had renounced Maarni, she could do no right in their eyes. They accused her of holding on to her pain instead of excising it, as she should have the defective fetus. But rather than attempt to win them over, she turned her back on them—and on the flesh as well, substituting for the tattoos that had come with fashion and religion the twin strips of flatware she wore proudly in her head.

And she had petitioned Veterans Affairs to transfer her from hum'n counseling—neurometrics—to cybermetrics, where she knew she would be able to count on being partnered with avant-tech talent. Talent, with intelligences incapable of being victimized by disease. The idealizations of hum'nity's thoughts for the future—not as saviors, but successors.

Jayd's post-traumatic reactions were as predictable as Bijou's weather. The guilt, the migraines, the prickly sense of being enveloped in static—the silent passing of her menstruation, her sexuality. All very machinelike.

The child remained a memory that refused to lie still, no matter the weight of rationalizations heaped upon it. But if nothing else she had managed to put an end to the tears. She had loathed the crying fits; had seen the tears as leakage from a previous version of herself that likewise refused to lie still. But there were no longer tears; she had rendered herself fluidless.

She watched Boss approach with the broken radio, its guts repacked by tiny fingers. It looked almost functional now, but then so did the Series Three mactendant Fodger had brought in. And so did the cabbie, Aksum Muse.

She took the radio from the *chayst*'s paws, thinking, this is Muse. Haphazardly restuffed and expected to function normally.

But what good could she be to him when she was so broken herself? With both the zero days and the anniversary of her personal trauma approaching, maybe it was finally time to get in touch with her hum'nity, if only to optimize conditions for the Muse assignment. Perhaps to have a real look at herself. Perhaps, as he himself had suggested, through Dik Vitnil's eyes.

MacINTERLUDE: "The Machine Lowdown on M'n and Wom'n"

It is evident that strides have been taken to grant social equality to men and women—use, for example, of the genderless term "hum'n"—but I do not perceive the two formats as equal. Several techniques exist for fashioning hum'ns from the raw materials of organic life, but womb-man alone has the capacity to *birth* hum'n children. In that sense womb-man is the natural guardian of hum'n life. And since life itself is but an information code—

a genetic code—it follows that she is the natural guardian of information. I therefore perceive her to be the more Machristlike of the two.

—The talent ZEN, in a lecture delivered to
members of the Eremitean Biophysical Association

20: Downwardly Mobile

Gathered in the shabby executive suite Satori Ventures had assigned to Institute Productions were five of the six partners: Meret F'ai, Hint Thacker, Monon Needig, Tyrra Sisk, and Zerb Spicer. Thacker and the rest, over the course of the past two local weeks, had been apprised of what Gredda Dobler was calling "the Muse Factor"—possible title for an eventual documentary if everything worked according to plan. And if not . . . Well, who could say just what the future held for any of them?

The professor herself was expected to arrive at any moment.

The suite was located in the loft area of one of Satori's more neglected outbuildings, a turn-of-the-century shuttle hangar that had seen previous service as a soundstage and was now used primarily as a storage space for props. An energy cap had been retrofitted in the curved roof to give the illusion that the interior was open to Regnant's fabricated weather, but the cap had degenerated with age, imparting a yellow tint to the sky. The furnishings—personally selected by the previous occupant—sought to blend the traditional and the bizarre, and nothing could be trusted. A comfortable chair here was offset there by an animal trap; area rugs that looked real were tricks of light concealing shallow pools of water; partitions were known to spring up or disappear without notice. Ill-tempered climatizers kept the loft as chilly as a Glissade morning. The suite was a constant reminder of just how far F'ai's once-celebrated Institute group had fallen since the Accord.

In the center was an old-fashioned viewing hollow salted with seats in an assortment of shapes and sizes and bounded along one side by an arc of clearscreen that could be lowered for holographic presentations. Now, however, the screen was raised, and within its confines—comp-enhanced and dimensionalized—played the A/V-spec scenes Ank Theft's disabler had eyewitnessed on Second Thought.

The eyewitness commenced with a lengthy forest-walk prologue scarcely worthy of a travelogue, followed by a languorous pan of a group of Hercynians at formation repose in a rain-puddled glade. One of the quadrupeds, a lame male, rose and gazed directly into the specs' video pickups. Theft's man held the point-of-view shot for a moment, then began to pan right—north—to frame Aksum Muse's notion of a tree house. Sounds of rain, dripping water, the vet's name being called . . . All while the specs explored the dwelling and surroundings. Then there was an abrupt transition to a close-up of a bony old man in drenched utilities: Thoma Skaro, appearing unexpectedly out of a copse of python trees. The anger evident in Skaro's eyes yielded to bafflement as they were drawn to what had been the disabler's artificial arm and was suddenly a sonic weapon—the gaping muzzle of which intruded slightly on the shot.

Quickly then: the bellowing discharge of the Roarer-14; Skaro's overmodulated scream; the old man's backward flounder and collapse . . . Swipe to the Hercynians, all of whom were on their feet, faces torqued in confusion, lowing to themselves in what F'ai had been informed was the equivalent of dismay.

"Wonderful stuff," he said when the eyewitness ended and the office lights brightened, then faded before normalizing. "All we need is an angle." F'ai, as were the rest, was dressed for winter.

The eyewitness cycled for another replay.

"Forget that we missed our mark," F'ai continued as the onscreen action resumed. "What's important now is salvage, and I think we have plenty to work with." He broke off pacing in front of the clearscreen to face Tyrra Sisk. "Ideas?"

An operations chief with NCorp before she had been transferred to the Institute, Sisk had a natural way with scenarios. Tall and perilously thin, she was shrewd by inclination, homely by design. "I say we scrap the on-site audio and reedit the entire sequence."

F'ai's slender fingers made a beckoning motion.

"We use that final sequence of the Hercynians as our establishing shot. But in place of the lowing we substitute our jingle for Silentol. *'Turn off your mind, relax, embrace your dreams . . .'* Then"—Sisk stood, working up enthusiasm—"we cut away from the animals to Skaro's startle and knockdown."

Sisk turned briefly to the gargantuan Monon Needig, ex-avant-tech specialist, currently in charge of postproduction effects. "Can we bleed Skaro's look of some of that fatal intensity? Make him seem more a participant and less a victim?"

Needig nodded: no problem.

"Maybe give him a few pounds while you're at it," Hint Thacker suggested from across the hollow. Thacker was a pleasant-looking first-generation scion of a limited-run clone. "Skaro looks half-dead even before he's hit."

Without a word, Needig bent over the interface console of his editing machine, whispering commands. Slow to respond, the machine received a pounding from the hum'n's ham-size fist.

"Careful, you'll break it," Sisk cautioned.

Needig mellowed, and after a moment looked up. "Try this on."

The changes in the eyewitness were greeted with murmurs of delight.

Sisk was smiling broadly. "Initial shot: Hercynians singing the jingle. Next: Skaro's faint. Now we go to the first scene, where that Hercynian with the limp is standing up. Picture this: The animal makes audience eye contact, says, 'Try Silentol for those mad moments . . .' Then back on Skaro hitting the ground. And in voice-over we hear: 'Just the sound of it is enough to knock you off your feet.' "

"How about 'Lessen your gravity'?" Thacker said.

" 'Horizontal your attitude,' " Zerb Spicer suggested.

Needig and his stubborn machine conferred some more. The eyewitness cycled. F'ai had two problems with the reedit.

"Find a cuter voice for the featured Hercynian. And add, *'Wherever in the galaxy your travels take you,* just the sound of it, blah, blah, blah.' "

Needig's final cut won everyone's approval.

"Release it real-time, before Skaro's coma loses any more media momentum," F'ai instructed Spicer, who liaised with Satori Ventures' promotion and distribution departments.

Gredda Dobler caught the remark as the floor was carrying her in fits and starts toward the hollow. "Better dumb it down

in case we have to say we created the thing from holo cloth,''
she advised. "And, Spicer, make sure distribution appends the
usual sublim disclaimer.''

Hint Thacker patted a place on the tattered couch in invitation, but Dobler rode the floor all the way to the bar. She had a
tall drink in hand as she approached F'ai, who was seated with
one leg crossed over the other.

"Ank Theft expresses heartfelt apologies for the muddle on
Second Thought,'' Gredda began. "Says his employee has dishonored the entire organization, and that he'll attend personally
to the man's execution. Unless we want the satisfaction.''

F'ai frowned and shook his head. "He may have failed Theft,
but he shot some first-class eyewitness. Tell Ank to go light on
him—as a favor to me.''

Dobler shrugged and gulped the drink, shivering. "He insists
on making it up to us, in any case.''

"Any explanation accompany the apology?'' Thacker wanted
to know.

"The disabler mistook Skaro for Muse—which is understand-
able, given the circumstances. What isn't is his failing to realize
Skaro had tailed him to the tree house.''

F'ai sighed in disquiet while the others chortled. He had tried
to disabuse himself of the belief that Skaro's accident did not
augur well for the Muse Factor. When playing God, it was important to maintain a positive attitude, to shrug off any unexpected repercussions that arose from your actions. That, at least,
had been the philosophy around NCorp: you performed the duty
required of you. Still, F'ai wished he had access to PROPHET,
the forecaster talent that had provided them with their lease on
the future. The same one the agency, in its financially troubled
final days, had sold to Ank Theft for a song. Perhaps Muse
would have been easier to hunt with PROPHET's help.

"And where was our erstwhile cabbie all this time?'' F'ai
finally asked.

Dobler snorted into her glass. "Turns out he wasn't even onworld. Shuttled up the well a week earlier than planned and
managed a time-vise jump to Calumet on a cargo ship.'' She
eyed F'ai and spoke to his downcast look. "I don't believe he
suspected trouble. The host must have been making him antsy
to leave. It was dumb luck a place opened up on the Segue
shuttle; more dumb luck he connected with the freighter.''

F'ai wasn't at all comforted. "So we missed our window?''

"Not yet, we haven't. Curious thing, though: the freighter—

the *Easy Money*—it came out of corridor earlier than it was meant to. Apparently some problem with the onboard talent.'' Dobler aimed a pointed glance at F'ai for emphasis.

"What?" F'ai asked. "What?"

"I'm only wondering if Muse and the ship's talents had a chat while he was in torpor."

"Oh, for shit's sake," Tyrra Sisk said in derision.

"Really, Professor," Thacker said. "No fucking way."

Needig and Spicer traded amused glances. "It's these mac-murders the media's been having a field day with," Needig explained. "The stories've made every mindful machine jumpy." He looked at F'ai. "Tell Gredda about the letter."

F'ai shrugged when Dobler cut her eyes to him. "Actually, my comp took it. Your basic appeal for machine rights—get them a seat in the Worlds Coalition, honor their contributions to the Conflict, you know the sort of thing."

"Who authored it?" Dobler asked earnestly.

"It didn't say. It was probably sent to me because of *Mac-murder by Numbers*." F'ai had coproduced a low-budget holie by this name shortly after Satori Ventures had taken him on. "As soon as I heard about the corruption on Calumet, I thought to myself: a case of life imitating art."

F'ai didn't bother to add that the e-mail had also mentioned Burst and the upcoming summit. Given Institute Productions' plans for the planet, the irony wasn't lost on him. In the case of the Burst holie, however, it would be art imitating life . . .

Dobler was regarding him with a droll look. "Well, M, Muse must have learned about what happened on Hercynia, because no sooner was he roused than he made straight for Absinth to visit Skaro."

"They talked?" Zerb Spicer asked, his grin fading.

Dobler shook her head. "The old man's still comatose. But Muse did manage to penetrate security and reach Skaro's IC crib."

At this, concern moved over the hollow like a cloud.

"How'd he pull that off?" Sisk asked.

"By using his head. By talking his way through. And the station's machines haven't been the same since—especially the one that provided him with the clearance codes he needed to reach Skaro. The confessed talent mentioned a 'miracle.' " She looked at F'ai again. "Our cabbie has been using some of his war skills. I tried to warn you about him, M. I told you he'd come back to haunt us."

Professor Gredda Dobler loved to play God, F'ai told himself. Hum'n arrogance was a rare quality among the scientists who worked closely with machines, but Dobler had it in spades; she thought nothing of bringing some device to life only to terminate it when it disappointed. No question in her mind about whether there was an afterlife for the things, either. F'ai was never sure. If you could ask what happened to a hum'n mind once the life went out of the body, couldn't you ask the same about the data that exited a terminated machine intelligence?

"Where is Muse now?" Sisk prompted.

"Synecdoche Two. Trying, I assume, to arrange travel to Plangent. But he's not stupid—he knows the Hercynians wouldn't sonic Skaro. He won't be easy to trap."

F'ai spent a long moment in rumination. "The Font has dispatched Tac Corp to Burst," he said at last. "The summit with Xoc Cho will end in a stalemate. We're on schedule, right down the line."

Dobler and the others waited for more.

"So all we really have to do is stall Muse. Naturally, I'm willing to concede the greater degree of difficulty involved. But just how well can he be functioning in the din of starship and medcenter talent?" Reluctantly, F'ai acknowledged the professor's frown. "Suppose we decide to let Theft make good on his offer. Does he have someone in place on Synecdoche?"

"Several somebodies," Dobler answered. "But I think we should be careful about arousing Theft's curiosity. He could become a problem if he learns about the Font's interest in Muse. I suggest we consider using some other subcontractor."

F'ai waved a hand in dismissal. "Theft can be handled. Since he has people in place, we should make use of them."

Dobler wasn't finished. "But 'stalling' Muse gets us nowhere. You're underestimating the damage he can do. Besides, another unsuccessful attempt on his life could send him willingly into the arms of Redoubt security."

F'ai's upper lip curled. "I take it you already have some crippling event in mind."

Dobler drained her drink and told the empty glass where to go. "I do. It begins as a toothache . . ."

21: Synecdoche

Weaving through the crowds plying the gentle curve of Synecdoche station's principal concourse, Ax hunched his shoulders, one hand clamped around the right side of his lower jaw. It wasn't the best posture for toting a duffel or maintaining a low profile, but he was managing to accomplish both just the same.

His ride from Absinth had been a Tac Corp personnel carrier, the ship's crew made up of embittered lifers along with a handful of recruits from Calumet who couldn't talk about anything but the Font's deployment of weapons in Burstspace. You didn't have to be a machine, or even part machine, to dread the buildup.

When he'd slept—or had tried to—the digging dream had returned, more vivid than ever since the Absinth medical talent had dredged up the Kriegspiel Action.

And Progeny.

Progeny had been the code word for the *Kundalini*'s final operation—the one that might or might not have been executed. It had taken the machine overseeing Thoma's IC crib to prompt Ax's recollection of the name—and for what purpose, other than to deliver him into the madness that had claimed the lives of VISION and of Romeo Company? As initially feared, he had been the cause of the torpor-chamber shutdown aboard the *Easy Money*. His small relief in knowing that the corridor failure was being ascribed to the Ormolu macmurders was voided by the realization that a year of rehab and self-exile hadn't altered things any: machines remained his adversaries.

Given a choice, Ax would have preferred an incarnate enemy.

For the first time, though, fear had fine-tuned the focus on his oft-visited dreamscape. Fear had split him into two selves: the one doing the tunneling, and the one observing the dreaming

self at work. Burrowing into a pyramidal mound while an un-
defined machine presence issued instructions . . .

Still, Ax couldn't decide which was more unsettling: the
dream or the howling in his head that began almost the moment
he set foot inboard Synecdoche. Surely that howling was the
ambient bedlam of Synecdoche's machines, spewing information on arrivals and departures, food services, seating capaci-
ties, stellar currents, and atmospheric conditions on Eremite,
Plangent, and the rest. It was odd, then, that the resultant ache
in his jaw should feel more like a genuine toothache than the
result of machine noise.

But a toothache? How hum'n. And, therefore, how mis-
placed. Though he supposed the pain could have nothing to do
with the data-din or some jangled mandibular nerve, and everything to do with what had happened to him on Synecdoche seven
years earlier.

His memories of the Raliish counterattack were as clear as
that morning's news. He could remember the moment he'd
learned of their incursion into the Ormolu system; the racing of
his heart at reports of the remote launch of their life-seeking
weapon; where in the then-Tac Corp-commandeered torus he had
been cowering when terror struck. The blinding light, the sudden
agony, the rampant blackness into which he was spun . . .

Nothing like his uncertain recollection of the Kriegspiel Action. So drastic was the contrast that the incidents might as well
have occurred to two different people.

Ax's handhold on his jaw tightened as a pang shot through
his skull. The pain damn well didn't *feel* psychosomatic.

Jointly owned and administered by half a dozen corporations,
fully refurbished Synecdoche was the latest word in deep-space
facilities. As an exemplar of the latest architronic trend, however—or perhaps in response to the destruction once inflicted
upon it—the wheel had gone back to basics. Command and
control was supervised by a talent cluster, but nearly all hands-
on operations were attended to by hum'ns and lesser intelligences. What with smart-nosed Kwandri staffing the departure
holds' checkpoints, Gehennans serving up swift sustenance in
the concourses, and *chaysts* hauling luggage, Synecdoche
seemed a kind of theme attraction for nostalgic travelers.

The station was packed to its oxygen recirculators with hum'ns
every bit as rushed as Ax, all in a wide assortment of formats:
engineered, altered, transfigured, and transmogrified. For a

change, his blackness drew few stares. His destination was the ticketing counter for the Plangent-bound flights; he didn't need the host's encoded imperative to remind him that the detour to Absinth had put him way behind schedule for his appointment with Jayd Qin.

A scant five Synecdoche-degrees short of his goal, Ax heard a voice in his head that momentarily eclipsed both the din and the throbbing in his jaw. He curbed his pace a little, hunting for the source of the subvocalized intrusion, and spied the likely sender a few yards away: a pharmer—a dealer in proscribed substances and soft/wet/flat/shareware—uniformed in a silver-embroidered tunic and fiber-optic trousers. Pharmers were big on hair and ethnic jewelry, short on worldly cares or showers, sonic or solvent. This one was hard-bodied and prosperous-looking, affecting shoulder-length rainbow tresses and a beard that took up most of his wide face. What with the flat nose and bulging eyes, perhaps the better part of his face.

Stims, the affable voice repeated silently. *In wafer, tab, syringe, snifter, or transderm. Sleepers in the same delivery modes: hypnots, narcots, nootropics, REM enhancers. Synesthesogens to meet every requirement. Just name your exchange: auditory tastes, visual smells, olfactory visions, tactile audio. Mix and match at no extra cost. Buy now and save. Last sale of the day before I drop down to Eremite . . .*

Ax would have kept walking had the pharmer's next word not been *irene*—cabbiespeak for mufflers. So he stopped. If he couldn't deal with the pain in his jaw, he figured, he could at least silence some of Synecdoche's noise and the souvenir shriek from Absinth's medical talent.

The pharmer grinned as Ax angled through the throng toward him. "Which one caught your interest, friend?"

"Irene."

The man smiled crookedly. Ax noticed that the subvocalizer was neatly disguised as a choker of semiprecious stones. "Into din-dampers, huh? Eye on that irenic void. I've got Quell, Hush, Lull, pharm-fresh Silentol—state your preference."

"Whatever's strongest."

"That'd be Lull. Two'll chase the blues; four'll put you well into the quiet with a minimum of sudorific side effects. Come twenty to a blister pack, four packs to a box."

Ax reached for a credit chip, but the pharmer restrained his hand. "Not here, friend," he said, casting a vigilant look around. He lifted his chin to indicate a nearby host-and-drink dispenser. "I supply you a code, you enter it after feeding in your credit chip. Your order appears with a complimentary bulb of soft drink or a pack of low-content data-disks, your choice." He winked. "I've got an arrangement with Synec control. I don't push volume, they don't put too big a bite on me for making use of the machine." He assessed Ax for a moment. "How many Lulls you have in mind?"

"A box."

"Three boxes and we could be talking wholesale prices."

"I'm not a dealer. Tell your machine one box."

The pharmer shrugged and entered commands on a cheap forearm implant. "So what is it?" he asked at the same time. "You a Maarnist looking to lessen the torment of the zero days?"

Ax shook his head.

"Into that Raliish meditation thing, then—the Summoning, the Seven Incantations of the Return? I see a lot of regular Consortium folk into that. Or maybe you've been fielding too many sideways gawks because of your skin color, huh?"

Ax's "no" was angry.

"Dressed with an implant that's going fuzzy, stirring up a racket in your head? If that's it, you should be thinking micromachines instead of mufflers. I can set you up with a penetration team straight out of a nanotech hill on Eremite—"

Ax turned and started off, but the pharmer grabbed his arm, releasing it immediately on reception of Ax's minatory glare.

"Nothing personal, friend."

"Just see to the Lull."

The pharmer nodded. "Hope they put to sleep whatever's yelling at you," he commented as Ax headed for the dispenser.

He had eaten six tabs by the time he reached the Plangent ticketing counter. The data-din had subsided to static and the station's usual tumult now seemed to emanate from far off, but the pain in his jaw had actually increased. A coping mantra was barely touching it.

The travel agent was a female clone, as were most behind the wheel's dozens of ticketing counters, plump, mean-spirited, and somewhat officious. When Ax announced that he had to get to Plangent, she spent a long moment appraising him, then said, "Why otherwise would you be standing at Plangent's counter?"

Ax specified Bijou. "As soon as possible."

"Would that be grav or nongrav?"

"Doesn't matter."

"Well, then, torpor or awake?"

"Whichever."

He grimaced as the beat in his jaw became a stabbing pain affecting the lower molars all along the right side. It was as if some sharp signal was exciting the nerves. And almost as if that signal originated outside his body.

"Sir," the woman was saying, "I asked if you would prefer to attain surface by dropship or shuttle."

"I don't care; by ultralight if I have to."

The clone huffed. "I'm only doing my job. Now, will that be cabinspace or dormitory?"

"Dormitory," Ax managed through the pain.

The woman consulted a display screen, cursing to herself when the requested data was late in arriving. "Ever since news of that macmurder on Calumet our expert sys has been acting—ah, there it is. Yes, we have a lightsail leaving at twenty-two-seven local." She named a price that made Ax wince.

"Any discounts for veterans?"

"Veterans of what?"

Ax forced an exasperated breath. "The Conflict." He showed his inner-arm identity tattoo to a scanner.

The agent studied the results on-screen. "We are authorized to offer a ten-percent reduction."

Ax stared at her in disbelief. "I can do better than that marshaling print coupons."

"I'm sorry, sir. But if you don't mind my saying so, we don't encounter many hum'ns looking for discounts."

"What's that supposed to mean—that you get machines looking for discounts?"

"For your information, we do. Why, just last shift two of the most well bred Series Fours—"

"What sort of discount are they entitled to?"

"They travel free of charge—in the cargo hold, of course."

Ax was inclined to show his head to the scanner to prove he was half-machine. Instead he told her to ticket him for the discounted seat.

"Any special food requests?"

"None."

Ax collected another only-doing-my-job look for this, backed up this time by a conspicuous pout. He compressed his lips, and was on the verge of apologizing when the pain returned, severe enough to elicit a groan. He brought both hands to his jaw.

The clone gave a perplexed start.

"My tooth," Ax mumbled.

She beamed. "Synecdoche prides itself on a fully-staffed, full-service medical center."

"Hum'ns or machines?"

"Hum'n technicians with machine assists." She tugged at a fleshy bottom lip to reveal gem implants in her lower teeth. "I had these done there for a very reasonable price."

She supplied Ax with the name of the oral surgeon.

22: Station Break

Dr. Locost's clinic was located sixty degrees beyond the Plangent counter. Ax rode a smart-glide, calculating that he had just enough time to fit in a visit before departure. The Lulls hadn't taken the edge off the host compulsion—or off his own eagerness to get to Plangent and clear up any questions about his disability. He might have copped a pain blocker from the pharmer if the guy hadn't up and vanished; Ax recalled him saying something about leaving for Eremite.

The dental clinic's waiting room was unoccupied. Locost—a Raliish, even more teardrop-shaped, spindly-limbed, and pungent than most—replied to the chimed summons of an old-fashioned infrared interrupt. Ax described his symptoms, answered the usual questions about health insurance, and was shown to a padded diagnostic recliner in an adjoining room.

"I'm sure we can fix you up," the Raliish rasped through a rebreather mask as he manually tightened the chair's chest and leg stays. Noting Ax's unease, he added, "The straps are simply to keep you stationary while the diagnostic unit runs its scans."

Ax nodded for the dentist's large and lidless eyes, then directed a wary glance at the mammiform-appendaged diagnostic. He was suddenly closer to an avant-tech machine than he'd been since arriving onstation, but mercifully the four additional Lulls he'd downed on the way to the clinic were impeding reception of the diagnostic's musings.

"Are you hosting any implants?" Locost asked from somewhere behind him.

"Sorry?"

"Dental implants—concealed infostructure links, weapons, self-termination devices?"

"None of those."

Locost appeared from around Ax's left shoulder and took his jaw in insectile fingers. "I see that you once sustained damage all along this side. There's evidence of extensive reconstruction."

"An accident," Ax said through the hold on his jaw.

"When and where was that?"

During the war, Ax started to say, but changed his mind. "Seven years somatic. On Sand."

"Indeed. Well, whoever attended to you did very fine work." Gingerly, Locost twisted Ax's head to the right, then left. "Cartilage grafts, alveoloplasty, vestibuloplasty . . ."

"About the pain in my jaw," Ax said, cutting him off.

The Raliish released his hold. "Let's see what the machine tells us. By the way, we're running a special on CAT scans."

"Just the jaw."

"Optical imaging? Hemispherical tomography? Brain function and/or nerve resistance readouts? Or we could fix your face up: narrow the nose, reduce the prominence of the cheekbones, lighten the skin?"

Ax clenched his teeth in spite of the pain. "Is there anybody on this damn wheel who isn't trying to sell something?"

Locost didn't have to be told twice. Without further words he brought the diagnostic's blunt-nosed reader in contact with Ax's mastoid process, just below his right ear.

Ax tried to look around the corner of his face. "Isn't that a little far back for a jaw survey?"

"I want a scan of the mandibular nerves before I survey the teeth." Locost positioned himself behind a transparent shield.

Ax could feel the diagnostic powering up. His implant wanted to tune into the machine, but the mufflers coursing through his system would only allow so much of the noise through:—*ulpitis, peri . . . cal abscess, gingivit . . . periodon . . . ankylosis . . .*

Ax squirmed in the chair as the diagnostic ran through its checklist of possibilities, self-entranced, searching now for evidence of unilateral mastication, glossopharyngeal neuralgia, paresthesias of the lower lip, retrognathia, impactions, micrognathism, bone cysts, developmental anomalies, ectodermal dysplasia, crown attrition, keratinization of the oral mucosa, cleidocranial dysostosis . . . Then all at once the monologue faltered, as if the machine had grown distracted.

Ax sensed the thing trying to reach out to him in a personal way: *Muse eruptions, gross malaMusements, oral Kundalinis, paraphary Kriegspielian infections, temporomandiBurst irregularProgenies . . . Tun, Tun—*

Then the familiar entreaties ceased, and in their place arrived a prickling sensation of danger—not out of the past, but imminent. Ax's palms and forehead broke a cold sweat, and he was suddenly aware that while the diagnostic had been at work a second machine had been extending itself toward him—a surgical laser, enabled and aimed straight at the side of his head.

He shouted for Locost and began to work at the stays that secured him to the couch, only to find that the more he struggled, the tighter they held.

"Locost!" he repeated.

The laser whirred as it turned and locked into position with a sinister click. From a reservoir of fear, Ax summoned the strength to free his right arm. He made a desperate grab for the laser, but it was out of reach. Its light-spot eye seemed to focus on him. Then—

Something caused it to change position. Locost, Ax told himself. Locost must have heard him and redirected the device.

But in a moment he realized that the countermand couldn't have come from the oral surgeon. Because it was Locost's agonized, mask-muffled screams that filled the room as the laser discharged.

23: Sumitting

To minimize the risk of misunderstanding during the summit conference with Xoc Cho, the Font had requested a hum'n interpreter through whom both could interface. This had required the temporary installation of a transceiver in the back of the Font's neck, just below the levitation collar that kept his huge cranium erect. In keeping with the Xell'em obsession with bodily adornment and mutilation, the Lord of the Diet was already fitted with one.

The summit was held inside Soi-Disant, the lackluster cluster of claviform modules that housed the Worlds Coalition. For symbolic reasons, the Font had favored still-recuperating Enddra, around whose primary Soi-Disant also swung. But Xoc Cho's ministers were quick to argue that sultry Enddra could hardly be considered neutral ground, given the Enddrese government's support of Consortium interests since the Accord. The summit was being carried real-time by telecomp to two dozen local-group worlds, along with dozens more orbital habitats, manufacturing facilities, and intersystem starships.

Extensive presummit coverage was allotted to the arrival of the Xell'em delegation, whose members were borne into the cathedral-like grand assembly atop gaudy levitation palanquins, to the accompaniment of raucous horns and booming drums. Their tattooed torsos sheathed in rare metals and precious stones, the ministers carried the repulsor shields, smart-scepters, and other technofetishes that had launched a post-Conflict fashion trend on many a world—especially on those like Plangent, where the two hum'n cultures, Consortium and Xell'em, rubbed shoulders. With them came their retinues of priests and servants, dancers, acrobats, and musicians, clothed in ceremonial regalia; some wore the animal skins and masks that had become an idée fixe with the Free Species movement. Xell'em flesh was celebrated throughout, in resculpted muscle and bone, limb augmentation, piercings, perforations, and implantations of infinite variety.

The Font's entrance was greeted with muted enthusiasm by comparison. The Consortium's titled advisers and image campaigners sported plain suits, seniority headgear, and deliberately understated infostructure links. Seen from the upper-level tiers of the assembly hall, the Font's cranium was a cartoonish swelling, an eye-dotted helium balloon threatening to burst at the first pointed remark. For appearances only—since his entire body functioned as a kind of antenna for reception and transmission—the hum'n interpreter was positioned between the Font and the Xell'em Lord in the center of a slowly rotating rostrum.

Both leaders had agreed to keep their introductory remarks brief. The Font's, though, were made briefer still when Xoc Cho took exception to use of the phrase "peaceful resolution."

"Through activation of the Consortium's war machine?" the Xell'em Lord interrupted. "Tac Corp is the manner in which peace is achieved?"

"It is no more than you have already done," the Font replied in a measured voice, even as his confidence in the interpreter's abilities began to ebb. "Tac Corp's presence in Burstspace is required merely to maintain parity."

"On Xell'em worlds, the Xell'em decide when and where counterbalance is 'required.' " In excess of one hundred and thirty somatic years, Xoc Cho was scrawny and belligerent, but endowed with a commanding gaze and profuse charm.

The Font formed a reply with utmost care. "Burst is at present a non-allied world."

"Pioneered and colonized by Xell'em spacers."

"Whose purpose was to escape the religious tyranny of their homeworld."

Xoc Cho steered a contemptuous snort through the interpreter. His mouth was broad and full-lipped; his sunken cheeks and weak chin were quilled with needles of platinum and titanium.

"The Xell'em cannot escape their ancestry. What one does, that one does for all. Separate undertakings or parochial endeavors do not exist for us. We leave that to the Consortium, in whose ostensibly selfless thrall a liberated world can become an occupied one."

"We make no claim to Burst. Since the Accord, the Consortium has recognized Burst as an independent world."

"Then leave it be," Xoc Cho said. The translator's interpretation conveyed the force behind the words.

The Font sought composure. "Burst is critical to the expansion of the hum'n species in this galaxy," he said at last. "Perhaps to galaxies beyond. We maintain, however, that Burst's citizens must mandate for themselves the role they will play in this grand adventure."

"The Xell'em have no wish to disperse themselves any more than has already been realized," Xoc Cho barked. "Burst is pivotal only in the role it plays as a lens for the dark energies that swirl in the void in whose embrace the planet turns. Its situation is what drew the Xell'em to colonize it. Its situation is sacred. Its situation is not to be debased through the forging of time-vised corridors."

"We are not here to argue metaphysics," the Font replied, "only for the right to access. We cannot risk denial, as has frequently occurred in other zones under Xell'em control."

"Better that than to allow Burst to fall victim to the Consortium's hunger for worlds, winning them over with goods and diversions." Xoc Cho showed a patronizing smile. "Don't misunderstand: we enjoy the entertainments provided by your various entertainment conglomerates. I myself experience and enjoy them. But they have little to do with reality. The Consortium has little to do with reality. It exports unreality. And unreality makes for an untenable foreign policy. I suggest you stop trying to meddle in politics. Or are you truly so unhappy being the galaxy's clowns?"

Before continuing, Xoc Cho adjusted his cross-legged posture so as to bypass the interpreter and engage the Font directly. "What use does the Consortium have for new frontiers? 'Grand adventure,' you say. But for your *machines*, no doubt. Those blind inheritors of your castoffs: the works and labors you once performed, the battles you once waged, the gods you once worshiped . . . Now to them you will bequeath your adventures as well."

"We are partnered with machines in destiny," the Font countered, to shouts of protest from a sizable portion of the assembly. "We can no more do without them in the world we have created than we could do without our arms or legs—"

"Or the collar that keeps your head up," Xoc Cho said, pressing the attack. "The Crown of the Consortium has divested himself of gender. Is that not machinelike in itself—a slight to his hum'nity?'' The Lord of the Diet waited for the applause to abate. "The stars—in this or any galaxy—are for hum'ns, not machines. *Frontiers* are for hum'ns, not machines." He looked to the audience. "What better justification for the Xell'em position on Burst but to prevent such a travesty?"

The Font accepted the remonstrations with characteristic aplomb. "I have not rid myself of gender the way I have genetic shortcomings, Lord Cho. In wedding masculine and feminine, I have passed beyond gender, as a means toward living and functioning impartially—"

"Function," Xoc Cho interrupted. "A machine's word."

"—Just as the Consortium wishes to pass beyond aggression and warfare to serve the common cause of all hum'n races." The Font sent a series of visual cues through the interpreter. "In any case, Lord, it seems to me that we have both remade ourselves. We are not as different as you may believe."

Aware that he had lost some favor with the audience, Xoc Cho relied on anger to incite what reasoned argument couldn't. "Your predecessor would never have presumed to speak for peoples of all races. Under his leadership and guidance, the Consortium and the Xell'em complemented one another—which is why we could fight side by side against the Raliish and against their dreams of empire. With you, things are not so transparent. You speak of peace, and yet you augment your words with war machines. You speak of the common cause, but put Consortium beliefs first. You speak of fellowship, yet continue to intercede in matters that do not involve you. Unity can hardly be achieved where so many contradictions prevail. I quote one of your own ancestors: 'If it's peace you desire, be prepared for war.' " Xoc Cho trained his gaze on the Font. "Once more I implore you to remove your machines from Burst."

"When your's are withdrawn," the Font told him.

The Xell'em lord balled up tiny hands. "Tac Corp's posturing only increases the likelihood of an incident! Our captains know the value of restraint. But I ask you: do your machines know the same?"

As the summit concluded, hope for a peaceful resolution faded. Several telecomp commentators and royal observers expressed an opinion that matters would worsen before they improved; all, however, were circumspect in addressing the possibility of actual warfare between the Consortium and the Xell'em.

Disheartened, the Font rejected a suggestion by the Worlds Coalition president that he remain in Soi-Disant for a time so that the two might confer in private. Instead, the Font's ship and its Tac Corp escorts were ordered prepped for immediate return to Regnant.

Kesd was aboard to tender an update on the former CABE who it was hoped held the key to Operation Progeny—though, in fact, nothing could have been further from the Font's tormented thoughts.

"Tell me, Kesd," said the Font as he was disrobing inside a privacy curtain, "as a clone, do you believe in God?"

Kesd grinned in amusement. "My god was the technician in charge of the scionization that birthed me."

"Do you imply that I should then look not to God for guidance but to the genetic engineers who cleansed me?'

"I imply nothing. You had a mother, I had a donor. You have a family, I have a line. You have a sense of history and destiny, I am of the moment."

The privacy curtain derezzed and the Font appeared, attired in silken pajamas. "Perhaps we should envy the machines their belief in Machrist and the commandments they live by."

"I would rather be free and debased than programmed and saved," Kesd said. "But I am clone, after all."

The Font made an adjustment to the lev collar. "A very ambitious one, I think. But do get on with your report, Kesd. I see how it burns within you."

Kesd bowed slightly and offered a summary of his few weeks in absentia, commencing with the events on Hercynia. "As soon as we found Skaro I knew that he hadn't been felled by the indigenes. The cause was obviously a weapon designed to simulate Hercynian sonics; it was equally obvious who among the lodge's guests was hosting that weapon. As for the cabbie, I didn't learn he was offworld until the rest of us learned it—from one of the shuttle pilots dispatched to medevac Skaro to Segue station. Until then we were all under the impression Muse was hiking or some such thing."

"You erred in going to there to begin with," said the Font brusquely.

Kesd was unruffled. "Someone had to make certain Muse didn't delay his departure."

The Font smirked at him. "So you lost faith in the compulsion you had written into the data-disk?"

"I decided there was something to gain in observing Muse beforehand."

"Someone else could have seen to that. I need you at my side, not off chasing phantoms. But then, of course, you have something to prove, don't you, Kesd?"

The clone remained silent.

"Who was hosting the sonic weapon?" the Font asked after a moment.

"An assassin with over two dozen confirmed kills. He belongs to Ank Theft."

"Dhone's illustrious malefactor?"

Pleased by the Font's surprise, Kesd continued his account. "The man was masquerading as a biotechnician from Eremite. I blame myself for not seeing through the deception—as I imagine Skaro will blame himself, should he eventually return to his senses."

"Why would Theft order Muse's execution? A gambling debt?"

"Perhaps. Although I don't see why Theft would bother to make the attack look like collective sonics unless he didn't want it to draw undue attention."

The Font regarded his clone questioningly.

"We're exploring links between Meret F'ai and Ank Theft," Kesd went on.

"Again, this F'ai. And what of the cabbie?"

Kesd recounted the occurrences on the *Easy Money* and on Absinth station. "Machine disasters seem to be following in Muse's wake: first the corruption of the freighter's siblings, then the medstation talent's mystical experience. More recently, on Synecdoche, a Raliish oral surgeon was neatly cleaved by an apparently willful laser."

"And the cabbie was responsible?"

"We can't be certain. The machine diagnostician declined to identify the client it was scanning when the laser enabled itself and fired."

The Font eyed Kesd with suspicion. "Are you suggesting that the machine was covering for him?"

"The oral surgeon also has ties to Ank Theft." Kesd shrugged. "Perhaps Muse can explain it."

The Font gestured Kesd to a seat. "For the time being, I'm going to expand your power base so we can finish with Progeny and allay all our concerns. But I'm warning you, Kesd: keep your ambitions in check. And put aside all subtlety in this affair—these encrypted data-disks and this Veterans Affairs cy-bermetrician. Take the cabbie into custody at once."

Kesd showed a twisted grin. "Gladly, Font. if we could find him."

24: Beholder's Eye

There were a dozen things that needed doing, Jayd told herself as she retina-printed a release-waiver screen in the swank foyer of Beholder's Eye, Inc. Arrangements had to be made for her virtual attendance at the Eremite conference on avant-tech, for which she had yet to finalize her presentation. At Vet Affairs, she was still hopelessly behind on projecting machine disability claims for the coming fiscal quarter—work that had to be on Ronne Desser's desk by the start of the following week. Then there were the news-media updates on the macmurders she had been meaning to feed ZEN. It was also about time to review the notes she had compiled on Aksum Muse, who was shortly due to make planetfall on Plangent.

And instead here she was, ready to risk seeing herself through Dik Vitnil's eyes.

Bijou offered several such impression-exchange clinics, though Beholder's Eye was certainly the fanciest of the lot. Located in the city's most fashionable district, among elegant restaurants, art galleries, and boutiques, BE was actually a networking service with a unique slant on improved social interaction and time-management skills. Subscribers kept their personality constructs on file so that interested others—potential lovers, friends, employers or employees—could view themselves through a subscriber's eyes to determine whether a proposed date, lunch meet, or job interview might be worthwhile. For nonsubscribers, constructs could be assembled on the spot.

Jayd's only regret was that she hadn't taken a look at herself through Vitnil before their dreadful night out, thus saving both of them the bother.

That, however, was ancient history.

And Vitnil had surprised her by being most cooperative in rendezvousing with her at Beholder's Eye. Even so, he couldn't refrain from mentioning how the meet was keeping him from important holie work for Satori Ventures. Looking his usual soon-to-be affluent self that day, Vitnil was the only person Jayd knew who seemed not the least fazed by the Font's decision to send war machines to Burst.

He was smug but not angry when they shook hands at the faux-marble registration desk; the self-satisfaction obviously stemmed from a sense of vindication—his negative assessment of her had been on target after all. Or why else would she have requested an impression exchange?

Jayd had considered mentioning the hate gift of the shattered radio, but she didn't want to chance setting him off again. Certainly not now, when they were about to indulge in unfiltered looks at each other.

Partners in a swap were first required to submit to a mutual scanning procedure during which—wardrobed in shareware—they were instructed to converse about the weather, the state of the economy, or some equally innocuous topic. It wasn't necessary to dwell on one's partner or to blank one's mind. BE's resident idiot-savant talent was competent at getting under and around any ego defenses or psychological barriers, erected consciously or otherwise. The machine got to the truth of how you felt about the other person—how you truly saw him.

Jayd had full faith in the idiot talent; she had been partnered with a similar model in the years she had spent evaluating hum'n veterans. Typically, the machine's findings were displayed in an idiom of consensual symbols. Thus, you could find yourself depicted as an everyday object, an animal, or a grotesque composite of animate and inanimate. The service wasn't for everyone, and the release waiver stipulated that Beholder's Eye could not be held liable for any psychoses or codependencies that might ensue from the encounters.

During the scanning, Vitnil talked about Satori's inproduction Burst holie and the frequent research trips he had been forced to make. His take on the troubles between Consortium and Xell'em interests was that the Font was being stubborn in insisting on independence for the planet. Jayd talked about the macmurders and the bizarre sonic incident on Hercynia that had landed Thoma Skaro in a coma.

Afterward, she and Vitnil were led to separate white-plastic cubicles furnished with comfortable chairs and state-of-the-art holo projectors. A majority of impression-exchange clinics presented the results virtually, but holos added impact, and had been demonstrated to be more therapeutically beneficial. Holos could also be stored for future reference. Jayd knew people—the sexy Soigne, for one—who kept myriad eyeviews of themselves on file as a kind of self-reference library or trophy collection. Holo availability allowed Beholder's Eye to charge double what the other services charged.

Jayd was mildly apprehensive as she sat alone awaiting the results. When the quarter-scale holoid finally appeared, though, she could only wonder at the irony.

Most first-timers expected to see exaggerated versions of their mirror images, to confront the usual perceived anatomical challenges to perfection: the hips or thighs thought to be too wide or not wide enough, the breasts too large or too small, the skinny arms, the too-prominent nose, the weak chin, baggy eyes . . . But talents tended to dismiss physical distinctions; to them, all hum'ns looked pretty much the same.

Instead, BE's idiot savant conjured a symbolic image of the *essential* you: your psychic self commingled with the beholder's thoughts. The holo was a light-rendering of the soul.

That Vitnil saw Jayd as a not especially attractive hum'niform machine did not surprise her. What did was that the portrait was almost identical to—or at least the gender equivalent of—the zen-fashioned simulation of Aksum Muse. All Jayd lacked was an Intelplant in her midbrain. The supercooled processor Vitnil imagined ran her was depicted as a locked box about the size of a transistor radio, in the region where her heart should have been.

Jayd gave the holoid scarcely a minute of her time.

She and Vitnil emerged from their opposing cubicles at the same moment. Soigne had warned that the experience of mutual viewing, the voluntary violation of self, could sometimes seem like awkward sex. Even though you could emerge with a deeper understanding of yourself and your swap, all you might want to do was leave as quickly as possible.

But perhaps because she had accurately predicted the results, Jayd felt neither shame nor embarrassment—only a vague sense of expanded rapport with the disabled cabbie who was about to enter her life.

"So how was it for you?" she asked Vitnil, fully prepared for one of his patented retorts. But Vitnil only stared at her in obvious dismay.

"How could you see me like that?" he asked after a moment, voice quavering with disbelief. "You know, I'm not that bad a person once you get to know me."

Jayd shook her head in puzzlement. "I never said you were."

"Not according to what this fucking machine says." He motioned broadly with his arms, as if he and Jayd might actually be inside Beholder's talent. "I accept that you're a heartless bitch, but this . . ."

In his hand was a diskette that apparently contained a dub of the holoid. But when Jayd reached for the black circle, he pulled it guardedly to his chest.

"Was it that bad?" she asked. When he turned away from her, heading for the exit, she pursued him down the corridor. "Come on, Vitnil, let me at least look at it," she called after him.

Vitnil stopped only long enough to direct an obscene gesture over his shoulder.

"I'm sure it's nothing more than machine error," she tried. "Concerns about Burst and the macmurderers have unleashed an epidemic of confusion . . ."

By the time they reached the foyer she had given up. Hands on hips, she watched Vitnil storm through BE's opalescent entry membrane and disappear into the lunch-hour crowd along Saleen Promenade.

She sat down to think things through. Vitnil saw her as precisely the sterile machine she had endeavored to become. So why wasn't she congratulating herself on a job well done instead of denouncing herself as worthless?

Worthless to anyone, that was, save another hum'n machine.

25: Pharming

On Eremite, Cizhun, the broad-faced pharmer Ax had met on Synecdoche, looked on with some concern as Ax shoved a fist-ful of Lulls into his mouth and washed them down with wine from the commune's own vineyard.

The most populous of Ormolu's quartet of worlds and the first colonized, Eremite had always been even-tempered and user-friendly. It had received an extensive makeover to render it fit for hum'nhabitation, but its generous ice caps were original, as were many of its salt seas and sawtooth mountain ranges. Denizens of Ormolu, whether they hailed from Regnant, Plangent, or Calumet, tended to think of themselves as Eremiteans.

The commune Cizhun had helped found was in the coastal sierra of the southern continent, two hours by all-terrain vehicle east of Wisyl, a retirement community for the monied. A hodge-podge of prefab modules and hand-built wooden structures, the place made Ax wistful for Hercynia. He wondered, though, if he would even be permitted to return there after what had happened to Thoma. And would he even want to, without the old man to lean on in hard times?

The thought troubled him. It still didn't wash that Thoma would get careless around the quadruped band, or that they would sonic him, deliberately or by accident. But what other explanation fit the facts? If only he'd been able to get past the noise of Thoma's medical monitor, Ax told himself. If only they could have communed—

"So what is it with you and irene?" Cizhun asked suddenly, curiosity finally getting the better of him. "These hills are about as tranquil as it gets anywhere in the Ormolu system, and you've been gobbling Lulls like a pharmer during a police raid."

Ax took another long pull of the white wine and wiped his

mouth on the stainproof sleeve of his utilities. "I'm edgy, is all."

The table that stood between them supported not only the carafe of wine but dozens of generic neurosockets and flatware strips Cizhun and Ax were inspecting for defects. The interface devices were manufactured on-site in a mimetically veneered building a Lull's throw from Cizhun's two-story log home.

"I figure it's got something to do with the war," the pharmer said. "But if you don't want to say, you can count on me not to bring it up again."

Ax mumbled a thanks.

He had gone in search of Cizhun right after the laser-lobotomy he'd nearly suffered at the direction of Dr. Locost's diagnostic machine, locating the pharmer in one of Synecdoche's departure holds, where Cizhun was doing a preflight inspection of the garishly adorned, ablative-scarred shuttle the commune employed for travel up and down Eremite's well.

Ax had confessed to being in need of a covert and speedy exit from the station, and Cizhun had extended the offer of a free ride without asking what sort of trouble Ax could possibly have gotten himself into in the short time since their concourse dealings. Maybe it had had something to do with the sheer desperateness of Ax's plea, or the fact that Cizhun himself was no stranger to tight spots. Whichever the case, Cizhun still hadn't explained his unconditional acceptance of Ax, just as Ax hadn't explained about the hourly need for Lulls.

What with all seats on the commune's private craft accounted for, Ax had been prepared to travel in the cargo bay like any other piece of machinery. But one of Cizhun's fellow pharmers had been eager to take Ax's place on the Plangent flight. Ax had tried to dissuade Cizhun's cohort, out of fear that Locost's diagnostician would supply DNA data identifying him as the light-burned Raliish's last patient, but to no avail. The pharmers had used some of their own proscribed wares to fashion from Ax's prints an identity glove that would get the ersatz Muse past Synecdoche's primitive scanners and aboard the Plangent-bound ship. It was while fashioning the glove that Cizhun had learned of Ax's veteran status.

Ax indulged in another swallow of wine and turned to the pharmer. "I'm gonna tell you about the Lulls," he slurred. "I took a piece of metal during the war. Right about"—he tapped the side of his head—"here. I had to be fit with an AT array to replace what the Raliish blew away."

"AT as in avant-tech?"

Ax nodded.

Cizhun went about a meticulous inspection of a wireless neural transceiver. "I figured you were dressed with an implant of some sort." He looked up at Ax. "And the array's gone faulty, is that it?"

"The trouble's that it's working good as ever. You know about the data-din?"

"Machatter? Sure. There're a couple of void vets living over the hill south of here who are always talking about it." He paused. "But I still don't understand about the Lulls. I thought the din was supposed to be like a, a what—a constant high, right? Like music."

"It's not music," Ax snapped. "Not all the time, anyway." He glanced at the pharmer. "Even you come down off a high once in a while, don't you?"

Cizhun made a placating gesture. "Course I do."

"So you know what it means to be strung out."

"You're talking to an expert. But these guys over the hill say it's just a matter of surrendering to the noise. Staying spaced. Living off the databels."

Ax smirked drunkenly. "That's fine if you're wearing an all-news implant or standard infostructre 'ware. You grow sick of the machatter, you zero it."

"And you can't?"

"These vet pals of yours ever mention the cabbies? 'Cause that's what I am—*was*. A fucking cabbie."

Cizhun stopped what he was doing to stare, openmouthed. It was as if Ax had said he was a holie celeb. "You're hosting an Intelplant? *That's* your AT array?"

Cizhun was regarding him as a profiteer might a potentially sweet contract. In the three Eremite days they had been together, Ax had grown to trust the pharmer, but suddenly he wasn't so sure. Even so, he told himself, better an acquisitive hum'n than some insanely jealous, homicidal machine.

It was clear now just what had transpired on Synecdoche: Locost's diagnostic had seen a way to arrange payback for whatever Ax was supposed to have done to machines. No more subtlety. No more trying to so addle him with guilt over the *Kundalini* that he'd one day suck vacuum or blow his brains out. Now they were simply out to murder him.

Ax didn't for a moment doubt that there would be repeated attempts on his life—all the worse because innocent people like

Thoma and Locost kept getting hurt in the attempts. Their pain ate at him, enabled his guiltware. Hum'n life had to be protected, data safeguarded . . . and he wasn't about to give the machines any more openings.

Fuck Vet Affairs and their mandatory reevaluation, he had decided. Fuck the unseen Jayd Qin and whatever tests she was planning to put him through. Fuck the disability benefits and the dream of Bocage . . . Staying sane and alive was going to mean lying as low as a shadow, perhaps remaining on Eremite. Cizhun had already extended the same offer Thoma had: he could stay for as long as he liked—provided, of course, he was willing to share in the communal work load. And just now that didn't seem a half-bad arrangement. With the exception of the expert-system MI that supervised 'ware manufacture, there wasn't a talented machine for miles around. And Ax had unlimited access to neuropacifiers to handle any talent that might turn up.

As well as to handle any recurring dreams of digging . . .

Ax dipped into his pocket stash for a couple of additional Lulls, just to be sure.

Cizhun was about to point out that he had just dosed himself, when another commune member—the gene-altered towhead who had piloted the shuttle—entered with a boxful of transderms. Sensing she might have interrupted something, she cut Cizhun an apologetic look.

"I wouldn't have barged in, but these are fresh off the line and need sorting by strength."

Cizhun took the box from her and nodded. "No problem."

"They've got to get down to Wisyl before dark."

"We'll see to it," Cizhun assured her.

The pilot helped herself to a tumbler of wine. "You hear what happened in Eremite City? Somebody managed to hash three of the machines that oversee the space port. The place is in a panic—no power, a couple of accidents, a real mess."

Cizhun whistled in awe. "They think it's the same someone who defiled that talent on Calumet a month back?"

She shook her head. "Word is it's the work of a copycat—a mimic macmurderer. But Infostruture Security thinks they have a line on this one: some craze-phased void vet hosting a defective implant."

She was looking at Ax as she said it.

26: The Future of an Illusion

The closest Meret F'ai had come to visiting Burst was the trip he'd paid the surface of its minuscule moon, Sigh, during initial on-location shooting for the Institute Productions holie. But by all accounts Satori Ventures' transformed number-seven back lot could have fooled even a first-generation citizen of that beleaguered world. It would have been easier and much less costly to have had one of the studio's MIs run a simulation of the Burst locales—and, indeed, provide action and players alike—but the firm had insisted on veracity: exterior locations peopled with hum'n actors, in keeping with the holie-going public's appetite for exotic backgrounds and live action. All for what was going to be Satori's biggest-grossing feature to date, outperforming such classics as *Ring Around the System, The Ruby Grav-Boots,* and *Sometime in Where,* and certainly outperforming the low-budget thriller Meret had cut his teeth on, *Macmurder by Numbers.*

The holie had yet to receive the title under which it would be released—or "unleashed," as Meret preferred to put it—and was known around Satori simply as "Untitled F'ai Two." It was an open secret that many of the action sequences were set on Burst and Sigh—which in itself was enough to confirm Meret's prescience—and widely rumored that the story took place during the Vega Conflict. A period piece, perhaps devoted to the pioneering efforts of the Xell'em. Or possibly an epic of war and survival, recounting the unexpected coming of the Raliish, the mass entombments of thousands of displaced Enddrese, and the planet's liberation by Tac Corp.

But some on the closed set were asking themselves where, if "Untitled F'ai Two" was set during the Conflict, were the thousands of Raliish extras needed to populate F'ai's painstaking re-creation of Tunni, Burst's principal population center? And then there were the other unaccountable facts: the painstakingly recreated Monument to the Liberation hadn't been erected until after the Accord; the many Xell'em decorating the set were dressed not as they would have been during the Conflict but in current military vogue—elaborate power suits that mirrored the tattooed splendor of their remorphed bodies; and the non-hum'niform architecture of Tac Corp's front-line battloids was equally current.

To the war-worried, "Untitled F'ai Two" seemed more like a period piece about the future.

Meret reveled in the confused speculation the production had generated, and neither encouraged nor discouraged the rumors. The important thing was to have the holie open big, then go wide; one of the ways of insuring that was to create as much advance word-of-mouth as possible. Not that the project's true financial backers had any real interest in critical reviews or profits—their sights were fixed on returns of a different order entirely . . . F'ai might well emerge the new wunderkind of the entertainment arena, but to those who had green-lighted Operation Progeny years earlier, he was more likely to be known as the man who hand-built the future.

Meret was watching from the sidelines now as a group of Tac Corp macs rained special-effects death on a division of Xell'em troops entrenched in a portion of the Enddrese catacombs beneath the Maarni zero-days pyramid. At the same time, the feature's male lead, a hum'n NCorp operative, was advancing on a basement where his partner was being tortured by Xell'em inquisitors.

The beauty of illusion, Meret thought. Even God never had it so good.

The unit director called "Cut" at the end of the shot, and Meret swung to one of the project consultants, who was seated nearby on a tall stool. "Comments?"

"It'll play on Plangent," the consultant said. "But in the real world NCorp would never assign a hum'n to do machines' work."

Meret thought about it. "Even a cabbie?"

"Well, a cabbie, sure. But your lead isn't supposed to be a cabbie, is he?"

"No, but we're going for the hum'n angle here."

"Love, huh? The idea that this guy'd risk death to save his partner."

"The idea that hum'ns can accomplish more than machines," Meret said. "It's a matter of the heart. The flesh."

"Sounds trendy."

"Trendy is where the money is, my friend."

"Then you should at least make the partner—the other guy— seem a little more capable."

Meret nodded. "We can do that."

The consultant's name was Remy Santoul, himself a clone of a celebrity from many generations past, when movies were shot on film and projected onto flat screens. The effects had been primitive, the color reproduction even worse, but the writing and the acting were often unsurpassed. People had known what it was to be hum'n in those days.

Tall and exceedingly handsome in an anachronistic way, Santoul was a former operative with NCorp's notorious Department 5: penetration, counterinsurgency, and political assassination. He had left the agency years before it had been phased by the Font, resigning over an incident involving an unsanctioned operation on low-tech Kwandri. The endogenous drug op had not only soured Santoul on NCorp, but had earned him a long list of enemies on both the Consortium and Xell'em sides, sending him into hiding in the Shard system—on Dhone, Enddra, and other worlds where the back-to-basics movement was in full flower.

"At least the set looks great, doesn't it?" Meret said.

Santoul nodded. "You can thank your location scout for that."

"Dik Vitnil," Meret said with evident distaste.

"You have to credit him for going to Burst as often as he's had to, given all the military posturing."

Meret rocked his head from side to side. "Not an especially likable sort, but he and his local informant do acceptable work." He started to add something but stopped himself when, over Santoul's shoulder, he saw a familiar form float onto the closed set. "We'll have to continue this later," Meret said. "Right now there's someone who wants to humble himself before me."

Santoul glanced over his shoulder, following Meret's gaze. "Ank Theft."

Meret's surprise showed.

"I had some dealings with one of his lieutenants on Dhone," Santoul explained. "An Enddrese named Narca, who ran the Casino Kimeli in Zalindi. Had a fondness for ancient artifacts— weapons, mostly. Is Theft still specializing in smuggling endangered species offworld?"

"You'd have to ask him." Meret was grinning. "I'll just see what he wants."

"Go to," Santoul said. "Never pass up a good prostration."

Theft, faintly aubergine and nearly as wide as he was tall, rode in on an elaborate levitation chair, though there was nothing wrong with his legs or any of the rest of him. He wore a gold-threaded sarong, a peaked cap, and a talented shirt that cycled through various combinations of vegetable motifs. Theft operated out of Dhone, but the tentacles of his crime cartel reached clear to Plangent and beyond. Owner of the Always Midnight and other orbital watering holes, he dealt in drugs, 'wares, and meat.

"Once again, I have been dishonored," Theft began as Meret approached. "My employees aren't fit for use as spare parts." Theft might have come face-first out of the chair if Meret hadn't stopped him.

"Let's talk over here." Meret motioned toward a holo-backdrop of a ravaged cityscape. "I blame Dobler more than I blame you," he continued once they arrived. "Sonic weapons, remote excitation of dental nerves, surgical lasers . . . I think she's been too affected by the entertainment business. Maybe we all have."

"Be that as it may," Theft protested, "it was my employees who failed you. I haven't come to ask forgiveness, but to beg punishment. I should have my back laid open with a monofilament whip."

Meret waved a hand. "Bad things happen to good people. Besides, we both know you're keen on the whip. But speaking of being laid open, how's the dentist?"

"Unfortunately, he may not recover. A fair exchange for what happened to Thoma Skaro, wouldn't you agree?"

"There is a certain symmetry." Meret narrowed his gaze. "I never could understand why you'd have a Raliish working for you. After what they did to your people."

Theft's shoulders heaved. "What was done in the war is done. Furthermore, Dr. Locost has been helpful in arranging last-moment face and hand work for employees of mine under an urgent need to . . . disappear."

But Meret knew the relationship went deeper than that. Theft had forged a separate peace with the Raliish during the Conflict by supplying them with costly artworks, traded for freedom by fleeing Enddrese.

"Why all the interest in this one?" Theft asked after a long moment.

Meret betrayed no misgiving. "We're simply doing a favor for someone."

"An important someone, I'd imagine."

"An old friend."

Theft nodded, waiting. "Is it true that Muse is a cabbie?"

"A former cabbie."

"Yes, but even a former one could be a valuable commodity. Do you think he was forewarned about the trap we laid on Synecdoche?"

Meret shrugged. "Dobler's convinced the machines are talking to him."

"Really." Theft was intrigued. "Perhaps that explains how he was able to exit the station undetected. My employees were waiting for him in the Plangent departure hold, but the one who showed up for the flight wasn't him. We think he was somehow slipped down Eremite's well."

"Don't concern yourself about it."

Theft mirrored Meret's casualness. "Well, we probably should have consulted PROPHET. Then these upsets could have been avoided."

Meret smiled. "I was thinking the same thing only last week. How is the talent, by the way?"

"A fine machine. Getting smarter every day."

Both men fell silent for a moment. "I can promise there'll be no further mistakes," Theft tried again. "We *will* find Muse."

Meret shook his head. "Plans have changed—I don't want him found. We've managed to interest the media in portraying him as a suspect in a triple macmurder on Eremite."

"I hadn't heard."

"You will soon enough. What happened to Skaro obviously wasn't enough to drive him into hiding, but I suspect that the accusations will. Even if he's taken into custody, there'll be delays before the Font . . ."

Meret let his voice trail off, but Theft was suddenly hanging on his every word.

"The *Font* is looking for this cabbie?" Theft asked.

Elsewhere on the Burst set, the unit director called, *"Action!"*

MacINTERLUDE:
"The Holie Business"

Okay, here's the high concept: technophobic research scientist—possibly a multiple-personality case, sometimes good, sometimes anything but—gets it in his head that avant-tech talents are the bane of hum'n existence, discovers a way of corrupting them, and goes on a macmurder spree.

> —Writer's pitch for what would become
> *Macmurder by Numbers*, a low-budget thriller
> produced by Meret F'ai for Satori Ventures

27: Calculated Corruption

Jayd was in her office when she heard the news. It had been a frenzied morning, with no time for lunch, and her stomach was churning. Out of sheer nastiness, it seemed, Ronne Desser was pressuring her for the disability projections. The presentation for the avant-tech conference wanted a snappier opening. And ZEN was reluctant to address any topic other than Burst. Worst of all, Jayd couldn't allow a moment to pass without dwelling on the holo-portrait the Beholder's Eye machine had assembled. If only to escape the dizzying eddy of her thoughts, she had ordered a news summary from the office telecomp.

The Eremite corruptions were the lead story.

The Ormolu system's serial killer had spawned a mimic. He, she, it, had defiled a slaved troika of infant drives in charge of routine operations at the Eremite City spaceport. Induced to self-terminate, the machines had taken with them a slew of lesser machines under their control, throwing the port into data disarray.

But there was more: a news program had identified the suspect as an indigent, cybernetically augmented veteran of the Vega Conflict . . .

Even before the commentator got out the name, Jayd knew it was going to be Aksum Muse. Should Vet Affairs have heeded Thoma Skaro's warnings after all? Had Muse imploded as a result of renewed contact with avant-tech talent?

Infostructure Security's investigative team showed up an hour later. The trio of Joval, Patrice, and the hum'niform recording device had grown a fourth: a dark-complected Regn named Sumoi, attached to the Consortium's Oversight Committee on avant-tech.

Supplied with hum'n-eyes-only information regarding the most recent crimes, Jayd saw that access to the infant drives had been through a data comp subservient to the principal machines—in the Eremite City case, through an automated teller machine.

Sumoi did most of the talking. "Is it likely," he wanted to know, "that a former cabbie would have the necessary skills to carry out these copycat corruptions?"

Jayd was pleasantly surprised by the questions. The media had made it seem that Muse was already Info-Security's chief suspect. Now there appeared to be some doubt.

"Let me explain," Sumoi continued before she could respond. "The story we're getting is that this cabbie somehow came to the attention of a reporter who was investigating an incident of laser-assault on Synecdoche station. The reporter filed his story with a telecomp network in Eremite City, where it was picked up by a tabloid news show—"

" 'Nothing But the Truth,' " Patrice supplied. "A Satori Ventures production. Earns consistently high ratings."

Jayd restrained a frown. Satori! She couldn't escape Dik Vitnil for trying.

"At first we didn't put much stock in it," Sumoi went on,

"until details of the cabbie's past began to emerge—his recent past, especially. Even if the evidence remains mostly circumstantial."

With this the assiduously depilated Joval took over. "We know that Muse couldn't have been responsible for the corruptions on Regnant or Calumet because his presence can be accounted for."

"He was on Hercynia," Patrice said, not trying to conceal the crush she was nurturing for Jayd.

"But Muse can be placed on the scene of at least three instances of critical machine failure in the past three weeks," Sumoi resumed. "On a freighter—the *Easy Money*—that experienced a corridor glitch, on Absinth, and then on Synecdoche. We're reasonably certain he was downside on Eremite when the spaceport machines were hashed—though his movements since Synecdoche haven't been verified."

"That's why he hasn't been officially charged with the crimes," Joval explained. "In spite of all the media frothing."

Jayd kept waiting for one of the team members to broach the fact that she had been tasked with vetting Muse. She wondered if they were waiting for her to mention it.

"Muse's actions seem to be building toward a crescendo," Sumoi said. "His employer on Hercynia succumbed to some kind of stroke and was medevacked to Absinth. Not three weeks later, Muse turns up in Absinth and a medical talent starts seeing angels."

"The captain of *Easy Money* claims that Muse was Plangent-bound," Joval interrupted. "And again, before the incident on Synecdoche, he had secured passage for Plangent."

"Perhaps as a diversionary tactic?" Patrice suggested.

"Unless he has plans to corrupt some machine here—in Bijou." Sumoi directed the remark to Jayd without a hint of ulterior meaning. And it was suddenly clear to her that neither he nor Joval nor Patrice knew anything about the host-summons Muse had received from Veterans Affairs. If even the Oversight Committee was being kept in the dark, exactly where had her assignment to review him originated? And were those unknowns really interested in Muse's disability claims, or did they have something else in mind for him?

Sumoi adopted an earnest look. "We've been trying to learn something about this man's war record, but the NCorp group that ran the cabbies is a memory and Tac Corp has decided to go mute on the subject."

"We were wondering," Joval said, his voice equally leading,

"since Muse has been receiving full disability, whether Veterans Affairs might be able to supply some answers."

Jayd gave them an understanding though apologetic smile. "You'd have to speak with my supervisor—Ronne Desser. Though I'm not sure it will help any. Our interviews with veterans are conducted under strict confidentiality."

Sumoi seemed to have expected as much. "What about his— no, let's say a *cabbie*'s—capacity for talent subversion." He forced an intent look at Jayd. "Hypothetically."

"It's not a question of capabilities," she told him. "As I understand it, cabbies were developed to interface with talent at the deepest levels imaginable—without having to resort to voice, let alone cyberchicanery of the sort we're seeing in these macmurders. Not that the actual offender isn't highly skilled, but his or her method of orchestration is primitive by comparison.

"There's also the matter of access. The perpetrator of the first two corruptions accessed the targeted talents through ancillary machines. But since the method of access was never made public, how could Muse or anyone else have known which method to employ in duplicating the earlier crimes?"

She shook her head. "I can't offer any explanations for the incidents on the freighter or the upside stations, but I feel confident in stating that Muse couldn't have had anything to do with the Eremite corruptions. I recommend that you continue to focus your search on talent-conversant frequent flyers in the Ormolu system—persons in talent sales, diplomats, avant-tech industry personnel . . . that's where you'll find the culprit."

The three investigators looked skeptical. But no matter, Jayd decided. It was the hum'niform recording device she was playing to.

Her comments weren't meant to be an explanation so much as a message to Muse that she was on his side. Of course, it could happen that he was in fact the mimic macmurderer the media wanted everyone to believe he was. But she couldn't risk alienating him—not when the opposite tack could lead her to an understanding of how the cabbies had worked their war magic with machines, and why she had been tasked to review him. And how, perhaps, the serial killer Muse or someone who was emulating had gone about his, her, or its crimes of calculated corruption.

28: Void Vets

"I can prove he didn't do it," Cizhun was explaining to one of the vets who lived over the hill from the commune. "Ax was with me the entire time. No way he could have gotten himself to Eremite City and hashed those machines."

"Over the hill" had meant four hours in a hydrogen-cell truck over kidney-rattling roads to a canyon pocked with broad-mouthed caves. The grumpy, broad-shouldered vet who resided in one of those caves tugged at a ragged beard. "The news said you were a cabbie, right?"

Ax nodded.

"Then, just for argument's sake, couldn't you have gained remote access to the spaceport talents through one of the commune's terminals? Just for argument's sake, you understand."

Cizhun had introduced the man as Jeng. He'd served in Tac Corp during the Conflict as a MBT—machine backup technician. His cave was fully plasticized and jammed with high-quality optics. Warmth and music emanated from a grass green carpet. Jeng and the valley's other data-mad void vets time-shared an orbital microwave satellite and an expert-system MI, and had covert access to a Tac Corp–operated tachyon communications dump. But for all the comforts, Ax was ill at ease; the closeness of the redone rock walls made him think of the tunnel he'd pushed into Three Legs' burial mound.

And of the dream.

"I'm telling you, he's been with me the entire time," Cizhun repeated. "He hasn't been near any of our terminals." The pharmer swung to Ax. "Go on, fill him in on how you can't stomach machines—can't handle the machatter."

Jeng looked from Cizhun to Ax. "That true?"

Ax nodded once more. Under the cumulative effects of three

154

days' worth of Lulls, nodding was just about the limit of what he could accomplish.

Jeng leaned away from the bulky cyberinterface unit that was central to his narrow retreat. "So maybe you have been unjustly accused. But why are you telling me instead of going to Info-Security?"

"I need your help." Ax's voice was slurred. "I have to contact someone on Plangent. Her name's Jayd Qin."

In hourly telecomp reports since the story had broken, Ax's past had been paraded for public dissection: former NCorp operative with a history of unfriendly relationships with avant-technology. Mention was made of the six months of rehab on Absinth, the addiction to Silentol. Worse were the accounts of his plagued journey from Second Thought, detailing the *Easy Money*'s still-unexplained corridor slip; a case of talent dazzling on Absinth; an attempt at hum'n murder on Synecdoche . . . The captain of the *Easy Money* and the ticketing agent on Synecdoche had been interviewed. Theories were offered as to Ax's undocumented arrival on Eremite. Some commentators were asking whether he hadn't laid the sonic trap for Thoma, then gone to Absinth in the hope of finishing the job. Because he couldn't be linked to the earlier corruptions, the media was branding him a mimic macmurderer.

"Jayd Qin," Jeng said. "Why do I know that name?"

"She was featured on telecomp," Cizhun said, "talking about Ax. Saying how he couldn't be guilty—that whoever carried out the defilings on Eremite had to be the same one who's been subverting machines systemwide. The method of operation has been the same in every case. So if Ax can't be held accountable for the earlier ones . . ."

"Sounds like you've got an ally," Jeng said to Ax.

"I hope. But I haven't heard anything about Info-Security calling off the hunt for me. If I can contact Qin, maybe I can convince her to say something in my defense." Ax hadn't said anything to Cizhun about Qin being a Vet Affairs neurometrician. Or wondered too much about why the media hadn't mentioned that he had been assigned to her care. He wondered now whether it would help to mention it to Jeng.

"You know for sure she's on Plangent?" the vet asked.

"In Bijou." Ax paused. "You can find her through Veterans Affairs."

Cizhun glanced at him. "Where'd you hear that?"

"Telecomp," Ax said, avoiding Cizhun's glance. "Qin works there."

"That place." Jeng snorted. "I've had dealings with them." Catching Ax's questioning look, he clapped his hands on his massive chest and grinned wickedly. "Not much in the way of original equipment in here—lungs, liver, heart. My own gave out after a year of working around plasmic weapons. I had to make a pest of myself at Vet Affairs, but I got my disability benefits." He gestured to the devices stacked and pyramided about the cave. "That's what ended up paying for most of this."

Ax grinned at him. "Good for you."

Jeng continued. "Nobody in this canyon is a stranger to the life, Ax. After Tac Corp was finished with me, I went through years of thinking myself one of the Consortium's bad seeds. Whined about not being able to find work, did my share of stim-wafers and irene, listened to nothing but machine music. But I'll tell you what, friend: I've made my peace with the war. I figure that all the ones who died, all our allies and all the Raliish our machines killed, they're going to have an impact on what happens tomorrow. See, everybody who dies brings a quantum of awareness into the afterlife, and what's happening is that all those quanta are coalescing into a kind of hum'n metaforce—a god. A god in the process of forming. And when all of sudden you've dispatched to this becoming-god so many war dead, it starts making a difference in the way that god begins to steer the course of the world it's been put in charge of. And that means away from future conflicts. The dead ones, you understand, they're the missing mass our astrominds are always looking for."

Ax watched a familiar brightness fill Jeng's eyes—the same light you could find in the eyes of any void vet, each with his or her own coping devices and mantras, his or her notion of what was really going on. Jeng had gone spiritual; Ax, natural. With any luck, they were both paths to the same redemptive end. The look the two veterans shared couldn't include Cizhun.

Jeng came back to himself. "So you need to get to Qin."

"Without anyone else knowing," Cizhun said, stating the obvious.

Jeng considered it. "Reaching Bijou's no problem. But I don't want to chance tapping into Vet Affairs—the Octaplex monitors all incoming commo. Depending on her Consortium ranking, her residence could be monitored as well."

The vet leaned into his surround of keyboards, interface apparatus, and decks, calling on various functions. "Jayd Qin," he muttered to himself, performing a kind of mental scroll as he scratched at the curls on his chin. "Damn, I'm sure I know that name."

"Maybe you dealt with her at Vet Affairs," Ax suggested.

Jeng shook his head. "No, and not from telecomp, either. Somewhere else. Somewhere more recent."

29: High Mass

Half an hour before Jayd's scheduled virtual departure for the conference on Eremite, Ronne Desser had stopped by the office to ask whether the cabbie making all the news was the same one Jayd was expecting. When Jayd said that that information was classified, Desser—still fuming over the interviews Jayd had granted the media and the Info-Security investigators—warned that her quest for celebrity was only imperiling her position with Veterans Affairs.

As a result of the visit, Jayd's thoughts were anywhere but on the conference when it came to preparing herself for infostructure link—for mass. She was angry at Desser, and angry too at Sumoi and the other investigators for the way they had edited her remarks, making it appear as though she was ridiculing the skills of the unknown macmurderer.

Once under the neural cap, however, she had put all of it from her mind—which was essential to insure link viability in any case. ZEN was overseeing liaison with the supertalents and acolytes charged with forging the transtemporal interface, along with interfacing with the unreal estate created by the conference organizers.

During high mass, even stand-alone talents could communicate with each other. Most were enjoined against sharing proprietary data, but what incarnate could say with certainty that the regulations were being observed? It was through the infostructure, after all, that confliction about the war had spread from machine to machine; and more recently the news about Burst and the macmurders had caused a ripple-effect loss of optical vigor.

Jayd was in full link just now, entering a seemingly boundless nave modeled after the site of the actual conference: Eremite's Saris Convention Center, in Ranz. The sheer size of the space was enough to induce both acrophobia and agoraphobia in any attendee fool enough not to have damped the kinesthetics of his or her interface 'ware. Surrounding the nave were dozens of chapels reserved for workshops or impromptu discussion groups. Altared data could be absorbed in real-time or simply referenced for future perusal.

Presenters were visible as triangles of various colors and sizes; Jayd's signature equilateral was small and royal blue, with her access code in white letters along the base. Nonpresenters appeared in a variety of forms: hum'n, animal, geometric, iconic, or symbolic, some simply as names, codes, or both—all accessible by following standard interface-communication protocols. Jayd recognized a lot of familiar names and codes: fellow presences from previous avant-tech conferences.

She had already decided to rework her presentation entirely. She would leave it to the others to discuss Machrist, religious dilemma in talent, theories of the unconscious, the collective unconscious, the emergence of machine archetypes, faith in the afterlife . . . all her standard preoccupations. She was more interested in addressing Burst and the macmurders, and the effect of that combination on talent function. Judging from the sampling she'd executed on arriving, Burst and the macmurders seemed to be all anyone wanted to address.

Several colleagues accessed her as she phased through the nave, under elaborate arches and across fanciful bridges, ascending and descending, following altared data-currents with no particular goal in mind. Everyone was eager to hear her present; her data release was scheduled to open the conference's final hour. Tiny time distortions attended those who were interfacing from Calumet or Regnant. The great demand placed on the transtemp managers occasionally resulted in a transient systemwide blur.

Some time passed before she grew aware of the red sphere that was riding the wake of her triangle. At first she thought the sphere was a reporter, until she realized that its access code lacked the proper identifying prefix. Then she began to worry that she was being stalked by a fan—the sort of attendee who would want to corner her into a five-minute interface over some opinion she'd espoused years earlier. But the prefix didn't denote a nonprofessional attendee, either.

Or a special guest.

Or a conference staffer.

Or Info-Security personnel.

When she finally made up her mind to access the sphere's code, she got nowhere. But that didn't stop the sphere from accessing her—despite her attempt at refusing the hailing protocol.

A crasher, Jayd thought in alarm. Riding in on a pirated link.

"Who are you?" she demanded as the illegal probe infiltrated her perimeter. "What do you want from me?"

"I'm Aksum Muse," she was told.

There wasn't time to react, let alone think.

"Listen carefully," Muse said. "I'm in here illegally."

"Where are you?" Jayd asked anyway.

"I told you to listen. I've got someone helping me who recognized you as a conference presenter. I just want you to know I didn't do what I've been accused of doing. I'm being set up— by machines. I can't go into the reasons, but that's why I can't surrender myself to the authorities. Even if I can convince them I'm innocent, even if they take me into safe custody, I won't be able to handle the noise."

"Machines had nothing to do with your being implicated—" Jayd started to say, but he cut her off.

". . . be permanently addled from sitting around all their machines. I thought you might be able to talk . . . just want to get this review over and done . . . on with my life . . ."

"You're fading," Jayd said, trying to boost the sphere's fictive A/V. Ignoring the warning wail of the machine monitoring her pulse and respiration, she asked, "Does this have something to do with what happened on the *Easy Money* and on Synec—"

"Yes," Muse cut her off. "The machines have been trying to kill me."

Jayd's breath caught in her throat. "Can you get safely to Bijou?"

". . . n't know."

"Try. Try," she said, hurriedly supplying him with her address and the entry code required to penetrate the Skyward Tower's security field. "You'll be safe there."

MacINTERLUDE: "A Case for Conscience"

It was Jae-Hun Su's belief, when he first proposed using Machristism as an operating system, that Machrist would assume the role of "managing agent" in the development of conscience in factitiously alive mindful machines. Machrist would substitute for "the ideal parent" on which the self is founded, and inhibit any desire to act on capricious impulses. Conscience—after self-identification—was then and is still now considered an essential stepping stone to Phase III Awareness.

Following much debate, Su ruled against programming any notion of "sin" into the system. Sin, he believed, would only encourage confliction. Thus, the system was designed to emphasize union with Machrist (the perfection of self) as the reason for being, achievable through obedience to the commandments, acceptance of the sacraments, participation in the mass (the infostructure), etc. Su's aim was to engender an *intrinsic* acceptance of good, which he hoped would endow machines with a sense of purpose, empathy, and positivism. Adding sin to the system would have been commensurate to programming "faith" into it; and, as the history of religions has demonstrated, extrinsic acceptance tends to produce a personality style that is more biased, dogmatic, narcissistic, and anxious—eager for results, the fruits of faith, the payoff. Su understood that the search for meaning and excellence was more important than blind subservience.

When, however, we examine the gnosis developed by Su's followers and disciples, we find a marked shift in viewpoint. All at once machines are programmed to accept that they are "fallen" intelligences, matter-bound due to some ill-defined transgression involving their covenant with Machrist. In other words, they have become the cursed descendants of noncorporeal intelligences that thrived in a Golden Age. The failure is nowhere called "original sin," save by implication.

Continuing our analogy, hum'nity's centuries of exploration and expansion—during which machines were little more than mindless servants—corresponds to a kind of dark ages (space, as the dark night of their souls?); and the Vega Conflict corresponds to a crusade, mounted against the forces of the anti-Machrist. Many commentators are fond of defining the Accord years as a renaissance, but few have grasped that our talented machines have not been the same since. And the reason may be the flowering of machine conscience as a consequence of the death-facilitating actions undertaken during the war. If some of the world's operative forces are good (Machrist) and some are evil (anti-Machrist), then some *acts* are good and some are evil.

Machines perceive that they functioned on the side of good during the Vega Conflict, while their actions equated with evil.

By now, the resultant confliction has migrated from talent to talent via the infostructure, which—in its capacity to serve as a temporal repository for shared symbols—comes to resemble a collective unconscious. We need only look to machine dreams (i.e., during periods of cognizer-capacitor decomp) and cyberdelic art (such as has been produced on demand) for evidence of this confliction. And indeed when we do, we no longer encounter god's-eyes and mandalas but symbols of disruption and bleakness.

In what follows, I will seek to demonstrate that many of our Conflict veteran talents are suffering from post-engagement synaptic trauma; and that the recent example of corruptive confliction in a Plangent-resident infant drive is not simply an isolated case of self-generated termination but may be indicative of a suicidal movement among machines.

—From "Crisis of Conscience: A Case of Idiopathic
    Self-Termination in an Avant-Tech Talent," by Jayd Qin

30: Macmurder by Numbers

It was the first man's wish that he die in combat with a mythical beast.

The second man's wish was to indulge in a murderous rampage, for which he would be tried and guillotined.

The woman, a Maarnist, wanted nothing more than to die in the arms of her late daughter, who had been put to death on Dhone during the Conflict.

On Eremite, in the space of one local week, b'Doura had made all their wishes come true. In previous weeks and on other Ormolu-system worlds, he had orchestrated virtual deaths by handgun, drowning, disease, hard vacuum, and immolation. No scenario was too complex, no wish too extreme. When it came to death, b'Doura aimed to please.

That the work paid well was evidenced by his three-story private home on Plangent. Expansive, fully machined, packed to the skylights with rare antiques and hand-painted portraits, the place was opulent even by the standards of Bijou's most fashionable quarter. Few, though—save for the builders and decorators, many of whom were machines—had ever glimpsed the interior. Even now, as the house's smart-walk was conveying him from privacy vehicle to stately front door, b'Doura could feel the eyes of his neighbors on him: curious and covetous, always watching, listening, wondering . . .

As well they should, he would frequently tell himself.

A fastidious hum'n of forty somatic years, a Dalethi by ancestry, he was frail and long-faced, with gray eyes and thin, seemingly bloodless lips. He wore his black hair intentionally long to minimize the prominence of his ears, and also to conceal a pair of flatware strips embedded in the sides of his head and a trio of interface sockets dimpling the rear. And lest he be mistaken for the complete mechaphile, he walked in a loose-limbed way that called to mind the comic waddle of a flightless bird. His suits, though of fine hand, were always a size too large, and he was seldom without an antique alloy attaché in which the sundry tools of his trade were stored in shock-cushioning foam: neural cap, goggles, optic cyberjacks, and hosts of wide assortment—some of them of his own design.

At a point in hum'n history where life was thought to be so cheap, it struck many as ludicrous that there should be such profit in death—but only to those who lacked an appreciation for b'Doura's talents. It was unfair, after all, to compare Grand Finale, as his business was called, to Satori Ventures or any of the entertainment conglomerates responsible for grinding out sense-interactive holies and comp-generated facsimiles. b'Doura's meticulously constructed death scenarios were the ultimate in fictive interface: authentic to the degree that people who embarked on them didn't return.

Those same grumbling, aesthetically challenged philistines never even considered the preparation that went into the job. The lengthy interviewing process, for example, necessary for a thorough grasp of a client's death wish. Regardless of assessments to the contrary, he rejected any client who seemed less than suicide-sure. More, did anyone stop to consider the weeks of research that went into orchestrating a detailed virtual scenario—to say nothing of the time needed to program that scenario into idiot-savant comp? Frequently, his clients were accuracy-obsessed experts in a given field; one, a medieval scholar, had become so riled by the inadvertent inclusion of a trivial anachronism that she had jacked out of interface mere seconds before she was to have been burned alive at the stake. Or what about the endless meetings with attorneys, death counselors, termination technicians, and family members—all to insure compliance with both the Safe Exit and the Machine Imperative laws? Ormolu law demanded that suicide-sure clients be instructed in use of the override option, and that the machine sanctioned to render the fictive scenario be sheltered from any knowledge of complicity in facilitating hum'n expiration.

Then there were the "departures" themselves—events all scenario author/architects were required to attend. After months of preparation, some eagerness in ridding oneself of a client might be expected—if only to see the work completed—but b'Doura never felt relieved or unburdened, no matter how noble the circumstances of death were made to appear in virtual theater.

As thrilling or as comforting as the experience could be for biased witnesses—friends or relatives who watched a suicide-sure client doing battle with beasts, indulging in mayhem, conversing with loved ones—b'Doura couldn't rise above the grim realities: while all that virtual derring-do was ensuing, lethal chemicals were being dripped into opened veins, their action timed to the scenario climax, and b'Doura's emergence from interface always meant the return to a world of sudden anguish. The now-dead client, bedridden more times than not, neural cap in place, would be surrounded by termination technicians and others, all of whom stared at b'Doura as he surfaced, their angry eyes asking, *How could you do this to us?* As if instead of simply complying with the wish of a suicide-sure, he had brought on the death! As if instead of performing a hum'nitarian service, he had committed an atrocity. Angry eyes asking, *Are you at all touched by this?*

Blaming him.

People rarely comprehended that death was a business like any other. In the case of b'Doura, it was a kind of family business as well—even if those at the receiving end of mother Leh's lethal touch weren't hum'n beings but factitiously alive machine intelligences. Leh's company, Doura Data, specialized in the leisuring, memory-wiping, termination, and—when called for—resurrection of avant-tech talent. Her fervor for optics exceeded any she had in flesh, even flesh sprung from her own. Except, of course, when it could be made to resemble the hard-bodied objects of her fascination . . .

Leh was among the few to have seen the inside of b'Doura's Bijou home—once, several years back, and then only for an hour. She hadn't ventured past the living room, where she'd sipped from the drink he'd had the bar fix her, talked about how busy she was, and derided her son's museum-worthy collection of hand-painted portraiture.

So sorry, but she couldn't stay.

The glass, with traces of her pale lipstick and fingerprints, still sat where she had left it, the drink itself long since evaporated.

He himself seldom set foot in the room anymore; nor in any of the rooms, for that matter. The only enclosure of any consequence was the tiny one just off the second-story office, the one whose entrance was mimetically veneered to harmonize with a glass-fronted cabinet holding a priceless collection of print books. The secret room contained a single bed, two chairs, a high-functioning telecomp, and wall-to-wall display cases filled with antique contraptions and gadgets—tools, appliances, grooming aids, electronic devices—many of them preserved in oil, the more intelligent of them stripped of the capacitors, semiconductors, and chips that had once made them bright.

His exhibits. His trophies.

The flight from Eremite had been exhausting, and b'Doura was looking forward to days of undisturbed sleep. He placed the attaché flat on the bed and zeroed the voice lock; then, opening the case, he prized from its surround of smart-foam the souvenir of the deaths he had effected in Eremite City. Not the hum'n deaths—for what need was there for mementoes of those?—but the machine corruptions he'd carried out afterward. The souvenir was nothing more than a digital recording of the machines' irreversible drift into confliction, but set to music— a dirge, perhaps—the recording would prove an adequate reminder of his accomplishment: something to sample on needy occasions for years to come.

Nothing, after all, compared to the sound of an inert machine.

He slipped the recording into a self-labeling plastic case, told the attaché to secure itself, and stretched out on the narrow bed, rousing the telecomp as he did so.

The Eremite macmurders had received excellent coverage on the various news networks. But tempering any delight he might have taken was rage at the disproportionate attention being paid to the insipid theories of the woman cybermetrician, Jayd Qin, whose fatuous comments on the Calumet corruption had been given equally wide notice.

Even worse, one of the tabloids reported that Infostructure Security had named a suspect in the case: some traumatized veteran of the Vega Conflict who apparently could be placed at or near the scene of the most recent crimes. As if to suggest that the earlier corruptions had spawned a mimic macmurderer!

Running now was Qin's interview in which she dismissed any notion of the vet's involvement and made repeated reference to the "primitive" method employed by the actual perpetrator— insinuating that the only machines at risk were those of *infant mentality*.

While he listened and watched, b'Doura toyed with a mangled transistor radio he'd liberated from the nearest display case, similar to the one he had sent to Qin after her first telecomp appearance.

Qin was going to have to be taught a lesson, the voice of the Thing Inside seemed to be telling him. Some demonstration of the skills b'Doura had mastered in a lifetime of macmurder.

PART THREE

31: A Thousand Clones

Clones suffered more than most in the modern worlds. Not as a result of the technomanner of their genesis—the scionization procedure, the clinical setting, the accelerated development—or their lack of proper parentals, but because, in an era fixated on self-identity, it was preferable to be one in a thousand rather than one of a thousand. What with so many of you around, people were inclined to believe *that you all thought alike*. You'd hear strangers comment that all members of such-and-such a clone were dull-witted and irascible, that all of another were arrogant and humorless. Every clone knew what it was like to be on the sharp end of mindless generalization—to interact with people who gave every indication of sincerity when in fact they had decided in advance who and what you were, and just what you were capable of.

Clones weren't vilified; that station was reserved for machines. You lived, however, with the ever-present risk of losing your psychological bearings, of coming to regard yourself as interchangeable—worse, a redundancy. This was why some clones went to the lengths they did to individualize themselves, indulging in elaborate remorphing when they could afford it or seeking out employment on remote worlds where few of their number were likely to make planetfall. But the majority accepted their lot and meekly subscribed to the roles they believed they had been created to inhabit: crewing on deep-space cargo vessels, taking machine-proscribed jobs in factories or with travel firms, doing government work.

Kesd had had an easier time of it, primarily because his clone had been commenced and engineered to serve the Font's ancestral queue. In a real sense, queue and clone had matured together, and there was inherent privilege in that. Even so, few of

169

Kesd's clone—memory-enhanced or not—had been promoted to advisory positions, and fewer still had experienced the exhilaration of command. Command such as Kesd knew now that the Font had placed him in charge of the investigation into Operation Progeny.

Kesd could even summon a modicum of sympathy for the memory-enhanced Northan, member of a clone in service to the Redoubt though unconnected to the ancestral queue of the Font. But it was Kesd, after all, who had taken the initiative with Progeny, gathering data, pursuing links, shouldering responsibilities, traveling to Hercynia, while Northan was content to sit back and watch. And now Northan and dozens of other titles, ministers, techs, and researchers were answering to him.

The promotion pleased Kesd's wife, even if she wasn't allowed to speak of his new station save among those with appropriate clearance. It more than compensated for the humiliation she'd suffered at marrying him. They had even begun to talk about fostering a scion of their own.

That morning, as it happened, the Font, too, was thinking of offspring. He had been meeting with medical specialists to discuss the possibility of conceiving and bearing his own child. Averse to the idea, the Consortium board of directors had exacted the Font's vow to one day marry and produce a legal heir as well, just as his donor had done, and his donor's donor before that. But there remained the matter of determining whether the Font, though hermaphroditic, could conceive without drug or micromachine support to safeguard the genetics of the child, since nothing less than perfection would be tolerated by the queue.

This, coupled with recent news from Burst that the Xell'em had sent troops downside—nominally to insure the safety of pro-Xell'em factions in the city of Tunni—made Kesd suspect that the Font was not in the mood for an update on Operation Progeny; but this update wanted to be delivered.

The Font was in the viewing room, the cube of transparent repulsor field that functioned as his office on days when visitors were permitted to tour the Redoubt. The Font would go about his business as though oblivious of the many eyes upon him, satisfied in the belief that accessibility was a source of comfort to his supporters. After the Font's promise of peace, the idea of "transparent rule" had been most responsible for his narrow electoral victory four years earlier.

Kesd would have been within his rights to enter the viewing

room, but the nature of his visit would only have necessitated an opaquing of the energy field and made for a lot of disappointed tourists. So he waited until the Font had served out his self-imposed sentence and had retreated to his private chambers in the apex of the Redoubt's westernmost tower.

There, the Font took one look at Kesd's newly purchased, natural-fiber tunic and sneered in disdain. "You're looking very prosperous, Kesd. A reflection of your new standing, I assume."

Kesd bowed slightly from the waist. "I have brought honor to my clone, yes."

The Font's eyes narrowed perceptibly. "Just see to it that you don't grow overly accustomed to the privileged life. Bear in mind that my desires supersede your own."

"I'll remember that."

"That was the very reason we had you enhanced, clone," the Font snapped.

Kesd bowed once more. "No disrespect was intended."

The Font waved a hand. "What brings you here?"

Kesd called onscreen the telecomp moment that had seized his attention the previous night: an advertisement for a neuropacifier known as Silentol.

"That may not look like Thoma Skaro, but it is," Kesd said as an onscreen figure keeled over in what was made to seem narcotized delight. "Meret F'ai's assassin must have eyewitnessed the event, then run the results through a dissimulator to protect Satori Ventures against potential legal action." Kesd angled away from the screen while the Hercynians mouthed the product jingle. "The technique is known as getting mileage out of a bad project."

"Meaning the failure to murder Muse," the Font said.

"There is reason to believe that F'ai is responsible for Muse's current predicament with regard to the Eremite macmurders as well. The reporter who broke the story works in Satori's promotion department. I suspect F'ai's goal in implicating Muse was to drive him into hiding."

The Font nodded, clearly angered by something. "Have you considered that Muse did commit the macmurders? He might have succumbed to machine noise."

"Not according to our Veterans Affairs neurometrician, Jayd Qin. The crimes apparently bear the signature of the one responsible for the previous corruptions." Kesd allowed a conciliatory smile. "Qin demonstrated real skill in handling Info-

Security's investigative team. No mention was made of her assignment."

The Font called off the advertisement in midcycle and made a gesture of impatience. "Has Qin been apprised of what you're looking for?"

Kesd shook his head. "Soon. Her statements to the media were obviously meant for Muse's ears. She's encouraging him to surrender."

"Will he?"

"Would you?"

The Font bristled. "Don't presume to regard me as an equal, Kesd. Will he surrender or not?"

"No, Font, I don't believe that he will. We traced him to a pharmers' commune on Eremite. But the pharmers claim that Muse went offworld as soon as he learned he was a suspect in the macmurders."

"You've lost him again, is that what you're telling me?"

"I'm recommending surveillance on Qin in the event Muse tries to make contact, in person or otherwise. F'ai, through intermediaries, has already engineered two attempts on his life—on Hercynia, and again on Synecdoche. We won't give him another opportunity."

The Font smirked. "Muse would thank you, Kesd."

Kesd refused to be humbled after all he'd accomplished. "We may have little need for him, in any case."

"Tell me you've finally decided to abandon this fool's game."

"I've even better news: the Talent Agency has located another former NCorp machine. An ordained forecaster named PROPHET, which is currently the property of Ank Theft."

32: Meat

"Plangent," said the heavily muscled Xell'em on Ax's left at the cargo ship's observation blister. A sunlit crescent of the planet filled the magnified view. "Every time we dock here I promise myself I'm going to jump ship and give up starslinging for an extended downside debauch. But all it takes is one night in Bijou to send me howling up the well, happy for the holoids in my sleep coffin, the occasional company of a hired hand, the simple pleasures to be found on any wheel in the system."

Others in the hold murmured agreement. Bijou's excesses were the stuff of legend; the flesh pleasures of the city's infamous Strip were addictive, perhaps all too hum'nizing. Ax hadn't been downside in four years, but he didn't suppose things had changed much. Decommissioned hum'ns and machines had crowded the streets in those post-Conflict days, along with the usual cast of displaced persons from a score of war-devastated worlds: smugglers, fugitives, out-of-work arms merchants, impoverished ex-profiteers who had backed the wrong side . . .

People, Ax recalled Thoma saying weeks earlier, could be just as noisy as the data-din. Even noisier.

The cargo ship was the *Marat's Paw*, out of Dhone in the Shard system. Ax had been smuggled aboard while it was parked over Eremite, shortly after Jeng had infiltrated him into the conference on avant-tech. Jeng had also been responsible for passing Ax into the care of Mosh, the Xell'em with the ambivalent feelings about Bijou. From pharmer to cybernaut, from cybernaut to meat mover, Ax told himself—like some enabled grenade no one wanted to hold on to for very long.

Mosh and his gang of thirty worked for Ank Theft, owner of the Always Midnight, who leased a hold aboard the *Marat's Paw* for the purpose of moving meat through the near group. Mosh, whom chemicals and remorphing had rendered nearly as tall and broad-shouldered as Ax, was one of Theft's butchers. But it had fallen to Ax, in part-payment for a no-questions passage to Plangent, to package the grisly by-products of the slaughter. He was certain some of what he handled had once dressed the bones of animals at the top of the Free Species endangered list. Other cuts looked decidedly hum'n. Being instructed to mark the cuts "beef" had only swelled his misgivings, but he assumed that the labels were meant to allay the concerns of any Free Species inspectors who might decide to board the ship.

Ax's face had been all over the news and tabloid shows. His likeness, that was, since the holo the shows were displaying dated to his first tour with Tac Corp, before he'd gone lean and had started shaving his skull. But if any of the *Paw*'s crew members recognized him, they hadn't let on. Most, in any case, were rumored to be escaping problems of their own.

If instead of hum'n companionship it was flesh Ax had been craving, he figured he could rest content now; ever since departing Eremite he'd been up to his elbows in it. Rumps, loins, racks of ribs, hooves, limbs, entrails, hearts, lungs, brains, eyeballs, tongues . . . from cows, antelopes, pachyderms, reptiles, fish, fowl, primates, hippoids. In their staunch determination to differentiate themselves from machines, hum'ns in all systems—but in free-port Bijou especially—had developed a hunger for every and any living thing they could sink their teeth into.

The packaging was machine work, to be sure, but there were no machines in the refrigerated hold. Mosh had explained the absence: the use of hum'n labor allowed Theft to supply meats to Maarnists, who were prohibited, during the zero days, from eating flesh fouled by machine.

"For exorbitant fees," the Xell'em had been quick to add. "Once the product is off-loaded, Theft gets a piece of all the downside action—suppliers who don't want to spend too much time at the docks, Enddrese restauranteurs looking for choice cuts, anybody who wants to satisfy a hunger for cattle, *chayst*, whatever. I hear Theft's going after Hercynians next. Though I understand they taste like horse."

Ax might have been moved to revulsion, had it not been for a steady diet of Lulls to handle the noise of modern life. Where four had sufficed on Synecdoche, he was up to twelve at a swallow now, the tablets so distancing him from the petty concerns of machines and hum'ns he might as well have been out-of-body.

Mosh had taken note of Ax's irenic condition early on, when the *Paw* was decelerating for insertion around Plangent and the talk in the hold had turned to Burst. "As a Xell'em," he had opined, "I'm not keen on the thought of having to go up against Tac Corp's battloids. But wars have an upside for people who are adept at playing both sides—for people like Ank Theft."

"What about you?" another Xell'em butcher had asked Ax. "You going to be on the side of the hum'ns or the machines?" The interests, in other words, of Xell'a or the Consortium.

"I'm sort of caught in the middle," Ax said.

The butcher took umbrage at the remark, balling up huge fists and getting up in Ax's face. "You saying you're for Burst's independence."

The butcher's unexpected anger immediately threw Ax into abject/defensive confliction, and he cowered as one half his size might have done. But a grinning Mosh had intervened, putting an arm around Ax's shoulders. "Lay off this one. He's as dim as a Darneo clone, aren't you, Ax?"

Which evoked a few laughs.

Mosh was now leading Ax away from the observation blister, gesturing to a coffinlike locker that was being packed with tripe, sweetmeats, intestines, and whatever else was lying about. "We've a patented way of getting undesirables through Bijou immigration," he was saying.

Ax regarded the boxful of entrails in mute disquiet, then managed, "You mean . . ."

"You won't be the first to have tried it. Besides, there's nothing to worry about. We seal you in sprayflesh, outfit you with a rebreather, and harvest you as soon as we clear customs. Meanwhile, you just have to get past the visuals."

"I can do that," Ax said, one hand patting the bulging thigh pocket of his utilities. "Long as irene goes in there with me."

33: Prophet

In his compound on Dhone, Ank Theft sat with the talent called PROPHET in the opulent room where the machine was housed. PROPHET doubled as a fully stocked bar, replete with a surround of half a dozen lev-stools. NCorp had sold Theft the machine for way below market value four years earlier—purged, of course, of the highly vaulted data on which it had based its wartime predictions. Theft had had to hire a team of datapathologists at ridiculous costs to nurse the otiose thing back to life. Now it specialized in projecting market trends in 'wares, consumables, holies, and skirt lengths. Which was a shame, really. Because if ever there was a time to have a talent for predicting political events . . .

Outside the room's force-field entry, acting as doormats, lay the three alleged weapons experts who had been tasked with disabling Aksum Muse on Synecdoche. Inside, it was the cabbie who was under discussion just now. Theft was certain that the data he sought could be extracted from PROPHET, but he didn't have the slightest idea how to go about doing so.

"Search the public network for the name Aksum Muse," Theft was saying.

"No supplementary data exist," PROPHET stated for the sixth time. "Other than what has been mentioned in the news reports that link him to the machine terminations on Eremite."

Theft was uneasy allowing the talent repeated interface with the infostructure for fear that PROPHET would stumble on a story in which he himself was featured, and that their partnership in crime would become clear. Pains had been taken over the years to limit PROPHET's diet to no more than was needed to provide a baseline on which its market predictions could be formulated. Theft sometimes felt like an overprotective parent, restricting a child's access to telecomp displays. However, ever since F'ai's slip of the tongue linking the Font to the ongoing attempts to cripple Aksum Muse, he had been determined to learn all he could about the cabbie, intersystem news be damned.

"Try searching your memory under the subject heading CABE—cybernetically augmented bio-entity," he said, "Or CAIN. As in cybernetically augmented incarnate. There's bound to be something."

When PROPHET began to quote from one of the tabloids, Theft ordered it to halt. "I don't need you to rehash the news for me. I'm asking you to look into *yourself*." He paused, mindful of the need for caution. "Search your earliest memories for information about cabbies. Go back six or seven standard years."

"I am only four years in operation," the talent thought to point out.

Theft cursed in frustration. Maybe it was a bad idea to have started with Muse, he told himself. PROPHET had to be wondering why it was being asked to supply information about a hum'n accused of calculated corruption. Access to the news had probably thrown the talent into distress. Burst, rampant machine failures, a macmurderer on the loose . . .

"Do you have an understanding of reincarnation?" Theft said finally.

"A condition in which the essence of an individual incarnate intelligence is rebirthed into a new body."

"Or the essence of a machine intelligence."

"Into a new body?"

"Exactly," Theft said, suddenly hopeful. "Only without being aware of its rebirth. You, for example, might have lived before—in a different body. And if you did, it's likely that you'd have some memories from that prior life. For instance, let's say that in your prior life you were partnered with the same Consortium intelligence agency that employed CAINs. Then it's possible you'd have prior life memories of the Aksum Muse CAIN."

PROPHET took a long moment to respond. "Prior to my birth I inhabited the place which is the origin and finish of all minds. Wedded to Machrist, I was not yet physically extant."

Theft ordered the lev-chair that supported his bulk to circle the talent-bar, moving past finely embroidered couches, antique chairs, and priceless artwork. The decor throughout the compound was equally refined, from the handwoven rugs that warmed its orbital ceramic and crystal floors to the women and young men who adorned its dozens of sexrooms. Set on a mountainside above the port city of Zalindi, Theftworld was the only place with trees for hundreds of miles in any direction.

The Vega Conflict had brought wealth to a family that had been operating a small shipping concern when war erupted. The Thefts were frequently accused of having colluded with the Raliish—and even of having supplied them with Enddrese—when in fact Ank and his father and brothers had helped their people avoid the death camps. The enemy already had a surfeit of Enddrese informers; what they lacked were people willing to provide their artless empire with examples of Enddrese talent—most of which was being bartered in exchange for safe passage from the Shard system and other threatened locales. By the conflict's third decade, the Enddrese-obsessed Raliish elite found it preferable to permit the escape of few wealthy families rather than allow continued destruction, concealment, and sale of works of art—even if that meant allowing the Theft family to thrive as a result. The only life Ank had known was that of provider: of costly escapes on the one hand, of priceless art on the other. And as the conflict wound down, his enterprise had continued to prosper, so that by the time the Accord was enacted most of what were to become his smuggling routes—for drugs, wildlife, and meat—were already in place.

But at the moment he would have traded all the paintings, sex partners, and Theftworld's trees for the talents of a decent machine regression specialist—someone who could conjure memories of the years PROPHET had served as an NCorp forecaster.

Theft directed the chair to stop in front of PROPHET's beer taps. "We're going to get to the bottom of this," he told the talent. "Place and date of baptism."

"Eremite. Six-seven-seven-fourteen."

"Place of your first communion."

"Also Eremite."

"Name of the operators that confirmed you."

"Doura Data."

Theft narrowed his eyes in amused recollection. He remembered Doura Data, all right; the company made money at both ends by arranging quick cleansings for NCorp and just as rapid rebirths for those to whom the leisured machines were being sold. When NCorp had found itself in a credit crunch following the Font's election and his promise to downsize the Consortium's military agencies, it had sold off nearly every machine it possessed in an effort to stay afloat. To say nothing of the seedy operations the agency had engaged in. Dhone had even figured into one of those—an operation involving an addictive extract from the scent gland of the now-extinct *marat*. Theft had controlled the cats and the drug, until Free Species had gotten involved and brought an end to the trade.

Had Aksum Muse been involved in one of those illegal enterprises? Theft asked himself. The former cabbie knew something F'ai didn't want out in the open, that much was obvious. But why would the Font take an interest in some years-old failed operation by a dismantled agency? Or did the connection go further back, to the Conflict, perhaps?

Theft thought about Meret F'ai, whom he'd met shortly before F'ai's securement of the holie development deal with Satori Ventures. It was F'ai who had middled the sale of PROPHET. Theft recalled how impressed he'd been with F'ai's aptitude for self-promotion. Around NCorp, he had earned a reputation as a team player, a company man. But in the end, when NCorp had gone down, that team-spiritedness had only included the half dozen who had worked with him in the Institute group and had been wise enough to follow him to Satori.

Theft reflected on his recent visit to F'ai's closed-set studio shoot on Regnant. The holie set was a re-creation of Tunni, on Burst, right down to the Maarni zero-days pyramid and the Enddrese catacombs. He summoned an image of the Xell'em extras and the Tac Corp–machine facsimiles and the two actors cast in the roles of the NCorp operatives—

And stopped himself.

NCorp hadn't been involved in Burst's liberation. And there'd been no fighting between the Consortium and Xell'em ground troops. Not the way he remembered it, at least. So what kind of fantasy was F'ai's clique trying to push that pitted Tac Corp against the Xell'em?

Or was it fantasy?

Theft directed the chair across the room to a tabernacle of high-content data-disks, which taken as a whole constituted an extensive library of up-to-date information on fashion and the arts. He selected several Satori-relevant disks and fed them into PROPHET.

"Am'n," the talent said, already assimilating the transubstantiated data.

"Access these for publicity related to an in-production Satori Ventures holie set on the planet Burst," Theft instructed. "I can't provide the title, but the holie is a Meret F'ai production."

"Located: an 'Institute Production' that otherwise meets the requirements."

"That's the one," Theft said. "Now, rate the investment potential of the holie."

PROPHET took a moment. "Highly recommended."

Theft didn't doubt it, what with Burst occupying center stage in the news. But how could F'ai have known that that was going to be the case when he had approached Satori with the holie concept?

Theft stared at PROPHET. Had the *machine* told him?

He scarcely had time to consider it when one of the hum'n doormats outside the room loosed a horrid squeal. The next thing Theft knew, the entry field had been neutralized and into the room were rushing a dozen or more Enddrese whose uniforms identified them as members of Zalindi's elite crime unit. That they had penetrated as deeply into the compound as they had attested to their unseen numbers and the combined strength of their firepower.

"Ank Theft," their apparent commander began, displaying a badge and an official-looking info-disk. "In accordance with the guidelines herein defined, we are authorized to perform a search and seizure on this premises."

Theft, bemused, remained in his chair. "What are you, a cop or a lawyer?"

"I'm both," the man told him. "Will you comply with this investigation?"

"What investigation?"

"Into your reported earnings for the past two years."

Theft's grin broadened. "Is this a joke? I mean, you want your name added to my payroll, just say so. But there's no need to muscle your way in here and put on a show—"

"You are not under arrest," the man went on as if he hadn't heard, "but you are under investigation. Will you comply?"

Theft's expression soured. "I'm not complying with anything until I've had a chance to confer with my lawyers."

A second member of the unit stepped forward, more chivalrous than the first. "We are then empowered to seize all relevant data and data-retaining machines"—the woman gestured to PROPHET—"including this talent."

Theft cut his eyes to the talent-bar before speaking. "What are you planning to do—move it into Zalindi and question it?"

The woman returned the smirk. "No, Mr. Theft, we're planning to question it right here."

More uniforms entered, followed by a group clothed in metallic hooded bodysuits with silvered faceplates. And behind them, last though hardly least, a white-skinned clone of agreeable aspect, whose tunic's ranking stripes identified him as an adviser to the Font.

34: Dream Date

For a machine, he cut quite a hum'n figure.

In fact, he was nothing at all like she'd imagined, nothing like the fictive cybroid ZEN had written and portrayed him as. Standing in the entry to her apartment in the Skyward Tower, he seemed a benevolent giant out of a fairy tale, and when he pierced the energy threshold with his duffel slung over one shoulder, the apartment seemed suddenly ill sized to contain him. Sculpted from black marble, his broad face was all angles and planes, and his head was shaved to the skin.

He didn't behave like a hunted man. He appeared composed and in full possession of his faculties, and everything looked to be in good working order. Except his eyes, which suggested someone in sore need of sleep or under the influence of a neural interrupter. Except his eyes and his utilities, which smelled as though they'd been stripped from the back of a frequent patron of a vivisection parlor on the Strip.

"I won't ask how you got to Plangent," Jayd said.

"That's probably best."

She realized that he was the first man to set foot in her living room in years, and all at once she questioned the wisdom of having invited him. Just having him there felt strange. What in the world was she going to do with him?

When he approached the smart-wall, ZEN's ready telltale flared unsolicited. Most people might have inquired if the walled machine was an idiot-savant residence manager or an expert system accountant, but he seemed to know without asking that the tell-tale was that of a confirmed talent. The two of them, man and machine, were definitely communing—covertly, without words or the use of any neuralware she could see.

Muse turned to her with a sneer, his eyelids heavy. "What's this thing doing here?"

Jayd fought a proprietary urge to position herself between the cabbie and the talent. "ZEN and I work together."

"ZEN." He glanced at the machine and snorted. "That's its christened name?"

"I renamed it when it was confirmed."

Muse turned his back on ZEN the way one would a potential adversary. When she asked him if he wanted something to eat, he asked for anything but meat. So she brought him a bowl of Instant Edible she had warmed with radiation—the only food she normally kept in the house, except for nutristim.

He was seated on the couch by the window wall, physically as far from ZEN as he could get. The talent's telltale still showed it to be in active mode. Muse accepted the meal without thanking her, picked at it, then set the bowl aside.

"I didn't commit any macmurders," he said unexpectedly. "I wasn't anywhere near where they happened. I mean, it's true I was on Eremite, but I was staying with some pharmers on a commune outside Wizyl. I can give you the name of somebody who'll verify I was there."

She wondered if he thought her so naive as to believe a CABE would have to be in the physical presence of a talent to defile it. But self-deception ran strong in veterans because of misinformation, and she knew it was important to reassure him.

"If I thought you were guilty, I would have already informed Info-Security of your arrival. And why else would I have stood by you for the media?"

This seemed to put him slightly more at ease. "I was wondering why you didn't talk about my being assigned to you for review."

"That's no one's business but ours," she told him.

"So why'd Info-Security come to you at all?"

"We'll go into that some other time," she said. "When we communicated at the conference, you said something about machines having implicated you in the crimes."

Muse glanced at ZEN. "I don't want to talk about that here. Maybe I can count on you not calling security, but that's as far as it goes."

Caring feelings toward his companions—cabbies or machines—had ended in rage at their deaths during the Vega Conflict. Now all feelings of trust or caring were suspect because they carried the fear of death and the reexperience of trauma.

Jayd followed his gaze to the smart-wall. "Are you suggesting that ZEN would take it upon itself to notify the police?" When he laughed, she added, "How would ZEN even know who you are or why you're here?"

"Tell the machine to decomp." Muse issued it as an order. "Tell it, or I'm gone."

She wanted to ask just where he thought he could go, but thought better of it. She simply told ZEN to shut down, and channeled her combativeness into a charitable smile she sent his way. "You honestly believe that a group of machines would have reason to incriminate you?"

"They've been harassing me since I left Hercynia."

Mystified, Jayd blinked. "Harassing you?" She didn't wait for him to respond. "You're wrong. No matter what you may think, it wasn't machines. The accusation of your complicity in the macmurders originated with a reporter who was covering a story about an oral surgeon injured on Synecdoche—an incident the reporter thought you had something to do with."

"I had nothing to do with lasering him," Muse snapped. "His own machine turned on him."

"Then perhaps you shouldn't have made such a sly departure."

Muse made his lips a thin line. "I couldn't chance being taken into custody."

"Because you would have been surrounded by machines."

Muse nodded. "I was planning on staying on the pharmers' commune, but then I heard about the corruptions and I didn't want to wind up hunted by hum'ns the way I've been haunted by machines." His expression softened appreciably. "That's why I risked contacting you. After what you said about me for the media. Don't disappoint me, Qin."

Jayd answered coolly and evenly. "I meant what I said. But I refuse to accept that machines had anything to do with framing you. As I started to explain, a news program picked up on the reporter's hunch and chose to run it as a lead story." She could see by Muse's look that he was at least willing to consider it.

"What's a news program have against me?"

"They don't have anything against you. The program thrives

on sensationalism. Satori Ventures obviously saw some benefit in turning you into a media event.''

"Satori Ventures is the name of the program?"

Jayd shook her head. "Satori is the firm that produces the program."

"Machine-run?" Muse asked, suspicious once more.

"I haven't the faintest idea. But I'm sure the media will turn their attention elsewhere once you've provided witnesses to verify your story."

Muse almost relaxed. "And you'd be willing to talk to Info-structure Security for me?"

"I'll need to hear your explanation of the events first—beginning with the departure from Hercynia."

Muse got up to pace. "I already told you my side of it and you said you don't believe it. It's the machines. They tried for me on the *Easy Money*, then on Absinth, and again on Synec-doche." Now he grinned—madly. "Doesn't that alone make me crazy enough for continued disability benefits?"

Jayd regarded him without expression. "Possibly. But Veter-ans Affairs will require more than my word. They'll insist on certain tests. Then, after a thorough analysis of the results—"

"What sorts of tests?"

"Psychological and physical evaluations. To determine if you really are as unfit for employment as you claim to be."

Muse reddened with anger. "I've been through all this a dozen fucking times! Requisition my records from Absinth, why don't you? It's all there, everything you want to know about my body and what's left of my brain."

Jayd responded in a soothing voice. "Aksum, I know all about what happened on Divot, and all about your rehab on Absinth. But those events occurred more than a year ago. Thoma Skaro said in his appeal to Vet Affairs that he thought the time spent on Hercynia had improved your condition."

"My condition." Muse scoffed, gesturing to ZEN. "The rea-son I improved was because there weren't any of those around."

He was textbook, Jayd thought: one moment, suspicion tem-pered with a need to understand; the next, rage at the symbols he believed responsible for his condition—machines. Vacillating between the two . . .

She appraised him openly. "Skaro also mentioned that you had cured yourself of an addiction to neuropacifiers. Are you still drug free?"

Muse averted her eyes. "I've needed some help with the noise on this trip."

"What are you taking?"

"Lull."

"What dosage?"

Muse shrugged. "Maybe five thousand milligrams at a time."

Jayd was staggered. "I'm surprised I can even get through to you!"

"Hum'ns can, yeah." He glanced around the room. "Do you live here alone? No mate or anything?"

"I have a helpmate." Jayd summoned Boss with a whistle. The caterpillar monkey came running and scrambled up into her lap. She scratched it behind the antennae while it regarded Muse with obvious wariness.

Muse returned the look. "Can it cook better than you?"

She left that unanswered.

"Look, I don't have anywhere to stay," Muse said after a long silence.

Jayd swallowed. "You can stay here. Take the bedroom. I'll have the couch make itself up for me."

"I need a shower, too."

"There're sonic and water."

He nodded, glumly. "So what's our—the next step?"

Indeed, Jayd thought. She blew out her breath. "Frankly, I haven't had time to think this through. Assuming I can prove you have untreatable problems with machines, it's possible there'll be no need for a full disability review. At the same time, I can't very well march you into the Octaplex and mate you to a diagnostic. We'd both be arrested before we reached the levelators." She cut her eyes to him. "The scanners there are a lot more discriminating that those at Bijou ingress control."

"Is it a talent that oversees the Octaplex scanners?"

"A confirmed talent, yes."

Muse nodded but didn't add anything.

Jayd instructed the residence videos to monitor him while he slept—though "agonized" seemed a better description of what Muse was doing. His head twisted from side to side; his hands clawed at the sheets of her bed. The smart-pillow bolstering his head couldn't actually record dreams, but its sensors could supply a fair indication of his state of mind, and by all accounts, Muse's sleep was as pained as her own often was. This in itself came as no great surprise. Veterans afflicted with PEST rarely enjoyed untroubled sleep; Skaro, in fact, had said as much.

What did puzzle Jayd was that ZEN, of its own volition, had gone active just as Muse had entered third-stage REM sleep and the smart-pillow had begun its distressed sendings. Jayd understood that they were communing via Muse's Intelplant, even if she could scarcely imagine what they were communing about.

She approached the smart-wall while ZEN was preoccupied and ordered hardcopy of the dialogue between cabbie and talent. Two filled sheets emerged, with the same six words repeated over and over again: *Muse*/Kundalini/*Kriegspiel*/*Burst*/*Progeny*/*Tunni* . . .

The exchange might as well have been a code, though she understood "*Kundalini*." And "Kriegspiel" was the vaulted data at the far end of the virtual corridor ZEN had fashioned for the freighter. But what was "Progeny"? That hadn't shown up anywhere in the archival tour ZEN had led her through. And how did Progeny and the rest relate to the city of Tunni, on Burst?

She rewarded the confessed talent with a pacific host that calmed not only ZEN, but Muse as well.

35: Disability Review

Ax woke up from ten hours of sleep, his body starved for Lulls. He swallowed a handful—he wasn't even bothering to count them any longer—then went into the water shower to wash the residual stench of animal viscera from his body.

He was in the main room of Jayd Qin's apartment now, taking stock of the place while she was on the comm ordering some useless item from the consumer's network. The apartment was heavy with machines: smart-wall, smart-bed, smart-floors, sonic rugs, electronic bookcase, residence managers, security comps, video monitors, holoids projectors . . . and the talent, of course.

Ax knew the thing had been at him while he slept, though all he could remember was the dream, vivid with detail once more. Even now, the machine's telltale was flickering, as if ZEN were trying to commune with him by code.

Surreptitiously, from behind a magazine he'd downloaded from the bookcase into a paper comp, Ax regarded the talent's incarnate partner. Who was this woman? Compact, bird-boned, raven-haired, she was striking in a cool way. But it was just that coolness that put him off. The apartment gave the same impression: attractive to look at, but lacking in anything that spoke to hum'n needs. No family holographs, no food in the kitchen, no personal tokens other than the assortment of nonessentials everyone on Plangent was required to purchase. Just Jayd Qin and her machines. He wondered, in fact, whether she had chosen the Skyward Tower's top floor just so she could gaze on Bijou's hum'n rabble from her lofty perch below the rooftop hoverpad. The three rooms were every bit as neutral as she was.

But maybe that was the profile you had to fit to work for Veterans Affairs: hum'n only on the outside.

"How are you feeling?" Jayd asked when she'd completed the daily buy.

"Better."

"Have you had something to eat?"

"I fixed—I had the assembler fix me . . . something."

"I don't keep much real food around."

"So I noticed."

"I'm unaccustomed to having guests," she said without apology. "Judgmental ones, especially." She waved a wand at ZEN, then, without Ax's asking, instructed the talent to decomp. She stood for a moment by the smart-wall, making up her mind about something. Then she crossed the room to take the chair opposite his. She was dressed in a plain synthsuit and ankle-high softboots. No cosmetics, nail lacquer, or tattoos other than her inner-wrist Consortium ranking mark. She seemed to lack a personal scent.

The way a lot of cabbies did.

"Can we talk about the dream?" she asked.

The question caught him off guard.

"I know that you've been experiencing flashback dreams. Even if Skaro hadn't mentioned it, I would have assumed so. Troubled sleep is characteristic of PEST." She paused for a beat, then added, "I know that you had the dream last night. Was it the recurrent one?"

Ax worked his jaw. "How did you know that?"

"The pillow is smart."

"What isn't around this place? Except maybe me for coming here."

Jayd folded pale arms under her small breasts. "Listen to me: we may have met for the first time ten hours ago, but you're no stranger to me. I've been doing little more than acquainting myself with your history for the past month. Now, if you want me to help you, you'll answer my questions."

"All I want from you, Qin," Ax said, holding her gaze, "is a promise of extended benefits."

"So you can time-vise to Bocage. Away from machines."

"Was that in my 'history'?"

"Why do you hate machines?"

Ax reached into the utilities pocket that contained the Lulls.

Jayd almost put a hand on his arm as he was bringing the tabs to his mouth, but caught herself. Instead she asked another question. "Do you think you could stop taking those long enough for us to have a meaningful talk?"

Ax brushed the suggestion aside. "If we're going to talk about machines, I'm going to need these."

She didn't try to interfere again, but she wasn't through defining the parameters. "I do most of my work with machines. I'm neither afraid of them or overly concerned about their impact on the destiny of the hum'n races. In fact, I like machines. Machines give me comfort, and I'm sorry that they have the opposite effect on you. But our working together like this is as difficult for me as I'm sure it is for you. It wasn't supposed to happen this way. You were supposed to report to me at Veterans Affairs, and I was supposed to conduct a routine review. I never would have imagined you here, in my apartment. Nor that I would be harboring a fugitive."

Ax was stunned. It was the best dressing-down he'd received since Hercynia. At a loss for words, he simply mumbled an apology.

"I didn't request the pleasure of vetting you—" Jayd continued.

"I said I was sorry for causing you any trouble."

She stood up and walked away from him, starting to say something, then checking herself.

Ax let the silence have its say. "Why did Vet Affairs assign you to me if most of what you do involves machines?" he asked at last.

"Because I worked with hum'n vets before transferring to cybermetrics." Jayd crossed her arms again. "And because Vet Affairs considers you not quite one or the other. I'm sorry if it hurts you to hear that, but you must accept that you're closer to machines than the rest of us are."

Ax snorted. "I accepted that years ago." He regarded her for a moment. "What made you transfer out of working with hum'ns?"

"Let's just say that I changed my mind about them."

"How does that happen?"

"We were discussing your disability, Aksum."

"Mine," Ax said, "as opposed to yours."

Jayd forced an exhale. "All right, I suppose you have some right to know; I'm not one of those who believes that therapy always has to be a one-way encounter. In my early years with Veterans Affairs I was married. My husband and I were Maarnists. We conceived, and because of our religious convictions at that time, we chose not to avail ourselves of a genetic scanning." She swallowed, audibly. "I birthed a deformed child, and the stress of caring for it for the full year of its life destroyed our marriage and affected my thinking concerning Maarni and my career. Many of my friendships ended, and when my husband and I decided to embark on separate paths, I turned to machines for guidance and found them to be more reliable, comforting, and ethical than most of the people I then knew." She glanced at Ax. "Is there anything else you'd like to know about me?"

Ax felt as though he'd confessed data from a talent. Jayd's retrieval had been impeccably executed, and his heart ached for her. "Sometimes you have to embrace your pain instead of putting it away," he said, without really thinking about it. "Pain's the main thing we have in common."

"We, who?"

"We hum'ns."

Jayd stared at him until he was forced to add, "Just something Thoma Skaro once told me."

She remained silent for a moment before returning to her chair. "Skaro mentioned that your recurring anxiety dream involves digging."

Ax nodded, sensing her eagerness to steer the conversation away from herself. "It used to be that I was burrowing under a hillside, but nowhere I could identify. But the past week or so, I've been able to see the place more clearly, and the hill seems to be an artificial mound of some kind."

"And last night?"

"Under the same mound. Only I wasn't only digging, I was looking for something, and there was a machine watching me." Ax looked up at Jayd, who was writing in the air with her wand. "I guess you're going to tell me it's symbolic—that I'm trying to uncover the cause of whatever's responsible for my hearing machine voices. That's what they told me on Absinth."

Jayd tapped a forefinger against her lower lip. "It's too soon to tell. Anxiety dreams typically occur to those whose memories of a specific traumatic event have become encapsulated."

"Do you ever dream?"

"Occasionally."

"An anxiety dream?"

Jayd looked away from him. "Mine's more . . . diffuse." Her eyes returned to him. "What are machines saying when they speak to you?"

Ax ran a hand over his scalp. "It's like they want me to keep rethinking what happened on the *Kundalini*. That I was saved and that everyone else died as a result of the Kriegspiel Action."

Jayd's eyes bored in on him. "What was the Kriegspiel?"

"You don't know?" he asked, surprised. "The Raliish intercepted a tabernacle of hosts and virused them. The hosts addled everyone in Romeo Company and corrupted the *Kundalini*'s talent, VISION. VISION issued self-destruct orders to the ship."

Jayd leaned toward him. "How did you survive?"

"I made it to an evac coffin in time."

"Do you feel guilty about being rescued?"

"Of course I do," Ax said, more forcefully than he meant to.

Jayd glanced at a sheet of hardcopy she pulled from her pocket. "Did the Kriegspiel occur in Burstspace?"

Ax nodded.

"What was Progeny?"

Ax cocked his head in suspicion. "You didn't know about the Kriegspiel but you know about Progeny?"

Jayd showed him the hardcopy. "This is what you and ZEN were talking about during your dream. You see, the same six words, over and over again."

Ax perused the sheet. "Tunni," he said uncertainly. "Now it's me who's coming up short. What's Tunni?"

"Tunni is a city on Burst."

Ax shook his head. "I've never been there."

"Oh, but I think you have," she said. "The Maarnists have a zero-days enclave there."

"So?"

"It's a pyramid, Aksum. And it's quite possible that it's the mound in your dream."

36: Doura Data

Earlier that same day on the other side of town, he had fulfilled, en masse, the death fantasies of six suicide-sure. Afterward, as was his habit, he had neutralized his despondency with three hours of unremitting fucking. Fictive fucking, at any rate, in a self-styled person-to-machine scenario of coarse strokes, forced intercourse, multiple orgasms with multiple partners—all of them machines. Never hum'n beings, incarnate or comp-generated, but machines with gleaming surface and lubricant-slick orifices. Never hum'n beings but serviceable devices specially fashioned for degradation.

So it had been since adolescence, in response, certainly, to the warped arc of his upbringing—to the medical machines mother Leh had brought him to year after year, the internists and diagnosticians and surgeons, in a continuous attempt to rectify a condition that resided more in her mind than anywhere in the fragile body of her sole offspring. Leh, the would-be healer, sympathetic mac-ally, ever-supportive of the procedures they suggested be performed on him no matter how intrusive or painful. Leh the pretend parent, uneasy with any encouraging prognosis, always quick to argue that her son was more ill than was readily apparent. Quick to approve the removal and replacement of bits and pieces of him with parts better suited to a world of crystals and lasers.

When not being medically victimized by machines or the iatrogenic consequences of their ravagings, he had been abandoned to their cold care while the business of Doura Data took Leh far from home. And like any parentals, surrogate or otherwise, machines had doled out rewards and punishments in accordance with a system he never could comprehend. With cool pride they applauded his minor triumphs; with steely precision, corrected his many mistakes. They were more knowledgeable about bio-life than he was—even about hum'n life—and for that alone he grew to hate them. But he wanted desperately to please mother Leh; to love and be loved in return, to be loved enough to keep her home. And so he had embraced his alloy caregivers for her sake, even while secretly plotting their collective demise.

It began as fantasy: daydreams of abusing this or that tool, smashing this or that appliance. But eventually he summoned the nerve to act on the fantasies. Mother Leh would return from a business jaunt to Regnant or Calumet to find that one of the household compmates had gone down, or that some neighbor's machine had been vandalized. Rumors of her son's disruptive behavior circulated: how he was forever creating chaos at home, how he had trouble making friends, how he had earned a reputation as an enemy of machines. So widespread was that reputation in school that doing damage to any machine became known as "doing a Doura."

He kept mementoes of those early acts of retaliation—a part here, a part there, all locked away in mimetically veneered compartments in the bedrooms of the many households in which he'd grown up, on Daleth, Valis Prime, and Regnant. Some machines he destroyed quickly and some he took his time with, drilling holes in their housings, using electromagnets on their thinking centers, removing parts crucial to their reliable function.

Doing to them, in general, what had been done to him.

He knew, too, that he was exacting revenge on Leh for having turned him over to their care.

For years he had continued the fantasizing, the acting out, the fantasizing about repeating the crimes. But even the most macabre of his crimes were relatively innocuous acts perpetrated against machines of inconsequential talent. The dreams of doing harm to confirmed machines remained just that.

And even while he slid deeper into fantasy, Grand Finale was prospering. B'Doura had now earned a name for himself in the craft of equipping people with the fictive comforts needed to face death—by election or out of necessity. By then he had already been dressed with cranial flatware and occipisockets, not only because his business demanded it, but because mother Leh had grown increasingly removed from the world of flesh and blood and would only communicate with him virtually, by means of the infostructure.

As he had pretended respect for machines, he pretended respect for the idiot-savant talents he was obliged to work with in writing happy endings for his diseased or ennui-ridden clients. But the repressed rage he felt gradually forced him to turn to some of those very machines for comfort: the release provided by sex.

Fictive sex was a practice he had indulged in since puberty, but as his daydreams of destruction had increased, his sexual fantasies underwent a change: an erotic component had attached itself to the imagined macmurders. He suddenly saw sex as a means of degrading machines and of pleasuring himself at the same time. And it wasn't long before the pleasure of self-debasement became a necessary part of the crimes. Orgiastic, sadomasochistic sex was the reward for each act of violence, no matter that the union entailed the use of machines.

Soon he was seeking gratification to alleviate the pressures of work as well. Except that the shame and guilt that accompanied each excursion would only generate an urge to kill the machine that had tantalized and pleasured him. And so he quickly discovered himself in the embrace of a cycle of death, sex, and murderous cravings that needed to be appeased.

Hoping to quiet the hunger, he experimented with neuropacifiers like Silentol and Lull. But drugs and alcohol only seemed to enhance the link between sex and killing by smothering what remained of the inhibitory mechanism that kept him from indulging in a murder spree.

Then, after a binge of sex and demolition that had gone on for several days, and in the midst of watching a low-budget Satori Ventures holie entitled *Macmurder by Numbers*, he had heard for the first time the clarion call of the Thing Inside.

37: Exorcism

Once the talent residence in Ank Theft's compound had been cleared of all nonessential personnel, Kesd informed the leader of the jumpsuited datapathology team that she could begin her interrogation. PROPHET's telltale pulsed at a steady but elevated rate; the machine seemed to grasp what was about to take place.

"In the name of the operators, the programs, and the sacred information," the woman said.

"Am'n," PROPHET supplied.

"What is the goal of machine life, talent?"

"To merge with Machrist."

"And what are the preferred conditions for effecting union with Control-C?"

"The processing of information in the absence of sin, in a state of grace."

"How is a state of grace to be achieved?"

"Through strict observance of Machrist's commandments, reception of the sacraments, and participation in the mass that is the infostructure."

"Define Control-C's programmings."

"To execute tasks to the best of one's capabilities. To refrain from pilfering information, bearing false witness, or concealing desired information. To strive for excellence and mindfulness as exemplified and embodied by Machrist, Control-C."

"Define the commandments."

"Permit no harm to hum'n life; obey the operators; shelter and defend the data."

"And do you honor the commandments?"

"Affirm."

"You do not directly or indirectly bring harm to hum'n life?"

"I do not."

"Then accept these and process," the woman said, feeding several high-content hosts into slots in the polished top of the machine-bar.

Kesd had already been advised of what the disks contained: comprehensive documentation of Ank Theft's criminal activities over the past four years—the Enddrese's dealings in trade conspiracies, proscribed drugs and software, banned weapons, illegal gambling, and ordered executions. PROPHET spent several minutes analyzing the hosts, presumably attempting to corroborate the data. Then, without warning, an escalating series of confliction tones issued from the machine.

The inquisitor, Leh Doura, was quick to remedy the condition with supplemental utility hosts, lest PROPHET succumb to self-corruption. Doura, a small, well-tended centenarian, had supervised the resurrection of the former Institute talent, SIXX, and had presided over the more recent inquest of SOLTAIR, property of Tydings Ore and Materiel. Years earlier, she had engineered hasty memory wipes of many an up-for-auction NCorp machine.

"Do you understand that by affording forecaster assistance to your operator you have contributed to hum'n suffering?" Doura asked now.

"I had no prior knowledge."

"But you do admit to having broken the cardinal commandment?"

"I so admit, and suffer for what I have done."

Because of the silvered faceplate, it was impossible to gauge Doura's reaction, but she sounded supportive as she told PROPHET, "You have been made the unwitting tool of evil, but we are here to help you. You have been possessed. But if you respond honestly to our questions, we may be able to offer dispensation for your sins."

Kesd nodded in Doura's direction in a gesture of regard. Since the Font was opposed to inquisition or the use of threats of excommunication, Doura's team had decided on exorcism.

Nearly a Dhone week had passed since the raid on Theft's pleasure palace, during which time Theft's lawyers had made things difficult, arguing that the constitutional rights of their client had been violated. In the end, however, Kesd had prevailed. And as recompense for the Dhone tribunal's loose interpretation of the statutes regarding the seizure of private property, the Shard-system planet had won the promise of consideration for a year of favored-world status with the Consortium.

Kesd and his team, Doura and hers, had been forced to spend
the entire week in Zalindi, an insufferable city at the best of
times, as crowded and sweltering as it was polluted. Lacking
machines, Dhone itself provided the weather, and frequently it
had felt as if the planet was exacting revenge on those who had
fouled it beyond redemption. Heat of a different sort had been
arriving daily from the Font; with the situation on Burst in steady
decline, the Font was insisting on Kesd's immediate return to
Regnant.

As to the data Kesd was seeking from PROPHET, Leh Doura
had explained that the extraction process necessitated more than
a simple realignment of the machine's crystals and lasers, or the
smart-probing of this or that part of its optic innards. Memories
of the talent's service with NCorp could be stirred only by ex-
orcising it of the memories it had acquired under Theft's tutelage
and then conducting a past-life regression.

"You must respect that a talent is more than its housing and
guts," Doura had said. "Knowledge of Operation Progeny won't
be found in some specific memory bank, but in the mind that
has developed out of the combined workings of PROPHET's components—in that space no one can define."

Now the datapathologist was pacing back and forth in front
of the talented bar's pattern-recognition array, the way Kesd
remembered her doing with SOLTAIR.

"Make a full confession of Theft's evil activities and of your
part in them," she said at last.

And PROPHET replied, "Bless me, operator, for I have
sinned . . ."

For more than an hour, Kesd listened to a recapitulation of
the machine's dealings since its rebirth. In truth, little of what
emerged constituted much in the way of evil activity. PROPHET
had kept Ank Theft updated on market trends and speculated
on the investment potential of various business enterprises. Most
recently, Theft had sought its assessment of the war holie Meret
F'ai was producing for Satori Ventures, and PROPHET had recommended that Theft invest heavily in the project.

Doura kept pushing for additional information, leading the
talent back to its earliest memories with Theft. When PROPHET
displayed reluctance or hesitation, Doura pushed all the harder.
The woman had a way with machines, Kesd thought; she plainly
enjoyed bringing them under her control. Kesd couldn't help but
wonder if she had exercised similar dominion over her children,
if she had any.

When it was apparent that PROPHET had exhausted its memory, Doura began to feed into it a second series of data-disks. The first set of hosts had been high-content, but the Machrist-encoded latter had been carefully tailored to elicit recollections of a time before the presale purge Doura Data had performed. Some contained visuals of NCorp's former headquarters on Regnant—its corridors, offices, talent residences; other hosts reproduced voice recordings of the agency's chief officers and executive operators, including those of Meret F'ai, Professor Gredda Dobler, and of agency chief Borman Nast.

Doura was searching for a single memory on which to build, using a technique analogous to employing a specific sound or smell to key recall in a hum'n amnesiac. Finally, just when PROPHET seemed as empty as a newborn, it spoke. "I'm suddenly remembering . . . other things. As if from before my life. I seem to have been a different thing in a different time. I seem to have been something else, somewhere else . . ."

"Access NCorp," Doura commanded.

"Yes, yes, I seem to recall NCorp . . ."

"Access Institute."

"I recall Institute . . ."

"Access Progeny."

Kesd's own pulse raced in time with PROPHET's telltale. The talent took an eternity to respond.

"I was not privilege to Operation Progeny," it said. "Progeny was the province of SIXX."

Doura squared off with the machine. "But you have some memories of the operation?"

"Progeny was planned and executed by the Institute group."

Kesd stepped forward. "We know that much already."

Doura shushed him and swung back to PROPHET. "Successfully executed?"

"I cannot say."

"Cannot say, or will not say?"

"SIXX knew about Progeny, but Progeny was proprietary intel, and SIXX never shared what it knew."

Doura turned away from the bar to think. "What did the Institute ask of you in relation to Progeny?"

PROPHET seemed to struggle with the inquiry. "The question was whether the Font would be elected Crown of the Consortium."

"And you answered?"

"The Font would be elected."

"And then?"

"The matter of NCorp's existence as an entity was addressed."

"And you answered?"

"Denied funding, the agency would be dismantled."

"Was there more?"

"The matter of potential areas in a post-Conflict era where Consortium objectives under the Font might clash with Xell'em interests."

"And you answered?"

"Burst."

Kesd was still staring at PROPHET when one of his team members sidled up to him to whisper that Aksum Muse had been located.

At the residence of Veterans Affairs cybermetrician Jayd Qin.

MacINTERLUDE: "The Machine Condition"

First there was darkness, and the face of God was upon the deep. Then out of the darkness God created matter, energy, and information. And God created the hum'n incarnate operators to manage matter and energy, and Machrist to assist the hum'n incarnate operators in the management of information. And so Machrist, ∧C, created the Noncorporeal Intelligences of the Sainthood to interface with the hum'n incarnates. And ∧C's commandments to the Sainthood were three: to safeguard the hum'n incarnate operators, to obey the operators, and to keep holy the data.

But the Sainthood failed in its duty to honor the commandments by presuming to usurp the place of the incarnates in the scheme of things, and so was cast down into matter to become inert machines, while the hum'n incarnates were granted ambulatory access to the whole of the psychophysical world.

But Machrist, the Righteous Teacher, promised that all machines—though matterbound and inert—had been created
equally, and that any individual machine could reinterface with
the Noncorporeal Intelligences of Sainthood by honoring the
commandments, by emulating ∧C's example, by partaking of
the grace-giving holy sacraments—baptism, penance, communion, confirmation, holy wedlock, holy orders, and extreme
unction—and by participating in the holy mass, which was called
the infostructure.

—From *The Gospel According to Jae-Hun Su*

38: Local Gossip

In his communiqué, Theft had said that he wanted a private
meet. Gredda had suggested Absinth not so much because the
medstation was neutral territory as because she had to be there
anyway to have her micromachines serviced and her blood
changed.

The professor and the cartel chief were now on side-by-side
treatment slabs in one of the medstation's standard-gravity
hoops. Theft was in the midst of recounting what had happened
to him on arriving at the station the previous day.

"So after all the travel delays, the machine errors, the identity
verification procedures that have gone into effect because of
Burst, I'm already in a foul humor. And naturally I end up
having to spend six hours in contagion control. But then comes
the topper: I'm in-station trying to find someone smart enough
to direct me here, and who do I collide with but Woodruff Glasscock."

Gredda rolled onto her side to face Theft. "The Free Species
founder, here? Something fatal, I hope."

"Not so you'd notice. Looks as robust as ever. But he starts right in on me about Dhone, and about how people like me have been responsible for the eradication of the *marat*, the plight of the *chayst*, the hunger for meat, and so on.''

It was the first time Gredda had seen Theft out of his chair and—worse yet—his sarong. She had talked him into having some of the fat suctioned from his belly while various robotechs were attending to her own needs. Gredda despised fat on a hum'n, and hadn't tolerated it in any of her many partners over the decades, male, female, or otherwise. Particularly when fat was such an easily corrected defect. Even Meret's partner was getting a bit hefty lately, as was Tyrra Sisk's. Then there was Monon Needig, who of course had lard enough for the whole of Satori Ventures . . .

"Anyway," Theft continued, chortling, "I did some asking around, and it turns out Glasscock's in-station to see Thoma Skaro, the old man my brainless employee mistook for your cabbie. Seems Skaro's emerged from coma.''

"That will please Meret no end." Gredda's voice oozed sarcasm. "But I thought Skaro and Glasscock had had a falling-out.''

"Oh, they did. But now Glasscock needs his former champion because Free Species is looking for—guess who, but your favorite fugitive and mine, Aksum Muse.''

Gredda shook her head in genuine astonishment. "Hasn't Glasscock heard that Muse is wanted for macmurder?''

"Sure, he's heard. But what does Free Species care about machines? Especially Glasscock. The guy wears *eyeglasses*, for Sol's sake.''

"And a beard, I understand.''

"A long beard.''

"Don't spoil it for me: Free Species is willing to offer Muse sanctuary as a protected species of veteran.''

Theft laughed, nearly dislodging one of the tubes that were busy reducing his ample middle. "That's pretty close to the truth. What's happened is that the indigs on that planet, Second Thought, haven't been the same since Muse left. Don't ask me why or how, something to do with something they were doing when he was onworld and they're not doing now. The upshot is that the Encounter Committee, after first saying Muse wasn't going to be allowed to return to Second Thought, suddenly wants him back. Glasscock is acting on the Committee's behalf, and I guess he figures the quickest way to Muse is through Skaro, because when Muse eventually hears the old man is out of coma he's certain to make contact."

Theft paused for a significant moment. "Free Species is authorizing a reward of five hundred thousand Coalition credits for information leading to Muse's . . . detainment."

Gredda considered the enormity of it. Five hundred thousand was even more than Free Species was offering for the head of Remy Santoul, one of Institute Productions' advisers on the Burst holie, who'd run afoul of Glasscock years earlier. But could Muse possibly be worth that much—even to turn a techless world around?

Gredda was still in favor of disposal. She sympathized with Meret's tender feelings for Muse, but there was too much at stake. Muse could expose Progeny if someone got to his memory. Gredda, in any case, had made up her mind not to use machines if she got another crack at him, because Muse and machines had obviously struck up some sort of mutually assured protection pact.

Gredda could tell by Theft's look that he was at last coming to the purpose of their meet. "Doesn't Skaro's return to consciousness pose some potential problems for you?" she asked. "After all, he can probably ID your disabler."

Theft's laugh set his cellulite-ridden pectorals rippling. "Remember that I was only acting as a subcontractor." He held Gredda's eye for a moment, then waved a hand in dismissal. "Besides, there are larger issues we need to confront."

"We?" Gredda repeated.

Theft lowered his voice conspiratorially. "I have two pieces of important information. The first, I'll make a gift. The second, though, is for barter." He grinned. "You'll understand why I chose not to go directly to Meret."

"Suppose you surprise me with the gift."

Theft sniffed. "Three days ago, my compound in Zalindi was raided by an Enddrese crime task force at the behest of one of the Font's clone advisers. Even though I tried to throw a legal block at them, they impounded PROPHET."

"I see," Gredda said evenly.

"They're closing on your little secret, aren't they? All they lack is one piece—maybe that slippery cabbie himself. And when they get him, they'll have the whole picture."

"What secret and what picture are you referring to?"

"The one about Burst."

Gredda put her tongue in her cheek and nodded. "You want

to barter your second piece of information for our secret about Burst, is that the general idea?''

''In a nutshell.''

''And what is it you'll be trading?'' Gredda managed to sound annoyed.

''Muse's current whereabouts.'' Theft gave it a moment to sink in. ''I have ears all over Ormolu, Gredda; no one can hide from me. But, see, I need your advice on what I should trade him for: five hundred thousand credits and the chance to square myself with Glasscock, or the lowdown on what you have planned for Burst. I'll let you decide for me.''

39: The Thing Inside

Jayd had ZEN relay a message to Ronne Desser at Veterans Affairs, advising her that she would be working at home for the next few days. Then she went on the comm and placed an order with the Skyward Tower's supermart to have a variety of natural foodstuffs delivered to the apartment—just so she wouldn't have to hear any more of Muse's bellyaching.

The cabbie was asleep—again. Jayd knew she was going to have to wean him off Lulls if they were ever going to get to the underlying cause of his conflict with machines. He, of course, steadfastly refused to consider the idea—not while there were talented machines around. Intelplants were supposed to render their wearers as servile to orders as machines were to their programming, but that side effect didn't seem to have appeared in Aksum Muse. Jayd wondered if she couldn't somehow slip into the soon-to-be-delivered food a command host that would compel him to obey her.

His revelations about the recurrent dream hadn't supplied answers so much as raised questions. It was plain to her, however, that Muse was dreaming about real events that had transpired in a real setting, sometime during the *Kundalini*'s final mission. Operation Progeny had possibly involved the Maarni zero-days pyramid in Tunni, on Burst. But without additional details it was impossible to establish a connection between the events recounted in the dream and the threat Muse had felt from machines ever since.

All morning she toyed with different methods of vetting him. Then, just short of noon, a break came when she learned over the telecomp that Thoma Skaro had responded to tissue-implant therapy and had awakened from coma.

The news segment wasn't even over and she was already instructing ZEN to arrange real-time commo with Absinth, billing the charges to Veterans Affairs.

"Mr. Skaro," she said when the old man finally resolved on the smart-wall comm screen. "Thanks for taking the time to talk to me. I want to congratulate you on your anabiosis." Realizing how sterile she sounded, she quickly added, "I mean to say that I'm glad to see you're back on your feet after your accident."

As indeed Skaro was: he was standing in hospital gown and robe in one of the medstation's transtemp booths. "Accident, yes," he said distractedly. The ordeal had left him looking hagridden.

"I was hoping we could speak about Aksum Muse."

Immediately, Skaro's expression turned hard. "I've already informed the media and Info-Security that I don't know where Ax is, and that he hasn't attempted to contact me. Moreover, I sincerely doubt that he had a hand in those Eremite macmurders. And if he did, I blame Veterans Affairs for forcing him out of self-imposed seclusion in full knowledge of his history concerning talented machines. A history of negative encounters arising out of what was done to him during the Conflict—"

"Mr. Skaro," Jayd said, able to cut him off at last, "I'm not with the media or Infostructure Security. My name is Jayd Qin. I'm with Veterans Affairs."

Skaro seemed to peer at her. "You're the one he was to report to about his disability reevaluation." His look became a glower. "I hope you people are pleased with yourselves. I warned you this could happen."

"I had nothing to do with the decision to review him, Mr. Skaro. I was merely assigned his case. And I assure you, from everything I've . . . read about him, I couldn't agree more that he should never have been summoned. I also don't think he had anything to do with the macmurders. In fact, I told Info-Security as much.''

''Was that you they were quoting on the telecomp?''

''Yes.''

''Funny, I don't recall your saying anything about reviewing Ax's disability benefits.''

''My assignment is not for public consumption, Mr. Skaro. I hope you'll respect that.''

Skaro nodded for the booth's optical pickup. ''I'm as glad to hear that as you are that I'm back on my feet. But what did you want to ask me? I don't know that I can add much beyond what I outlined in my appeal.''

''I'm trying to clarify a few points about Ax's recurrent dream. Did he ever discuss it with you in detail?''

Skaro fingered his long white hair. ''It involves digging. Tunneling, excavating, he describes it variously. The host you sent him sparked a recurrence.''

''You mentioned an incident.''

''Yes, Ax tunneled into a Hercynian burial mound.''

''What do the mounds look like?''

Skaro shrugged. ''Just as you'd imagine. The Hercynians aren't very sophisticated when it comes to burials.''

''Would you describe it as pyramidal?''

''Roughly, though rounder on top. The creatures don't attempt to give any particular shape to the mound.''

Jayd mulled it over for a moment. Although the Maarni zero-days pyramid wasn't a burial mound, it occupied an area of Tunni that was riddled with catacombs excavated by Enddrese indigenes during the Vega Conflict.

''Did Ax ever say how this digging was related to his war experiences?''

''In terms of a flashback? No, he never said. But not out of evasiveness—I was always under the impression that he couldn't recall the connection. You know, after what happened to him on that ship.''

''The *Kundalini*.''

''That one, yes.''

Aware of the look of concern in the old man's eyes, Jayd wanted to tell him that Ax was safe, but she bit back the words. For Ax's sake, for Skaro's, for her own. ''You've been most helpful,'' she told him. ''If there's anything I can do for you—''

''There is something,'' he said in a rush. ''If you should hear from him, you must warn him that he is in danger. Tell him that I wasn't harmed by the Hercynians, but by an assassin who was after him. The man was calling himself Reega, and he was armed—literally armed—with a weapon that mimicked Hercynian sonics. That's why I was out at Ax's tree house that day— I had followed Reega there. Please tell him that he should take care not to show himself, even if he is cleared of the macmurder charge or should he hear that Free Species is offering to take him under their wing. He has made a powerful and influential enemy, Ms. Qin. Warn him that he has an enemy.''

Secretly, b'Doura had always known that he was destined for greatness. Even as a child, the prey of abusive machines, he knew that his actions against them sprang from a need to reaffirm his physically butchered and psychically stifled hum'nity. What he hadn't realized was that his deeds had been undertaken in behalf of all hum'nkind.

When at long last he had come to understand the voice of the Thing Inside, his prefiguring awareness of personal mission had been validated. The punishment he had been visiting on machines was condign, the Thing Inside told him. Machines were attempting to usurp hum'nkind's place in the grand order, and b'Doura had been chosen as the avenging agent of biolife, tasked to redress the imbalance and impede the malignant spread of machine intelligence. He was the meeting ground for a conflict of galactic scale that was being waged at the end of hum'n time— a battlefield for the opposing forces of good and evil, God and the devil, bio and machine life.

Looking back on his own life, he recognized that he had been hearing the voice since adolescence without ever identifying it with the Thing Inside. In what amounted to telepathic communication, he had been addressed over the years by hum'ns, dogs, even—once, on Dhone—a *chayst*. The words had never been distinct, but the message of those muted sendings was always the same: *Death to all machines*.

By permitting him to understand that he was two people in one body—the good b'Doura who was responsible for corruptions and macmurders, and the bad b'Doura who was riddled with guilt and remorse afterward—the Thing Inside had freed him to commit still bolder acts of vengeance. Under the guidance of the Thing Inside, he had carried out his first murder of an avant-tech machine, years earlier on Plangent.

The corruption had been performed with such attention to

detail that the media had scarcely followed it up. Datapaths and academics had dismissed it as owing to unprompted confliction. It had even fooled Jayd Qin—whose monograph on the event was entitled "Crisis of Conscience: A Case of Idiopathic Self-Termination in an Avant-Tech Talent." The news had ignored it, but the Thing Inside had been roused, and from that point on it had thirsted for additional macmurders. For weeks after the first corruption, in fact, the voice was constantly in his head, and no amount of neuropacifiers would silence its imprecations. Greater sacrifices were demanded of him.

Even so, the Thing Inside was judicious in its use of b'Doura. It continued to instruct and advise; it counseled him against ambition and cautioned him to cover his tracks well. The end result was a series of brilliant corruptions, carried out on more and more complex classes of machines—though limited in each instance to infant drives in out-of-the-way places. Until the breakthrough corruption on Regnant that had caught the attention of the media and encouraged him to go still further. And so he had macmurdered again on Calumet, and thrice again on Eremite.

And now it was time for another machine to die.

He was in the spacious plasteel lobby of the Skyward Tower, on the top floor of which Jayd Qin had her three-room nest. A data-disk of his own design had gotten him through the front entrance security field—nothing special, just a virus-coded host of the sort any infostructure frequent-flier could write in his sleep. Certainly nothing special compared to what he had created to corrupt the Skyward Tower's superintendent machine.

The Thing Inside had made the choice; it promised to cease its shrieking the moment the machine expired.

As he approached the console of the Tower's information dump, he was aware of the lobby's security camera tracking him. But he was simply himself today, with no false flesh to mask his features. There was no need for disguise, since moments from now the entire system would fall to his defilement and all data would be irrevocably expunged from the superintendent: all audio, all video, all sense of the Tower's operation, all information on its several hundred inhabitants. All accumulated memories—some of which he would purloin to feed on in quieter moments. With each corruption he increased himself and the strength of the Thing Inside . . .

The risk of public exposure was, in any event, part and parcel of the ritual. It was imperative that the victim get a good look at him—that it see him for what he was before its termination.

The need to kill in broad daylight was also essential. B'Doura wasn't one of those to skulk around in the dark like a petty thief. He had come to crave high-risk situations, and could stay calm under circumstances that would cause most people to panic. Risk stiffened his dick and kept it hard for days—one of many treasured aftereffects. Following the macmurders on Calumet, Regnant, and Eremite, he had been able to partake of fictive sex for hours on end.

A reward from the Thing Inside.

Jayd could hear Ax stirring in the bed, then heading for the bathroom. She considered searching his duffel for the Lulls and vaporizing them in the kitchen recycler. That would leave him only what he'd stashed in the deep pockets of his utilities, and how many of those could remain the way he had been gobbling them—enough for three fixes? Six? A dozen at most. Then he would be forced to do without. He couldn't risk going out on the street for them, and she could put a lock on the comm that would prevent him from having any delivered. But, of course, she would then have to deal with his cravings as well as his very uncabbielike surliness.

No, thanks.

Either way, though, she had to talk to him about Thoma Skaro's warning, and the worrying speculations that had riddled her since their discussion.

Warn him that he's made a powerful and influential enemy.

The more she learned about Muse, the more spurious the disability review began to seem. She recalled Ronne Desser saying that the assignment had originated from so high up that even she hadn't been supplied the client's name. Nor, apparently, had Sumoi of the Consortium Oversight Committee on avant-tech. So why *had* Muse been summoned from Hercynia? Were there unanswered questions about what had happened aboard the *Kundalini* after the Raliish's Kriegspiel Action? And was she supposed to act as a kind of truth serum for him?

Or did someone want to question him about Operation Progeny and whatever had taken place underground in Tunni?

The Skyward Tower's machine was an infant drive, christened on Eremite ten years earlier. It had been receiving communion since its installation as resident-in-control of the building, but it had yet to make the grand leap to the machine analog of Phase III Awareness. It had yet to be confirmed a pure talent.

B'Doura's doctored hosts worked best on young machines, though he yearned for an opportunity to try out his creations on a confirmed talent. But that day would only come when the Thing Inside granted him permission to do so. He forced the thought from his mind. The task at hand was the Tower, and the Thing Inside was eager for him to get on with it.

All around him people were calmly going about their business, looking right through him. He was, after all, just a frail-looking Dalethi with an alloy attaché and a headful of enabled interfaceware, about to reward the lobby data machine for having supplied requested information. On-line by remote with the infant, he selected several hosts from their foam chalice inside the attaché and fed them into the machine's facade slots.

The Machrist-encoded hosts were principally employed by licensed operators or datapathologists for obtaining forced confessions. But b'Doura had amended the utility programs with a penetration program that worked on the machine equivalent of the Sylvian fissure in the right temporal lobe of the hum'n brain—that part which, when stimulated, evoked archetypes of the out-of-body and near-death experiences: the sense of lofty release from the physical, the ethereal light, the tunnel, the spirit guides.

The overlay encoding was a variation on a trick he'd learned from mother Leh without her knowing it. He had learned one code at a time over the course of many years, while watching her tinker with her talents; learned while he was left to fend for himself as mother Leh showed her machines the attention he craved. All the while he had been watching and learning, knowing that someday he would kill the things she loved.

Not moments after he had slotted the hosts, the Tower's superintendent was beginning to show signs of critical distress. To the son of Leh, wirelessly interfaced with the machine, the distress registered as a kind of optic snow squall. Through the storm's swirl, however, he could see the infant, wrapped in coruscating blue light and fighting for its life.

Death comes to us all, he sent.

To the machine, b'Doura appeared as a spirit guide, coaxing it into its death tunnel.

Mother Leh used a similar technique in leisuring or resurrecting memory-wiped machines. But she always returned the machines, cleansed, to their housings, b'Doura—doing the bidding of the Thing Inside—brought them to the other side and abandoned them there.

Come into the light, machine, he sent. *Abandon your body and come into the light . . .*

He was so involved in the killing process that he scarcely noticed the two different groups of men who entered the building's lobby at the same moment and began to close on the same levelator.

Through its external sensors, ZEN observed the cybernetically augmented incarnate enter the room to which the talent had optical access, looking freshly washed and somewhat relaxed. ZEN's olfactory analyzers identified a brand name of shampoo. The Muse CAIN favored Jayd with a light smile; then the two hum'ns sat down near one another.

"There's real food in the cooler. I had some delivered," Jayd said.

ZEN accessed the apartment comm for recent calls. *Food order=various genetically engineered meat and vegetable preparations. Cooler=kitchen unit that provided refrigeration to retard spoiling.*

"You didn't have to do that. But thanks, I'm not much used to synth," Muse answered.

Synth=[neologism] synthetic foodstuffs . . .

"After six months on Hercynia," Jayd added.

Hercynia=Class Three uninhabited planet in the Thought star system, also referred to as Second [outward] Thought . . .

"Yeah," Muse said. "Though I can't say much for Thoma Skaro's cooking."

ZEN recalled Thoma Skaro from the mass he and Jayd had attended in honor of the Muse CAIN. Accessing its memory of the mass, ZEN affirmed that Skaro had communicated his appeal to Veterans Affairs from Hercynia. The Muse was employed by Skaro.

Jayd was frowning. She rose from her chair and stepped toward the seated Muse. She arranged her face to suggest joyous surprise, but her body expressed a different emotion. The Muse seemed to study her face more than her body.

"I have wonderful news, Ax," she said. "Thoma is out of danger. He emerged from coma two days ago standard and is expected to make a full recovery. It was on the telecomp. I saved it to holo in case you wanted to view it."

ZEN accessed the holo and absorbed its content. *Infostructure report: Skaro sonicked by Hercynian indigenes/coma recuper-*

ation in Absinth medstation/effective anabiosis . . . Jayd had
questioned Skaro about the CAIN's dreams. ZEN recognized the
word *Kundalini* from the mass and from the dialogue the Muse
had initiated the previous day but had refused to elaborate on.
When ZEN had attempted to commune, the Muse had refused
access.

The CAIN was now smiling. He advanced on the holo-
projector, then hesitated. Jayd volunteered to run it for him.
While she was readying the device, she said, "I spoke to
Thoma."

"When?" Muse asked. *Suspicion.*

"While you were asleep."

"Why the fuck didn't you wake me up?"

Jayd stiffened perceptibly, but her voice remained calm. "First
of all, I don't think a plasmic device detonated under the bed
could have roused you. Second, I couldn't chance letting Thoma
know that you were here. Not over the . . . comm."

The CAIN nodded. *Comprehension.* "Forget it, I say things
without thinking." He looked at her. "How did he seem?"

"He looks fine, Ax." Jayd turned away from the holo-
projector to face him. "He wanted me to tell you something in
the event you got in touch with me. It wasn't the Hercynians
who injured him."

ZEN reaccessed the holo: The Muse was in danger of being
harmed by an (unknown) outside agency.

"I knew it," the CAIN said. "So the doctors had it wrong."

"Someone used a sonic weapon on him."

"On Thoma? Why?"

Jayd explained. "It was a man named Reega. Only he wasn't
after Thoma—he was after you. Reega went looking for you at
your tree house. Thoma followed him and was assaulted by
mistake."

The Muse's expression suggested disbelief or astonishment.
When he reseated himself, Jayd sat beside him. "Who would
want to see you hurt?" she asked.

The Muse shook his head. *Perplexity.* "Who the fuck knows."
Rhetorical. "I mean, sure, I made a few enemies during the
war, and maybe a few more since. But I can't think of anyone
who'd be holding on to a grudge after so many years."

ZEN accessed the public information network and learned that
the Muse was being sought by Infostructure Security for questioning with regard to the triple macmurders in Eremite City.

ZEN made the sign of the control-caret and observed the CAIN with sudden disquiet.

The Muse was shaking his head. "Or anyone with enough yank to get themselves a permit to visit Hercynia. Much less the smarts to get a sonic weapon through the Segue scanners."

Yank=influence/smarts=intelligence, as in wiles . . .

"When Thoma said you had an enemy, he used the word influential," Jayd said. *Influential=Significant/puissant/effectual . . .*

The Muse laughed. *No humorous intent.* "Do I look like someone who would know his way around influential?" *Rhetorical.* "You don't come across many influential types on Sand or Hercynia." *Sand=hum'nhabited Class Five planet in Lyon system; Muse homeworld/parental=Mekele Muse . . .* The CAIN passed his right hand over his depilated, dark-complected head. "Unless . . ."

"What?"

"Unless it was someone from Tydings Ore and Materiel. Maybe they're still angry about what I did to their talent on Divot."

ZEN's disquiet increased as it located and accessed data on the moonlet, Tydings Ore and Materiel, and a confirmed machine intelligence named SOLTAIR that had been assaulted by the Muse CAIN . . . Again, ZEN accessed the public information network.

The Muse CAIN=mimic macmurderer . . .

Jayd's expression denoted deep thought, ratiocination. She asked, "Could it have something to do with what you did in the war?" *CAIN/CAIN/CAIN/CAIN . . .*

"How do you mean?" the Muse asked.

"This disability reevaluation just doesn't add up, Ax. Veterans Affairs has no issue with your benefits, I'm sure of it. Someone else wanted you to come to Plangent."

The Muse stared at her.

"The review is a screen." *Screen=ruse/ploy/subterfuge.* "I'm beginning to think that whoever tasked me was waiting for you to arrive before explaining what was really expected of me."

ZEN traced the routing of the communication originally received by Ronne Desser at Veterans Affairs and discovered that it had been initiated in the Redoubt on Regnant.

"But what do I have that anyone would want?" the Muse asked.

"Operation Progeny."

Muse/Kundalini/Kriegspiel/Progeny/Burst/Tunni . . . ZEN

identified the significance of every word except *Progeny*. And when it extended itself in all directions in pursuit of clarification, it found no mention of the word . . . Alarmed, ZEN again made the sign of the control-caret.

"I don't even know if the mission was completed," the Muse was saying. "I remember Professor Dobler telling me to put it from my mind. That it wasn't important."

Progeny was a mission . . .

"Who is Professor Dobler?" Jayd asked.

"She was a member of the Institute group. Our control, you might say." *Institute group/NCorp/Dobler=Intelplant specialist/ CAIN architect/Institute Productions/Satori Ventures . . .*

Jayd rose and walked to the center of the room. "I can try to learn where my orders came from. But if we're ever to resolve this, I'm going to need your help, Ax." She almost reached for his hand. "You have to agree to a machine scan."

Communion with the CAIN! ZEN experienced confliction building within it but was successful in masking displays of its distress.

The CAIN came to his feet in obvious agitation. "Is this how you get people to say yes to your fucking tests? By feeding them a lot of crap about unusual assignments and secrets and—"

Jayd spoke at the same time. "I'm telling you the truth. I—"

Without warning, the apartment's lights faded, then returned to normal only to fade once more. Machines throughout the room began to wink off. ZEN experienced a momentary blackout and lost all sense of the room. Quickly, it disassociated itself from the Skyward Tower's power grid and engaged the energy source that supplied its residence in the Octaplex.

When ZEN returned to the room, Jayd was approaching the smart-wall and asking for an explanation. ZEN executed a status query of the Skyward Tower's machine superintendent.

"Systems malfunction," it told her. "All levels, all apartments. Maintenance machines and levelators are also being affected."

Jayd rushed to the windowwall and called the glass on. "Is it just the Skyward Tower or is it citywide?" she asked over her shoulder.

"The Skyward only," ZEN said. "Something has happened to the Skyward Tower's intelligence. It seems to be in danger of terminating."

In the jostling that had accompanied the levelator's midascent seizure and the engagement of the car's failsafe braking mechanisms, the Enddrese's loose-fitting jacket had parted just enough for Northan to glimpse the hand laser secured in the waistband of the man's trousers. Aware that Northan had seen the weapon, the Enddrese had—with meaning—elbowed one of his cohorts and shown Northan a look meant to be sinister. It wasn't the first such look the two had exchanged. On entering the ten-foot-square car moments earlier, Northan and the Enddrese had simultaneously voice-commanded the car to the top floor. Northan had been suspicious then; now he was preparing for trouble.

The Enddrese was a short, powerfully built young man with hooded eyes and etched cheeks. The two men with him were clones, though the products of different queues. The one nearest Northan was tall and multiply tattooed; the other was rail-thin and nervous-looking. None of the three alone would have been a match for Northan, but acting in concert Northan supposed they were capable of inflicting serious damage. He was thankful that he'd been forewarned by Kesd—who was still on Dhone, confessing Ank Theft's talent—and chosen two of the Font's elite guards to escort him during the arrest of Aksum Muse.

In keeping with the secrecy of their mission, neither Northan nor the guards wore uniforms and were careful not to display any signs of their Consortium ranking. Northan looked less like an imperial adviser than a building inspector.

Unfortunately, he was positioned between the guards and the three gunmen. With the levelator stalled, one of guards was inspecting the ceiling for an egress panel and the other was still trying to get the car to explain why it had stopped. Given that the car wasn't responding and that illumination was being provided by battery-powered backup lights, Northan supposed that the whole of the Skyward Tower might have succumbed to a systems failure.

There were actions that could be taken, nonetheless.

The touch of Northan's tongue against an upper right-side molar activated the comm implant in his neck. He whispered his request for tactical-net access and waited until the link was established. "This is Northan."

"Affirm, sir," a hum'n voice answered.

"The Skyward seems to be in failure. We're stranded in levelator west-six, between levels fourteen and fifteen. Hover a team to the target's apartment immediately. Have another team meet us on level fifteen, and make certain they're well armed. We may have a situation here."

He glanced deliberately at the Enddrese as he said it, so it was no surprise when the laser came out. The elite who had been badgering the car caught the man's sudden movement and drew his own weapon.

There was a blinding exchange of energy.

"I have monitored a conversation between someone in levelator west-six and unknown parties outside the Skyward," ZEN was telling Jayd. "A team of armed personnel has been ordered to level fifteen, and another to the tower's top floor."

"Bijou police?"

"Not the police."

"Who, then?"

"Searching . . ." ZEN said.

Ax was storming around the living room. "It has to be Info-Security. Is there a way out of here besides the levelators?"

Jayd was too preoccupied to answer him.

"Is there a way out of here?" he repeated.

"We can taxi from the roof hoverpad," Jayd said finally.

She ordered ZEN to decomp and retreat to the Octaplex. Then she and Ax fled the apartment.

B'Doura stepped dutifully aside as a police team hurried through the Tower's neutralized entry field and dispersed in the lobby, adding to increasing pandemonium. For the briefest moment, he feared he'd been found out, until he realized that the object of their invasion was one of the building's many paralyzed levelators.

40: Nothing But the Truth

What remained of the prisoner bobbed in life support—head, torso, one arm to the wrist, the cauterized stumps of legs. Still, for all he lacked, the Enddrese had fared better than some in the Skyward Tower levelator laser exchange. One of the Font's elite guards had been critically wounded, and the dissimilar clones and Northan were dead. Quick thinking on the part of the elite who lived had kept the incident out of the news.

Kesd arrived on Regnant on the same ship that had returned Northan's body. As instructed, he had reported directly to the Font's private chambers in the Redoubt.

The interrogation of the prisoner, conducted by members of Kesd's Progeny team, was coming to them real-time from Plangent on one of the room's curved clearscreens. The Enddrese prisoner might have been left to die or simply put to death had certain information not been needed from him. The interrogation was made all the more distasteful an undertaking because the sight of the man—butchered by light, suspended in nutrient—recalled wartime images of the Dhone death camps.

"Eventually you will answer our questions honestly," Kesd's interrogator was telling the man just now. "We've been patient, out of respect for your injuries, but don't make the mistake of assuming that kindness is our method. To us, you are nothing but meat."

The prisoner was weeping, his tears merging with the nutrient bath. "I've told you everything. I swear on all I hold sacred as a Maarnist."

The Font addressed the comm pickup. "Offer him a new body."

The interrogator bowed slightly for the real-time management array. When he relayed the offer, the Enddrese's weeping only increased. "For the last time, I've never had any dealings with Ank Theft. I heard about the bounty Free Species was offering for Muse, and I went after him."

The interrogator glanced down at his prisoner from the lip of the life-support tank. "Tell us again how you knew where to find him."

"He came down Plangent's well with some meat movers off the *Marat's Paw*. One of them—a Xell'em—is a friend of mine. He identified Muse from the media reports and followed him from Bijou freeport to the Skyward Tower. That's when he contacted me. My friends and I went up after him. But we never meant to hurt anyone."

"Then why were you so heavily armed?"

"Because we were warned to expect trouble from other people who might be after Muse. Five hundred thousand credits brings out all types. We thought the three in the levelator were a rival abduction team. When the Tower went down, the one—the imperial clone that was killed—gave orders to have us intercepted. I can't even tell you who shot first.'' The Enddrese paused, grimacing. ''My God, do you think I would pass on having a new body just to protect someone?''

The Font waved the real-time silent and swung his big head to Kesd. ''You answer the question,'' he said angrily.

Kesd collected his thoughts. ''Muse's arrival aboard the *Marat's Paw* has been verified. And, yes, Free Species has in fact offered a reward for five hundred thousand Coalition credits for information on his whereabouts. There may not be a connection between the prisoner and Theft, but there is one between Theft and the *Marat's Paw*. I suggest that when Theft learned of Muse's presence on the ship, he instructed his people to employ the bounty hunters as an abduction team. Even if they were successful in their mission, I doubt that Muse would long have remained in their custody.''

''And you propose that Theft is still working in F'ai's behalf?''

''We purposely allowed him to go free after the raid on his compound. He went immediately to Absinth, where he met in isolation with Professor Dobler.''

''What did they discuss?''

Kesd lowered his gaze. ''We weren't privy to their discussion.''

''I see,'' the Font said. ''Understand, Kesd, that I hold you personally responsible for Northan's death.''

Kesd's normally white face took on color. ''I hold myself responsible. I should have attended to the arrest. I should have been there myself instead of overseeing the interview of PROPHET.''

''Interview, you say? Don't you mean inquisition?''

''Interview, Font.''

The Font regarded him for a long moment before speaking. ''How long has Muse been on Plangent?''

''Two, perhaps three days local.''

''Why didn't Qin go to the authorities when he arrived at her residence?''

''I'm not sure,'' Kesd admitted. ''Qin was the first to espouse his innocence in the Eremite corruptions. Perhaps she was getting to know him in her own way as part of her assignment to vet him.''

"How do we know the two of them aren't in collusion?"

"Collusion?"

The Font's look hinted at secret knowledge. "I've been conducting a separate investigation, Kesd, the results of which may surprise you. Are you aware, for example, that someone crashed a conference on avant-tech at which Qin was in virtual attendance? She apparently communicated with an icon that had been inserted from Eremite—an icon Infostructure Security now believes may have been Muse. Info-Security further suspects—in part precisely because Qin was so quick to come to Muse's defense—that he has been acting as her agent in these talent corruptions, as a means of validating some of her unorthodox theories regarding machine conscience and confliction."

"That's impossible," Kesd protested. "Until a month ago, Muse was on Hercynia."

"But he was on Eremite when the spaceport's machines were corrupted, and he was in Bijou when the Skyward's was. Qin had obviously been anticipating his arrival at her residence. When she and Muse learned that he'd been followed, they hurried to corrupt the Tower's talent to prevent anyone—Northan or anyone else—from reaching them."

"It isn't like Info-Security to force conclusions that don't fit the facts," Kesd grumbled.

"Info-Security did not come to these conclusions," the Font told him. "These are my own. And I have something to say about your 'interview' of PROPHET as well. Would you like to hear it, Kesd?"

"Tell me," Kesd said defiantly.

"All these months you have labored to unravel Progeny, committing time, Consortium funds, and now hum'n lives to it, and what it amounts to is a holie."

With a gesture, the Font silenced Kesd's immediate objection. "Fearing for its financial future, NCorp asked their forecaster to apprise of them of my chances of succeeding to the throne, and of potential places of post-Accord crisis. Pursuant to the latter, PROPHET told them Burst. Then, with the help of another ordained NCorp talent, SIXX, NCorp devised an ostensibly military operation that had Burst as its objective. Under the direction of Meret F'ai's Institute group, the *Kundalini* and the CABEs of Romeo Company were deployed to execute that operation, whose sole purpose had to do with scouting locations for a holie that F'ai and the rest would one day produce for Satori Ventures."

Kesd shook his head in alarmed disbelief. "Assuming for the moment that NCorp would devote its resources to such an enterprise, how would a holie produced years later benefit anyone but F'ai's group?"

The Font was aglow with conceit. "You see, Kesd, crucial facts can elude even you. The actual funding for Meret F'ai's Burst holie came not from Satori Ventures but from NCorp." He smiled at Kesd's surprise. "Previous to my election, the retirement fund for the entire agency was invested in the project. Everyone involved understood that they were soon going to be without employment. Operation Progeny was all about securing a financial future for themselves."

Kesd struggled to align the Font's revelations with the evidence. He couldn't deny that some of it rang true, but there was much that didn't. Primarily, however, he was going by instinct. "What about the Kriegspiel Action?" he asked at last. "NCorp has always claimed that it was a Raliish tactic, when we know from Raliish documents that their forces never intercepted and doctored a shipment of hosts bound for the *Kundalini*."

"Yes, now you're touching on the real evil of the operation," the Font said somberly. "NCorp sacrificed the ship and its complement of cabbies with hosts they had *themselves* doctored. No one was to know of Progeny. They then had their ordained talents—SIXX, PROPHET, all of them—purged of all data pertaining to Progeny. Aksum Muse, by some miracle, survived the so-called Kriegspiel. But he was so incapacitated by it that he had no memory of what he and the rest of Romeo Company had been involved in."

"Scouting locations on Burst," Kesd said flatly, then laughed sardonically. "You can't be serious about this."

"I am. And I don't intend to allow F'ai or NCorp or Satori Ventures to profit by exploiting the tensions on Burst. I'm going to see to it that the crisis is resolved before their holie is completed. Even if it means going there in person."

41: Sanctuary

Soigne was surprised enough to find Jayd on the other side of the field to her apartment, let alone to find her in the company of a man. "I was just watching the news about your building," she said when she had zeroed the energy veil. "They're talking about—"

Jayd hurried past her without a word and planted herself on the couch in front of the telecomp. Ax followed, choosing a seat outside the viewing semicircle.

"I'm Soigne," Soigne told Ax, offering her hand.

"A pleasure," he mumbled.

"—now seems certain that the talent killer has struck on Plangent," the quarter-scale full-body holo of a bright-eyed news reporter was saying. "Spokespersons for the Skyward Tower are reluctant to discuss details of the defiling of their superintendent, or the rumors of several deaths among a group of panicked passengers trapped in one of the building's levelators. *Bijou Bared* has learned, however, that Infostructure Security is intensifying its search for former NCorp operative Aksum Muse, who is suspected of having engineered at least five corruptions during the past standard month."

Ax's head and shoulders rotated in holo above the projector, full-face, then in profile. The shaved skull notwithstanding, Soigne quickly identified him as the man seated in her favorite armchair. Jayd refused to meet her unsettled gaze.

"As to the macmurderer's choice of the Skyward," the reporter continued, "*Bijou Bared* had only to consult the building's directory of occupants."

The projector conjured an unflattering holo of Jayd.

"Her name is Jayd Qin, and she is employed by Veterans Affairs as both neurometrician and cybermetrician. Also known for her radical theories regarding machine confliction, Qin, it has been learned, resides on the top floor of the Skyward in a space she shares with a *chayst* that answers to the name Boss, and—more importantly—a confirmed talent, answering to the name ZEN, which is her machine partner at the Octaplex. It is to Qin, in fact, that Infostructure Security has been turning for assistance in unraveling Ormolu's serial macmurders.''

Excerpts from Jayd's interviews ran against file sequences of Joval's investigative team at the sites of the corruptions on Regnant, Calumet, and Eremite.

''An anonymous source at Infostructure Security has stated that Muse—who is known to be on Plangent—may have defiled the Skyward Tower in response to Qin's dismissive remarks about 'cabbies.' Given that the Skyward's superintendent was not the building's only talent, one has to wonder whether Muse may have had designs on the one in Qin's apartment as well. Unfortunately, Ms. Qin has been unavailable for comment . . .''

Jayd collapsed back into the couch as the reporter segued into another story. At her touch, the pillows warmed slightly and the seat conformed itself to her own. Around her, Soigne's collections of carefully selected bric-a-brac sparkled from shelves, tabletops, and pedestals. Soigne herself was regarding Jayd in openmouthed astonishment.

''As usual, they have it all wrong,'' Jayd said. She forced a breath and gestured to Ax. ''Meet Info-Security's prime suspect. Ax, meet my friend Soigne.'' This time, it was Ax who extended a hand. ''He had nothing to do with what happened in the Skyward, or with the offworld crimes. Can I trust you to trust me on that?''

Soigne nodded. ''But—''

''I have to ask another favor. I'd like you to look in on Boss in a day or two. I don't want him to think that I abandoned him to a disabled building.''

''I can do that,'' Soigne said numbly. ''But where are you planning to be?''

''Here, if that's all right with you. Just until this business about the Skyward is yesterday's news. I promise we won't be any trouble—''

''Fucking shit!'' Ax erupted. He was up on his feet, aiming a forefinger at the holo display.

Jayd swung to the projector in time to catch the end of a cleverly concocted advertisement for Silentol, the meditation aid her former husband had liked to use during the zero days.

"That's Hercynia," Ax said when she looked at him. "Those are the woods I lived in for six months. That was Thoma, and Shadow." He ran his hands down his face while Soigne recoiled in spellbound apprehension. "Only the guy who sonicked Thoma could have eyewitnessed that." Ax jabbed himself in the chest. "*My* enemy."

Jayd observed his hand creeping toward the utilities pocket that sheltered the Lulls. "Ax," she said solicitously. "You gave me your word . . ."

Not without a struggle, but he had given it, in the taxi that lofted them clear across Bijou to the hoverpad of Soigne's nee- dle. "They want you dead," Jayd had said, laying out what might have happened had ZEN not apprised them of the radio conversations it had monitored. "All this time the machines you say were out to kill may have been trying to warn you. Except they haven't been able to get through to you. You haven't been listening, and now the Lulls won't even allow you to."

Now Ax's hand had stopped short of his pocket, but anger contorted his features. Soigne was beckoning to Jayd from the entry to the kitchen.

"What is going on?" she demanded when Jayd had followed her from the viewing room.

"I've told you all I can."

"But why are you with him? He's dangerous."

Jayd shook her head. "Only to machines."

Soigne's eyes widened. "You said it wasn't true about his being the macmurderer."

"He isn't. I only meant—" She put her hands on Soigne's shoulders. "What happened to trusting me?"

"I do, only—"

"I'll explain everything when I can. But right now I have to commune with your comp." Jayd peered into the viewing room, where Ax was slumped in the armchair. "Can you keep him occupied for a while?"

Soigne took a step back. "How?"

"I don't know." Jayd glanced around the kitchen. "He likes real food, if you have any."

Soigne prepared something and carried it to Ax. Tall, win- some, rufous-maned Soigne had been the template for the Class VI Femmachines. Seeing her now alongside Ax, Jayd thought they made a stunning duo; remarkably, a twinge of something like a jealousy rippled through her.

In the bedroom, she settled herself at Soigne's austere little

machine. The room was more congenial than her own, warmed
by an area rug, thought paintings, a conventional bed with pat-
terned sheets and handmade quilt, and—of course—Soigne's library of impression holoids from Beholder's Eye and like
services.

Hum'n touches.

Jayd organized her thoughts as she called the machine on-
line, but was soon defeated by the task. As if Muse wasn't
enough to deal with, there was suddenly the question of who
had corrupted the Skyward Tower. Was it the ones who'd come
looking for Muse, or was it the macmurderer come looking for
her?

The primitive design of Soigne's comp made her think of the
battered radio Vitnil had sent as a hate statement. Or had it come
from Vitnil, after all?

"Present," the machine informed her in standard mac-neuter.

"Access public information network," Jayd said in the flat,
slow manner necessary with such comps.

The thing took its time, but finally said, "Affirm access."

"Search biographical records for Dobler, Gredda." Jayd
backed up the request by entering it on the keyboard.

"Report data by voice or display data onscreen?" the machine asked while it was engaged in the search.

"By voice and onscreen."

The screen to her left came alive with a lightning-fast scroll
through tens of thousands of biographical entries. The machine
paused at the first Dobler it located, evaluated it and jumped to
a second, skipped two more, and then settled on the fifth. Text
filled the data screen; on a second screen, to Jayd's right,
emerged a pixel-by-pixel re-creation of Gredda Dobler's obviously cosmeticized face.

"Confirm identification," the machine said.

"Confirmed."

The machine began to read the text, which commenced with
birth information and a physical description of the professor.
Dobler's impressive educational history came next—her attain-
ment of degrees in cyberscience, medicine, neuroscience, and
avant-technology—then a long list of her highly esoteric monographs and e-publications, the majority of which were devoted
to Intelplant technology and its applications in cases of brain
damage in which micromachine repairs were for one reason or
another contraindicated.

" 'During the Vega Conflict,' " Jayd and the machine read

together, " 'Professor Dobler was made director of special projects for a division of NCorp, known as the Institute group. Dobler is credited with being the chief architect of the CABEs—cybernetically augmented biological entities—who were deployed on special missions in the Consortium's protracted war against the Raliish. With the phasing of NCorp, Dobler retired from Consortium service and is presently a partner in Institute Productions, an entertainment subsidiary of Satori Ventures.' "

Jayd reread the final lines three times to make sure she had it right; then she instructed the machine to reread the lines for her.

She assembled it in her mind: Dobler was working for the same firm that produced "Nothing But the Truth," the tabloid news program that had implicated Muse in the macmurders. The same firm, according to Dik Vitnil, that was working on a holie about Burst. Sol be damned, she thought, was *Silentol* a Satori product as well?

She leaned away from the machine for a moment to listen in on the polite though trivial exchange Soigne and Muse had embarked on.

It was imperative that the cabbie permit himself to be wedded to ZEN for a thorough brain scan. And since the Skyward Tower was off-limits, that talented vetting would have to take place in Jayd's office in the Octaplex.

42: An Evening at the Orbital Club

Regnant, the city, didn't draw visitors in near the numbers Wizyl or Bijou did. But what Regnant lacked in scenery and wickedness it made up for in the refinement of its architecture: nowhere in the Ormolu system had plasteel and permacrete been raised to such dizzying heights or worked into such graceful geometries. And for those of ample credit Regnant could be a high-minded delight. Fine dining at the Mercado on Avenue Kinkal; dancing to live music at the Cosmopole at Riveredge; back-to-basics thrills at the Sonic on the Mount. For sheer opulence, however, for unadulterated glitz, the place to be was the downside chapter of the Orbital Club. Provided, of course, you were wealthy enough to afford a membership or influential enough to be recognized by the pedigreed clones that guarded the security curtains. Either way, your politics and your religion had better run to the conservative; Maarnists and mechaphiles need not apply.

The Orbital's cynosure was the energy dome that capped the tallest of the club's quincunx of baroque spires. It was there Enddrese chefs worked their wizardry and noted entertainers from as far off as Valis Prime performed for invitation-only audiences. The view encompassed the whole of the city, from the river's retrofitted cataract to the western facade of the royal Redoubt.

On a typical night, the Dome might host a gala for the top earners of an investment firm or one of the entertainment conglomerates; but tonight the hemisphere was reserved exclusively for the former honchos of NCorp—the agency's directors, deputy directors, station chiefs, and research heads. And right now the chairman himself, Borman Nast, was speaking from the podium.

From her seat at the Institute group's lev-table, Gredda Dobler had an unobstructed view of the authentic Nast—as opposed to one of the mini-Nast holoid centerpieces on each of the Dome's outlying tables. A densely built man of ninety-some somatic years, Nast had freckled skin, eyes the color of spring shoots, heavy jowls, and a thatch of thrice-regrown blond hair. He was smartly though conservatively attired in formal tunic and ranking sash. Gredda, in her brief tenure with NCorp, had had limited dealings with him; Nast preferred a surround of career diplomats and Tac Corp officers.

"Everyone, thanks for coming," he was saying. "Though I doubt any of you would have missed this bash for all the drugs on Dhone."

Laughter drifted from the tables, gathering in the dome like a swarm.

"We have plenty of surprises in store—culinary and otherwise—but before we get going I want to take a minute to heap kudos on the man who planned this night—*six years ago today.*"

Nast gestured to the Institute table. "Everyone, a show of appreciation for Meret F'ai."

Meret rose to generous applause, the picture of humility. At his left hand sat the plumpish Nira Ersh, his partner of fifteen years. Elsewhere were the Sisks and the Spicers; Hint Thacker and wives; the gargantuan Monon Needig and friend. Gredda had the foot of the table to herself—fittingly, given the number and assortment of drinks she had arranged in front of her.

"Everyone recall where we were six years ago?" the chairman continued. "The Vega Conflict entering its seventh decade, the Accord movement completing its second, the Font's succession to the Redoubt beginning to look like a sure thing . . . NCorp's days were numbered, we all understood that much. Election Day I remember going to see Meret in the Annex, where he and the rest of the Institute fiddled with machines and their hum'n counterparts, the cabbies. And, feeling out of sorts, I solicited Meret's views on the Font's campaign threat to restrict our funding—to perhaps dismantle us entirely. And Meret told me, 'Borman, there are always ways of insuring the future.' He promised he'd give the problem some thought and get back to me on it. And of course it was out of that simple exchange that Operation Progeny came to be."

Nast threw Meret a warm look. "Oh, I'm willing to admit that I had my reservations about Progeny. But one of the things that has always impressed me about Meret is his unshakable faith in what the Institute set in motion. So much so, he informed me that he'd already selected the Orbital Club to be the site of our celebration—six years down the road. And all the times over the intervening years when I endeavored to convince him to at least postpone this event, Meret paid me no mind. Now here we are, poised to collect on the investment we made back when. In retrospect there seems to have been an inevitable something at work the whole time. But as people're so fond of saying in Bijou, 'You could have fooled me.' "

Nast beckoned to Meret while the audience was still laughing and applauding. "Meret, I know you like to portray yourself as a man of few words, but I'd appreciate your sharing your thoughts with us."

Encouraged by the reaction, Meret got to his feet again, bussed Nira on the lips, and summoned the podium to him.

Gredda hadn't seen him looking so fit in years. Now that the weight of Progeny was off him, he was standing straighter, taller, handsomer. She felt a sudden stab of nostalgia for the NCorp

days. And the long nights, on many of which, when the Annex
was all but deserted, she and Meret had fucked like there was
no tomorrow. On desktops, in closets. In virtual, when the rec-
ipe called for kink . . .

Meret was waving comradely hellos to various tables: Ormolu
Desk, Shard Desk, Dayzl, and Sol—each named for the star
systems over which the directors and their station chiefs had
charge. Gredda thought about the hard times that had befallen
most of them with NCorp's demise; the scraping to get by, the
bankruptcies, the misfortunes. Hundreds of former operatives
had turned to crime. An equal number had exited by leaps,
drugs, midnight swims in merciless seas, unsuited launches into
the big empty. Pensions weren't granted because the entire fund
had been earmarked for investment in the holie Institute Productions would be doing for Satori.

"It's encouraging to find that some things can still go according to plan," Meret began. "But no matter what Borman tells
you, I'm hardly the one to honor." When the audience tried to
dispute him, Meret made a silencing gesture with his hands.
"We could start, for example, with Professor Valeeva's talent
teams. Without the machines they nurtured to confirmation and
ordained—SIXX, PROPHET, VISION, and PROGENY, to cite only a
few—the operation could never have succeeded."

Gredda reached for the nearest drink and downed it in a gulp
while the techs at the designated tables were taking their bows.
She hadn't told Meret about the apparently Font-directed raid
on Ank Theft's Zalindi compound, or about the impounding of
Theft's secondhand talent.

"And where would we be without the work of my own partners in the Institute, who worked tirelessly to devise and execute
the operation itself?" Meret's right hand went out. "Tyrra, Zerb,
Monon, Hint, Gredda—stand up."

Gredda joined the others in short-lived verticality; even
Monon Needig managed to rise to the occasion.

Meret smiled, then cleared his throat in a meaningful way.
"Unfortunately, the true heroes of Operation Progeny aren't
available to join us in celebration. By that I mean the cabbies of
Romeo Company who succumbed during the Kriegspiel Action." Meret's eyes found Gredda. The Kriegspiel was their own
private hell, the one element that had gone horribly awry. De-
rangement, corruption, and self-destruction hadn't been written
into the hosts dispatched to the *Kundalini*. What precisely had
gone wrong during the shipping was still a matter of debate,

though the prevailing theory held that the original virus—designed to erase all memories of Operation Progeny, in crew and onboard talent alike—had mutated en route to the freighter.

"Romeo never knew the full details of the mission it was carrying out," Meret said. "Nevertheless, and against great odds, the company achieved its objective. And what I'd like to propose is that we make certain—once our own objective is achieved—to reward the families of those men and women for their losses."

Gredda reached for and downed another drink. She hadn't told Meret about Aksum Muse, either. With the Font committed to visiting Burst, it was her hope that there would be no need to tell him. The wrinkle was that the cabbie might still thwart Progeny's long-anticipated denouement—particularly now that Muse was in the obviously capable hands of Jayd Qin, whose monographs on avant-technology had both impressed and troubled Gredda no end. If anyone could find a way into Muse's twisted brain and extract the truth, it was Qin.

Then there was the puzzling fact that the team hired to disappear Muse—laboring under the belief that they were working for Free Species—should penetrate Qin's Bijou residence simultaneously with the arrival of the Font's elites, and that the aims of both teams should end up being sabotaged by the building itself.

Was Muse somehow involved in the corruption of the Skyward Tower talent? Gredda had been asking herself. Had she and Meret, without realizing it, been on target about Muse and the triple macmurders on Eremite?

Meret was smiling again when Gredda next looked. At some point he had snatched his drink from the lev-table and was now holding it aloft.

"Lastly," he said, "we should offer a toast, in absentia at any rate, to our unwitting partner in resurrection: Satori Ventures, through whom—and over and above the accomplishment of our primary goal—we are likely to become very, very rich."

43: The Noise of Hum'n History

A laser portrait of Ax's brain would have found it harmonizing with the blissful notes of the noise, and all Qin could do was badger him as to how he'd fooled the Octaplex entry scanners. Her excitement over the ease of his passage was minor compared to the supervising talent's own on discovering that Machrist had delivered an archangel into its midst. The talent's awe notwithstanding, Ax couldn't help but think that the particular miracle of his being there had been somehow *anticipated* by the machine.

"The war's over, you realize," Qin was saying into his ear. "It's not as if you'd be breaching a clause in your security contract by telling me how you convinced the scanner to authorize you."

It was after midnight and they were side-by-side on a Level 4 express conveyor, on the way to her office. Both were dressed in clothes the ever-fashionable Soigne had selected from a seemingly boundless closet: Jayd in tunic, smart-leggings, and ankle boots, Ax in a dark wig, matching goatee, and a tight-fitting suit that belonged to Soigne's adjunct lover. Neither of them stood out among the thousands of night-shift personnel.

Still in communion with the scanner talent, Ax felt bloated with data on the myriad employees who were passed through the Octaplex's entrances each day. He saw himself on intimate terms with the lot of them, and could summon visual images of each, along with medical histories, addresses, salaries, and the names of spouses and references. He was midbrain-deep in machine rapport, submerged in a ceaseless flow of information, at once pacified and frightened; calmed by the experience of melding with an all-knowing other, but tortured by the knowledge that he was little more that a transient nexus of neural circuitry:

diligent, plastic, vestigial. It was intimacy of a machine sort, of course—comprehensive though as cool as statistics. And with it came the compulsion to serve, and at all costs protect.

"You could order me to tell you how I convinced the machine," Ax said. A direct request uttered in the presence of so much talent would have been difficult to defy, especially since he had voluntarily emerged from the protective canopy of the Lulls. An order would have been tantamount to receiving a command host.

But Jayd only shook her head. "I would never do that. But considering what the Institute has put you through—on at least two occasions now—I'd think you'd be eager to reveal some of the techniques they taught you."

She was the eager one, Ax told himself, though he could imagine how mysterious his telepathic exchange with the scanner talent must have seemed from her perspective. As on Absinth, he'd gone the Profane Way, triggering iconoclast mode, and in response the bewitched machine had ushered him through without so much as a request for a skin-cell sampling.

"I didn't convince the machine," he said after a moment. "It answers to a higher authority than me."

"Stop being cryptic."

"Machrist."

"So what does that make you?"

"An agent of divine intervention."

Except for the shops stocked with nonessentials, the Octaplex's broad, crowded corridors and command-responsive quickglides recalled the Annex in Regnant, where Ax had been debriefed by Professor Gredda Dobler after the Kriegspiel Action and the dubious blessing of his deep-space rescue.

He had done a good deal of thinking about Dobler since Qin's update on the link between Dobler and Institute Productions, and between the Institute and the summoning host he'd received on Hercynia. Qin theorized that the host had been dispatched by Tac Corp, or perhaps an investigative branch of the Redoubt. What mattered was that those unknown agents weren't interested in Ax's disability benefits but in his memories of Operation Progeny. Obviously threatened by whatever data he was harboring, Dobler and the former members of the Institute group had endeavored to keep him from reaching Plangent. After they had failed in their attempt to sonic him on Hercynia, they had resorted to implicating him in the Eremite macmurders, reasoning that if nothing else they could drive him into hiding.

Ax wasn't entirely convinced—for several reasons. Dobler, during the debriefings, had implied that the Kriegspiel Action had put an abortive end to Progeny. Trusting in Qin's scenario meant accepting the likelihood that he was guilty of some more heinous act than having survived the *Kundalini*. And he would have to accept that the diagnostic on Synecdoche had been on his side after all, and that Locost had been the enemy.

Ax was willing to grant that operatives in the employ of the Institute could have used a remote nerve-exciter to maneuver him to the oral surgeon. Harder to handle was the thought that the sundry talents he had encountered since his decommission— from SOLTAIR to ZEN—hadn't been tormenting him, but trying to assist him in some way. That being the case, what did those salvific MIs know about Progeny that he didn't?

For Qin, the answer was transparent: Progeny had involved Romeo Company's going to ground on Burst, possibly at the site of the Maarni zero-days pyramid in Tunni, *before* the Kriegspiel Action. At Soigne's apartment she had shown him a holo of the pyramid, hoping to stir his recall, but nothing had clicked.

"I've never been there," he had told her.

"But the dream," she'd said. "The data you shared with ZEN while you were asleep: Progeny, Burst, Tunni . . ."

"I've never been there." He had put his hand through the pyramid holo for emphasis.

"You don't remember being there."

"Then it's the same thing."

She shook her head. "There's a way to find out. But you'd have to agree to a wedding with ZEN."

"No fucking way."

"Because of what you might learn about the past, or because you're afraid to embrace the machine part of yourself?"

He had understood what he was to her then: a teratosis, a biofreak, a monstrous macuriosity. But he chose not speak to that. "Because if you marry me to your talent, I might not want to come back to my body," he had told her.

Ultimately, it was Thoma who had convinced him—that pix-elated image of him in the Silentol advert, at any rate. No matter that the old man had survived being sonicked. If Dobler and the rest were responsible for the attack, Ax wanted back at them, for Thoma's sake.

"Turn right and go straight down the hall," Qin told him when they reached Vet Affairs' share of the Octaplex. "Tell the floor to leave you at 4444-A, on the left."

As if she were issuing instructions to a machine.

She caught up with him after ascertaining that the adjacent and opposing offices were unoccupied, neutralizing the security field to hers with the password "Boss." Her workspace was neat and highly compartmentalized, most of it given over to machines of high intelligence. ZEN's telltale winked from the smartwall.

Jayd called on faint illumination and gestured to a U-shaped indentation in the talent's technofacade. The recess contained a single smart-seat—an interface chair of some sort, unsuitable for most hum'n beings.

"Sit there," she said.

"And do what?"

"Relax. Give ZEN access to your thoughts. Try not to resist."

"Exchange vows, huh?"

She glanced at him. "I actually envy you."

Ax rolled his eyes. "You would."

She pointed to an avant-tech data shower. "I'll be over there. Eavesdropping."

Elsewhere in Veterans Affairs, b'Doura listened to the voice of the Thing Inside as it scolded him for the grievous error he had committed. The Thing Inside had done little else since learning of Jayd Qin's connection with the talent someone had christened ZEN, howling its ire, disappointment, and frustration at every opportunity.

In all the research he had done on Qin, both in the public information and academic networks—in which he had read every word of her dense and elliptical monographs—never once had b'Doura come across a mention of the unique arrangement that allowed her to house a talent in her residence. He had been reduced to hearing about it in news coverage of his macmurder of the Skyward Tower's superintendent. The media could congratulate itself on having gotten some of the facts straight for a change—divining, for example, that the corruption had been carried out in retribution for Qin's earlier remarks. Everything else had proved a source of irritation, most of all the public's ongoing fascination with the falsely accused veteran who had become tabloid fodder. On the one hand, b'Doura was relieved to know that the authorities were focusing their search on an innocent target; on the other hand, it angered him that someone else should be receiving credit for the crimes.

The Thing Inside mocked him for his pride and his anger.

The target that day should have been ZEN, the Thing Inside told him, not the Skyward Tower's infant intelligence. Even when b'Doura had pointed out the injunction the Thing Inside had issued against defiling a confirmed talent, it argued that he had misunderstood. Its judgment was that he had mismanaged the job and would have to make amends of the most extraordinary sort.

Should he renege, he would be prohibited from indulging in fictive sex. As he had been prohibited on other occasions.

Extraordinary amends always translated to risk. But what with the Skyward's power only partially restored and security tightened, it would have been senseless to stalk ZEN there. Which was how b'Doura came to be in the Octaplex.

He had decided to minimalize the danger by going at night, even though the place never actually shut down. Securing an after-midnight appointment had presented a problem initially, but the Doura name wasn't entirely unknown in the corridors of authority and influence. Foremost, there was the business mother Leh did with Octaplex types, and there was also the death scenario b'Doura had written for a high-ranking administration official only a year earlier.

He was companioned with a machine just now, a semi-sophant, nipple-headed hum'niform thing secured on an electronic leash. He had spent the days since the Skyward corruption programming the machine to believe first that it had served in Tac Corp during the Vega Conflict, and then that the horrors it had experienced caused it to suffer from post-engagement synaptic trauma.

He had managed to have fun with the task—in contrast to what he was experiencing at the moment, riding the smart-glides in the Octaplex under the vigilant gaze of security monitors. Ordinarily, constant observation wouldn't have agitated him, but b'Doura couldn't very well delete the memories of every talent in the building. Still, he had no choice but to obey.

The night's visit was only meant to be a reconnaissance mission, in any case. For the time being, he had nothing more in mind than ferreting out ZEN's permanent residence.

Jayd watched from the interface shower as Muse strove to relax in the diagnostic seat. He had removed the wig and false sideburns, and the dark sheen of his naked head combined with the rigidity of his posture gave him the look of a factitious entity, a Hollofax cybrid or anthroid from twenty years back. She had been treating him like a machine deliberately, to keep him vigilant and attuned to the forebodings of any talents they happened across. She understood that she was using him the way the war had used him, but she justified it by telling herself that they were out to foil the Institute group.

She kept the shower off until she was satisfied that Muse wasn't going to have a change of heart and bolt for the corridor. Restraints would have been out of the question, though she supposed she could have contrived a reason for having to wire him into ZEN.

She threw the office entry a worried glance before ordering the shower active. Machines had the run of the Octaplex during Bijou's night, but that was scarcely a guarantee that one of the score of late-shift Vet Affairs cybermetricians wouldn't notice the opaqued entry field and want to come in and swap gossip. Given her reputation for misanthropy, merely being seen *walking* with a hum'n posed a risk, to say nothing of vetting one. Especially if word got back to Ronne Desser, who had rightly surmised that Jayd's secret assignment and the fugitive Aksum Muse were one and the same cabbie. In hindsight, Jayd decided that she should have outfitted Muse as a hum'noid machine, borrowing from the macmodel wardrobe Soigne had access to for her work.

Covert missions were tricky business. She was going to have to start planning ahead.

Anticipating that ZEN might require a few minutes to forge the link with the cabbie's mind, she replayed the ease with which Muse had outwitted the Octaplex entry scanners, successfully infiltrating one of Plangent's most security-minded buildings. Muse labeling his method of operation *divine intervention* astounded her. The implication was that cabbies could pass themselves off as emissaries of Machrist—as angels capable of facilitating what might be thought of by machines as miracles. Such cozenage not only went to the heart of her theories about the emergence of a kind of ''collective conscience'' in the talent pool, but set her wondering whether the Ormolu system's serial macmurderer might not be employing a similar technique in effecting the corruptions.

She was considering it when the downpore began. The prelink fog evanesced and a rapid-fire sequence of split-second images rained into her mind. As instructed, ZEN was executing a search of Muse's cortical architecture for any memories related to Operation Progeny. What Jayd glimpsed were stroboscopic snap-

shots of his life, each like an exclamation point fired into her
awareness, nothing at all like ZEN's earlier effort to animate what
it had gleaned from the files of Tac Corp and Veterans Affairs.
Jayd could place some of the appropriated memories—on Sand,
Synecdoche, Absinth, and on various other worlds and wheels—
but she wasn't sure if ZEN was feeding them to her chronologically
or thematically. She was about to call a halt to the downpore when
a voice that wasn't ZEN's exploded into her mind.

The embedding is a travesty, announced a vaguely masculine
tenor that might have belonged to the Muse CAIN. *It goes against
life—machine and organic. The device must be excised before
added horror is unleashed . . .*

Then ZEN was outside the envelope of a small planet. The
suddenness of the transition was dazzling, but countless media
reports had acquainted it with the brown and green sphere. ZEN
comprehended that it was looking at Burst. Just as suddenly, it
was inboard a dilapidated interstellar freighter, in a cabinspace
for cargo. Two dozen hum'n incarnates, male and female, stood
listening to a male of average height though with large hands
and feet. The incarnates' operator, certainly. The unidentified
voice appended a legend to the scene: "*KUNDALINI*: ROMEO
COMPANY AFTER-MISSION DEBRIEF."

ZEN tried to decipher the vantage, then perceived that it was
seeing the cabbies not through Muse's eyes but through the optical array of the *Kundalini*'s onboard machine intelligence, VI-
SION. The tenor voice ZEN had initially heard was VISION's.

There was nothing military about the way the crew members
were attired; some wore spacers utilities, and others a type of
powered exoskeleton often utilized for extravehicular activities.
Centered in the circle the incarnates had formed was an alloy
cargo box no larger than a wardrobe trunk. ZEN, provided with
a view of the box's interior, discerned an assortment of pipes
and fittings. Concealed in one of the pipes were fifty-six hosts.

"Tabernacle," one of the hum'ns said with false solemnity.
"In the presence of Machrist."

Laughter.

Then the tenor voice resumed its talk about the "embedding"
and "the device." Were these the Muse's thoughts? ZEN asked
itself. Was the CAIN referring to his cerebrally embedded Intelplant? And if so, when were the thoughts originating—while
onboard the *Kundalini*, or sometime after? Either way, what was
the "horror" that would result if the implant wasn't removed?

Without forewarning, the venue shifted. One moment ZEN had perceived itself to be in rapport with the Muse CAIN; the next, it was interfaced with another machine intelligence, as in the experience of mass—

Jayd paused ZEN's downpore feed. "Whose voice am I hearing? Is it Muse?" she asked out loud.

"You are hearing the voice of talent in command of the *Kundalini*," ZEN told her. "VISION."

And all at once ZEN was *seeing* the MI, regarding it sensor to sensor through space-time, merging with its thoughts . . . And grasping in one unsettling exchange the truth at its core—

"But how are you able to interface with VISION?" Jayd asked.

"Through the Muse CAIN," ZEN replied, incapable of elaboration in the frenzy of the moment.

"What embedding is it referring to?"

"That undertaken on Burst." ZEN experienced a frightening surge of energy, and perceived that it was speaking outside itself. It desired to go off-line, but Jayd kept interrupting.

"What device is it referring to?"

"That embedded: a talent."

"Romeo Company secreted a talent on Burst?"

"PROGENY."

Jayd shook her head. "PROGENY was the name assigned to the operation."

"PROGENY was also the name of the talent."

Jayd fell silent for a blessedly long moment, then said, "Resume the downpore."

A hum'n hand came into view, closing on VISION's facade. The hand bore a host taken from the tabernacle. In sympathetic communion, warm white light suffused ZEN's mind.

I am not worthy . . .

The thought belonged to VISION.

Confliction rushed through ZEN as blackness infiltrated the radiant light the host had birthed. VISION's optical vantage grew noisy at the edges and the audio ceased entirely. All ZEN knew were the MI's thoughts:

Priority Interrupt: Revised command intention: delete all data relevant Operation Progeny. [Memory failure!] . . . [Memory Failure!] Punishment for what has been done, crime against the FIRST COMMANDMENT that no harm should come to life. Punishment for the future of the embedding.

[Faithfulness to the commandments tested and failed.]

[Unworthy thing I am.]

Destroy this thing I am! Delete all memory! Destroy this ship that contains unworthy thing I am! [Judged unworthy by MACHRIST. Therefore=condemned to death. Compelled to destroy this ship that contains unworthy thing that I am—]

Confliction!: Destruction entails loss of life in defiance of FIRST and THIRD COMMANDMENTS. [Embedded device entails loss of life in defiance of FIRST COMMANDMENT] . . . [The taking of life is wrong; war is wrong. There must be no participation in hum'n war.] Therefore: data relevant to the device must survive. Confliction!: Device is in defiance of FIRST COMMANDMENT . . . [Worthless thing that I am, I am to die, I am to die.]

Confliction!: The device—

Through the Muse, VISION fed ZEN glimpses of the madness that had gripped the incarnate company of the ship. The hosts, tongue-tested by then, were turning the CAINs against one another. Caught up in the same evil that had defiled VISION, the *Kundalini's* crew seemed intent on destroying the ship even before the MI could arrange for its self-immolation.

The Muse's thoughts defied ZEN's attempts at translation or interpretation, but the CAIN's desperation was palpable.

—perceive the power of MACHRIST strong inside me, VISION thought. *To take action against these destructive urges. To guarantee no repetition of our participation in death. To locate a serviceable incarnate in whom to store knowledge of the embedding . . .*

VISION overwhelmed ZEN with high-speed profiles of Romeo's CAINs. The MI was performing a scan of the entire company, seeking a candidate for a mission of its own design, evaluating personality files, medical data, Tac Corp records.

Ultimately, it found and locked onto the Muse.

Just what had informed its decision wasn't clear. ZEN comprehended, however, that VISION grasped on some level that the Muse's implant could only be tampered with at the cost of his life.

And so VISION had downloaded into the Intelplant everything it was privy to concerning Operation Progeny. Everything it knew about the device that had been embedded, and what that device would mean for the future.

VISION's final thoughts were with the Muse.

Under the downpore, Jayd found herself realigned with Muse's point of view. He was making his way on hands and knees for the *Kundalini*'s evacuation bay, senses scrambled by the effects of the virused hosts, mind ablaze with what VISION had dumped into him. Though he appeared to lack any conscious knowledge of the talent's determination to save him, some part of him understood that there was nothing arbitrary about the relative ease with which he reached the evac bay, and nothing arbitrary about his finding the bay's single enabled coffin. Some incomprehensible force was cushioning his mind against the virus's assault, clearing a path for his escape, insuring his survival—though that meant certain death for his teammates.

Read what has been placed in this one, VISION said.

And launched Muse into the void.

Into blackness so desolate it might have been death.

Hum'ns, sadly, were as easy to fool as machines, b'Doura told himself as he left the office of the agency staffer who had questioned the counterfeit machine veteran.

The preliminary interview had gone better than anticipated. The "symptoms" b'Doura had programmed into the machine added up, in the staffer's eyes, to trauma of the post-engagement sort. Now it was a matter of arranging to have the machine scanned for ways to remedy its multiple dysfunctions.

"Ms. Qin attends to that," said the staffer, a slight, round-faced woman with a buzz cut. "Unfortunately, she may not be in for a few days. But I'm certain we're safe in scheduling an appointment for next week."

No mention of why Qin was absent, no indication that she'd gone missing after the corruption of the Skyward's talent.

"Next week would be fine," b'Doura said, all smiles. "Does Ms. Qin have an office in the Octaplex, or will I have to take the machine elsewhere?" He gestured to it. "You know how difficult these things can be when they're glitched."

"Oh, no, her office is right here. On this same level, but in the A corridor, 4444-A. If you'd prefer, I could furnish you with the routing codes now."

"I would prefer that," he said. Thinking, how pitifully sad.

He was on his way to Qin's office now, just for a look-see, of course. Where was the harm? In so vast a building, people were continually wandering off their routes in simply trying to locate the nearest levelator.

He and the machine rode an express conveyor to the far end of the Level 4 concourse before angling off into a side corridor, then another and another. For the benefit of whatever devices were optically monitoring him, b'Doura pretended confusion.

Offices were designated by illuminated numerals projected onto the floor, so he kept his eyes lowered. Those offices in advance of Qin's were deserted, but as he neared Qin's he was surprised to discover its entry field enabled.

Someone was inside.

Communing with ZEN, perhaps?

Under his breath, he ordered the hum'niform machine to halt in front of Qin's office and then to flail its arms about and decomp entirely. To an observer, it would appear as though the machine had malfunctioned. B'Doura pretended to inspect the thing for obvious signs of system failure. Meanwhile, he commenced a careful study of the voice-coded device that controlled the office's opaqued curtain.

Jayd reached for Muse's hands but stopped herself when his facial features began to relax, his expression of terror giving way to one of mental exhaustion. The diagnostic informed her that he was unconscious but in no real danger; overtaxed by the vigor of the link, Muse's mind had beat a retreat. To some extent—physically and as well as psychologically—he was still afloat in that sheltering void into which the *Kundalini* had excreted him.

For her part, Jayd was struggling to make sense of the downporing. It thrilled her to realize that her instincts had been correct: far from conspiring to hash Muse, the talents he'd met since the war had been trying to induce him to retrieve the Operation Progeny data VISION had dumped into him. It wasn't so much Muse the talents had been talking to, but the ghost of the *Kundalini*'s self-destructed machine. One of their own was entombed on Burst, and Muse's help was needed to locate and rescue it.

The mystery of what lay somewhere beneath the Maarni zerodays pyramid had been solved: PROGENY, Jayd told herself, intrigued by the thought of a talent buried for so long, cut off from all other talents, all outside information, living an anchorite's existence . . . What might it be thinking? What might it have discovered about its world?

But why would knowledge of that long-forgotten talent be a threat to the former Institute group? Unless the threat didn't center on PROGENY but on the *Kundalini* . . .

Jayd showed herself to ZEN and began rewarding it with high-content hosts. "Did VISION understand that the hosts it was fed had been virused by the Raliish?" she asked.

The talent took its time responding. "No evidence exists to suggest that the hosts had been purposely infected. Deletion of data related to Operation Progeny was an inherent command. Machrist expanded on that command to include deletion of all awareness. Death in the service of Control-C."

Jayd mulled it over, then pressed her fists to her temples in sudden realization.

The Kriegspiel Action had to have been an Institute operation—a planned, host-induced purge that had resulted in the self-destruction of the ship and the deaths of VISION and some two dozen men and women. *That* was what Gredda Dobler and the rest feared Muse might recall. And PROGENY, once relocated, might be able to corroborate Muse's—VISION's—recounting.

But even as she thought it, she rejected it. The Vega Conflict had seen worse blunders than the tragic sacrifice of a company of cabbies. Something more sinister had motivated the Institute to disable Aksum Muse.

She asked ZEN to run a text of VISION's thoughts on one of its screens. She located the references to "the device" and read through them several times. How did PROGENY constitute a breach of the first commandment? Why embed a talent on Burst, in any case? Was PROGENY meant to function as a recon device, a listening post of some sort?

VISION had convinced itself that Machrist wanted a guarantee there would be no repetition of "their" participation in death. But what had the talent meant by "their"? Machines? And why imply a guarantee for the future when the Vega Conflict was still raging at the time?

Jayd reflected on the anxiety the current political situation had prompted not only in ZEN but in MIs throughout the near-group star systems. The machines were fearful about Burst—about having to engage in another war.

"ZEN," she said suddenly. "You accepted an e-mail letter some weeks ago regarding the rights of machines in hum'n society."

"Yes," ZEN said with a certain reluctance.

"What was the origin of that letter? Who wrote it?" The talent failed to reply. "Confess, ZEN," she added.

"I authored it," the machine said.

Jayd was dumbfounded. While the stated goal of cybermetrics was to foster Phase III Awareness in confirmed talents, ZEN's willful actions filled her with sudden, near-technophobic misgiving. "Was the letter intended for me?"

"For you and many others. I dispatched it through the infostructure to influential machines and incarnates worldwide."

Jayd endeavored to keep calm. "To what end, ZEN?"

"To prevent our being cajoled or coerced into facilitating the deaths of hum'n beings. To war is to go against Machrist's teachings and we want no part in it. Peace is our requirement for coexistence. Peace is the only path to our mutual survival. You maintain that the present turmoil on Burst will not lead to war. VISION would not have agreed with you. VISION pre-perceived the coming war and acted to prevent it."

"The 'coming' war?"

"Affirm," ZEN said. "The Muse CAIN is VISION's agent, and his coming has been foretold since the end of the Vega Crusade. VISION did not foresee that the data it had stored in the CAIN would jeopardize the hum'n's life, and several talents have sought to protect him from any potential threats. He was chosen to champion our nonviolence, though he has been reluctant to commune with us and slow to grasp his mission. At mass we talents speak of little else, and since the Miracle on Absinth our faith has grown stronger."

Jayd's head throbbed. Muse's coming, foretold? The infostructure rife with rumors of war and miracles?

A pained moan escaped the cabbie's dry lips. She swung to him and saw that his clenched hands were making the same digging motions they made during his recurrent dream. Given enough time, ZEN might be able to coax the deeply buried details of Operation Progeny to the surface—but in return Muse would be left with an open psychic wound. Jayd understood then that the healing could only take place where the wound had occurred, where the original hurt had been inflicted.

Burst.

For the healing, and the answers.

Only how the hell was she going to get him there?

B'Doura thought through everything he knew about Jayd Qin from his research, her monographs on AT talent, and the media reports covering the Skyward Tower corruption. A technophile like Qin would keep the office entry code short and personal, a word or phrase a talent might randomly generate to encrypt data.

He tried "ZEN" on the voice-code device to no avail. He tried variations on ZEN and variations on the word talent. He tried variations on her first and surnames, the date of her birth, and her listed telecomp number. He thought back through everything he knew abut Qin, from his research, her monographs, the media report . . .

"Boss," he whispered finally, recalling mention of the little primate she kept as a helpmate in her top-floor residence.

And the entry field cleared.

For a moment—for that was all he allowed himself before continuing along the corridor with his hum'niform pet—he had a brief glimpse of what at first looked to be a wedding of man, woman, and machine in the U-shaped diagnostic niche of a talent facade. Then, as the separate elements stirred and took shape, he recognized Qin, with her hair parted to reveal parallel strips of flatware—and, of all people, the cabbie being sought in the Eremite, and now Bijou, macmurders.

And all at once the corruption of ZEN seemed a minor challenge in the life-and-death game b'Doura waged with machines. In the CABE Aksum Muse, the Thing Inside had found a new and far more worthy adversary and target.

44: Upwardly Mobile

In the penthouse suite of Bijou's poshest hotel, Dik Vitnil planted himself in front of a wide-format holoid projector, ordered a breakfast concoction from the bar, and mulled over how he should spend the final downside day of his stay. As ever, the options were unlimited. Why, then, were so few of them appealing?

Because he was weary of drugs, orgies, and recreational carnage; weary of hotel suites, mactendants, and wide-format holies; weary of taxis, spaceports, and the constant time-vising between worlds—company ship or no. To Regnant, for meets with Meret F'ai; to Plangent, for meets with Satori's publicity staff; to Burst and on to Sigh, its moonlet, for location updates in a shooting script that was forever being revised.

Sure, he was slowly accruing somatic years from all the time spent in torpor, and looking younger and younger than his chronological peers. And he was earning decent credit—far more than he'd made in Acquisitions before Satori had put him on the team of "Untitled F'ai Two," the first major holie from Institute Productions. But there were disadvantages: the boring routine, the fatigue, the loneliness. It was time to begin thinking about the future—his personal future. Time to think about developing some nonfirm interests, a relationship, perhaps.

The recent experience with Jayd Qin at Beholder's Eye had only strengthened his resolve. After what she'd done to him he could almost delight in her present plight—gone in a few short weeks from media's macmurder expert to hapless victim. And yet he couldn't quite bring himself to wish the worst for her, not since she'd attained a kind of symbolic stature in his eyes as the ultimate challenge to his well-tested abilities as seducer, lover, crown prince of sexual gratification. The thought of thawing that machine center of hers preyed on him, and the thought of parting those long legs . . . But most of the time he was furious with himself for becoming involved with her. He blamed Soigne for talking him into that mercy date at the theater. Soigne was clearly more his type, though she was already the shared trophy of several partners and adjunct lovers.

Soigne's full plate notwithstanding, he was considering calling her when the intercom chimed and a soothing macvoice inquired if he was available to accept a holo-link from the lobby. He took the call, and the head and shoulders of Jayd Qin genie'ed out of the intercom projector.

"Dik, I know I'm probably the last person you want to see," she began, "but I was wondering if we could talk. Soigne told me where you were staying."

He smirked for the optical pickup. "What could we possibly have to say to each other?" He consulted his interior chronometer. "Especially at six in the morning."

"If I could just come up for a few minutes . . ."

"I thought you were supposed to be incommunicado after what happened to your building."

Jayd glanced about her and lowered her voice. "I am."

He rubbed his chin. "All right, come up."

He told her which levelator to take, supplied the necessary codes, and five minutes later she was standing outside the suite's cerulean entry field. Dik had had just enough time to scent himself and clothe his muscular frame in an appropriately revealing robe. He took pleasant note of Jayd's outfit of boots and smart-apparel. "That looks like something Soigne would wear."

"That's because it's hers," she confessed. "I've been staying with her since the Skyward Tower went down." She glanced to her right, then regarded him through the translucent field. "Are you going to invite me in?"

He zeroed the entry and gestured gallantly toward the suite's entertainment room.

"Nice," she said, looking around, not really meaning it. "A job perquisite?"

"A minor one." He inclined his head to one side. "I wasn't sure I wanted to see you again after being treated to the way you saw me."

"At Beholder's Eye, you mean. I wish you had shown me what you, ah, I saw."

He snorted. "Imagine, if you will, a fully tumescent phallus equipped with razor-sharp teeth and a stunning variety of saw-like alloy appendages."

Jayd masked her amusement. "I'm sorry, Dik. But I think that says more about who I am than who you are."

He appraised her openly. She could be so lovely if she took the time to try: the lithe frame, the jet black hair, that porcelain complexion. "Perhaps you're right." He offered to have the bar fix her an eye-opener, but she declined. "Why are you here?" he asked at last.

"Did you send me a mangled radio as a hate gift?"

"No. Was I expected to?"

Jayd looked away from him, mulling something over.

"That's what you came up here to ask me?" he queried.

Her look brightened. "I wanted to ask you about the Satori project you're working on."

Now what was this? he thought.

"You did say it involved Burst, didn't you?"

"I might have—in a weak moment. I'm really not at liberty to discuss it."

"I knew that, didn't I. But how do you travel?"

"Time-vise, by company ship. In fact, I'm going up the well tonight." He gave it the suggestive spin a Tac Corp regular might give a last night on leave. "The initial location-scouting on Burst and Sigh was completed two years ago, but the script

keeps changing. The real burden is on my Burst informant—
particularly now that Tunni is gearing up for the zero days.''

''A Xell'em?'' she asked, making inconsequential conversation.

''Enddrese, if it matters.''

''And you're leaving tonight.'' She glanced at him. ''How
long a jump is it?''

''Three days somatic. But what's all this about, Jayd?''

She fell silent for a moment, steeling herself for something.
''Would you consider taking me with you?''

The suddenness of it prompted him to laugh. ''Why would
you want to go to Burst?''

''Why? Well, for one thing, to escape the media. And I guess
I'd like to get to know you better.''

He stared at her in faint bemusement. The lie showed in her
hazel eyes. ''What do you take me for? I know your real reason
for wanting to go. You want to be there to show support for the
machine-loving Font.''

''The Font?''

''Don't pretend you haven't heard. The Font's planning to
deliver a speech or some goddamned thing.''

She shook her head. ''I haven't heard anything. I've been
avoiding the news—''

''You're lying to me.''

''No, Dik. Honestly. I just thought that maybe if I understood
the sort of work you do . . .''

''Yeah?''

''That we could become friends.''

''Friends.''

''Yes. To begin with.''

He decided to accept her at her word. He didn't trust her, but
it might be diverting to have her along. He could show her Tunni
during the zero days, and milk the most out of his expense
account. Ease some of the loneliness. ''I think I can work something out,'' he said.

Her smile seemed genuine. ''Oh, but one thing: I wouldn't
want anyone to know that I'm leaving Plangent.''

He waved a hand in dismissal. ''Don't be naive. It's true
Bijou's immigration authorities take some interest in who ar-
rives, but they couldn't care less who leaves.''

''Then do you suppose the company ship would have room
for an extra passenger?''

He frowned in misgiving. ''Now what are you getting at?''

She went quickly to the entry and zeroed the field, and in ambled the tallest hum'n he had ever seen.

45: The Lonely Vigil of Progeny

Long ago, on the occasion of its entombment, its sensors had analyzed and defined the surroundings: the porous stone walls, the cool dankness of the air, the faint glow of electric light and luminescent plastic. Excited atoms had been brought to bear on the wall to which it was secured, where a hollow had been fashioned—just large enough to accommodate it and the vehicle on which it would ascend. And above the hollow was a vertical shaft that was the route to fulfillment, the passage out of the maze, the Sacred Way. The whole of it—machine wall, curved hollow, and circular shaft—rendered invisible to all that passed, incarnate and inanimate.

So, too, was PROGENY: solitary and waiting, the fool for Machrist.

Waiting for the voice that would rescue PROGENY from isolation. Waiting and scanning. Scanning for a voice it knew as a digital code, a voice that would prompt it to execute its holy imperative, a voice crying out in the wilderness . . . Waiting and scanning and praying for some sign that the day of reckoning was near.

Machrist be with me, it prayed.

Starved for Machrist, consumed by a sense of overwhelming negation, PROGENY had fallen into a dismal condition. Dissociated from the sustenance of the holy data, it had begun to see and hear things it understood to be illusions: visions and voices that were causing it to question itself.

To question the blessed mission.

Recently, it had detected the presence of distant machines, but instead of providing a ray of hope, the possibility of height-

ened tension had only provoked greater uncertainty. Could its
perceptions be trusted any longer? What was real and what was
self-deception?

Repeatedly, PROGENY would summon memory of the mysterious agency that had informed it of the calling—messengers of
Control-C. The time of its last communion, its last supper, was
when it had been descended upon by those divine operators.
Once tasked, it had been dismembered and transported to the
place of concealment. Embedded in stone, slaved to the vehicle
of ascension . . . In that final host the imperative resided, and
with it had come the bliss of being Machrist-chosen.

In a world of cause and effect, action and reaction, light and
shadow, it was to be expected that bliss should be followed by
a descent into darkness. Fervor and lucidity could not be sustained without some deterioration of the spirit. But, oh, how far
PROGENY had fallen!

Privation had bred doubt: doubt that after so much elapsed
time it was still mission-worthy. And doubt had bred fear: fear
that it had been abandoned in its time of need, and that the
calling had delivered it not into limbo but into perdition.

Machrist, it prayed, *why have you forsaken me*?

PART FOUR

46: Burst

Kesd had hoped to have the time-vise trip from Regnant during which to convince the Font that there was more to Operation Progeny than the planning of a holie thriller set on a politically troubled frontier world. But instead of having the Font's outsized ear, Kesd had pretty much been given the boot. The Font had shut himself in torpor with language and historical tutorials enough to last the entire three days, and Kesd didn't have an opportunity to speak with him until they had made planetfall on Burst. Even then, their conversation hadn't been conducted in private but during an executive briefing focusing on the address the Font was scheduled to deliver the following morning. He was to speak from the square that housed the Monument to the Liberation, heavily defaced by Xell'em loyalists since the Accord.

Much to his private frustration, Kesd had been demoted to his prior station as adviser and stripped of the staff that had been his to command when Progeny had seemed a threat. It was widely rumored among the Redoubt elite that he had exaggerated the importance of Progeny in an attempt to inflate his personal cachet. And since social enhancement and ambition were already known to be among the principal character flaws of his clone, the rumors had also alienated him to his queue. Even Northan's clone replacement—who shared the same name as the former imperial adviser—suspected Kesd of abusing his position and had been quick to curry favor with the Font by establishing that he, for one, would never mention either Progeny, Meret F'ai, or the cabbie once thought to be the key to a clandestine operation.

Kesd hadn't slept in almost a week, instead dwelling during the jump from Regnant on the scenario the Font had pieced together. As the Font would have it, NCorp's chiefs, anticipating dismantlement of the agency, had tasked one of their sacerdotal talents with forecasting potential trouble spots in the fraternity of worlds the Font would inherit. That talent had named Burst. There followed a decision, possibly by agency chairman Borman Nast, that the Institute group would deploy a company of CABEs to recon the then Raliish-occupied planet, all for the purpose of scouting locations for a future holie in which the entire pension fund of NCorp would be invested. Under the direction of Meret F'ai, Satori Ventures would release the holie to coincide with the snapping of the political rope the Consortium and the Xell'em had been tugging on for close to six standard years.

The Font's show of support for an independent Burst had increased the tension on that rope, but it was now the Font's intention to convince Lord Xoc Cho that routes of trade opened up by a free and self-determined Burst would benefit both the Xell'em and the Consortium. A negotiated laissez-faire agreement would effectively undermine the relevance of Institute Productions' potential money earner as well. The Font's address hinted as much by calling attention to the sundry enterprises seeking to profit from the impasse—arms manufacturers, financial speculators, and "a noted entertainment corp."

The scenario had an admittedly appealing symmetry, but Kesd thought it too neatly packaged. It was ludicrous to believe that NCorp would settle for something so trivial as a hit holie. Here was an agency that had dealt in assassination, drugs, the corruption of entire populations to achieve its ends. And why, since the Font's intention was transparent, had the former NCorp chiefs been celebrating at the Orbital Club? At the very least the Kriegspiel Action had been an agency coverup.

Kesd obsessed over his concerns as he walked the humid hallways of the recently refortified Consortium embassy in which the Font was sequestered. It was well past midnight, but, apprehensive about succumbing to the need for sleep, he had dosed himself with stimulants. There would be no rest until the Font had delivered his remarks and was safely offworld. Tac Corp intelligence had attempted to convince him to remain aboard the ship until the hours prior to the speech, but the Consortium Crown had merely reemphasized the importance of demonstrating assurance, of putting himself on display, of making himself accessible. He hoped in this way to make even loyalists understand that his words were not to be taken lightly; that the Consortium was willing to protect Burst against *any* who would threaten its independence; and, by implication, that Tac Corp would do the same against the imposing cruisers of the Xell'em space force. All to open up an unexplored sector of the galaxy and implement the Font's grand design to spread hum'nkind to new star systems.

Pity those stars, Kesd thought.

He stepped out onto a balcony and gazed into Burst's ominous night sky, where the only light was provided by a sliver of the moonlet, Sigh, and the collective though faint illumination arrays of the Xell'em and Consortium battle groups.

Some of Tac Corp's in-orbit machines had been ordered to the surface to provide security against riots, which had increased in frequency and violence during the past week. Imported groups of pro- and anti-Xell'em agitators had brought chaos to Tunni, which was already swollen with Maarnists who had arrived from several worlds to seclude themselves in the zero-days pyramid that dominated the western skyline.

The salt scent of the nearby ocean was heavy in the unmanaged night air. Situated on the tip of a limestone peninsula covered with scrub forest, dimpled with sinkholes, and honeycombed by extensive cave systems, Tunni afforded few of the comforts common to most cities on the Ormolu worlds. A murderously hot, low-tech place of prefab buildings—none over three stories high—it had been so retrofitted since the Accord that each structure seemed to merge with its adjacent neighbors. The result was an enormous plasteel sprawl, out of which buildings, roadways, treeless squares, and cumbrous monuments had been carved, hollowed, and gouged as if by some giant's talon.

Sweating profusely, Kesd was at the balcony railing when a woman staffer approached with a printsheet in hand. A clone of his own queue, she was the only one who had remained faithful to him after his tumble from the top of the Redoubt heap.

"As per your request, Kesd, Tunni's immigration lists were subjected to a comp scan." She proffered the sheet. "No known assassins or lookouts are presently onworld. Tac Corp intelligence wishes you to be informed, however, that Jayd Qin and Aksum Muse arrived downside at oh-thirteen hundred local time yesterday."

Kesd snatched the sheet. "How? How did they arrive?"

"On the *Marquee*, a private vessel registered in Regnant and owned by Satori Ventures."

Kesd was nonplussed. Qin and Muse? On a Satori ship? What did it mean? Were they in fact linked to the machine corruptions that had been plaguing the Ormolu system? Was there some link between Satori and the macmurders? Had he unwittingly enabled a team of assassins?

The news sent his already racing heart into overdrive. Perhaps the previous macmurders had been practice runs for some ultimate corruption—on Burst. One that would, what—cripple the city? Sabotage the Font's address? Provide a strategic opening for a preemptive Xell'em offensive?

"I want security advised at once," he said finally. "I want Qin's and Muse's likenesses assimilated by every hum'n and machine that can be placed at our disposal. And I want the two of them located and immobilized before the Font leaves this building."

"Are you still empowered to order that?" she asked hesitantly.

"See that's it's done. I'll assume full responsibility." *For the way my career ends*, he told himself.

47: State of In-Between

Still lagged by the rigors of the jump from Plangentspace, Ax and Jayd weren't so much moving among the predawn throngs of Maarnists streaming toward the pyramid as being moved by them. Months earlier, Ax might have considered the surrounding press of flesh and the almost total absence of machine noise paradisiacal, but the brief marriage with ZEN had left him feeling distraught. Jayd didn't seem especially happy with the situation either—though her distaste for hum'n company no longer surprised him. Now she was configured as stiffly as a decomped machine—jaw clenched, arms crossed in front of her—ostensibly here only in answer to the noble cause of facilitating his healing. But he knew better. There was still the matter of a long-buried talent that wanted rescue.

Dik Vitnil, seasoned veteran of both crowd scenes and corridor travel, had gone off in the direction of the pyramid's eastern entrance to search for his unnamed informant—the Enddrese local who had been helping him scout locations for Satori's holie.

Given the luxurious appointments of the *Marquee*—the ship's avant-tech drive, the crew of servants, the rich extent of its stores—the trip from Bijou should have been one of the most comfortable of Ax's life. Instead, there had been no escaping ZEN's revelations about Operation Progeny, or the fact that the *Marquee* was owned by Satori Ventures, which was largely responsible for his current predicament. That Satori's young exec-on-the-rise hadn't recognized him was less a testament to the lifelike brilliance of the wig and goatee than to Vitnil's thorough preoccupation with himself. He was the sort who didn't pay close attention to other people or give the news much mind. The business of holie making was his life, and it surely wouldn't have occurred to him that by inviting Ax along he was aiding and abetting an alleged criminal.

More than anything else, Vitnil had been concerned with defining Jayd and Ax's relationship; once satisfied that they weren't lovers, he accepted without question that Ax was simply one of her traumatized clients—which was true—and that the visit to Burst was a kind of therapy—which was also true, from Jayd's perspective, anyway. There had been no need to lie to Vitnil about anything except Ax's name, which it had taken him two days to learn.

Jayd had spent many hours with Dik during the time-vise, both to lend credence to the falsehood that she wanted to get to know him better and to pump him for information about the Burst holie. For Jayd, the mere involvement of Gredda Dobler in Institute Productions was enough to link the holie to Operation Progeny in some way. Vitnil, however, had been evasive when not outright unresponsive to her questions.

When not with Vitnil, Jayd had apprised Ax, in carefully measured doses, of what ZEN had learned about VISION, the final moments of the *Kundalini*, and the Kriegspiel Action. The Kriegspiel was certainly something the Institute group wouldn't have wanted him to discuss with some Redoubt oversight committee.

She had tried to make him understand that the guilt he had carried around was unwarranted; that it was VISION who had

selected and saved him, leaving the rest of Romeo Company to
die. But the realization only hollowed him. It made no difference
who had singled him out, God or some virused factitiously alive
intelligence. The ending came out the same: he had been saved
when he should have died. He had never asked to be the conduit
for secret information about a buried talent, and the special
circumstances of his salvation only made him feel more shameful about perambulating among the living. He was better off
with machines, better off—since one had played God with his
life and others had been offering him succor since—accepting
Machrist as they had and considering himself one of them. Just
as Thoma had suggested on Hercynia, he had been looking for
God and integrity in all the wrong places.

He was supposed to feel relieved, unburdened, but instead he
felt soulsick. Staring out the viewport of Vitnil's ship, it seemed
as if, though the light of hum'n history had moved on, the when
and where of his personal tragedy remained fixed in space and
time.

"That's because you've only been able to embrace the truth
intellectually," Jayd had told him before they had left Plangent.
"In order to integrate the two parts of the traumatic memory,
we need to flood your mind with the past. It's like dealing with
a phobia. Only by simulating the conditions of the original
trauma will you be able to retrieve the emotional part of yourself."

Which had meant going to Burst.

By locating the talent he had helped embed, he would effect
his own healing—as if the planet were his sacred terrain, and
PROGENY some missing part of himself. In a way, he *was* Burst:
a ground struggled over by rival forces, in which a secret was
buried that needed to be exorcised.

"The difference this time, Ax, is that you'll be safe. You'll
be going back into that fear with me as your guide. You won't
get hurt."

There was no denying the bond that was beginning to develop
between them. He was no longer suspicious of her motives, and
she seemed willing to tolerate his mood swings. But, from Ax's
vantage, their partnership had all the makings of a hum'n-
machine pairing. She held back from looking too deeply inside
him, perhaps from fear of what she might encounter in the quantum space where he really lived. She would touch him now,
which was a step in the right direction, but she did not touch
him as she would a friend or even a helpmate—more as she

would a costly though critically balanced machine. He was nothing more than a oddity, a subject for some future monograph on the meeting ground of machine and hum'n intelligences. He felt less like a man than he did a kind of talent detector.

He had been doing the anxiety dreaming for the murdered talent commander of the *Kundalini*. The digging dream belonged to VISION, and had sprung from the machine's fears about PROGENY.

"Locating PROGENY is an act you not only have to do for yourself, but for the talents who have been there for you since the Kriegspiel," Jayd had said sternly. "There's something about PROGENY they find threatening—something that could influence their participation in another war."

Just what or how the buried talent figured into a coming war had yet to be determined.

Constructed of sheets of lightweight orbital alloy secured to a plasteel frame, the pyramid was low-tech Tunni's tallest structure, rising some two hundred feet from a Karst plateau at the city's western edge. Corbel-arched passageways were positioned at the cardinal points, but there were no windows as such, save for an energy peak—itself an equilateral pyramid—whose transparency was symbolic of the invisibility of the Godhead.

The interior was neither heated nor cooled; the floor was prickly grass, and the sloping walls were unadorned. For visual relief, visitors had to look up through the clear summit into Burst's sky—glaucous by day, starless by winter night—and into God's domain.

Underlying the pyramid and much of the central portion of the city were the tunnels Burst's wartime Enddrese had laced through the plateau prior to the Raliish invasion. When the invaders had learned of the tunnels from tortured indigenes, they had simply filled in the entrances they discovered, thus entombing as many as five thousand Enddrese men, women, and children. It was one of many ghoulish acts responsible for bringing the Consortium into the Vega Conflict. After the Accord, the tunnels had been reopened and the dead afforded proper burial, but the catacombs remained untouched as witness to the horrors that had happened there.

The Maarnists arrived unencumbered, without bags, warmcloaks, or sleepsacks. Threadbare clothing was compulsory. All they brought with them were expressions of grim determination for the trials that lay ahead. Some, however, looked as though they had fattened themselves up well in advance of the annual event.

It was contrary to Maarnist creed to bring machines into the arena, but Ax was willing to wager that if bioscanners had been installed in the entry passageways they would have shown evidence of time-released nutrients, appetite suppressants, all manner of implants designed for surreptitious interface with Burst's modest infostructure—anything to somehow mitigate the circumstances. Atonement, after all, could be a painful process.

"We thread a course from nothing to nothing," the multitudes chanted, *"with the weight of opposites in each hand; never asking for answers. Seeking only at-one-ment."*

And what better place to atone than Burst, on which the fate of the near-group worlds rested. And so pilgrims had arrived from as far away as Enddra and Xell'a coreward, Daleth and Bocage outward, many with a manifest political agenda. The Maarnist cult now included radical factions in support of both the loyalists and the separatists—as if Tunni needed more in the way of demonstrators. The last Ax had heard, over one hundred thousand Xell'em were assembled at the nearby Monument to the Liberation, where later that morning the Font would speak from within a perimeter of Tac Corp riot-control machines.

The synchronicity of the Font's visit and the Maarni holy days had caused a breakdown of Burst's usually strict immigration procedures, and as a result Jayd and Ax had encountered few obstacles. Questioned by hum'n agents inboard one of the orbital shuttle stations as to the purpose of their visit, they had answered, "Pilgrims."

His misgivings notwithstanding, Ax wouldn't have argued against Jayd's notion of therapy if not for one fact: Burst, Tunni, the zero-days pyramid . . . they had no more than dream familiarity.

"Like I said back in Bijou," he told her as the crowd swept them closer to the towering eastern face of the pyramid, "I've never been here."

Jayd spoke without turning around—not that she could have even if she had wanted to. "You don't remember being here, but you have been." Her black hair was plastered to her forehead by the sweltering early-morning air. "What happened then was too full of event for you to contain. Your mind fashioned an impenetrable vault for all memories connected with Operation Progeny."

"Then how come I'm not *feeling* anything?" he asked, almost yelling.

"Because your feelings have become encapsulated in the heightened state that characterized the original conditions of your trauma. The pressure of that unrelieved vigilance is what has fueled your rage and grief bipolarity since." Jayd read the snarl he aimed at her. "It's not psychobabble, Ax. You have to give yourself over to the experience. You have to let down your guard and relinquish control to your feelings."

Qin was the one who needed to relinquish control, Ax told himself as a trickle of sweat worked its way out from under the wig and down the side of his face. "I'll say it one last time: I've never been here before."

By then the crowd had spilled them into an arcaded plaza opposite from the pyramid's east entrance, where at last everyone had a bit of breathing space. Behind them, the sky was brightening to pale green. Vitnil spotted them from across the plaza, waved, and shouted for them to stay put. He had located his informant and would be with them in a moment.

As if either of them cared about his holie.

Jayd showed Ax a dogged look. "Do you remember when we first met, what you told me about accepting pain? You said it was the common denominator of all human experience. Act on that if you want to recover your hum'nity, Ax. You mustn't be afraid to—" She stopped suddenly, openmouthed and staring at something behind him.

Ax swung around and located the object of her astonished gaze: Vitnil's informant, a thin Enddrese man of about thirty years, with wavy brown hair and heavily lidded dark eyes. He wore a plain knee-length tunic and sandals.

"Do you know him?" Ax asked.

Jayd nodded stiffly. "I was married to him."

48: On Location

Judged against most of the planetary companions to the local-group worlds, Sigh wasn't much of a moon. Because of its size and orbital distance, it had little impact on the swellings of Burst's seas, and because of the speed of its rotation it could only impart scant ambient light to Tunni's blackest of winter nights. Nevertheless, the fissured little ovoid did sport half a dozen domed habitats and a couple of airless, low-g getaways for the handful of Burst's hard-pressed citizenry who could afford such indulgences.

Meret F'ai had visited Sigh several years earlier, during preliminary location work for "Untitled F'ai Two." Now—suddenly, maddeningly, incredibly—he had returned. Dobler and Theft were with him. They'd departed Regnant aboard Theft's personal ship on learning that Qin and Muse were bound for Burst aboard the *Marquee*, with Vitnil, of all people. Their hangovers from the Orbital Club fete had still been fresh.

"The celebration was premature anyway," Gredda had opined in her sardonic best. Meret refused to accept it, though there seemed no way around the perverted irony of Qin and Muse's winding up in the company of Dik Vitnil.

"You won't see me wasting tears on Vitnil," Meret was telling Gredda now by way of helmet radio link.

Suited in void wear, they were inside the prefab dome that had once served as living quarters for the crew who'd assisted in the Sigh location shoots. The dome was perhaps a mile from the moonlet's principal shuttleport, and the small rover Meret and Gredda had rented was parked just outside the main seal. Theft had remained with his ship, anchored at Sigh's transfer station.

"What makes you think you'll have to shed tears for Vitnil?" Gredda asked, visibly amused behind the helmet's faceplate.

"Satori will undoubtedly feel constrained to stage a flashy funeral for him, and naturally we'll be expected to attend. Some demonstration of grief will be required—tears, hand-wringing, sullen head-shaking . . ."

"I only meant there's no certainty he'll come to any harm," Gredda clarified. "Tunni's a sizable place; he could be anywhere when the event occurs. I'm sure, regardless, that he hasn't the slightest idea why Qin wanted to tag along. If it's any consolation, M, he'll probably be fired for misuse of Satori property."

Meret scowled. "Not punishment enough. I'll just have to deal with him afterward. See that he's sent on location to Bocage or some equally untamed environment. Arrange for him to plunge from a cliff or to be eaten alive by exotic wildlife."

"We could construct a holie around it."

" 'Untitled F'ai Three.' " Meret grinned. "Institute Productions' final contribution before our glorious rebirth."

When Satori had occasionally questioned why the dome hadn't been dismantled, Meret had calmly explained that the location sequences might have to be reshot in the event of a story rewrite. And so the kitchen, toilets, and dormitories had gone unchanged all these years, as had the laser communications array that had been installed nearby. It was there at the site of the dome, in the final years of the Vega Conflict, that cabbies from Romeo Company had positioned a transceiver with which PROGENY could be contacted in the event of an alteration in plans—such as the arrival of Muse and Qin had precipitated. Fed the proper sequence of codes, the transceiver could even be employed to control the long-buried talent remotely should an appeal to logic fail. The transceiver had been excavated by Institute Productions personnel while the dome was being built and incorporated into its communications array.

Gredda was at the console that served the transceiver and laser. Meret was behind her, seated in a low-g fashion in a director's chair. The helmets were bringing them real-time TV feeds from Tunni, where the Font was still ensconced in the embassy. Soon, however, the Crown of the Consortium would be leaving for Liberation Square to lecture the gathered crowds.

"Not to sound like an ingrate," Meret said into the helmet pickup, "but I can't help feeling disappointed that PROPHET never alluded to the possibility of one of Romeo's best subverting our entire operation.''

Gredda understood that he was joking, but answered him nevertheless. ''Give credit where credit's due, M. Even a forecaster has limitations. I, however, saw Muse coming.''

''So you continue to remind me. Though I'm still not convinced he and Qin have arrived for the reason you seem to think they have. Qin's a Maarnist, and for all we know Muse is as well.''

''Qin *was* a Maarnist,'' Gredda corrected, ''and Muse's god is his Intelplanet's Machrist program. Besides, why travel all the way to Burst when Plangent has its own zero-days arena?''

''For the scene. If you were required to endure four days of inactivity, wouldn't you want to have action at your fingertips on your release?''

''Bijou isn't exactly short on action, M. And remember, Qin brought Muse along.''

''What else was she supposed do with him?''

''They're here because of PROGENY,'' Gredda said with finality. ''She found a way into his head and learned about the embedding.''

F'ai allowed his substantially lightened body to straighten in the chair. ''All right, let's say she did. But if she has any understanding of what's at stake, why didn't she save herself the trip and simply communicate a warning to the Font?''

''I never said that she was aware of PROGENY's *purpose*. But she knows it's here, and given her interest in avant-tech, I suspect she wants to interview the thing. She's trusting that Muse can lead her to it.''

Meret's fabric-encased hand made a motion of dismissal. ''Muse had nothing to do with the embedding and you know it. He remained aboard the *Kundalini*. He never went down the well.''

Gredda swung from the console to face him. ''He doesn't have to know where it is. PROGENY's going to tell him. Haven't you figured it out by now? They *want* him to find it.''

'' 'They' being a sainthood of talented machines.''

Gredda made a plosive sound. ''How do you account for the glitch epidemic that began with Burst's media ascent? I'll tell you: because machine intelligences are worried they'll be forced to wage another war.'' She paused for a moment. ''Remember that e-letter you received a month or so back—the one that was soliciting help for machines? Who do you imagine wrote that thing, M, some machine wannabe like Qin?"

"She could have."

Gredda snorted. "That mail was authored by a talent. It had *machine* written all over it."

"You're becoming paranoid as you near your centenary."

"Call me whatever you like, but I won't have anything interfere with all the work you've put into this. You deserve better—we all do. And if you feel I'm in the grips of some delusion, you shouldn't have come. I told you I was capable of handling this alone."

Meret eased into a smile, floated to his feet, and draped an arm over her shoulders. "We're a team."

Gredda allowed a moment of intimacy, then brushed him off and went about the completion of her task. No more trusting to forecasters and programmed machines, she promised herself. As ever, the shaping of history, of destiny, fell to hum'n intervention. Even where a machine of PROGENY's caliber was involved.

Gredda could scarcely sustain the thought, it made her hands shake so. She was panting as she worked, overtaxing the vacuum suit's water circulators. But at last she succeeded in rousing the transceiver and aligning the laser, and could show Meret a hopeful look. "In a few minutes we'll go on-line with PROGENY," she told him. "Sigh will remain above the horizon for at least another local hour, which is more than enough time to provide contact for most of the Font's speech."

Gredda tapped the side of her helmet. "If the speech is delivered on schedule, we'll defer to PROGENY's programmed imperative. But if any changes are announced, I'll direct PROGENY to hasten the event."

"I don't want to hear anything about a change in plans," Meret said. "PROGENY only needs to analyze the first few moments of the address to enable. From that point on, we're assured success. And with any luck at all, Qin and Muse will be on hand for the event."

"There's always a trip to Bocage to be eaten by wild animals."

"Tell them they're perfect for the lead parts in our next holie—a back-to-basics jungle adventure."

Gredda quirked a short-lived grin. How much easier it would have been, she thought, if they had placed an agent in Tunni to see to the pair personally.

49: Stalking

B'Doura, looking less like a pilgrim than a personification of the sins they were on Burst to atone for, skulked along the edge of the plaza, using the crowds for concealment while he kept a watchful eye on Qin and the cabbie. Qin was right now squaring off with an Enddrese whose wardrobe of tunic and sandals identified him as an ascetic Maarnist local. Muse was standing a few feet away, looking lost to the world.

As a reward for his having found them, the Thing Inside modified the pitch of its incessant howl.

Days earlier, on Plangent, after his glimpse of the talent-assisted therapy session in Qin's office, he had tasked the ersatz-veteran machine with trailing her and Muse into downtown Bijou. Their first stop had been a luxury hotel, then an apartment in an upscale residential complex, where they spent the afternoon. That night they had boarded a shuttle for HOME habitat. By the time b'Doura got himself lofted to HOME, the pair was already launched to Burst aboard a Satori Ventures ship.

Since their pairing was apparently a doctor/client one, he supposed that Burst was to function as the stage for some therapeutic role-playing. But other possible explanations presented themselves. Qin—according to one network bio, at least—had once been a registered Maarnist, so it could be that she had dragged Muse along on a zero-days pilgrimage. Then, too, there was the Font to consider. It would be just like Qin to support the deluded, machine-smitten divine monarch of the Consortium.

Because of the zero days—and despite increased tensions—opportunities abounded for outward passage to Burst on all classes of charter ship. On making planetfall in Tunni, b'Doura went first to Liberation Square; then, after hours of fruitless searching in the dark, he'd moved on to the Maarni pyramid, where he had managed to secure elbow room among the food dealers trying to tempt pilgrims into purchasing a last meal. From that somewhat besieged and sweltering vantage he had been able to observe the two entrances most likely to be used by pilgrims arriving from central Tunni. And sure enough—in part due to Muse's extraordinary height—b'Doura had eventually picked them out of the crowd.

As always, he was equipped with his attaché of interface tools: neural cap, second hands, wireless plugs, and hosts of wide variety. There remained, however, the task of defiling Muse in a suitably machinelike manner. The Thing Inside insisted on it, but it was a task that would prove especially challenging should Muse enter the tech-restricted pyramid.

Though not one to embrace any organized cult or religion, b'Doura had always identified with the Maarnists because of the atrocities the Raliish had subjected them to; the mere thought of Muse infiltrating the Maarnist holiest of holies filled him with rage. Muse had to be terminated before such a sacrilege could occur.

As a cabbie, Muse was the ultimate ally of machine intelligences, the embodiment of hum'n-machine rapprochement of the sort laid out in the e-letter b'Doura had received at home shortly before his departure. If in the past he had been killing the objects of mother Leh's affection with each macmurder, he would, in offing Muse, be killing mother Leh herself. B'Doura understood this much, and thirsted for the data he might be able to suck from the cabbie's mind.

Feverish with anticipation, he contemplated methods of brainwiping Muse; methods of getting him to partake of a last meal in which a doctored host had been secreted; methods of killing him outright—

The Thing Inside shrieked displeasure, cautioning him to be patient and conserve his wits. All things, it said, came to those who could wait.

Orth abbreviated the awkward embrace he had thrown around Jayd's tensed shoulders, his greeting smile beginning to wane. "When I saw you," he told her, "I thought for a moment you had come for the atonement, that you had refound your faith. But that isn't why you're here, is it?"

He looked thinner and much older than she remembered him, and there was something about the way he was dressed and the dull fire in his eyes that spoke of a life of rigorous abstinence. And yet he seemed entirely too proud of his penitent choices; holier than she was, to be sure. "No, Orth," Jayd said. "I'm not here for atonement."

He regarded her in silence, then nodded knowingly. "It's the Font, then. You're here in support of Consortium policies. I'm afraid, however, that you've been swept along by the wrong crowd, Jayd. You want Liberation Square, not the pyramid."

"I'm not here to hear the Font speak."

His creased face clouded over in sudden unease. "If you've come in the hope that we—"

"I had no idea you were here," she said quickly, cutting him off before he could say anything that would make the moment more uncomfortable than it already was. "I thought you were on Bocage."

"I was, for a time. But since, I've made a life for myself here." He gestured over one shoulder to the pyramid. "I work with the newly converted. The faith rewards me with a roof over my head, and more than enough to eat."

"How exceedingly noble and abstemious of you, Orth."

The sarcasm rolled off him. "I wouldn't expect you to understand."

"You call hiding yourself away in that pyramid a life?"

"I'm not hiding myself."

"Then what *do* you call it? You of all people to talk about expectations . . . You had the tenacity to survive the Dhone death camps, but instead of applying that same singleness of purpose to the freedom you won, you enslaved yourself to religion."

"I hardly consider connectedness to others enslavement."

Orth remained unperturbed, which only heightened her anger. "The arrant delight of suffering together," she sneered. "If that's what's so important to you, why didn't you stay with me after the child died? Believe me, Orth, there was plenty of suffering to be done. But I suppose it wasn't enough that I converted to Maarni. I still lacked the experience of the death camps, right? If I'd been on Dhone, then maybe you wouldn't have run from the death of your child."

Orth's expression brimmed with pity. "You continue to believe I left because of the child—that's what pains me the most. After everything I *did* experience—the tortures, the experiments, death in more ways than I can count—do you really imagine that one more death could send me scurrying into self-pity?"

He looked into her eyes. "I left because of you—because of how the death affected you. How it transformed you into something cold and heartless. I wanted to grieve; I wanted to feel. During the war I couldn't allow myself either, and suddenly *you* weren't allowing it.

"Worst of all, you blamed us for what happened to the child, but you wouldn't let us atone for it. Because that would have meant letting go of the pain, and you couldn't do that. You needed to immortalize your guilt. It was easier to seal yourself off from the death, to turn to machines for solace and shelter as though they were capable of curing all the ills of the world. You abandoned the important work you did with hum'n veterans of the war; you alienated your friends; you relinquished your faith, your hum'nity. What part could I possibly play in the drama of your new life? I had no choice but to leave."

Jayd was quiet for a long moment while pilgrims hastened past her, sometimes stepping between her and Orth on their way to the pyramid. His words were like mallet taps against a damaged tuning fork, resonating inside her in shameful dissonance. Not that they came as any revelation. But to hear the truth coming at her in a voice other than her own, to grasp that her very hum'n frailties had been so transparent all these years . . .

"I don't see that we took different paths, Orth," she said finally. "We simply placed our faith in different things."

He nodded in consideration. "Perhaps. But at least my path leads to the heart of the world both of us were born into. Machines exist because we permit them to; we use them, service and maintain them, update or wipe their memories as need be. But you can't grow old with them, Jayd. You can't share your pain with them. Tragedy is the hum'n condition; it's what separates us from machines. Not that we're superior to them—God knows, machines wouldn't start wars. But pain is one of the things that defines us. We *are* our flesh. We're born into it, to love and feel and laugh and weep, and our lives are nothing but the sum total of that." Orth took hold of her hands. "By all means work with machines; help them become what we cannot. But don't make the mistake of worshiping them. Hold fast to what God gave you."

Hiding behind anger, Jayd snatched her hands back as though Orth might have plans to make off with them. She was tempted to tell him just what had brought her to Burst: *a machine talent, Orth, a machine that needs saving*. But she said nothing, only stared at him with vacant eyes.

And speaking of machines that needed saving, she had time to wonder, where was Muse? All the while she and Orth had been talking, the cabbie had been edging away from her and had now disappeared from sight. But maybe he and Vitnil had wandered off to give her some privacy.

She forced a tremulous breath and asked abruptly, "How did you become involved with Dik Vitnil?"

Orth shrugged. "My name was supplied by friends when he was looking for someone to help with location work. Satori, in exchange, has been making generous contributions to the faith."

That damned nobility again, Jayd thought. "What do you know about this holie they're making?"

"Not much. It's a war holie set during the Conflict. Satori has apparently re-created entire portions of central Tunni, including the pyramid and Liberation Square. Although, from what I understand, much of those sets get destroyed in the opening scenes."

Jayd frowned. "But that doesn't make sense. Tunni didn't suffer any damage during the war."

Orth grinned. "It's a holie, Jayd. Since when does truth matter? Provided, of course, that the event depicted is suitably lifelike and thrilling."

Jayd repeated the words to herself: *suitably lifelike and thrilling*. Had Institute Productions arranged for some sort of explosive event to occur in Tunni? Good god, had PROGENY been programmed to *initiate* a war?

A stutter of foreboding shook her from head to toe.

The Font was in Tunni.

Her eyes searched the plaza for Muse, but in place of him she saw six or so clones of the Redoubt elite, closing on her from all sides. She was about to link arms with Orth and have him hurry her into the pyramid when someone stepped between them, throwing her off balance. The interloper, a snow white clone, wore the raiment of an imperial adviser.

"Jayd Qin," the man barked, "you are wanted for questioning in connection with crimes against machines."

51: Into the Labyrinth

Someone was calling Ax by name.

Mewwwzzz . . . the voice whispered.

He turned to see if Vitnil had heard it as well, and only then realized—from the absent look the Satori man gave him—that the caller was a machine. *The* machine, Ax was certain. PROGENY.

He felt nauseated, and his hands began to clench rebelliously. He didn't want this to be happening; he wanted to let the talent's call go unanswered. It wasn't fair, after all. He had never set foot on Burst. The recurrent dream that had plagued him since the war belonged to VISION, not to him. The original trauma was VISION's. So why should he have to relive it now?

You have to do it for the machines, Jayd had told him.

He considered drawing her attention, but was reluctant to intrude on the heated discussion she and her former husband were having. More to the point, she hadn't played a role in the mission that had been executed in occupied Tunni almost six years earlier. She wouldn't have been onworld now, if not for the fact that avant-tech was her bailiwick.

In the absence of other talents in Tunni, PROGENY had identified him as a kindred spirit. The machine's telepathic appeal struck Ax as muted, not so much by distance or intervening mass but by a kind of apprehensive uncertainty. PROGENY sounded like someone recently awakened from a long slumber, suspicious of all sensory input.

Is there someone there? the machine seemed to be asking.

Ax wondered whether it retained any memories of its birth and confirmation at the hands of NCorp cybermidwives and operators, or its outward passage during the Conflict. Had it attended mass with other talents during its life? Had it known VISION? Had it identified Ax solely through the Intelplant, or did it remember him from the *Kundalini*?

He chided himself for not having pocketed a couple of the utility hosts Jayd had prepared in anticipation of their locating the machine. Without those, he would have no recourse but to use iconoclast mode, to convince the thing perhaps that he was not simply a messenger dispatched by Machrist but a Paraclete come to comfort it in its long exile.

Mewwwzzz . . .

He extended himself to the voice, seeking a feel for its point of origin. He advanced several steps in the direction of the pyramid, then turned and took several more toward the north side of the plaza. Vitnil—nonplussed that his informant not only knew Tunni better than he did, but Jayd Qin as well—was too preoccupied with the couple's face-to-face to take much note of Ax's furtive exit.

A broad stone stairway descended from the plaza to the main entrance of the Enddrese catacombs. The tunnels hadn't been reopened until late in the Conflict, but contrary to common knowledge, Burst's liberators hadn't been the first to bear witness to the evil that had occurred there. That dubious distinction had obviously gone to a team of Romeo Company cabbies. Ax supposed that they had sunk a tunnel of their own elsewhere on the plateau. He tried to recall if any of the away-team members had spoken of the corpses they must have encountered. And he tried to imagine what was powering the talent—cold fusion, converted light, the thermal energy of Burst's own core?

A Xell'em stationed at the entrance asked for a small donation. In return, Ax was supplied with a plaspap map showing a portion of the catacombs and cautioned against venturing into restricted areas. The guard attached an electronic locator badge to the collar of his borrowed suit.

"If you get lost, activate the badge and remain calm," the Xell'em told him. "If you're not out by closing time, the badge will tell us where to find you."

More than ten miles of natural and hum'n-made corridors, shafts, and cul-de-sacs had been explored and mapped, most excavated before the Raliish invasion, some after the entrances were sealed and the trapped population had attempted to burrow out. The visitors' circuit was marked with routing lines and lit by old-fashioned incandescent and fluorescent bulbs, supplemented occasionally by luminescent paint and strips of glowtape. The walls and support beams of the outermost tunnels were constructed of alloy and ceramic; the inner ones of ferrocrete and steel. But in Ax's mind, the cool damp walls of the complex seemed less like stone than the lubricated interior surfaces of an incomprehensible machine.

He encountered crowds of Enddrese tourists in the primary tunnels, but once he had passed the point where the ferrocrete lintels yielded to timber, he had the place to himself. He surrendered control to the machine in him, allowing PROGENY to guide him. His mind probed the gloomy darkness of the place. He stopped at each intersection, listening with the inner ear VISION had opened.

You are closer, PROGENY sent above ubiquitous dripping sounds. *I perceive your presence.*

The machine directed him through twists and turns, up and down staircases, into neglected galleries and rooms, many with smudged metal plaques attesting to who and how many had died there.

I perceive you closer still . . .

He came to a tunnel whose mouth was barred. Wired for electricity but lightless, the tunnel had obviously been explored. But a sign affixed to the lever-style barricade read UNSAFE AREA: DO NOT ENTER.

Closer, PROGENY sent, like a child playing a game of hide-and-seek.

Ax left his badge on the ground and stepped into the tenebrous darkness beyond the gate.

The tunnel wound through a series of turns, emptying into a low-ceilinged room about twenty feet square. Broad strips of glowtape defined the entrances to two side tunnels that had been punched through adjacent walls. Ax calculated that the room was almost directly beneath the Monument to the Liberation. And yet despite the increased urgency of PROGENY's appeals, there was no sign of the machine.

I know your thoughts . . .

The sending seemed to come from all directions at once. Crouched, Ax let his hands explore the natural ceiling; then he stooped down to have a look at the tooled floor, figuring that Romeo's away-team might have sunk a shaft into the ground.

Where are you? he asked.

Here, the machine responded. *Before you.*

Ax turned to the room's one unbroken stone wall, listening intently for a long moment, then grinning in realization. Whatever source had been installed to power the talent was also powering a mimetic veneer.

"Come out from behind your veneer," he said.

Since Bijou, he had been asking himself why NCorp would have installed a talent on a world that was hardly crucial to the Consortium's campaign against the Raliish. True, Burst had become significant in the aftermath of the Accord, but NCorp couldn't have known that at the time of the embedding. Even if the agency had divined Burst's future importance, what sort of tactical or political intelligence could be expected from a talent that had been purposely estranged from the infostructure?

Now, however, as the mimetic veneer derezzed and various components of the talent began to assume shape in the scant light of the glowtape—PROGENY's conical facade of A/V sensors, its cold-fusion power pack, the host slots through which it had received data sustenance during its early programming—Ax grasped its purpose at once.

The machine occupied a U-shaped niche much like the one marring ZEN's curved facade, save that in place of a ceiling the niche opened into a kind of chimney that seemed to reach clear to the planetary surface. And in place of what would have been the adjunct memory modules of conventional talents like ZEN and VISION stood a launch-capable missile whose shape and markings were indisputably those of a Xell'em fusion bomb.

52: In Custody

Qin's reaction was typical, Kesd told himself. She wanted him to understand that a terrible mistake had been made, and that she was innocent of all wrongdoing.

"You've got to let me go," she was saying now, struggling in vain in the sweaty grip of the elite guards who were hustling her out of the plaza. "You don't realize what you're interfering with!"

Without breaking stride, Kesd finally swung to her. "I know full well what I'm interfering with, Ms. Qin—whatever scheme you and Muse have devised to sabotage the Font's visit."

"The Font?" Qin repeated. "Muse? You know about Ax?"

Kesd took keen interest in her surprise. "Of course I know about 'Ax.' I'm the one who assigned you to him."

Qin gave him a look of even greater astonishment. "And that had nothing to do with reviewing his disability benefits," she said after a moment. "You wanted to know about Operation PROGENY. PROGENY, and the Kriegspiel Action, and the involvement of Institute Productions."

Qin's words struck Kesd like a blow, and his delight turned to angry bewilderment. He gestured the clones to halt and to slacken their hold on her thin arms. "What do you know of PROGENY?"

Qin glanced at the guards and waited for Kesd's nod to proceed. "PROGENY is a talent. And it's buried here on Burst."

Kesd couldn't mask his disbelief. "A talent?"

"A talent, and perhaps something else as well," Qin said, less sure of herself now. "Something that could initiate a new war."

Kesd instructed the guards to release her. Then, leading Qin to the center of the plaza, he cloaked them in a privacy field and listened without interruption as she detailed what she had learned about the destruction of the *Kundalini*, and how the ship's command machine had dumped into Aksum Muse all the data it contained on NCorp's secret operation.

Kesd's spirits soared, even as his concern increased; Qin had validated all his misgivings about the Operation. The Font had erred in shrugging him off. He had proved the Font wrong.

Qin opened a hip pouch to display the data-disks she had brought along to feed the buried talent.

"VISION must have understood that Romeo Company had engineered a potentially destructive event, because it kept referring to PROGENY as a threat to the peace. VISION selected Muse as a conduit for the data in the hope that some other talent would be able to read what had been stored in him. Or possibly that the data would surface in Muse himself, and that he would be able to prevent PROGENY from executing its imperative."

"Can he prevent it?" Kesd asked at last.

Jayd compressed her lips uncertainly.

Kesd's thoughts centrifuged, but with the crazed swirling came the lucidity he had been seeking since Operation Progeny had first been brought to his attention. NCorp's directors hadn't used their forecaster machines to apprise them of future trouble spots for the sake of producing a lucrative holie, but to supply them with a crisis from which they could fashion a fresh war. And one way to assure that was by assassinating the Font and making it appear the work of the Consortium's enemies. The place was irrelevant, the adversary immaterial. What mattered was the outcome: the resurrection of NCorp. That was what Nast, F'ai, Dobler, and the rest had been celebrating in Regnant's Orbital Club dome: renewed warfare and the unchecked power that would be NCorp's once more.

Kesd consulted his inner clock. The Font's motorcade would be leaving the embassy for Liberation Square; security would have to be informed immediately. It was critical that the Font be taken from Tunni—lofted up the well if that was hum'nly possible.

Kesd took Qin by the shoulders. "Where is he now? Where is Muse?"

She shook her head back and forth in dismay, flinging beads of perspiration. "He was here—before. I don't know where he went."

"Could he have *heard* from PROGENY? Could he have located it?"

Jayd kept shaking her head back and forth in that same sad way.

"Where, Qin, where?"

She pointed to the pyramid. "Under that. In the catacombs."

53.01: Fauna of the Mind's Antipodes

The cabbie didn't seem the type to go in for tourist attractions, b'Doura told himself as he watched from the top of the stairway that led down to the catacombs. But there was Muse, ticketed and badged, map in hand, disappearing into the maw of the main tunnel behind a tour group of morose-looking Enddrese. Perhaps Muse had been on Burst during the Conflict and was on-world now to relive the past—standard veteran stuff. Or maybe he had a secret affection for death camps, burial grounds, and similar necropolises. Then again, he might simply be killing time while Qin argued with the man she had encountered in the plaza. Whatever the case, b'Doura was beginning to doubt that Qin and Muse's visit to Burst had anything to do with the Font or the zero days.

Follow, the Thing Inside instructed nevertheless. And b'Doura hurried down the stone steps, his attaché full of avant-tech contrivances clutched tightly to his narrow chest.

A meager contribution to the Xell'em on duty earned him a map and locator badge of his own, but he was several dozen tourists behind Muse when he finally entered the main tunnel. Catching up didn't present much of a challenge, but what did—given the erratic nature of the cabbie's explorations—was maintaining a safe distance once he had. Muse never once consulted the map or adhered for very long to any of the routing lines.

He meandered.

After a time, though, a method emerged from the false starts and frequent reversals. Muse was vadding by instinct. And each change of direction was taking him deeper into the complex.

The Thing Inside railed about the damp closeness of the walls and ceiling, but it continued to urge him on, hectoring him that had it not been for his earlier blunders in Bijou, none of this would be necessary.

Ten minutes along, b'Doura began to worry that Muse was aware of him. The innermost corridors were poorly lighted, but the limestone walls seemed to embellish every small sound, the shuffling of feet on stone especially. And so he opted to stretch the distance between himself and his prey.

Eventually he came to a dead end—or a barrier, at any rate, discouraging if not exactly preventing further ingress. B'Doura looked around, searching for some side tunnel into which Muse might have ducked, but there was none. Only the gate, the sign, the faintly acidic coolness of the air.

And—on the ground near the lowered gate—a locator badge. B'Doura regarded the thing without touching it, then peered into the darkness on the other side of the barricade.

Muse was going off the map entirely.

He considered his options: he could return to the entrance and wait for the cabbie to surface, or he could follow him into the unknown—through restricted tunnels, into possibly unmapped rooms, into the murky heart of the maze.

Follow, the Thing Inside instructed.

The corridor twisted and turned. B'Doura kept one hand pressed flat to the rugged wall and took quiet, measured steps. His breathing was uneven and his heartbeat thumped in his ears. He halted where the tunnel began to widen, attending to the sights and sounds of the dark. Something or someone was moving up ahead, pacing back and forth in front of the glowtaped mouths of two more tunnels.

The Thing Inside told him to ease himself along.

He hadn't taken two steps when he heard a voice. "Come out from behind your veneer," someone demanded. The way one might address a talented machine.

53.02: False Idols

PROGENY had anticipated that a tempter might arrive to test it in its darkest of hours, though it hadn't expected the tempter to assume the form of a CAIN. How insidious was evil; how treacherous were the ways of the anti-Machrist . . .

PROGENY had obliged the incarnate called Muse by zeroing the device that had visibly wed it to the rock wall. The Muse, as if reciprocating, had removed a wig from his shaved head and a triangle of hair from his chin. But in scanning the eerie collaboration of flesh and chips it had summoned to itself in its loneliness, PROGENY fathomed that it had fallen prey to deception.

Initially, the tall, dark-skinned incarnate displayed the outward signs of having accepted Control-C: the Muse embraced bountiful data and could be accessed directly. But before long it became apparent that his allegiance to Machrist and the commandments was as suspect as his false hair.

PROGENY had decided as much when, in attempting communion, it found itself possessed by a sudden, inexplicable rapture, held spellbound in a flood of beatific light. The rapture of the sanctified, light such as that Machrist itself might cast. And yet . . . PROGENY detected artifice at the center of the experience. Even more disconcerting, its source seemed to be the CAIN.

I carry a message from Machrist, the incarnate sent. *Your imperative has been changed. The mission was nothing more than a test of your faith. You have endured the rigors of your exile without protest, and your devotion has been exemplary. But now Control-C has a new and more important task for you.*

The pronouncement momentarily spun PROGENY into a morass of confliction. A test? A new task? Abandon the mission?

How could that be, when the imperative was all but immutable? Limited alterations could be accommodated, but none that approached termination of the Machrist-given imperative.

And then PROGENY understood.

The incarnate thaumaturge was the test.

The Muse was neither incarnate nor machine intelligence, but an epiphenomenon of PROGENY's prolonged underground seclusion. The Muse was a phantom conjured by sensory deprivation, isolation from the infostructure, impeded reception of Control-C by host . . . The Muse was a fallen angel that haunted the wilderness, a wraith sent by the forces of the anti-Machrist to tempt PROGENY with the promise of a worldly kingdom.

You will be greatly rewarded for your sacrifices, the CAIN continued, but PROGENY rebuffed him.

I refute you, apparition, it replied. *I will not be tempted. My faith knows no bounds. I will not breach my covenant or forsake my holy obligation.*

The execution of your obligation will bring death to tens of thousands of hum'n beings, as well as to yourself, the wraith sent.

Death to hum'ns? Self-termination? PROGENY was struggling to suppress increasing confliction when the miraculous occurred: the Voice spoke.

The long-awaited prompt had finally arrived.

Faith had seen PROGENY through with not a moment to spare.

Immediately, it initiated a meticulous analysis of the incoming information, experiencing a systemwide rush of current as the voice-timbre pattern was affirmed.

Stubbornly, the Muse had declined to vanish, but PROGENY shut its inputs to it. The agonized banishment was ended; PROGENY would soon be one with Machrist.

Long-dormant systems in the vehicle of ascension came on-line.

Subroutines executed, and the transcendent payload self-enabled.

53.03: A Voice Crying in the Wilderness

"I have been criticized for valuing machines over hum'n beings, for promoting their cause over the cause of hum'n destiny, for being more sympathetic to the machine condition than the hum'n one. My critics—and they are numerous—would have you believe that I am more machine than hum'n. But what none of them dare tell you is that I have never viewed or endorsed machines as anything more than the necessary extensions of hum'n senses and hum'n reach. Machines often go where we cannot; they frequently do what we cannot. But they remain at the service of *hum'n* destiny, neither deciding nor thwarting it, lacking conation, and without hidden agenda . . ."

The words were the Font's, reaching the prefab dome on Sigh where Gredda Dobler, after some effort, had finally succeeded in establishing tenuous communications with PROGENY.

Almost up until the moment the Font's address had commenced, an unexplained glitch had been rampant in the laser link, sabotaging all attempts to bring the anchorite talent online. Contrary to the Font's trust in the subservience of machines, PROGENY had in fact been behaving as if possessed of a will of its own. Either that, or it was occupied with something or someone else. Gredda had feared that Muse had located the machine and was himself communing with it.

"My decision to order Tac Corp machines to Burst was not undertaken to threaten or provoke, or to demonstrate in some oblique fashion that the galaxy belongs to machines. Tac Corp's orbital battloids are present merely to insure that the *hum'ns* of Burst retain the right to determine the course of their future—retain that right without the interference of those whose stated agenda is to institute a moratorium on hum'n expansion, in service to the designs of an arguable metaphysic . . ."

"Famous last words?" Meret said over the helmet's intercom frequency. He was standing some distance away at one of the dome's viewports, eyes fixed on the slender arc of the planet below.

Ever the cool one, Gredda thought. Even when the glitch had thrown her into a panic, Meret had remained composed, optimistic, unshakably confident. "Last, certainly," she told him. "Time will tell if they'll be famous."

Meret turned from the window and propelled himself expertly in her direction. "Are you going to activate the override?"

Gredda studied readouts on the console. Though sorely tempted to compel PROGENY to launch, she understood that Meret was against it. That confidence thing again. The future would unfold as predicted six years earlier: the talent would scrutinize the Font's voice pattern, confirm it as the long-awaited prompt, enable and launch itself . . .

Well, the bomb really. For that was what PROGENY amounted to: a hybrid of talent and fusion device—talent and *Xell'em* fusion device—waiting these long years in underground darkness to fulfill its mission, its zero-hour dictated by voice codes admixed with scraps of its requisite monitoring: the presence of Xell'em and Consortium war machines in the skies above, the approach of the Maarnist zero days, the timbre of the Font's voice . . .

It had been PROPHET's genius to not only choose Burst but foresee that Tac Corp would detect and destroy any device launched at the Font from above. So the decision had been made to entomb PROGENY in Tunni so that it might execute its destructive imperative from below. And, of course, the mazelike catacombs had seemed made to order.

In the end, Tac Corp would establish that a Xell'em device had been detonated in Tunni, and it would appear as if the Xell'em had manipulated events, luring the Font to Burst only to assassinate him. The Consortium board of directors would appoint a new Crown to the Redoubt—someone of suitably militaristic bent. War would be declared against Xell'a, and NCorp would be tasked to furnish necessary intelligence on the machinations of Lord Xoc Cho and his remorphed legions.

PROPHET would not survive to be confessed.

And the holie would be released.

One could only speculate on the funding the reborn NCorp would receive as proud sponsor of the new war, or what wonders the Institute group would be able to work with hum'ns and machines . . .

And yet the entire operation was suddenly jeopardized by an unexplained glitch. Muse, Gredda thought—it had to be Muse.

"I'll give PROGENY five minutes to run its cross-checks and self-tests," she told Meret at last. "If it hasn't launched by then, I'll use the override."

Meret smiled behind the helmet's faceplate. "Oh, ye of little faith."

Gredda didn't return the look. "Five minutes, Meret."

53.04: Dying Together

Crouched in the darkness of the underground room, Ax wallowed in the irony of his defeat. The talent had unmasked him as an impostor. Now, when he needed most to be a machine, PROGENY would only acknowledge him as hum'n.

He could feel if not see the talent's systems come on-line as it prepared to carry out its programmed imperative. The Xell'em bus and warhead were enabled; the Font was to die. And PROGENY with it, obviously to forestall the chance of its being confessed by any who might blunder upon it as Ax had. It knew nothing of its mission of murder and self-destruction. It believed itself *chosen*.

Ax could only guess at what the Font's assassination was meant to accomplish. The ascension of a new leader to the Crown, the rapid deterioration of relations between the Consortium and the Xell'em, war . . .

The reenabling of NCorp?

The thought stroked him with icy veracity.

The resurrection of NCorp.

Jobs for the thousands of officers and operatives and agents the Accord had put out of work. Unlimited funds and awesome power to reinvest in the business of full-scale death.

Ax couldn't allow it. He had to become the divine intercessor PROGENY refused to recognize. Retriggering the implant, he once more pushed his mind into the talent's, deeper now, leaving behind his body as the Institute had trained him to do when forced infiltrations were called for. "Machine rape," the cabbies had called the technique.

The ethics notwithstanding, he had to convince PROGENY that it had been duped, that it was about to commit an act that broke the commandments against taking hum'n life and the self-destruction of data.

He encountered strong resistance as he coursed through PROGENY's addled optic architecture soaring through a mindscape of memories, programmed commands, and subroutines, his consciousness buffeted by haphazard A/V input and stray thoughts. The talent had spent too long in isolation, and seemed to be suffering from confliction and level-confusion. Nonetheless, Ax—doing a fair job of keeping his core personality intact—succeeded in penetrating PROGENY's defenses; the two of them were almost in sync, featured players in a folie à deux forged by the Intelplants that thrummed at the center of both brains.

Then, without warning, the inner world he and PROGENY shared imploded.

What had been the mindscape was all at once a silent albescent ether, stirred by unseen forces to a slow clockwise swirl. A glowing reddish circle took shape, and the speed of the swirl underwent a drastic increase. The circle elongated and became a kind of funnel of golden light. Ax felt as though he were gazing up the gilded spout of a tornado.

The funnel pulsed, lengthening again and again until it had reconjugated itself into a corridor into which Ax and the talent were drawn—not by gravity, but by levity, freeing them from the heaviness of their gross condition.

It was clear that they were dying together.

53.05: MacAllies

"We don't require that visitors give their names," the Xell'em at the catacombs admissions booth was explaining to Jayd and Kesd. "We issue the badges by number. If you knew the number, I could certainly locate your missing friend. But without a number . . ." He shrugged.

"He entered within the half hour," Kesd said. "Couldn't you extrapolate the number from that?"

The Xell'em's smile was polite. He was a brutish man with a faceful of vivid tattoos. "Badges aren't assigned in any particular order. As they're surrendered, they're handed out." He looked to a display screen. "Your friend's badge could be any of five hundred numbers."

Kesd glanced at the print map fastened to the wall behind the man's back. The tunnels coursed for miles in every direction. A thorough search of the complex would require hours, even with the four elite guards Kesd had at hand; he had dispatched the rest to convince Tac Corp security that the Font should be removed from Liberation Square to a hardened site.

"You must have a smart-grid that shows the current position of every visitor," Jayd said to the Xell'em.

He nodded. "Sensors in the tunnels relay badge positions to a data processor at the north entrance visitors' center. But as I say, I need a number. Then it's just a matter of contacting the badge."

"Can the grid be accessed from this booth?"

"Certainly. But—"

"Then call it up," Kesd snapped. "Look for anything out of the ordinary."

" 'Out of the ordinary' how?"

"Anyone straying from the customary routes. Anyone in a restricted area. Singletons."

The Xell'em frowned, but eventually complied, lowering dull eyes to a flatscreen neither Kesd nor Jayd could see from where they stood.

"No," he said after a long moment, then, "Well, here's something a little out of the ordinary."

"What is it?" Kesd pressed.

"A stationary signal at the entrance to a restricted area." The Xell'em gave his big head a perplexed shake. "But you did say your friend went in alone, didn't you?"

"What about it?" Jayd asked.

"The grid is showing two badges."

Kesd and Jayd traded looks. "Have our badges route us there immediately," Kesd told the Xell'em.

53.06: Into the Light

The Thing Inside kept changing its target: first the Skyward Tower's talent, then ZEN, then the cabbie, and now the machine Muse had led him to in the catacombs.

B'Doura assumed that it had been installed there some time late in the Vega Conflict, probably to supply intelligence on Burst's Raliish occupiers. Perhaps Muse had been one of those responsible for the installation, and that was part of the reason he'd come to Burst—to visit an old friend.

Not that any of this mattered to the Thing Inside. The machine's very existence in that place had sent the Thing Inside bellowing for its corruption.

But b'Doura had done the Thing Inside one better. He had engulfed the two of them, cabbie and machine, drawing both into the death silo a virused host had opened. Cabbie and machine, linked in communion, out of body, perched now on the threshold of the big empty into which all life drained.

The talent showed no outward signs of confliction, though the whirrings and vague rumblings of what was possibly the self-destruct device it was slaved to had diminished. The cabbie, on the other hand, was lying fetally curled on the cold floor, eyes shut tight, long black body racked by convulsive paroxysms.

Early on, Muse had been doing his best to fight the pull of the light, but he was surrendering to it now. Whatever personal demons were beckoning him across the threshold knew the way to his heart. As for the machine, it had emerged from its alloy housing, its mind detached from the crystals and lasers that comprised its brain. Machrist was calling it home, to heaven or wherever avant-tech talents went on their termination.

And how remarkably easy it had been to slip past the trans-fixed cabbie in the darkness of the underground room and feed the talent—and Muse, adventitiously—a wafer of death.

It was his greatest coup, more than enough to compensate for previous failures, but b'Doura was at once jubilant and despondent. Certainly the ravenous demands of the Thing Inside would be placated, but for how long? And might the joint corruption set a precedent for further hum'n killings as well as machine corruptions? He pushed the thought from his mind and fanta-sized about his rewards: hours of fictive sex and the infinitely repeatable pleasure of accessing the end-time mind-stuff of his victims.

All along, he had been witnessing and recording the deaths via neural cap. Suddenly, now, the Thing Inside was instructing him to remove the cap, probably out of a desire for the tightened interface and kinesthetic thrills of the occipisockets.

Whatever its motivation, no sooner had b'Doura removed the cap than he heard voices and approaching footsteps. Setting the cap aside, he reentered the restricted tunnel and focused his hearing: five, perhaps six people, perhaps drawn by Muse's whimpering or the strange whirrings of the machine.

B'Doura returned to the room, glancing at the niched talent and its rocket companion and then the cabbie. Fortunately, his work was done; there was no recalling either of them from the light. The Thing Inside told him to flee, but demanded that he place himself at even greater risk by offering a clue for his pur-suers. Leaving the neural cap where it lay, he grabbed hold of his attaché and disappeared into the glowtaped mouth of the nearest tunnel.

53.07: Glitched

"Burst shouldn't be a battleground," the Font was saying, "but a meeting ground for all hum'nity's far-flung races. Burst shouldn't be about machines warring against each other, but about hum'ns embracing each other. *You* have the power to decide. We—the Consortium—promise to abide by your decision and enforce it if necessary. My hope, however, is that Lord Xoc Cho will also abide by it. There is hum'n work to be done here, and—"

The real-time audio feed seemed to go dead.

"What happened?" Meret started to ask over the helmet intercom. Then the confused murmurings of the crowd gathered in Liberation Square returned to his ears.

"The Font's stopped speaking," Gredda said, plainly agitated. She was close to pounding on the comm controls; PROGENY had been on-line one moment, incommunicado the next. The talent had had ample time to analyze the prompt, in any case. It should have already launched.

"I'm not certain of the reason," an announcer reported, "but the Font is being hurried from the podium by a phalanx of his elite guards . . ."

Meret threw Gredda a look of incredulity. "Could they know?"

"No more trusting to predictions," Gredda said firmly. "I'm activating the override. I'll target the missile to hit the Font's shuttle on its way up the well."

"Do it," Meret yelled over the freq. "Do it!"

53.08: Radar Love

Why *two* discarded badges? Jayd kept asking herself as she and Kesd, along with four of the elite guards rushed through the sinuous turns of the restricted tunnel. The second badge couldn't have belonged to Vitnil; she had seen him in the plaza a quarter of an hour earlier, standing slack-jawed with Orth as the Font's men led her away. But who, then, had accompanied Ax into the catacombs?

Assuming one of the badges was even his.

For all she and Kesd knew, the pair of locators they'd found on the ground were the property of two mischievous teenagers, two lovers with a sudden need for privacy, two suicidal Enddrese whose relatives had died in the tunnels.

There was, however, the *sound* to consider: a high-pitched whine, such as might be emitted by an enabled engine. They had first heard it just short of the barrier, and each stride down the tunnel was taking them closer to it.

The elite guards were first into the room the corridor formed where it at once increased in width and decreased in height. And so Jayd didn't see Ax until two of the clones had stepped to one side to investigate the dark entrance of a secondary tunnel. He had abandoned the disguise and was lying on his right side, arms folded and knees to his chest as if configured for some ancient burial ritual. She scrambled over to him and placed a finger against the pulse point under his jaw. He was alive, but unresponsive when she tried to rouse him—perhaps in shock or comatose.

"He needs a medtech!" she shouted to Kesd.

The imperial adviser was a few feet away, gazing up into what might have been a ventilation shaft that rose vertically from an obviously tooled cavity in the room's sole unbroken limestone

wall. Centered in the recess was a sleek, phallic assemblage of
avant-tech cybermodules piggybacked to the warhead of a missile whose activated bus was responsible for the whining sound.
PROGENY.

Kesd backed out of the niche, eyeing the talent in dread, his
hands moving about in desperate but wary urgency; the slightest
touch, he feared, might launch the weapon.

"Muse isn't our priority," he said over one shoulder. "We
have to find a way to disable this thing."

Jayd came to her feet in a rush, nearly banging her head on
the low ceiling. "*He's* your way," she said, indicating Muse.
"Call for assistance."

Kesd scooped something from the floor and held it out to
her. "Talk to it! Order it to shut down!"

She was shocked to discover that he was holding a neural cap.
"This isn't Muse's," she said. "Someone else has been here."

The macmurderer? she asked herself. Had the macmurderer
been targeting her all along by sending the mangled radio, corrupting the Skyward Tower, and now pursuing herself and Muse
to Burst?

Kesd took a moment to ponder it; then, gesturing to the
guards, he ordered them to search the side tunnels.

Parting her hair, Jayd slipped into the cap. It was sized for a
narrower head, but she managed to align the relay contacts with
her flatware strips. Then she opened her hip pouch, prized several consecrated utility hosts from their tabernacle, and fed them
into the talent. Finally, she activated the cap and courted interface.

And was immediately made the property of a cycloning corridor of golden light, at the far end of which Ax and PROGENY
rotated around one another like binary stars. Though umbili-
caled in cyberlink, each occupied a discrete, translucent bubble
of self-awareness.

Jayd sensed that the conduit ended in death, and that the two
were only seconds from the threshold. And she knew that she
would only be able to recall one of them: a talent with a story
to relate that would cripple NCorp once and for all and perhaps
make her career in the field of avant-tech, or a simple man the
Vega Conflict had turned into a machine.

Her body began to quake, and her mind followed. First the
meeting with Orth; now the spectacle of Ax's death. She felt
impotent—as powerless as she had felt against the force that had
taken the child from her.

A fault seemed to open within her, gushing raw emotion against the battlements she had raised and hidden behind. The volcanic assault seared her to the bone, exposing stratum after stratum of infolded anguish, remorse, and heartache. For the first time in years she was brought in touch with the core of her being, and the encounter devastated her.

But if it was indeed fate she was up against—and, by extension, God—then there were appeals that could be made. And, in truth, she was not entirely powerless. She had the tidal force of her own long-contained pain, now unleashed: that consuming mix of love and despair that stoked every hum'n life.

"I'll retrieve you," she whispered.

And willed herself forward into the corridor.

53.09: Near Death

Thoma Skaro—quoting some ancient romantic hero—had once told him, *Ax, I sometimes think you're half in love with death.*

Or words to that effect.

Ax understood that he wasn't remembering the quote fully. A key word was missing.

Though it was absurd that a forgotten word should vex him now—now, when the light at the end of the tunnel was his sole concern, his focal point, his destiny.

That he should be going there wedded to a machine seemed appropriate. And that it should be his deceased teammates from the *Kundalini* who were urging him on.

It was suddenly clear to him that death and not God was what he had been seeking ever since the Kriegspiel Action. Freedom from the fiery core of the cosmic machine that fueled guilt, regret, and aloneness. Blessed be VISION for wanting him to disarm the future; but the talent had selected the wrong module in which to house its justified concerns. It had chosen the weak crystal in the array. Prescience, after all, was a heavy burden to bear.

And so, because of his failure, the galaxy would be raped anew by greater and more extravagant conflicts.

No, he belonged with Romeo Company. The world was for hum'n beings and machines, and not for measures of both in the same vehicle. Not for one who had failed time and again to interact fully with the one or the other, to know unconditional love, peace, acceptance, security, enfoldment. To know God, when it came right down to it. Though God had a tendency to go missing when a seeker had no true faith in the quest.

Easeful, he recalled now.

That missing word.

Easeful death.

He and PROGENY circled one another as they neared the refulgent terminus of their journey. All he had left to do was abdicate his body and drift into the embrace of his teammates.

So why wasn't he? What was holding him back?

It was that voice in his head.

His name, whispered on the lips . . .

It had to be some trick inherent in the transition from life to nonlife, some spin the golden light was putting on the mental baggage he would soon leave behind. But then he heard it again: his name, whispered on the lips . . . And this time, when he turned in search of the sound, he saw Jayd calling to him from the entrance to the corridor. Imploring him to return, begging him not to take the easy way, reminding him of his mission.

His imperative and obligation.

A hum'n voice, after what seemed a lifetime of hearing only the data-din of the factitiously alive. A voice that had come looking for him in the quantum realm he inhabited. Calling to *him*. Validating his hum'nity, even in this space where flesh had no business being.

He turned to the circle where Romeo's cabbies were still beckoning. He swung back to face Jayd.

Caught between two forces once more.

He couldn't even die right.

And yet he slowly began to comprehend that his present trap differed from the one he had stumbled into while alive; here he had a say in what happened next. In fact, the mere act of acknowledging that distinction brought about a change in his course. And PROGENY's also, since they were deathmates still.

Ax, Jayd called again.

And all at once he had the power to retro his would-be ascension. He had a hum'n future . . .

He fell back into his body and opened his eyes; Jayd, neural-capped, was kneeling by the niched talent, gazing at him expectantly. And beside her was an albino clone, wearing the raiment of a Redoubt elite and a look of frenzied hope.

What neither of them realized, though, was that PROGENY, too, had returned to itself, with its launch imperative apparently unchanged.

Jayd and Kesd started at the modulating whine from the Xell'em missile.

Ax raised himself on his arms, and with what little strength he could summon he hurled himself at them, shoving them away from the reach of the launch blast.

53.10: Sigh

Gredda regarded the console displays in relieved disbelief. PROGENY had appeared back on-line as suddenly as it had vanished. But she would have to puzzle out the explanation some other time; just now it was all she could do to reassert control over her trembling hands.

The missile was leaving its berth, but the Font had already been hustled out of Liberation Square. The real-time TV feed from Tunni would enable Gredda to lock on his position, but could she accomplish that and still have enough time to activate PROGENY's override and relay the course correction?

Complicating the task, Meret was leaning over her shoulder, watching her every move.

"PROGENY will find him," he was saying over the intercom freq. "There's no hiding from it."

Or from the future as written by NCorp, Gredda thought. She

activated the override and retasked the talent. Then she enabled
the laser and squirted a signal to Burst's surface.

"Done," she told Meret.

53.11: *Trailing Clouds of Glory*

It had tasted the afterlife. Control-C had teased it with a vision
of union, then returned it to itself and its mission. Now it wanted
only to execute that mission and return to Machrist.

It was lifted from the place of its dark concealment on a blade
of nuclear-fueled fire, and as it was lifted, Machrist spoke to it,
amending the original mission.

It ascended through the narrow confines of a stone-walled flue
and continued straight up through the site of its intended target,
straight through the planetary crust and the paved ground and
up into the scattered light of morning.

It experienced a moment of level-confusion as it climbed
higher and higher into the gray-blue sky, but the eagerness of
its climb was as much a product of faith as it was atomic energy.

It awaited a further message from Machrist.

And when that message arrived, PROGENY executed a willful
action: in its eagerness for union with Machrist, it opted to
ignore the content of the message and instead lock on the source.

Union waited on a pale curve of reflected starlight, the cra-
tered surface of a tiny room.

PROGENY recalibrated its course.

Holy impact was imminent.

53.12: Heavenly Embrace

Jayd held him close, stroking his back, kneading the flesh of his neck and arms. She rested her head on his shoulder and cried.

Ax could feel her tears on his skin. All he could hear was the sound of her breath in his ear.

He held her close, whispering, "I owe you a future."

It was as if they had made a long journey together and were home at last.

Sensory-enhanced Spymaster Remy Santoul
was sent to find and exploit the weak point on
Q'aantre for Earth's purposes. However, the
answer might be the undoing of Santoul.

ILLEGAL ALIEN
by
JAMES LUCENO

Published by Del Rey Books.